Edited by Linda Branam and Laura Jorstad
Cover Art & Design by Kate O'Hara
Interior Design by Eira Brand of Zipline
Published by Nikota Publishing House Incorporated
Distributed by Riyria Enterprises, LLC

ISBN: 978-1-943363-99-5

Copyright © 2025 Emilie Nikota
All rights reserved. This book or any portion thereof may not be reproduced or used in any manner whatsoever without the express written permission of the publisher except for the use of brief quotations in a book review.

THE ETHER WITCH
VOLUME 1: THE CASTING CALL

by
Delemhach

DEDICATION

To Liz, and David. The best in-laws I could've asked for, and who seemed to know before my husband or myself that we were in it for the long haul— just like a certain parental couple in this book.

CHAPTER 1

A COERCED COLLABORATION

From his bedroom balcony, Tamlin Ashowan stared out over the Alcide Sea.

The full moon illuminated the inky waters below his family keep, and a magical dusting of stars glittered brightly against the darkness.

Closing his eyes, he took in a deep, slow breath.

Everything was quiet save for the gentle, repetitive rush of water meeting the cliffside far below, and there was even a delicious smell of spring in the air. Everything was peaceful in the kingdom of Daxaria, with no wars, droughts, or plagues for more than a decade. The monarchy served its people well, and as a result, its citizens flourished.

So why did Tam, a future viscount and duke, twin brother to the soon-to-be queen of Daxaria, feel anxious?

He couldn't put his finger on it, but it was almost as though something big and important was about to happen.

That said, this particular evening didn't seem quite as charged as the day a little more than seven years ago when his sister, Katarina, had battled against a civil rebellion in the foreign kingdom of Troivack. Katarina had helped the Troivackian king and queen win the civil war and stop Aradia, the first witch and daughter of the Gods. Following her uprising, the first witch was imprisoned in a secret location in Troivack. Aradia's own twin brother, the devil, had been killed during the battle; however, as an immortal with divine blood, he had been reborn elsewhere. In an effort to find him, the Troivackian army partnered with their coven, the Coven of Aguas, and had apprehended several children who possessed mysterious backgrounds. However, it was difficult to discern if any of them were the devil… which meant he could still be at large, albeit in the form of a child.

Tam continued gazing out into the night, idly considering what could be making him feel so restless.

A soft knock sounded behind him, making him turn around.

Standing in the doorway was his mother, Duchess Annika Ashowan.

Once upon a time, she had been praised as the most beautiful woman in all Daxaria, despite being born and raised in Troivack prior to marrying an old Daxarian viscount. Viscount Jenoure had died a year after their marriage, leaving Annika to live as a childless widow for a time before she met a certain royal cook who just so happened to be a witch. And they also just so happened to fall in love. Luckily, due to Finlay Ashowan's contributions to the kingdom and his impressive magical power, he had risen through the noble ranks and became a beloved hero of Daxaria.

The famous couple were still spoken of often among Daxarians, and while she was no longer heralded as the most beautiful woman in the kingdom, Annika Ashowan had aged gracefully throughout the years—despite all the stress her daughter put her through—and still was quite energetic for a woman nearing her sixties.

"Tam? What are you still doing awake?" Annika called out softly to her son.

Tam gave his mother a half smile and faced her. "Couldn't sleep."

The duchess smiled back and gestured for her son to return to the warmth of his room. "Love, it's still technically winter, and firewood isn't cheap."

"Since when are we concerned about money?" Tam asked wryly, though he did retreat back into his chamber, closing the glass balcony doors behind him.

"You build wealth by being careful with it. Remember, if you respect money, money respects you."

Tam nodded along with the phrase his mother had often repeated during their budgeting and finance lessons throughout the years.

"Why are *you* awake then?" Tam gestured toward the two armchairs in front of the crackling hearth.

Annika lowered herself into a plush navy-blue armchair and touched her temple wearily.

"I've been going over the coronation details for your sister. Your birthdays are a month away, and a week after that she is going to be crowned queen."

"I still can't believe King Norman is entrusting Daxaria to her," Tam said with a bemused chuckle.

Katarina had always been the wild child of the Ashowan family. She had an incredible skill for getting herself into trouble, and that hadn't seemed to change as she grew older. Though she had learned to curb her more outlandish urges, and even channeled her abundant magical energy into studying swordsmanship, she was still too mischievous for her own good. Which meant that when she and the prince of the kingdom had fallen in love and wed, many people had grown concerned for the future of Daxaria.

"Well, King Norman is trusting that the council will help her and Eric a great deal," Annika replied reasonably.

Prince Eric Reyes. The man with more skeletons in his closet than in a postwar cemetery who had fallen hopelessly in love with Katarina seven years ago during their time together in the foreign court of Troivack.

Their romance had been beyond shocking, but the pair had barreled forward in ways that kept them true to themselves, and despite all odds? They were managing quite well—even with their three boys, a year apart in age—six, five, and four—who were every bit as troublesome as their mother. The boys worked together as a cohesive disaster to keep the world turning upside down as often as possible.

"Do you think Antony, Charles, and Asher will behave for the entire ceremony?" Tam wondered aloud after he and his mother had taken a few moments of silence to ponder the fast-approaching event when the Daxarian king would abdicate the throne.

The duchess smiled but emitted a brief groan at the thought of her three grandsons. "His Majesty assured everyone the ceremony would be kept as short as possible."

Tam laughed again and closed his eyes while settling back into his seat. "I bet His Majesty King Brendan Devark will have an opinion on the princes."

Annika shook her head and sighed at the mention of the Troivackian king. "I'm given to understand that King Brendan and Queen Alina's two boys are remarkably well behaved. Which isn't a surprise, but I think they will definitely bring to light Antony, Charles, and Asher's... *delayed* mastery of etiquette."

Tam grinned. "Kat's in for an earful from Alina, I bet."

Alina Devark, queen of Troivack, was Katarina's best friend and Eric's younger sister. As a result, there tended to be unfiltered opinions exchanged quite regularly whenever the couples were able to visit each other.

"Her Majesty Alina is more than welcome to try influencing the boys. Perhaps she has the energy to make a difference. I admit I don't have quite the same amount of vigor I used to," the duchess informed her son, followed by an uncharacteristic yawn.

Tam waved off his mother's words. "You seemed perfectly fine the other night when that man tried to strangle you."

Annika raised an eyebrow at the mention of their joint espionage work. "Lightly stabbing someone is not the same as teaching children. The latter is significantly harder."

Stretching his legs out in front of him, Tam eyed his mother's drawn features sympathetically. "I'll probably sleep soon. You should go try to do the same."

The duchess didn't respond straightaway to her son's gentle dismissal. Rather, she regarded him thoughtfully. Her brown eyes brightened as they keenly roved his face. Tam's slanted almond eyes looked like his father's, save for the coloring, which was the same as her own. His straight nose, his defined jaw... There were bits of both sides of the family there.

"Will you ever get married?"

Tam's attention had briefly wandered over to the fire as his mind drifted, but hearing the question, it snapped back to Annika Ashowan. After the moment of shock passed, he raised his eyebrows and rolled his eyes. "Not this again."

"A mother is allowed to wonder."

"Can you wonder in the morning, and maybe only three times a year as opposed to eleven?"

"Tam, your father and I are going to go traveling once you are officially made the duke, and I'd like to know that someone can be here with you. I know you always like being alone, but—"

"I hope you're aware of your hypocrisy," Tam interrupted dryly.

It was the duchess's turn to look unimpressed. "I at least had my assistant Clara, may she rest in peace, to rely on when I had no one. You haven't even gotten an assistant to replace Likon. It's been seven years. You need someone to help you if you aren't going to get married."

"I managed just fine when you, Da, Kat, and Likon abandoned me to go to Troivack, didn't I?"

Annika's tone sharpened. "You mean when you 'somehow' lost the wall of your father's office, part of the floor, and the desk full of paperwork? And all of us almost got arrested because of the number of important documents that vanished?"

Tam's tongue poked his cheek as he looked away.

Damn. He had really hoped that she had let that go...

He dropped his chin down before responding to his mother. "I can just wait until Likon—"

"Likon isn't coming home from Troivack. You know it. I know it. If only he knew it... Once he gets around to noticing he's fallen in love with Lady Dana Faucher, he's going to marry her. I wagered with her mother, Lady Nathalie, that they'll be married before the fall."

"Somehow I doubt that it will be that easy. Leader Gregory Faucher most likely will refuse to let a man who is completing a punishment of servitude for alleged treason marry his daughter." Likon had read Prince Eric Reyes's correspondence years ago to keep tabs on the prince when he was traveling with Katarina, and his nephew serving as the prince's assistant, Thomas Julian, had aided him in doing this. Things became even more serious when Thomas Julian was found to also be feeding information and assisting the first witch when she instigated the civil war.

Annika huffed. "Oh, he will. We just need to be a bit creative with convincing him."

Tam laughed.

He had no doubt his mother had devised several cunning, manipulative plans to sway the infamously gruff and protective military leader in Troivack to allow his beloved daughter to marry Likon, the Ashowans' adopted son. However, the handful of times Tam had met Gregory Faucher when he'd come to visit Katarina, Tam had gotten the distinct impression that he was not someone who could be duped easily. He chose not to comment on this opinion for the time being.

"Look, can this maybe wait until after my birthday? I—Wait. You haven't brought up the assistant thing in almost a year. And suddenly it crops up…" Tam's eyes narrowed. "Who is it?"

Annika smoothed the cream silk of her skirt. "Do you remember Eli? That boy that was helping Likon serve the Troivackian king…?"

Eli had been a young man that Prince Eric had known during his mysterious four year absence from the Daxarian court. They crossed paths again in Troivack when Eli had been tasked with assassinating Eric—unaware he was a prince—while enslaved to the Troivackian traitor Duke Icarus.

"Mm-hm," Tam responded impatiently.

"Well, the matter of Duke Icarus's estate has finally been settled, and the young man wants to become a citizen of Daxaria, but because he isn't revealing his parentage and he doesn't want to get entangled with the Coven of Wittica, Likon suggested maybe he work for you for a while."

"Why didn't Likon bring this up to me himself?" Tam questioned while leaning forward and resting his elbow on the armrest of the chair.

"Because he wanted me to discuss with your da whether or not the coven would permit a witch to live in Daxaria without revealing their magic."

"So we're offering to help and protect this Eli person when he starts the process of gaining Daxarian citizenship, and because Likon asked us, you're suggesting Eli work for me while we do this?"

"Yes."

"Again, Likon should've asked me. He knows I'd listen."

"You are terrible at responding to letters and you know it. Eli needed to prepare, if your answer was yes, before leaving Troivack for the coronation, so he could pack and say his goodbyes."

Tam continued staring at his mother warily. "He's already on the boat, fully packed, isn't he?"

"Not at all."

Tam didn't believe his mother for a second.

"He's already *in* Daxaria. They arrived at the castle tonight. The two of you can meet tomorrow," Annika finally admitted, though she still had the gall to act innocent.

Tam let out a moan and rubbed his face.

"Love, I know you're terrible with change, but you're always complaining about the amount of work you have. I have no idea why you insist on making your life harder." The duchess stood and stared down at her son.

Tam started his oft-cited list of why he preferred to not hire a new assistant. "A new assistant will need me to take time to explain things, and then they'll want to know about my magic, and—"

"Neither you nor Eli ever want to talk about your magic. There. It's perfect."

"That makes him suspicious."

"Why are you being so difficult?"

"I have a stubborn father and meddling mother; I've had to adapt."

Annika lowered her chin and stared disapprovingly down at Tam, who looked back at her unabashedly.

"Likon vouches for him. You said you would hire him if Likon requested it, and he has. I'm beginning to think complaining is just a habit of yours at this point."

"I only complain when someone forces something upon me."

Annika bent down and kissed her son atop his head. "You and your sister are more alike than you realize."

"Surprise, surprise. We're both hardheaded, we don't like being forced into things, and neither of us wanted the responsibility of leading a noble house or, say, a kingdom."

"You got the easier option, and yet you still complain more than Kat."

"No, Kat complains more, you just don't live with her."

Annika gently cuffed the back of her son's head. "If Likon says Eli is good, then I think he's good. Try to be appreciative that you have so many people wanting to help you."

Tam gave a halfhearted smile and rose from his seat to hug his mother.

"I'll try. But in exchange, you can't bring up marriage for another year."

Annika reached up and returned her son's embrace—it was a little tricky given that he had also inherited his father's impressive height and she was on the shorter side—but despite Tam's seemingly unenthused response to having a little extra help, the duchess seemed pleased and perhaps even a little relieved.

Tam, on the other hand, was already starting to wonder if perhaps the uneasy premonition he had been having moments earlier was a bad omen. He had only ever really seen Eli from a distance, and rumor had it that the young man kept his secrets just as well as, if not better, than the future duke of the Ashowan household.

CHAPTER 2

A BREAKFAST BOMBARDMENT

There was screaming, there was crying, there was maniacal laughter...

Gods... I didn't know Kat was going to bring the boys over. Tam groaned as he plunged his head under his pillow.

He could tell by the brightness of his room that he had slept in, but he didn't care all that much. He had acquiesced to his mother's insistence on hiring an assistant after all.

Determined to partake in a leisurely morning, Tam made a very conscious decision to try and wait for his nephews to settle down before he would join them all in the dining hall.

His efforts were thwarted before they could even commence by the sound of their pounding fists at his door.

"UNCLE TAM! UNCLE TAM! MY TOOTH IS GOING TO FALL OUT SOON! YOU HAVE TO SEE!"

Well, there's Charles...

"UNCLE TAM! WE NEED TO GO LOOK FOR STARFISH! YOU SAID LAST TIME YOU FOUND SOME!"

Aah… Antony…

"COME DOWN FOR BREAKFAST I'M HUUUUNGRY!"

And of course dear, dear Asher.

Tam rose from his bed, not bothering to make himself more presentable. His long hair hung around his face as was his norm, and he wore only relaxed trousers and a loose sleep shirt. He made sure the pendant on a gold chain around his neck was hidden before he opened his door and stared down into the three eager faces of his sister's sons.

Antony, the oldest, was growing out his red hair and already had a small ponytail tied off at the back of his neck, much to his mother's displeasure. His bright-blue eyes looked identical to those of his grandfather Finlay Ashowan, but the shape of his nose and mouth were entirely Prince Eric's.

Charles, or Charlie as he was occasionally called, had a mop of wavy dirty-blond hair and could have passed for a small clone of his father were it not for his golden eyes, like his mother's.

Then there was Asher. Asher's red hair was already touching his shoulders, and his eyes were hazel like Prince Eric's. They currently stared up impatiently at Tam, Asher's head already fallen back from impatience.

"Is breaking down your uncle's door really the proper way to greet him?" Tam asked with a raised eyebrow as he sleepily leaned his left arm against the doorframe.

"FOOD!" Asher moaned while seizing Tam's hand nearest to him and tugging it.

"After breakfast, we see the starfish, right?" Antony was very obviously trying to conduct himself with some measure of self-control and not bounce up and down.

Mum must've chastised him downstairs, Tam thought with a smile.

"LOOK!" Charles bared his teeth and stuck out his jaw, revealing a lopsided loose tooth.

Tam slowly crouched and squinted at the little pearl. "Huh. Should we tie it to Harold and see if he'll yank that out for you?"

The boys broke out in giggles at the mention of their mother's pet donkey, who still lived at the keep where she had grown up with Tam.

"OY!"

Tam looked toward the newcomer who was adding a shout to his morning.

Katarina Reyes—future queen of Daxaria, mother to three royal hellions, daughter of the famous house witch, hero in the foreign kingdom of Troivack—stood at the end of the hall wearing a pair of brown trousers and a white tunic with the sleeves rolled up. Her long red hair was unbound, and a sword rested on her hip as she stared at her brother sardonically, her golden eyes glinting.

"Come on. I'm hungry," she said tersely with a jerk of her head.

"ME TOO!" Asher wailed before flinging down Tam's hand and bolting to his mother. The young boy wrapped his arms around her left leg and pressed his face into her thigh.

Raising a judgmental eyebrow, Kat watched her brother as he straightened and yawned. "Gods, you sure took some time to get your beauty sleep. Why aren't you better looking?"

"Your spawn interrupted the process," Tam retorted as Antony latched himself onto his uncle's right leg. "Is your husband here with you for breakfast?"

"Eric's downstairs with your new assistant, yes."

"Grandpa made eggsin toast!" Charles informed his uncle excitedly before seizing Tam's other leg.

Tam attempted to waddle into the hallway with his nephews attached to his limbs, but found he was really only succeeding in having his pants pulled down.

"Eggsin toast, eh?" he retorted as the boys giggled.

Eggsin toast was a breakfast delight that Finlay Ashowan, in his infinite kitchen wisdom, had crafted ages ago. Cinnamon, nutmeg, eggs, and cream were whisked together, and then thick slices of crusty bread were soaked in the mixture before being pan-fried in pools of melted golden butter.

He served it with thick whipping cream, and it often had his grandsons running laps around the keep shortly thereafter.

"I might be convinced to have a slice or two of your grandfather's eggsin toast. Though, mind if I get dressed?" Tam added as the boys continued to cling to his legs.

"I'm surprised Mum finally wore you down, by the way. *You* agreeing to a *stranger* as your assistant? Did she ask you when you were drunk?" Kat scoffed as Tam stopped a short way in front of her.

"Close. Middle of the night, and she prefaced it by asking me when I'm getting married."

"Pfft." Kat grinned and put her hands on her slim hips. "Makes perfect sense now. Well, come on down and meet Eli. He's a lot like you, so it's going to be interesting to see which one of you is able to make eye contact first. I might even place bets with Eric."

Tam briefly glanced at his sister, unimpressed, and then tried unsuccessfully to get his nephews to release him—though Asher, who was grasping his mother's pant leg, was starting to look a mite enticed at the prospect of clinging to his uncle and making him drop his pants in the hall...

"Alright. Take these... monsters... downstairs and let me get dressed, will you?" Tam put a heartfelt effort into prying Antony's arms from his leg.

Kat sighed while patting Asher on the head.

"You heard your uncle, kids... he needs help getting changed."

"THAT IS NOT—"

Tam didn't get a chance to finish shouting as Asher took a flying leap, seized the front of Tam's pants, and dragged them down so that he stood in only his underwear.

Kat turned around and started to whistle while striding away.

Tam, watching her go, crouched down and drew his nephews closer. "New plan. I take you all down to look at starfish, and maybe a few sea snails end up in your mother's bed later, hm?"

The boys cackled and released their uncle at this proposed compromise. Taking advantage of the moment of liberation, Tam yanked his sleeping trousers back up and gave them a nod. "I'll be down for breakfast soon."

The boys were about to bolt off toward the stairs when Tam called out, "Oh, how does Eli seem?"

The three of them turned back around. Instead of their usual rambunctious energy, they seemed pensive, and all wore identical expressions.

"Who's Eli?" Antony asked at last.

Tam pressed his lips together.

Alright. Apparently, the young man is very *quiet.*

By the time Tam was dressed in his usual black pants, vest, and white tunic, and was making his way down the staircase, he could already hear the great commotion in the dining hall. Kat was shouting at one of her sons, Annika was trying to console Asher about something, and any other voices that could belong to his father Fin, or to the prince, were drowned out.

Tam paused outside the dining room doors. Closing his eyes, he took in a deep breath, readying himself for the chaotic onslaught of a meal with his family...

He stepped into the brightly lit stone dining hall, which was taken up mostly by a long wooden table. Tam didn't bother announcing his arrival or even venturing into the thick of whatever new disaster was unfolding at the far end of the table. Instead, he slipped into the seat nearest the door and waited for one of the serving maids to discreetly pass him some food.

He had already completely forgotten about the fact that his new assistant was supposed to be there, and was tucking in to enjoy his father's eggsin toast when the room suddenly fell quiet.

Tam stopped eating.

The maid to his left finished pouring his cup of coffee and returned to the kitchen.

Slowly, Tam looked down toward the end of the table where his parents sat with his sister, brother-in-law, and nephews. They were all staring at him wearing looks of mixed amusement, surprise, and confusion.

Unsure what could make them gape at him in such a way—and half concerned his nephews had pulled some new prank he hadn't noticed yet—Tam frowned and turned to see if anyone was behind him...

But was instead taken aback to find that there was another person sitting *across* from him at his lonely end of the table.

A Zinferan who perhaps had a Daxarian parent, based on the softness of his slanted eyes and pale complexion.

Though oddly, this person was staring at Tam, utterly transfixed.

They had both chosen the seats at the far end of the table away from the others, and upon locking eyes with the young man, Tam felt his heart drop to his stomach.

There was something familiar about this person... as though they had at one point spent a summer together as children. He felt like he could call out his name much in the same way he could call out Likon's, with the same assured knowingness... Only he didn't know it.

Distracted by this peculiar sensation, Tam tilted his head thoughtfully.

The young man gulped, as though nervous to be scrutinized in turn.

"Godsdammit. Fine. Eric, you win the bet," Kat grumbled from the other end of the table. "Eli made eye contact first."

"Katarina, language," Annika warned. However, she was sadly too late as her youngest grandson, Asher, perked up.

"GODSDAMMIT!" he roared as though about to charge into battle.

Kat winced and ran her tongue over her teeth as she sensed her husband, Prince Eric Reyes, slowly turning to stare at her with a very dry expression.

"Tam, that there is Eli. The assistant Likon and Eric recommend," Fin called out as Antony clambered out of his seat and tugged on his grandfather's sweater.

Tam didn't bother trying to discern what the lad was asking his grandfather. He returned his attention to Eli, who had averted his gaze to his breakfast plate and laid down his fork before picking up the napkin in his lap and wiping his mouth.

He looked like he wanted to flee, and Tam couldn't have felt any more sympathy if he tried.

"Great to meet you. I'm Tam. Feel free to go find your chamber with the help of one of our maids if you're finished." Tam pretended to sound flippant as he braced his forearms on the table and focused on cutting up his eggsin toast.

"If you are certain you don't mind, my lord, I shall retire for now." Eli rose, bowed, and took his leave, his footfalls remarkably silent on the stone floors.

Tam hated how he felt the burning eyes of everyone around him.

Godsdammit… I would've loved a leisurely breakfast…

Tam turned to a skill he had learned out of necessity; shoveling the rest of his eggsin toast in his mouth, downing his black, scalding coffee, and abandoning his seat in less time than most people would've taken to cut up their own food. "I'll go take a look at the revisions submitted to us by our merchants with regards to their profit shares with the new ship."

"Er… Tam, don't you want to know about your new assistant…?" Fin wondered aloud, his eldest grandson on his lap.

"I'll learn about him as we work together. Excuse me."

"You said we'd look for snail—I mean, starfish!" Antony burst out, betrayal bright in his blue eyes as he stared earnestly at his uncle.

Tam paused at the door and smiled at him. "It'll only take me a little while. Besides, you aren't finished eating, and your grandmother wants to wash your face after. By then, I'll be ready to go. Alright?"

Antony looked reluctant to agree, but a quick tickling from his grandfather had him forgetting any possible negative thoughts and reaching for his abandoned plate so that he might finish his meal from his new spot at the table.

Tam retreated from the dining hall, already feeling indigestion clogging his chest.

But he was used to it.

As much as he loved his family, he served them best from afar. Or in one-on-one exchanges.

He knew he was a constant source of worry for them with his withdrawn, introverted tendencies. Despite his efforts to combat his family's worry by being highly productive and working harder than any noble son in the kingdom, they still thought and spoke at length about how he could improve himself. Regardless, even though Tam refused to embrace his magic, and as a result held everyone at arm's length, he still wanted to be worthy of being a part of the famous, heroic family.

The future duke had just begun climbing the stairs to the upper floors when a voice called out behind him. "Tam, mind if we talk alone?"

His hands curled into fists in his pockets as he turned back around and gradually lifted his gaze from his feet to his brother-in-law, Eric Reyes. A flicker of anxiety and magic tugged at his chest, but he battled it back as best he could in order to maintain eye contact.

Eric surveyed Tam in his usual manner when no one else was around.

Calculatingly, emotionlessly, and distantly.

Tam knew why his brother-in-law behaved that way, but that didn't make their interactions any less awkward.

"Of course, Your Highness. Though if we could be quick, that'd be appreciated. I'd hate to upset Antony."

Eric bobbed his head, then gestured to the front doors that towered over them.

Apparently, it was to be a *very* discreet discussion if it warranted leaving the keep altogether.

Tam wordlessly descended the stairs toward the doors, distantly wondering if this had anything to do with his recent espionage work with his mother off in the city of Xava, or if the prince was going to want to talk about the new assistant, Eli.

Either way, Tam wasn't particularly excited about the conversation ahead.

CHAPTER 3

HELP OR HEADACHE

Tam and Eric Reyes stood outside in the wintry air that was only just starting to soften its cold edges in favor of spring. The two were perched at the edge of the front courtyard of Tam's family keep, where they could look down the cliff to the icy waters of the Alcide Sea.

"I owe Eli more debts than I care to count," Eric started casually.

Tam stiffened.

"Try working with him for a year," the prince continued. "By then, if you still don't think it's a fit, I'll find somewhere else for him to go, but it's hard with the coven already being displeased with Kat becoming queen. Witches aren't supposed to be in positions of power."

Tam didn't bother stating that he knew all this and had his own fair share of headaches involving the coven and his inheriting a dukedom—even if he had never disclosed the exact nature of his magical power as a mutated witch to them. Mutated witches were witches that didn't have magic that clearly aligned with one of the four elements. Rather, their powers usually incorporated all four of the elements to varying degrees, though they were often rooted more in one element than the others. For a long time, mutated witches were rare and looked down upon by the covens. But as centuries wore on, mutated witches became not only much more common, but also more powerful. Like Finlay Ashowan who was a house witch and could command the items in his home, sense what people craved, and create a protective shield around his home. There were some mutated witches who could speak to animals, or help regrow teeth if someone had any knocked out. The Coven of Wittica, the official coven of Daxaria, liked having the mutated witches report the details of their magic to better track the evolution of their kind.

At present, Tam was hoping that Katarina would flex her talent for being incredibly frustrating so that they wouldn't pay him and his lack of reported magic much thought.

"Are they still trying to determine who succeeds you in the event of your death?" Tam asked, trying to change the subject.

"Yes... They still think Charlie should take the throne. Apparently, despite his golden eyes, they think he has so little magical power that he may as well be human."

"Antony's abilities should come out soon."

"We think so, too, but he honestly shows no disposition toward any specific element. We know he's a hellion like his brothers, which some witches think could be indicative of a power, but with Kat as their mother, I'm inclined to disagree and state that's just his personality."

Tam didn't need to laugh. The comment was more factual than joke by that point.

"Time will tell what powers, if any, the boys have." Returning to the topic of Tam's new assistant, Tam hoped they could move the conversation toward its end. "I'll give Eli a fair chance this year. Though I want to know his parentage."

Eric grimaced.

Tam almost locked eyes with his brother-in-law as a result.

"He will reveal that eventually," Eric announced evasively.

"That is a great deal of trust in someone who works alongside kings and lords but doesn't have much to back him up."

"The way Eli looked at you, I would've thought you two knew each other," Eric mused lightly, though his hazel eyes were sharp on Tam's profile.

Tam gave his head a slight shake. "I probably just startled him when I sat down across from him." With his hands in his pockets, the future duke turned to face the prince more squarely. "My concern about Eli is that there may be something dangerous about him, or that his history will come back and give me more paperwork. I don't want to judge him. I just don't want any headaches."

Eric laughed while staring out at the sea. He looked tired but thoughtful, and his short beard gave him a wise appearance. "With how quiet you try to keep your life, it's a miracle you survived a childhood with Kat."

Tam didn't respond. He wasn't asking for much in terms of credentials or background from Eli. Future dukes usually had a baron or trusted viscount work with them. Not that any would be employed under Tam, what with his social reclusiveness, his reputation for endless working, and his father's commoner origins.

But he didn't really want another noble working for him anyway.

"Your father knows a little bit about Eli's background, as does His Majesty Brendan Devark, and both think it'll be a mutually beneficial pairing. I just promised Eli long ago he could choose whom he told, barring extenuating circumstances or people with a need to know."

"How am *I* not on a need-to-know basis, when I'm his employer?" Tam persisted, without bothering to hide his irritation at being left out of a decision, and barred from information that would directly impact him.

Eric clapped a hand on Tam's shoulder, still smiling. "Give Eli a bit of a break. He has even less say in his fate than you do right now. At least let him trust you on his own terms."

"But I can't trust him on mine?" Tam's hold on his patience was starting to fray.

Eric was momentarily taken aback. "Gods… Sometimes you're so much like your da, it's scary."

Tam said nothing, just turned and strode back to the keep without another look back.

It wasn't the first time—nor would it be the last—that his family did what they believed to be the right thing regardless of how he, the black sheep of the family, felt about it. They had never really overcome their impression that he needed to be managed due to his struggles socially, and in large spaces and crowds, even though he had taken on much of his father's paperwork.

He knew their actions came from a place of love and good intentions, but it was because of their kind intentions behind such efforts that often made it all the harder for Tam to speak up more firmly on what he was and was not fine with. In other words, despite his family being filled with lovely people, they could be very annoying.

Tam sat in his father's office with his back comfortably resting against the well-worn brown leather of the chair. It was quiet. The flames in the stone hearth had dwindled low, but the late-morning sunlight had warmed the room despite the faint draft creeping in around the tall peaked glass windows overlooking the sea and pale sky. A rustic mug holding black coffee sat a short way past Tam's right hand, its steam still curling prettily in the light.

Taking in a slow breath, Tam felt the corners of his lips lift despite the letters in front of him. A viscount and a baron were interested in arranging a marriage between Tam and their daughters, neither of whom he had ever met.

Not that he recalled anyway.

Peaceful mornings with coffee, the smell of parchment, and the sun shining outside…

They were some of the small pleasures Tam allowed himself to openly enjoy while alone.

As usual when he was surrounded with these comforts in blissful solitude, the coiled tension in Tam loosened, and he felt more at ease.

It was one of the many reasons he enjoyed his lunches in the office.

Alas, the dark-blue-painted door with its black, squeaking latch and hinges wailed at the arrival of an intruder.

Tam quenched the urge to immediately stiffen. He dropped the letter back onto the desk, already hoping whoever it was—most likely one of his parents—wouldn't ask about what he was reading.

It turned out to be his mother, and so the odds of Tam not being asked about what he was working on were Gods awful.

"My son, are you forgetting something?" the duchess greeted him with a tight smile as she clasped her hands in front of her gold-patterned skirts.

Tam frowned and tilted his head.

With Kat's coronation coming up, it was entirely possible there was something he didn't remember.

Was he supposed to send money to a moonshine merchant? Or was there a letter for the Coven of Wittica he had forgotten to send…?

Annika cleared her throat, and out from behind her stepped Eli.

The young man gave a quick bow to Tam and kept his eyes lowered.

Eli wasn't exceptionally tall, though he was taller than the duchess—not that that said much.

"You forgot to tell your assistant what you need his help with," Annika informed Tam, still wearing a smile, although Tam could tell she wanted to wag a finger in his face.

The future duke rose from his seat, his hands finding his pockets as he addressed his mother. "I don't have any work he can help me with right now. I'm just tending to… personal correspondence."

"Shouldn't your assistant know about your personal correspondence? As your *personal* assistant?"

Tam gave his mother a very firm look.

She knew why he had reservations about trusting the lad, and she of all people should've understood. In all of their espionage work together, she had always been the one reminding him to be very wary of people. The slight eyebrow raise she gave him argued that he should be able to get information out of Eli *because* of his own secret outings and work. Tam's irritable, quiet huff said that he didn't need to have *more* on his plate, inspecting someone who worked so close to him.

"You were going to reject the viscount and baron anyway," Annika said, verbalizing the silent argument her son was thinking, thus revealing she already knew exactly what he happened to be reading.

"Did you open my missives?" Tam implored, an edge entering his voice.

"No. I took a guess because the viscount and baron tried to speak to your father and me at the castle yesterday afternoon about whether you'd seen their letters yet."

Tam looked at the ceiling.

Sometimes, he hated living and working in such close proximity to his family… Alright, he often hated it.

"Eli, feel free to go have a seat by the fire. I'll have the maids bring you up a cup of tea. I'm sure you and my son will want to familiarize yourselves with each other. Now, if you will pardon me."

The duchess gave a cordial smile to Eli and then swept out of the room, closing the door behind her.

Tam's gaze moved to the stone fireplace as he released a very careful breath. He hoped it could maybe dispel some of his anger, as it was starting to stir up his magic. Plunking himself down in his chair, he rubbed the back of his neck, then his temple.

"Sorry, Eli. I don't mean to be an arse. I just don't like strangers being thrust at me." Tam couldn't quite bring himself to look at his assistant yet.

"It is no problem, my lord."

Tam grunted the instant Eli used the term *my lord*, and while he knew he should've apologized, needed to take a moment to rub his eyes.

"Please… have a seat… by the fire. I will… continue… working," he managed while barely resisting knocking his forehead against the desk.

"If you like, my lord, I would be happy to write the rejection letters on your behalf to the viscount and the baron."

Shaking his head with his eyes still closed, Tam waved the young man toward the chairs.

"Look, I'm sure you're brilliant, and you probably don't want this job, either—"

"I am grateful for Duke Finlay Ashowan's assistance."

Tam stopped, his gaze snapping up after Eli's wooden response, freezing the young man on his journey to the armchairs by the fire.

"Wait… You…" Tam stood. "You actually *don't* want the job!" A smile broke out across the future duke's face that made Eli lean away, his eyes still averted.

"My lord, I am of course grateful that I—"

"No, no. No, no. You don't want to be here, correct? Then you don't have to be here! I'd be glad to find you a place where you can do what you prefer! I know my da said something about the coven giving you issues, but I don't mind creatively adjusting some paperwork so you can enjoy a job you actually want!"

Tam rounded the desk feeling absolutely elated.

His father and mother couldn't object if Eli really didn't want the job!

The assistant flinched and gripped his hands together tightly in front of himself. "N-no, my lord. If I've offended you, o-or you think I'm unsuitable for the role, I apologize. I will work hard to make up for my shortcomings."

Tam stared at Eli carefully.

The young man really hadn't sounded all that happy to be there, but he definitely *was* desperate to stay there.

Odd.

Tam dropped his head dejectedly.

Perhaps he *was* becoming a little too secluded and difficult as he got older.

"Look, Eli, I—" Tam lifted his face to stare straight at the young man, and then was surprised into falling silent once more. He stared at the shape of Eli's jaw, the freckle dotting the top of his right cheekbone, his thick black hair and thin neck... Then he looked down at the young man's torso.

Eli nervously glanced at Tam and hastily looked away again when he realized how studiously he was being watched.

"Good Gods. How in the hell did *no one* catch on that you're a *woman?*"

The Zinferan stumbled backward in shock. "W-what do you mean, my lord? I am Eli, from Zinfera. I-I am eighteen years old, and I—"

"Does the prince know about this?" Tam asked incredulously, his mind reeling with whatever these implications meant.

Eli's wide eyes jumped upward. "I'm not a woman! I swear!"

"Eli?"

"Yes, my lord?"

"You don't have a bobble in your throat, you still have a high-pitched voice despite being eighteen, you don't have any facial hair—"

"That is not uncommon in Zinfera!"

"You don't even have a mustache. Eli. I am absolutely certain you are a woman, and I'm wondering how in the hell no one thought I'd notice—Wait. Is this a prank? From Kat? It is, isn't it? For fun, she bet her husband how long it'd take me to notice you were a woman! Of bloody course. Now that I've figured it out, does this mean you actually have a position with Prince Eric and not me?"

There was a tense moment of silence.

Then Eli collapsed onto her knees, bowing. "Please... Please do not tell anyone."

"You're jesting. Everyone has to—" Tam stopped talking when he saw how Eli trembled.

"Oh. Godsdammit. No one actually noticed? Shit. Please don't bow. Godsdammit, I'm sorry! I-I had no idea! My sister likes to play pranks, and I thought this was one of them!" Tam was already dropping down to a crouch as he rambled while holding up his hands in surrender.

"Please… Please do not tell anyone. Please. I've hidden this since I left Zinfera. If people find out… it means it might be easier to find me!" Eli explained in a near shout.

"Okay! Alright! Not a problem! I won't tell anyone! Please just… stop… bowing."

The end of Tam's words were then punctuated by the brisk opening of the door.

One of the maids stopped dead in her tracks at the sight before her.

She stared at Eli, who was still bowed on the floor, then at Tam who had his hands outstretched in the air.

"Erm… is this a bad time…?" she ventured squeakily.

Tam cringed. "Just a bit. Leave the tea on the small table and that'll be all, thank you."

The maid gave an uncertain nod, then proceeded into the office, set the tea tray down on the table between the armchairs in front of the fire, and took her leave, her eyes already darting to the hall as she left.

"Godsdammit, she's going to tell my mother."

"You think she heard us?" Eli sat up, worry bright in her eyes.

Tam's hands finally lowered as he looked at her. "No… but she'll think I'm being a real arsehole to you."

Eli nodded in understanding and settled back onto her haunches, grimacing.

"You… You swear you won't tell anyone…?"

Tam couldn't fully hide his sardonic expression. "How in the world does no one see that you are female?"

"Well… I think the Troivackian king knew by the time I left, but Zinferan women tend to be a little easier to disguise."

"Women who disguise themselves as men always decrease their age. Are you also older than eighteen?" Tam questioned directly.

"You know a lot of women who disguise themselves as men?" Eli returned instead of answering.

Tam gave her a tight smile. "Stories for another time. So. How old are you really?"

Eli's shoulders hunched. "Twenty-five."

"Mm-hmm. Alright. And... Prince Eric does not know?"

"No, he doesn't."

"Does the Troivackian king know all your secrets?"

Looking to the ceiling, Eli frowned pensively. "I don't think so...?"

Tam started to rub his face again while Eli seemed to sift through what appeared to be a great volume of secrets she was hiding about herself.

So much for a tranquil morning...

CHAPTER 4

AN OUTGOING ORIENTATION

As the carriage bumped and squeaked its way up the steep road through Austice toward the castle, Tam stared out the window. Most people would have been looking at the storefronts with their colorful painted, rounded doors and signs, or even at the people who traveled alone along the sides of the streets, but he looked blindly at the moving road.

Across from him sat Eli—if that was her real name.

An urgent missive had been sent to the keep. Since both of Tam's parents were already at the castle in Austice, the summons in the letter was undoubtedly for him—though the note had been vague.

He assumed the request had something to do with his sister's coronation, but given the day he'd had since discovering Eli was not a young man, but a woman, and that same damnable sense that an even bigger storm was brewing, he found himself already bracing for something awful.

Tam wondered if they were going to ask him to take over as Eric's assistant. Gods knew the Daxarian prince had gone through a number of them since his and Katarina's eldest son Antony had learned to walk.

The current king's assistant, Mr. Kevin Howard, had only managed to hang on and resist retirement as a result of King Norman emptying a staggering amount of gold into the assistant's possession... and Finlay Ashowan agreeing to supply the man with as much moonshine as he required. However, once Eric was crowned, both His Majesty King Norman and Mr. Howard were set to live out their days in peace, out of the court.

Eli's quiet voice broke through Tam's anxious thoughts, making him look away from the blurring cobblestones to the woman who kept her eyes turned to the empty seat beside him. "If you have reported to His Majesty or the coven the truth about my gender... I-I know I have no right to ask this, but could you please tell me now? I will accept whatever punishment is assigned to me. I just wish to mentally prepare."

Tam took in a small breath, almost making himself sneeze as a result of the dust the carriage wheels had stirred up along their journey. "I didn't tell anyone that you're a woman. You have my word."

She swallowed, looking wholly unconvinced.

At least she gives as much trust as she expects back, Tam noted wryly.

Just why in the world had she been thrust into his care?

No one ever paid him much mind, it was true... at least outside the realm of *What is wrong with Tam? Why can't Tam look up from his feet? Why does Tam hide from everyone and everything? Why are crowds and large spaces hard for Tam? Is Tam stupid? Is Tam touched with the power of the devil?*

Despite being wildly self-conscious over how obvious he was being presently, with his hands gripping into fists out of discomfort, Tam did his utmost to look at Eli as calmly as possible to ease at least some of the stress mounting between them in the vehicle.

"I didn't like the circumstances that brought you into my life, but I have no personal problems with you. Your past, and your secrets, I have no interest in getting involved with. I'm more interested in staying *out* of them, and I don't say that to be callous. I don't think you really want me getting close to you, either. I apologize if I've been rude." Tam bowed his head regally.

There. He had used a combination of honesty and noble respectfulness to draw clear lines as well as clarify his true thoughts.

As much energy as such an act usually took, it almost always paid off.

"I believe you. I do not know you well enough to have an issue with you, either. At this time, I simply have my own reservations that I've formed out of necessity. Thank you for your understanding."

An equally painful but effective response. Though Tam wondered if Eli's reservations were about everyone or the Ashowan duchy in particular.

Deciding that it wasn't his business either way, Tam nodded, and the ride resumed in silence.

"The Coven of Wittica and King Norman of Daxaria are both very reasonable and fair in their dealings. I'm sure you will be able to build the life you wish." Tam cleared his throat and pulled his shoulders back as he resumed staring out the window as they neared the castle.

Eli didn't say anything.

"You served under His Majesty King Brendan Devark for the past seven years, yes?" Tam asked next.

"Yes, my lord."

"How... How has Alina—Her Majesty—been doing?"

The informal use of the Troivackian queen's first name had Eli's eyes homing in on Tam's profile.

He could feel Eli's curious stare, and knew he should have been more careful when asking about Alina. It had just been a while since he could talk to someone about the Troivackian queen without people suspecting he was still mooning after her.

"Her Majesty had a difficult year after Her Highness Princess Katarina departed, but she has become quite renowned in Troivack. There has been some civil unrest as a result of some of her work, but she and His Majesty seem to be managing it well."

"I'm glad she's doing alright..." Tam smiled a little as he said the words to himself, his gaze already distracted.

With nothing else pressing to address, the rest of the carriage ride proceeded without another word shared between Tam and his assistant.

The castle in Austice was filled with its usual amount of chaos by the time Tam's carriage pulled up to its front steps. Even without exiting the vehicle, he could hear faint shouts coming from within the tall iron doors.

Eli paused in moving to get out of the carriage, a blank, dazed expression on her face that made Tam smile knowingly. While the assistant didn't explicitly show or say anything, Tam had a hunch about exactly what her thoughts were.

"Yes. Ever since my sister was crowned princess? It's always been like this. Our keep is actually the quiet place by comparison. Unless of course the three princes join her when she visits."

Eli cleared her throat and lowered her eyes in an effort to once again appear politely indifferent. "I see, my lord."

Tam's gaze lingered on Eli another moment while she kept her face turned down dutifully before exiting the carriage.

Footmen awaited him outside and he bobbed his head in greeting before, without thinking, he turned back to the open carriage door and offered Eli his hand.

The two footmen behind Tam balked.

Eli had just been starting to clamber out of her seat when she realized there was a hand offered to help her out... as though she were a lady...

She stared at it, and then at Tam, whose eyes were growing round as he realized what he had automatically started to do.

He gaped at her, frozen, as she sank back into the shadows of the carriage.

His mind racing, Tam cleared his throat, masked his dumbfounded expression, and said, "Eli, did you not bring the paperwork I told you to? I needed to review it prior to the meeting today."

Relief flooded the assistant's face as she leaned forward in a bow. "I apologize, my lord, the duke said he had already brought everything needed today to the castle. I was unaware there was more."

"Ah... It's—it's not your fault. I know it's hard having to go back and forth between my father and me," Tam added smoothly before dropping his hand and turning toward the castle doors.

He waited for Eli to finish exiting the carriage before he began walking, and he was relieved to see the footmen looking disinterested yet again.

On the steps to the castle doors, before the guards could overhear, Eli murmured. "My lord, you only found out my secret yesterday, was it really—"

"As of this afternoon I've known you as a woman longer than I've known you as a man," Tam defended seamlessly.

Apparently unable to refute that point, Eli dropped the topic, though Tam had definitely heard the tiny grain of irritation in her tone.

The two entered the castle that was bustling with servants all dedicated to their tasks of hanging large emerald banners with golden edging in preparation for the coronation. Fortunately, the staff had the help of Keith Lee, the royal court mage, who was using magic to help straighten the material. Other servants were scrubbing the floors and walls.

Tam hesitated venturing farther into the castle in order to gaze around the transforming room. While he normally wasn't able to lift his sights for very long in such a wide, busy space due to his magic, the excitement and liveliness of the room permitted it, though he also had to find an appropriate path up to the council room.

"Tam!" a familiar voice called out, and the future duke turned to see none other than a close friend of his father's, the head of housekeeping for the castle, Hannah.

The older woman had silvery-streaked blond hair that she wore piled atop her head with a few wavy wisps floating around her face. Her dark-blue eyes were clear and wide, and she wore a tidy but sensible cream-colored dress that gave her an almost heavenly look.

"Afternoon," Tam said with a smile.

"Are you here for the meeting?" Hannah asked, beaming back at him.

"That I am. Hannah, this here is Eli," Tam continued, noticing that Hannah was turning toward the assistant, who was already bowing to her.

"Ah, yes! We've met once or twice before when you came with His Majesty King Brendan."

"Yes, Ms. Hannah."

Hannah's eyes warmed fondly at the sight of Eli before she turned a questioning look at Tam.

"My mother hired her—him to be my new assistant," he corrected hastily.

The housekeeper's eyebrows shot upward. "Your mother wore *you* down?"

Tam looked at the ceiling briefly before letting out a long breath. "How should I get to the meeting without ruining any of your staff's hard work?"

Hannah grinned knowingly before turning and pointing to the left, where the banners were being hung. "We aren't cleaning over there until after we've finished decorating. Do you mind using the south stairwell?"

"Not at all. See you later!" Tam waved and set a brisk pace toward the perimeter of the entrance hall with Eli trailing behind him.

"Is there a reason you haven't had any other assistants since Likon?" Eli ventured in a curious voice, jogging to catch up to Tam's long strides.

The pair were already crossing behind one of the largest banners and moments later had stepped into the corridor, which thankfully looked a little less busy.

"I told you the first day. I'm not good with strangers, and I like working on my own."

"Likon says you complain all the time about how much work you have."

"I just wish there were two of me, but not much I can do there."

"I suppose one day you could have a son that would help."

"Did my mother pay you to say that?"

Tam could feel Eli's eyes snap up. "No. Apologies if I've—"

"Don't worry about it. Ah." Tam suddenly stopped in his tracks, and Eli almost bumped into his back.

Tam turned and quickly but quietly pressed Eli out the nearby doorway, down the stone steps, and—with his hand hovering just behind her back—toward the castle wall under the windows.

Eli blinked rapidly the entire way, looking confused about what in the world had prompted the strange exit out by the castle's rose maze. The soggy ground beneath their boots was just starting to turn green with the promise of spring.

Tam waited, and from above, the sounds of two people talking and walking by the window reached them.

Perhaps sensing that this was the reason for hiding, Eli patiently waited in silence while Tam fixed his gaze on the earth.

Once the voices were out of earshot, Tam cleared his throat. "Sorry about that. Shall we?"

"Is there a reason you are avoiding His Majesty King Brendan and Her Majesty Alina Devark?" Eli had identified the speakers easily enough.

Jogging up the stone steps, Tam resumed his former pace without batting an eye at the question. "The king isn't fond of me, and I'm already late for the meeting. I don't need to add an uncomfortable encounter to my day."

Once they had returned to the castle corridor and resumed their journey, Tam lowered his voice, then asked as casually as possible, "I understand why you'd want to lie about your gender when you were enslaved, but why did you keep lying about it?"

Eli winced and glanced around quickly. "It still seemed like the safest option. I know you've heard I don't wish to be found or return to Zinfera, and being a woman tends to… complicate matters."

Moderately surprised that he'd received the semblance of a straight answer, Tam decided not to push his luck any further. They reached the servants' discreet, winding stairwell and started to climb.

"Well, don't worry. Even if we do not continue working together, I'm sure you won't have to return to Zinfera under any circumstances."

Sadly, however, Tam's reassurance seemed to prod at fate in such a manner that it took exception, though he had no way of knowing this as they headed into the meeting with Prince Eric Reyes's inner council.

CHAPTER 5

A WEIGH-IN FROM THE WISERS

Tam and Eli sat at the farther end of the council room table that, as Eric's coronation neared, had grown more crowded.

At the head sat King Norman Reyes, the wise king of Daxaria, who had streaks of brown along his temples; his pointed beard looked much the same it had nearly thirty years ago, save for its lack of color. Age spots had appeared around his cheeks in the past five years, and his hands had become whorled, but the brightness in his hazel eyes still spoke of his quick mind.

On the king's left sat his assistant, Mr. Kevin Howard. The man was incredibly competent, but he had a distaste for the unpredictable and chaotic parts of life. Meaning that he had a *special* sort of relationship with the current duke of the Ashowan family—Finlay, the house witch—since the duke had a highly developed skill set when it came to stirring up all kinds of unprecedented occurrences.

Kevin Howard, now in his older years, had thinning white hair that still waved in places much as it had in his younger years. His dark-blue eyes remained sharp and intelligent, but were placed behind a pair of round, gold spectacles he wore because his vision had begun to blur with age.

On the king's right sat Finlay Ashowan. The duke was just past his mid-fifties and yet looked forty at most. This was a side effect of the curse his mother, a healing witch, had cast long ago to bring him back to life—the steep cost of such a spell being both her life and Finlay's vastly expanded lifespan. The curse element being that it was unspoken but widely known that Fin would outlive his beloved wife, and even possibly his own children. Fin's hair was still the same brilliant red it had always been, save for the white touching his temples, and his slanted almond eyes remained their electrifying light blue.

Beside the duke sat Captain Taylor of the Daxarian military, a man with a bushy salt-and-pepper beard. What hair remained on his dome-shaped head was a mere quarter inch long. He was a large man, and as he had aged, his muscles had given way to softness; talk of his retirement was growing more and more prevalent. While a bit socially clumsy, the soldier had a knack for rallying his men, and he also held a longtime friendship with Duke Finlay Ashowan, as once upon a time he had been sent to the house witch's kitchen to serve as an aide as punishment for his abysmal behavior.

Beside the king's assistant sat the prince, Eric Reyes, who looked as serious as ever, his arms folded as he sat back in his seat listening to the proceedings, his short dirty-blond hair was tidy and his beard cropped short. He had grown strong and hearty since his time in Troivack seven years ago. If anything, the soon-to-be king had only trained harder, thanks to his wife being overly enthusiastic with the sword.

Beside the prince was his friend and temporary assistant, Marquis Morgan Linsey, a nobleman in his thirties with light-brown hair, a lean face with freckles, and pale-brown eyes.

Finally, there was the visiting leader of the Coven of Wittica, Louise Riddel, a bespectacled woman in her early fifties with chestnut-brown hair and glinting green eyes. She had come into her position three years prior. She had a kindly round face, but the tightness with which she pinned her hair hinted at a disposition that might be a bit fierce.

"Lord Tamlin, thank you for joining us," the king called out regally.

Tam bowed his head. "Of course, Your Majesty."

He and Eli sat side by side at the farthest end of the table, away from the rest of the council.

"The reason we summoned you today is to try to make some headway with the coven's concerns regarding you and Her Highness Princess Katarina taking over positions of leadership and power, when doing so is outside the lifestyle that witches should be following, according to the will of the Goddess."

Tam nodded in understanding.

"It has been decided that Lady Katarina will no longer be a member of the Coven of Wittica after her coronation at the end of this month," Louise Riddel informed Tam, her tone dignified and ambiguous about any personal feelings she might have on the matter.

Tam straightened in his seat and frowned. "Why is my sister not here when this decision is being made?"

"She was," Eric replied calmly, drawing his brother-in-law's eyes to him. "She left shortly before you arrived due to some… issue… with the princes."

The council became momentarily awkward. Everyone looked pointedly around the room with its many bookshelves and tapestries.

Tam couldn't help but briefly speculate what his nephews' new source of mischief was. Surprisingly, it couldn't have involved anything happening with the banners in the front hall—he would have seen them.

"So Her Highness agrees to no longer be a part of the coven?" Tam continued after taking a quick breath and dragging his mind away from his sister's children.

"Yes. Of course, the princes are not expected to forgo their education from the coven should they prove to have abilities themselves. However, come the time of abdication and the naming of an heir, choosing the child without magic may become the precedent henceforth. At this time, however, the coven still holds the position that should any one of the three princes prove to lack any magical ability, by default he should be the next king," Louise explained. "If two of them do not have magic, the eldest will resume the throne."

"Are you wanting me to relinquish my place in the coven as well then?" Tam guessed. In all honesty, he had never felt all that attached to technically belonging to the coven. The only issue was that it subsequently brought up another important matter.

"Given that the Ashowan duchy gained its title in part thanks to its service to both the coven and the crown, your dismissal as a member of the coven was not our first inclination." Louise paused and glanced at Finlay Ashowan, whose stony expression warned Tam that whatever was coming next would not be good.

"However, you have not disclosed what your own magical abilities are, and while we understand that they are traumatic in nature, we do insist that you disclose any details you have about them, especially given the fact that you would be acting as a diplomat between the coven and the crown."

Tam felt an iciness twist his gut. His teeth clenched, and it was a brutal battle within himself to look and sound cordial.

"I understand that I would be in a position of great importance, taking part in the affairs of both the coven and the court here in Austice. However, I don't use my magic. Why does it need to be disclosed?"

"For the sake of the sensitive information you will be tasked with, but also for the safety of your king and fellow witches." Louise Riddel didn't look hateful or suspicious when she answered Tam, but she didn't look sympathetic either.

Tam felt his magic stir in his chest, and a new inner conflict started to tear at him.

"And if I refuse…?"

The tension in the air mounted, and Tam could sense Eli stiffening at his side.

Louise Riddel's thin lips pursed. "Then I am afraid we cannot condone you acting as the next diplomat of the coven. Sadly, this has other implications as well." The coven leader looked to the king, who was regarding Tam with an equally somber expression.

"Some council members are arguing that the dukedom should cease to exist after your father retires."

Tam's right hand curled under the table as potent anger surged forward. It was in no way helping his battle against the magical power already tugging painfully at the center of his chest.

"I have worked tirelessly for the dukedom since my father received the title. I have carried out all requests. Without his presence I've been a part of several negotiations involved with the Coven of Wittica. My preference not to reveal my abilities has never been an issue before. Why is it a problem now? Have my contributions and work not been satisfactory?" Tam's gaze bored into the coven leader's face.

The lines around Louise's eyes tightened as the air around Tamlin Ashowan took on a darker edge. "That is because up until your assumption of the title, your father would accept responsibility should anything happen. Once you are named duke and diplomat, however, that is no longer the case. Your abilities will be kept private between those who need to validate that you are not only in control of your magic, but that it does not pose a threat should something like what happened to Her Highness Katarina Reyes in Troivack happen to you."

An elite knight in the Troivackian court had attacked Katarina by throwing the potent drug known as Witch's Brew into her face, drugging her into a state where she lost control of her abilities.

Tam didn't bat an eye at this argument. "My sister had disclosed her powers, and when the attack happened no one knew what to do."

"But there was *some* understanding. Luckily, your father was able to intervene back then. But we don't know if your powers are so great that even Duke Finlay Ashowan cannot combat them."

"I'm not a threat." Tam's voice was hoarse. His skin prickled as he resisted the magic continuing to rise in his being.

He needed to leave. Immediately.

"Wouldn't Lord Tam be stripped of all titles by that logic?"

Everyone in the room was startled, as the interruption had come from none other than Eli.

With everyone still momentarily stunned, she bowed her head and continued. "You spoke about stripping his title of duke. Would his mother's former viscount house also be stripped?"

"That position was not specifically created to also bear the responsibilities to the Coven of Wittica, so no. He would still hold Viscount House Jenoure," Norman assured while eyeing Eli with a little more interest.

Fortunately, Eli's interruption had given Tam enough time to get a hold of himself. "Is this condition the only way I can inherit the dukedom? Or is there something else the coven would accept?" He didn't bother hiding his displeasure.

Giving a slight bow of her head, Louise responded, "At this time, that is the official and firm position of the coven."

Inside his skull, Tam's magic began an unholy buzzing as he sifted through any excuses he could use to get out of the meeting. Then the king spoke.

"There is another matter that we were hoping to discuss with you today, Lord Tam."

Tam forced himself to look at the ruler, and instantly felt his furious emotions ever so slightly soothed in the face of the man's gentle eyes.

Norman had always treated Tam kindly, and did his best to speak with him privately rather than in a group setting. It was a consideration that Tam had always appreciated, and he admired how observant and patient the king was.

"The Zinferan emperor has fallen silent."

Tam knew without looking that Eli had turned pale.

"He has been in poor health for years, and has outlived what all his physicians predicted. This means his court has had plenty of time to become divided. There is the expectation that a new ruler will soon be named, and there is even talk of the capital moving." The king stared at everyone grimly. "Zinfera has long been our ally, but this power struggle suggests great change. What is even more troubling is that his concubines are engaging in horrific acts, and, unfortunately, we do not have the grounds to officially intervene without risking a war. Sadly, the emperor is too proud, and his mind too compromised from his sickness, to listen to reason. However… we now have an excellent reason to become involved before there are any developments that may sour our dealings with them, with the help of Troivack."

Tam was relatively certain Eli had stopped breathing.

"Ancient beasts not seen since the first witch loosed them have been spotted in Zinfera. Allegedly, there is a dragon." Norman's gaze subtly moved from Tam to Eli, then to Fin.

Tam turned to his father, who gave his son an unreadable glance before returning his attention to the king.

"We need someone to investigate and gather proof of the dragon's existence, and to do so quietly."

With growing dread, Tam realized where the discussion was going.

"Lord Tam, Eli…" Eric started softly. "I have proposed that the two of you be the ones to gather the evidence we need while learning more details about what exactly is happening in Zinfera between the higher ranked nobility. Duke Finlay is too recognizable and would be discovered quickly, as he has traveled several times to Zinfera's court. Tam, with your black hair and the shape of your eyes, you won't be as noticeable. You, of course, will have assistance from Lord Jiho Ryu, your father's friend."

"Why does Eli need to return? Wasn't sh—*he* promised that he'd never have to return?" Tam demanded while his assistant's shoulders curled forward.

"Thank you for bringing that up, Lord Tam," Louise Riddel interjected.

Tam's gaze slid slowly to the woman. He was starting to feel a deeper dislike toward the coven leader.

"Your new assistant, much like yourself, has requested that he never has to share what his magical ability is."

"So? He doesn't hold a position of power," Tam bit back sharply.

"It makes acquiring Daxarian citizenship difficult, because he has also refused to share his parentage."

"He worked alongside the Troivackian king with no issue in the past seven years. Again, why does it suddenly matter now?"

"He was little more than a prisoner as they investigated the former Duke Sebastian Icarus's dealings," Louise Riddel supplied.

"Eli was captured, enslaved, threatened, Gods know what else, and then proceeded to help in the investigation voluntarily, while also serving the king without having any real freedom, and you think this is somehow *his* fault and needs to be punished?" Tam's voice had risen and gained a deadly edge.

Everyone leaned back in their seats.

Even rarer than Eli talking was Tam speaking loudly to anyone who wasn't his sister.

"Tell me, who here has fallen off a horse headfirst recently?" he continued acidly.

"Part of the process to complete his citizenship is that he serves as an assistant," Eric interjected calmly. "That means he needs to go with you, Lord Tam. We are also hoping he will be able to provide insight and information that will help you during your time in Zinfera. Neither of you will be expected to make a formal announcement of your arrival or attend court."

Tam said nothing.

He could tell this wasn't a request.

So he looked at Eli—and almost flinched.

She was staring at the prince, her eyes filled with betrayal, and hurt.

Eric at least had the decency to look apologetic toward his old friend.

Furious, Tam lowered his gaze.

He could refuse to take on this task, but that would work against his case to remain as the heir to the dukedom—especially as the new coven leader seemed determined to find out what his magic was, one way or another.

No one in the council room seemed to feel particularly good about the way things were going. Judging by the look on the king's face, he was debating whether he should press the matter or change the subject, but he was spared a decision when the door slammed open amid the loud objections of the guards.

Everyone's heads whipped around to see…

Lord Dick Fuks. The former chief of Daxaria's military. The man was legendarily mad as he was brilliant.

He stood with his arms straight out as though presenting himself, in his full one hundred years of wrinkly glory…

Completely nude.

"Fear not, Your Majesty! I'm here for the council meeting!"

Everyone truly was at a loss for words.

At least they were momentarily distracted from the tense discussion when faced with the legendary Lord Dick Fuks and his low-hanging fruit basket.

CHAPTER 6

THE UNDERESTIMATED UNDERDOGS

Tam stood outside the council room with the other members of the meeting while Lord Dick Fuks's son, Les Fuks, tried to convince the elderly man to return to his chamber and put his clothes back on. Lord Dick was wildly proud of his name, as he believed it built character and notoriety, and so he named his son Les Fuks, while his grandson Aster went by the nickname Ass Fuks.

The new earl, Les, had loathed the tradition, but his son Aster had wholly sided with his beloved grandfather.

As Lord Dick Fuks had aged, he had grown even more outlandish in his behavior, and for a while, many weren't certain if the former earl was simply being eccentric, or if he was perhaps falling into the terrible mental decay some men at his impressive age succumbed to. However, in the past year, it had become clear that he wasn't cooking with all the ingredients, much to Les Fuks's dismay. Before, he'd had a sliver of hope of helping his father toe the line of propriety, but recently... that was not the case.

So as Les Fuks waged another long battle with his father, Tam faced off with his own troubling parent. Eli stood off alone to give them privacy.

"Why the hell have I been working my arse off helping you run this dukedom if they are just going to take the title and lands right back? Does Mum know that they are proposing this?" Tam demanded, his voice quiet but angry.

"I haven't told her yet because I thought you should hear about it first," Fin said softly. "Tam, to be honest, I'm a little surprised that you care this much about it. You hate all of the public appearances the role requires—not to mention the work itself. If you become a viscount, you still have a title, and you won't have to worry about traveling to check on the schools, because the next diplomat would be taking over those duties. And you'd have to be the worst gambler alive to squander all the money your mother has saved."

Tam didn't speak as he stared blindly down the hall where the other council members and the king milled about, waiting to resume the meeting. Emotions burned in his throat, making it difficult to find the words. Finally, he managed, "Did you really think I'd be relieved to hear that because I have a problem with my magic, I cost our family this title?"

"Tam, it isn't your magic that's the problem. It's that you aren't disclosing what it does. After what happened with your sister in Troivack, it makes sense that they want to know your abilities."

"Despite all the work I already do and have already accomplished for the coven? Does my guarantee that my abilities aren't a threat to anyone other than myself mean nothing?"

"Tam... Are you *absolutely* certain that your abilities can't harm anyone? Without a shadow of a doubt?" Fin's blue eyes were intent on his son's face. Tam could hear the sincerity in his father's voice. If he answered that he was absolutely positive he knew the range of his magic, his father would support him in fighting against the council...

But he *couldn't* promise that.

Tam swallowed.

Seeing this reaction, Fin's expression filled with familiar pain. It was the same worried, loving expression that Tam had seen countless times before, whenever the issue of his powers came up.

"I'm on your side, Tam. I know you're a smart man, and that you just want to protect the family, but what if something happened while you were investigating the schools? You know we deal with vulnerable people all the time."

"Right. I get it."

"I will fight the council and the coven to ensure you keep the title of duke, and—"

"Don't." Tam turned, his magic in his chest rattling, wanting to be used. "I'll figure something out. It's me they have a problem with, not you. You just focus on your retirement plans with Mum."

"Tam, no matter what, I'm your father. I am here to help regardless of title or age, and needing help from others doesn't mean you're not capable. Trust me, if it weren't for other people I know, I—"

"You never would've been able to be with Mum. I know. I know you just want to help. I know *everyone* is just trying to figure out what's best for me, but I'm not a child. I'll decide that for myself." Tam stalked away from the council room, not caring at all that he hadn't asked to be excused by the king.

Seeing that her employer was leaving, Eli nervously started shuffling down the hall after him. She had to pass Fin, though, and the duke held up a hand to stop her.

"Maybe just give him a bit of time. I also was hoping to apologize to you about asking you to return to Zinfera." Fin gave a strained, sheepish smile.

Eli fidgeted with the seam of her trousers as she bowed. "May I request that I excuse myself from accompanying Lord Tam to Zinfera, and instead remain here in Daxaria to offer my assistance to you, Your Grace?"

"This is more Eric's—His Highness's idea than my own. I understand that, like my son, you have things you'd much rather keep to yourself, and I can't imagine what you have lived through. I've already argued these points with His Highness. I think right now the prince is desperate to have someone he can trust and that knows the Zinferan empire."

Eli didn't answer immediately, her eyes remaining lowered as something dawned on her: "Even if I wasn't serving Lord Tam… His Highness would've requested I go."

"I think so. I can arrange for you and the prince to speak more privately tomorrow if you like," Fin offered while raising his hand palm up in the air as though asking her if she'd like a biscuit with her tea.

The duke appeared to disagree with the idea of sending his son and assistant to spy on the Zinferan kingdom. While Eli appreciated that, she suspected the duke was being considerate more toward his son than toward her. After all, why would she matter when the greater powers of Daxaria said otherwise?

That was always how it was. She was shoved around wherever anyone with more power willed it. She just had to survive and make the best of it until she could be free.

"Thank you, Your Grace, but I'm sure His Highness will speak to me if he thinks it is worthwhile."

Fin stared at Eli as she bowed. A funny half smile tugged at the corner of his mouth. "You know… I think you and Tam might do really well together."

Straightening, Eli kept her chin lowered. "I appreciate your confidence in me, Your Grace. I hope that Lord Tam feels the same way."

Fin nodded idly, though his gaze remained on the assistant. The measured distance that Eli placed between herself and everyone was peculiar…

"Pardon me, Your Grace, I will go see if I should call for the carriage to take Lord Tam home or not."

Blinking out of his thoughts, Fin slipped his hands into his pockets and nodded. "Of course. I will see you back at the keep this evening unless my daughter invites me to dinner."

Eli bowed once more in response, then turned and hurried after Tam with the hopes of leaving with him in the very near future.

Tam sat with his back against the knights' barracks, eyes closed.

It was one of his favorite places to have a moment to calm down, as it reminded him of Captain Antonio, the former Daxarian military leader who had been like a grandfather to him and his sister before his death more than a decade ago.

With his magic no longer tearing at his insides, and his breath slow and even, Tam reluctantly turned his mind to the council meeting… until he sensed another presence.

He didn't have to open his eyes to know who it was. "You found me quite quickly."

Eli gave a subtle huff. "I would've come faster, but your father wanted to speak with me."

The tense note that entered her voice prompted Tam to look up at his new assistant. There was grimness in her eyes, and a trace of anger showed in the way her jaw was clenched.

"If you really don't want to go to Zinfera, you won't have to," he told her.

"The prince wills it."

"Then he can go if he wants it so badly. I thought you two were friends."

"As much as a prince can be friends with a refugee," Eli countered mildly.

Tam paused. As accepting as Eli was forcing herself to seem, the hardness behind her polite mask revealed her true thoughts.

"Daxaria isn't like Zinfera or Troivack. Commoners and nobility are quite close here. Just look at my father and mother. He was the cook."

Eli didn't respond, but Tam could tell she didn't fully buy that point.

Deciding not to prod at what was undoubtedly a sore subject, he instead rubbed his face while leaning forward. "I'll probably be in Zinfera for a few months. It could even be a year or more. Especially if they want me hunting down a dragon. Just tell me where you want to work and I'll find a way." Tam pushed himself to stand while Eli continued staring out across the sea of lush green grass and the pristine blue sky.

"My lord, I... I wanted to say thank you earlier, but I didn't have the chance until now." Eli turned suddenly and bowed.

Tam cringed. "Gods, for what? Or do you mean about not revealing that you're a woman?"

"I mean for objecting to my being forced back to Zinfera."

Tam momentarily balked, then recalled what had occurred in the meeting. "It's fine. Just so you know, you could've said the same thing. If you want something, you need to say so."

"I'm not in a position to—"

"Yes. Yes, you are. You are not a slave. You are a person. A person who has done nothing wrong and has had enough forced upon you."

"I'm not a citizen of Daxaria. I can still be thrown out."

"The instant you were placed in my family's care, that stopped being a possibility."

"Unless you or your parents decide to send me back."

"You'd have to do something remarkably terrible for us to do that."

Eli finally looked at Tam, and just as on the first day she had arrived at his keep, when it was hard for him to look away, he found his attention trapped. Why did she feel so familiar and comfortable? It was easy to look her in the eyes.

"You know, I've been thinking—" Tam broke off. "Battling against people shoving us around is great, but I think we could also maybe have a bit of fun in the meantime."

Eli frowned. "What are you suggesting, my lord?"

"Please stop calling me that," Tam insisted the second the words left her mouth. "Tam is fine. If we're in proper company, I understand, but for the love of the Gods it is painful to hear."

She raised an eyebrow, waiting for him to finish explaining himself.

"As for a bit of fun… My family, and the prince, threw us together because they don't know entirely what to do with us, and because we are both known for keeping secrets. Yes?"

Eli nodded slowly.

"What if we, through our combined efforts, give them a bit of a headache using these reasons against them?"

The assistant rounded on Tam, her head tilted. "Why would we do something so pointless?"

Tam looked to the sky with a sigh. "Juvenile act of rebellion? It's rather cathartic, and somewhat helpful."

"I hardly see how it could be helpful to us."

Tam grinned, startling her. She had heard rumors he was handsome but hadn't paid much attention. Now she realized just how true they were.

"Come now, you know better than anyone that the prince is being a donkey. What I'm suggesting is some harmless fun where no one gets hurt."

Eli opened her mouth to give a resounding no, when Tam leaned forward, his hands in his pockets, his face still smiling and his eyes twinkling.

"So? How about it? As my assistant, do you think you can help me?"

CHAPTER 7

A BELEAGUERED BARGAIN

The Zinferan assistant? *He* has five children back home?"

"He doesn't look old enough to have one child, let alone five!"

"What about the rumor about Lord Tamlin Ashowan? That he weeps anytime he sees sunlight?"

Tam and Eli sat in the well-hidden shadows of the second-story window as they heard the excited discussions taking place between the laundry maids and the maids tasked with scrubbing the floors on their way to dump out their buckets. It was the day after the council meeting, and it hadn't taken long for Tam's supposed mischief to take root.

"See? Perfectly harmless," Tam cited casually to his assistant.

"His Highness and your father know these rumors are fake."

"Exactly. Most of these servants will also know they are fake, but they don't want to quash them. They'll want to keep the rumors going because people love gossip, so they'll twist it using something they know to be true."

"That's irresponsible. What if they guess something that *is* true, or is hurtful?" Eli asked sternly.

"Lord Tamlin walks around in the daylight all the time! He's probably just going blind! That's why he doesn't look up very much!" The fervid retort of one of the maids down below echoed up to the future duke and his assistant.

Eli stared at Tam flatly, as though expecting him to look regretful in the face of such a ridiculous farce.

Tam merely considered the maid's theory while nodding. "It's better than people thinking I see death hovering over those who are about to die."

"Did you plant *all* the rumors that exist about you?" Eli risked a quick look down at the maids while craning her neck over the stone window ledge.

Tam shrugged. "Some. It was usually Kat who started things. I threw one out, here or there... But let's be honest. I *am* quite strange. There's power in no one knowing a clear thing about you. If they don't know where certain gossip originated, they'll assume there has to be a seed of truth to it. If you think the king and his council don't listen to rumors with some measure of seriousness, I'll be the first to tell you otherwise."

Tam pushed himself away from the wall and made his way down the castle corridor, his hands casually stowed in his pockets.

Eli reluctantly followed, her expression exposing her thoughts that maybe her new employer wasn't as serious and dour as she had heard. In a way, that was worse. Even his idea of mischief was surprisingly lackluster...

"Did His Highness really summon me on his own?" Eli wondered skeptically while eyeing Tam's back.

"He did."

Eli fidgeted with her pant leg before changing the subject. "By the way, the chest you packed with your books weighs too much for you to take with you to Zinfera."

Tam didn't say anything. "Did you try taking out the—"

"Yes."

"You don't know what I was going to say." Tam stopped walking and waited for Eli to catch up to him.

She regarded her employer flatly and squared her torso to him. "You were going to ask if I had removed the texts about the fish that Zinferans serve, which can be poisonous if not prepared correctly."

Tam stared back.

"Might I recommend removing the trilogy about the different soil types in Zinfera as well?" she prodded.

Sighing, Tam looked away. "Dammit… That means I have to read them this month before we leave."

"Pardon me, my lord, but why do you need to know those things at all?"

"It's worth knowing if what you are being served is capable of killing you, and it's also worth knowing the types of soil so that if I learn about the various plights of the tenants and farmers under the concubines, I can tell if they are fabricating anything or are hiding funds."

"My lord. That is the type of information an assistant could be learning for you."

"And is my assistant coming with me on this trip?" Tam asked in a mildly sarcastic tone.

Eli's fingers twitched as though wanting to curl into a fist. "It is an order from the soon-to-be king of Daxaria. Of course I will have to go."

Tam scoffed. "I'm willing to bet you gold His Highness will offer you the chance to stay here in Daxaria."

"That depends on his confidence in your ability to manage yourself in a foreign kingdom," Eli returned evenly.

Tam crossed his arms over his chest and raised an eyebrow. "Believe it or not, despite my bit of fun with starting rumors, I am a reasonably capable person."

"I never said otherwise, my lord." Eli bowed her head.

"Besides, as rumors get twisted, people reveal their true perception of you. Sometimes it's actually quite funny." The future duke resumed his walk down the corridor.

Eli appeared to consider his words briefly before darting to catch up.

She didn't have much time to respond, as the two of them reached the prince's office once they rounded the next corner. Tam wasted no time in knocking on the dark wood of the rounded door.

"Come in."

Giving one final glance down at Eli, Tam noted that she had already smoothed her expression to one of neutral submissiveness, her eyes fixed on the floor. A tiny half smile tugged at his mouth for a lone breath of time before he opened the door and entered the office. At least she had stopped wearing such a look around him when they were alone.

Three narrow steps wound up from the door into the tower where the office was located. The room was stone, but the ceiling, while not at the peak of the tower, had wooden support beams above. A fire that had been lit hours earlier kept the space toasty warm, and the many books that filled the shelves around the perimeter—save for the fireplace—helped insulate it.

"Ah, Lord Tam. My summons was more for a private word with Eli."

Eric was seated behind an ornate oak desk that was remarkably tidy with his paperwork, quills, and inkpot—most likely thanks to the prince's new assistant.

"I understand, Your Highness, but prior to you two speaking alone I want to say again that I strongly disapprove of forcing Eli to return to Zinfera. Sh—He can stay back with my father as I suggested, and I can complete this journey on my own."

"Your input is noted," Eric returned.

Silence rested over the trio for a beat.

"Well then, I will wait for you to finish." Tam addressed Eli politely, though he caught the flash of annoyance in her face, and knew it was because for the hundredth time since he had learned she was a woman, he had almost revealed the fact.

Once Eli and the prince were alone, Eric stood from his desk with a warm smile. "Have a seat. I already have tea brewed for you."

Eli inclined herself politely and obeyed, already wishing she were alone in her room back at the Ashowans' keep. Even if she technically didn't want to live in the same household as the duke's family, having a quiet space to herself was significantly more attractive than spending her time around Tamlin Ashowan or Eric Reyes.

Eli accepted the porcelain cup that the prince handed to her, her nose twitching at the musty smell. The drink should have had a sweet, mellow scent from the fine, matured leaves the prince most certainly had access to. He really had brewed it himself… and as an avid tea drinker, Eli knew she wouldn't be able to sip it without making a look of disgust.

She put the cup down.

Eric watched her and laughed. "Damn. Thought I'd improved."

"I should return to the Ashowans' keep soon so that I can continue helping Lord Tam pack for the voyage."

The prince's humorous expression shifted as he glanced down at the cup of tea in his own hands. It was rare for him to look so sheepish. "I'm sorry I made that request and didn't tell you about it sooner," he began without looking at Eli.

"As I said to Lord Tam, I understand I am in no position to make demands."

"That's a different attitude compared with when I found you enslaved at Duke Icarus's estate," Eric pointed out, his eyebrows twitching toward a frown.

Eli found herself regretting putting the teacup down. Without the delicate porcelain occupying her hands, she started to fidget, then forced herself to stop. "I had nothing to lose then and figured I'd be killed soon anyway. Hope is a dangerous weapon that hovers over someone powerless like myself."

Eric's frown of uncertainty turned to one of concern. "Eli, I really think you are in a much better position than you realize. The Ashowan family will protect you no matter what. I can't tell you everything about the type of challenges and battles they've faced, but there are very few threats they can't manage. With them as your employers, you'll be safe even in Zinfera."

Eli bit her tongue. She didn't want to tell her old friend he knew nothing about what she was afraid of, or how her life had been controlled by influential people when she herself technically should have been powerful as well. Just because he knew she was a part of the Zinferan royal family didn't mean he understood everything that had happened since she'd been abducted from the palace…

"I won't send you if you're going to hate me."

Eli's brown eyes snapped up.

Eric stared back at her intently. "I had honestly hoped that because you've been away from Zinfera for close to a decade, you'd feel a bit safer—especially because I'm not sending Tam to the capital. He'll be landing at the Ori harbor and traveling to Haeson from there."

Eli jolted in alarm. "The land between the Ori harbor and Haeson city is almost as deadly as the palace itself! Why are you sending him there?"

"Because Concubine Soo Hebin owns most of the towns in that stretch of land."

Eli involuntarily broke out in a cold sweat at the name. She swallowed back the telltale mouthful of saliva that rose as a warning that she was about to vomit.

"She is the most powerful concubine in Zinfera right now. And other than myself, the only family that is powerful enough to keep her in check is the Ashowans. I thought that you might want to help take away some of her influence, given that she was the one who arranged to have you sold, with the help of her cousin Lord Yangban."

Despite barely being able to think straight, Eli numbly realized that the prince either had learned something new about her past or was taking an educated guess at what had happened to her all those years ago.

"I'll stay here in Daxaria," she said.

Eric blinked in surprise. "Are you feeling alright?"

"Fine. Your tea just has an unpleasant odor. Is that everything for today, Your Highness?" Eli forced herself to wait for the prince to dismiss her. She desperately wanted to rush outside to be sick in private.

"You don't have to go to Zinfera," Eric reassured slowly.

Eli did her best to stand and bow in a calm fashion. The prince stood to walk her to the door.

"I admit, I was kind of hoping you'd stay a bit longer today and share your opinion on Tam… He's hard to read, and I've been trying to make heads or tails of him since resuming duties here in Daxaria." Eric glided into the new topic smoothly, his tone more jesting than serious.

"He is a nobleman who has isolated himself and occasionally gets bored as a result," Eli threw out without thinking.

Eric stopped in surprise at her blunt retort.

She bit her tongue, forcing herself to get a hold of her chaotic thoughts. "My apologies. I… I must still be recovering from the long journey from Troivack."

While the prince nodded vaguely, he didn't look entirely convinced. "It's alright. Though if you think Tam acts out, just wait until you meet Duke Oscar Harris of the Iones household. His wife isn't much better, either… They stay with the Ashowans whenever they come to visit, but the amount of repairs the Ashowans have to do to their keep after their every stay is alarming. You'll meet them soon."

Eli's hands curled into fists as Eric opened the door painstakingly slowly.

"Fingers crossed for you." The prince waved her toward the door with a grin.

As if her day wasn't bad enough. Eli stared stonily at Eric, and seeing this, his smile dropped.

"You're still superstitious about that? Alright, I take it back! Fingers are uncrossed!" He lifted his hands into the air in surrender.

Eli reached through the wretched anxiety that was storming her being. She knew this request from the prince held all kinds of opportunities, even if she was scared beyond reason. The timing would even work out for the better so she may as well just get it all over with. Bracing before she could stop herself she said, "You know, Your Highness, if you *promise* me Lord Tam and I won't have to go to the capital, Gondol, I'll go. But afterward? I want to be finished serving the Ashowans, finished with Troivack, and I want to go wherever I please in Daxaria and not be involved in royal politics ever again."

Eric's gaze turned imperial. "I see you've found your motivation to negotiate."

She held out her hand. "Do we have a deal?" Holding the prince's eyes, she waited, her heart in her throat.

After a moment of him scrupulously eyeing her expression as though trying to glean what had inspired this sudden shift in her, Eric grasped her hand and shook it. "You have my word. I'll deal with the coven while you're gone and work with Lord Finlay to make sure you don't have to wait the full year before being freed from your duties."

Eli bobbed her head as she fled the office into the bright corridor, relieved to hear the door close behind her.

However, she was a little surprised to see Tamlin Ashowan leaning against the wall with his arms folded. She had expected him to wait somewhere more comfortable.

They locked eyes.

Eli could tell he had heard everything she had just demanded.

Her right hand finally did close into a fist.

Well, so what if he heard? This is better for the both of us. I'll stop him from being murdered in Zinfera, and then we can both go our separate ways without owing each other anything.

She wondered if Tam would take offense to anything he'd heard, or pressure her for details about her discussion with the prince... She steeled herself for either reaction.

Instead, he pushed off the wall and turned away, looking completely disinterested.

"Come on, we might as well have lunch here before heading back to the keep."

CHAPTER 8

A SISTER'S SCRUPLES

T AM! Tam! Taaam, problem! Big problem!" Katarina burst into her brother's chamber, her long red hair flying around her. "He doesn't look old enough to have one child, let alone five!"

Tam had been in the middle of tying a black silk cravat around his throat. He was only donning it because of his sister's coronation that afternoon. So he was a mite startled by her presence in the keep—she should have been at the castle preparing.

He turned away from the mirror. "What's wrong?" What could have prompted her impromptu visit on one of the most important days of her life?

"Da wants to work as the royal cook again when he retires from the dukedom!"

Tam stared blankly at his sister. Was she jesting?

He continued gaping into her wide, desperate golden eyes.

No. No, she was not.

"Kat, don't you have hundreds of people at your castle waiting for you to be crowned today?"

"Yeah! They can wait! Good Gods, you know I love Da and his cooking, but he would technically be my employee and we both know he has an opinion about everything!" Kat started pacing frantically.

Tam noted her untucked cream tunic and loose trousers. "Did you come here wearing your sleep clothes?"

"Not important right now!" she barked in response.

"Kat, are you maybe overreacting to this because you're nervous about officially becoming queen?"

"Tell me, how would *you* respond if Da skipped on over to you and said he wanted to be your cook? Actually, that's a great idea! Can you tell him you'll hire him?"

"We still have Raymond."

"Raymond's going to retire in the next five years and you know it!"

Tam put his hands on his hips and stared at his sister flatly. "Kat... just tell him no, or ask Mum to convince him that he should spend his time traveling with her, or helping with the boys."

"Right... right... But Mum likes her alone time! If she decides it's a marvelous idea, I'm done for!"

"Kat, he'd be busy all day as the Royal Cook. You really wouldn't have to see him." Tam turned back to the mirror to take another run at tying the cravat that he loathed passionately.

"It's about boundaries, Tam! You of all people should understand that!"

"While I do, I'm not sure *you're* familiar with the concept. Especially given how you barged into my room without knocking."

The future queen of Daxaria scowled. "You know, I'm going to fill Mum and Da's heads with all kinds of helpful ideas while you're away. Suggest things like how Da should be the cook here and if Mum wants a granddaughter so badly, she should start looking for your future wife herself to save you the headache."

"You honestly think Mum *hasn't* contrived a bunch of surprise dates already? I know you're not the sharpest sword in the armory, but do you not know our mother at all?"

"Did she really?" Kat snorted, ignoring her brother's insult. "Gods, why didn't I hear about that?"

"Because you'd be annoying about it if you did. Now, go back to your castle. Get in a dress—or uniform, I don't care—and go become queen. Daxaria won't set itself on fire without your help." Finishing with the cravat, Tam steered his sister toward the door.

"Tam, what if I'm terrible at this?"

"You're walking perfectly fine on your own."

"No, I'm serious." Kat halted and spun round to look in her brother's eyes again. It was rare for the infamous wild woman to look so uncertain.

Tam's arms dropped to his sides as he let out a long breath, his attitude softening. "Kat, you'll be surrounded by the inner council, and they will have Daxaria's best interests at heart, and I'm sure your husband will curb your more... impulsive actions when it comes to acting as queen."

"You'd think that," Kat grumbled. "But that's the problem with having a husband who is outrageously in love with me. I'm relatively certain that if I wanted to pass a law that said people had to walk on their hands, he'd let me."

Normally Tam would be insulting her and making sarcastic remarks about her marriage in response to his sister's words, but the way Kat slumped forward... she seemed like a child terrified to get on a horse for the first time.

"I'm glad you're uncertain—"

"*Thanks!*" Kat sniped, openly offended.

Tam let out a snort and shook his head. "Kat, it means you're taking this seriously and aren't being cavalier about this responsibility. You are in charge of everyone's well-being now, and while I know you're happy you get to protect everyone, it *is* going to be hard. There are going to be a lot of difficult choices. It's not a bad thing to look to others for input and advice. You'll get the hang of it. Just don't ever stop taking time to self-reflect."

Kat stared at her brother quietly for a long while. "Gods, you sound like such an old man."

Tam rolled his eyes to the ceiling. "Right. I'm *absolutely* convincing Da to work as the royal cook before I go. Now get out."

Kat stuck her tongue out at her brother and whirled back around toward the door, her bout of vulnerability already past.

"Oh! How has it been the past month working with Eli?"

Tam moved his hands to his pockets as he considered how best to answer... The truth was, Eli had barely been around. He had more or less restricted her to working on the contributions the dukedom would make to the coronation, which had her running errands in Austice: receiving moonshine deliveries, helping Mr. Howard categorize gifts sent by noble families who couldn't attend, and so forth. Ever since he had overheard Eli's vehement desire to get as far from his family as possible, he'd done his best to ensure she didn't have to deal with them.

Which also helped keep her gender a secret. Annika Ashowan herself was busy, and whenever Eli was around, Tam ensured she was far away and that the duchess's reading glasses—the ones she swore she didn't really need—went missing every now and again. Really, he just had to help keep her secret until they were on a boat to Zinfera. Then Tam could rest a little before venturing into the foreign empire.

"Hello? Did you hear me? Are you ignoring me?"

Kat interrupted Tam's spiraling thoughts, forcing him back to the present. "Eli's fine, but there's no sense in getting attached. He's going to set off on his own once we return from Zinfera."

With a sigh, Kat reached out, intending to muss her brother's long, straight, silky black hair, only he batted her hand away easily.

"You're going to die alone at this rate. You know that, right?"

Tam gave a groaning sigh and resumed shoving his sister out of his room. "Go get crowned. Or don't, but at the very least, go make sure your children aren't doing something horrendous to the guests."

"Oyy! I left my boys in perfectly capable hands!"

"No one has hands capable enough to handle your boys. Go save whoever you dumped them on. I'll see you later." Tam put a little more muscle into his final shove, getting Kat out the door.

Kat cackled, but when she straightened and looked back at her brother who had braced his arms against the doorway blocking her from reentering, she said, "Thanks, Tam. I… I really am glad you're going to be nearby while I rule. At least I know one person around me won't be afraid to tell me when I'm being a dumb-arse."

"You're always a dumb-arse. Never forget it."

Kat flipped her middle finger in the air then skipped down the corridor, hands clasped behind her back.

Tam watched her retreat, shaking his head but smiling.

Daxaria was about to experience its most chaotic queen ever: a woman whose magical abilities helped her see in the dark; one who had inhuman strength, required little to no sleep, could absorb magical power directed at her, and could ingest nearly all poisons unharmed. And if she ever absorbed too much power? She could redistribute her power to enhance the capabilities of those nearby. That was all before mentioning her familiar, Pina. The cat ruled the heart of a stone golem, an ancient beast of the earth that guarded the kingdom by standing day and night out in the Alcide Sea—not to mention the heart, body, and soul of Cleophus Miller, the kingdom of Troivack's most legendary knight. The man had been made a diplomat to prevent him from abandoning Troivack entirely in his efforts to stay close to Katarina's cat familiar in Daxaria.

Ah... Kat's going to be an absolute menace to good society.

Tam leaned his shoulder against the doorframe to his room. His cravat was already pressing uncomfortably against his throat.

"Lord Tam."

Tam jumped at the sound of his assistant's voice, and half stumbled into his door frame, nearly thunking his head against solid wood. "Good Gods! How do you do that?"

Eli stared, nonplussed. "Do what?"

"I can normally sense anyone approaching me, but with you..." Tam willed his heart to resume a healthier beat.

Eli ignored Tam's exasperation and plunged on, business as usual. "Lord Tam, everything is finished for the preparations for both the coronation and our departure tomorrow morning."

"Wonderful. Thank you for doing that. You should go get ready for tonight now. Maybe have a cup of wine or moonshine before you go. If I know my nephews, things are going to take a lot longer if they're present for the ceremony, so best to be relaxed going in." While Tam had been talking, he loosened the knot from his throat with a subtle sigh of relief, and so didn't see the look of stricken horror on Eli's face until he looked up. "What's wrong?"

"Why would I be expected to go to the coronation?"

Tam stared dumbfounded. "Because you're my assistant. I need assistance in crowded, formal events more than any other time in my life."

"But why?"

The desperate pleading in Eli's tone mixed with her reluctance made Tam smile wryly. "Because I'm twenty-eight years old, a future viscount, possibly a future duke, and I don't have a betrothed. I want to be able to escape the reception without having to deal with any of the nobles who think I should marry their daughters, nieces, sisters… You get the picture, I hope."

"What can I do about it?" Eli asked with a grimace.

Tam bit back a laugh. He had come to know his assistant was wildly capable of hiding her true thoughts and emotions, but when it was just the two of them, she was marvelously upfront in her distaste for all manner of things.

"You, my dear assistant," Tam started while reaching out to rest his hands on Eli's shoulders. He felt her tense and noticed her cheeks turn a subtle shade of pink, but he ignored it when she didn't move away. "You are going to keep talking to me about the most boring things imaginable to chase away any woman that gets within three strides of me. If an ambitious father is trying to talk to me, I need you to describe the most disgusting foods and smells you've ever experienced in your life."

Eli scowled. "I'm not going to scare away women and their family members for you."

Tam raised his eyebrows and smiled. "Oh? Have it your way then. But you still have to come tonight."

He turned to his chamber without another look back, though he had the keen sense that Eli had opened her mouth to object further.

After closing the door with his heel, Tam waited and listened.

Sure enough, he heard soft muttering: "I don't even have anything to wear. The lout can repel women just with his awkward personality…"

He grinned and then called out, "Don't worry, I already had clothes sent to your chamber!"

Eli didn't speak again. Tam took it to mean that she had cast a withering stare at the door and then had gone to see if he had, in fact, prepared proper clothes for her to wear that evening.

Making his way over to the floor-length, gold-rimmed mirror in his room, Tam plucked up the black jacket he had draped over one of the mirror's posts and slipped it on, humming a tune to himself.

As much as he hated to admit it, it was fun having someone at his side who could be candid with him, especially when they wanted less than nothing from him.

"I wonder if Eli has heard the new version of our rumors yet…" Tam chuckled to himself as he imagined her trying to act unbothered by the outrageous turn their planted gossip had taken.

Who knows? Maybe tonight won't be as awful as I thought.

CHAPTER 9

A GUSSIED-UP GUEST

Tam stood almost completely squished into the back wall of the throne room. A woman with a light-green gown and very bony shoulders pinched his left arm, while another, rounder lord wearing a gray jacket kept swaying back into Tam's front. Then on his right side, awkwardly shoved because there was no space to be elsewhere, was Eli.

"I thought this event was invitation-only," she murmured beside him irritably.

Tam raised an eyebrow and slid a casual glance in her direction. A refreshing breeze brushed along the back of his neck from a stained-glass window that had been propped open behind him.

"It was. However, the coronations in Daxaria are normally held at the castle in Sorlia. They are holding it here in Austice because this is where Kat grew up, but the throne room and banquet hall here in Austice aren't as big as Sorlia's, so… here we are."

Eli winced as a young woman in a sunny yellow dress happened to crunch her toes with the low heel she wore. "Do you think the ceremony will start soon?"

Tam risked lifting his eyes to look over the sea of people toward the doors. There, guards stood waiting, sweat already rolling down their temples from under their steel helmets.

"Mm. Maybe. My guess is the boys are being difficult about wearing their official clothes."

Eli let out a long breath.

Tam lowered his attention to her. She had donned the clothes he had picked: a powder-blue vest with a fine silk coat to match. There was a linen tunic underneath, and tan trousers.

It was a becoming color on her, only…

Tam looked away hastily.

To him, it was plain as day she was a woman. Her delicate neck, the glow of her skin, the high cheekbones, the full mouth…

He cleared his throat and blinked.

Gods. He always was terrible around women, but hiding the fact that Eli was one made everything thrice as awkward.

Tam was spared from further rumination when some very poignant whispers seeped through the crowd. "So he *doesn't* have seven children?" one young woman asked with a gasp.

"No! Have you seen him? He is obviously too young for such a thing. No, he is one of Reese Flint's children, but from his time in Zinfera! I hear our former bard pulled every string in the book so that Lord Tam's assistant could come work here in Daxaria. With Reese Flint's backing, of course the Ashowans would take him in!"

Tam subtly chewed on the corner of his mouth as he felt Eli turn, ever so slowly, to stare up at him.

"My word! That does make sense! Though the Zinferan… he does look rather feminine for a boy, doesn't he?"

Tam looked to the ceiling and squinted, his magic only fluttering slightly as Eli's wide-eyed stare scorched the side of his face.

"My lord," Eli managed through gritted teeth.

Tam plastered on an innocent smile. "Yes?"

"Is this what you meant by *harmless fun*? People think I'm related to the bard that is famous for bedding every other woman in every kingdom."

"People were going to wonder about your parentage regardless! Reese Flint has so many children, it really isn't that outlandish a guess."

Eli emitted a faint growl in the back of her throat before turning to gaze angrily ahead again.

Tam fought off a laugh, but he didn't succeed in stopping his smile as he looked toward the thrones in the hopes that Eli wouldn't notice how humorous he found her irritation. He was vaguely aware of two young noblewomen observing their interaction and whispering fervently behind their fluttering lacy fans, but couldn't be bothered to care much.

"Announcing the arrival of His Majesty King Norman Reyes!" Mr. Kevin Howard, the king's assistant, shouted over everyone, instantly silencing the room.

All eyes swiveled to the doors, which opened with a loud clack.

Due to the king's shorter stature, Tam and Eli couldn't actually see him as he ascended the bright-red carpet of the aisle that led to the thrones.

That suited Tam fine.

He closed his eyes and simply enjoyed the feeling of the breeze behind him… until Eli's elbow found his ribs.

It had been subtle, but it made Tam's dark eyes slide back over to her. "I can't see anything," he murmured back as explanation.

"This is still not the time for a nap."

"I wasn't napping. I was concentrating."

Another huff from Eli succeeded in motivating Tam to fully open his eyes again. Which turned out to be a good thing, as Katarina and Eric arrived next, and they were significantly easier to spot.

Kat wore her official knight's uniform, adorned with two gleaming silver and gold medals she had earned: one for her contribution to Troivack's civil war, and another for her protection of Alina, the queen of Troivack and her best friend, as she had guarded the monarch on several occasions while putting her own life at risk. Not that she ever thought a reward to be necessary after any of those events—Katarina simply believed that was how things were meant to be.

Overall, the coronation proceeded remarkably smoothly. Even the three young princes followed their parents without anyone physically restraining them from getting into trouble.

At one point Antony yawned, earning a warning look from his grandmother, Duchess Annika Ashowan. Then Asher started tapping and scuffing his boots, until both Eric and Kat shot glances over their shoulders at him while they waited, kneeling, before the king as he began the process of abdicating his crown.

Yes, everything was proceeding according to plan…

That is, until both Kat and Eric rose as the new king and queen of Daxaria and faced their vassals with their prepared speeches. They didn't even get as far as opening their mouths before a series of shrieks sounded among the crowd.

Kat and Eric dropped their gazes to their sons, their expressions flat.

Antony, being the eldest, had long ago learned how to school his features to look as guiltless as possible.

Charlie was still developing this skill, and so he instead made an expression that was remarkably like his mother's when she was in trouble, looking away with his tongue poking the inside of his cheek.

As for Asher… He was already fidgeting nervously.

Tam immediately started scanning the crowd, pushing away from the wall.

"Do you see what's happening?" Eli asked him. The nobles in the audience were starting to sidle toward them, away from whatever trouble the three princes had caused.

"Nothing yet. My money is on them having accidentally released some mice, or—"

"Godsdamn—HAROLD! OUT!" Katarina roared while already descending from the dais toward the family donkey. Harold was looking quite lovely with a wreath of white flowers around his neck and more in his mane, behind his ears, and… a bow on his tail.

"Ah, it's just Harold," Tam finished with a grin as he observed the donkey start to nibble curiously on an older noblewoman's pockets. "Huh. She must have brought snacks to the coronation."

Laughs and more awkward shuffling took place as Katarina started trying to wrangle the donkey out of the room.

Eric was already standing in front of his sons with his arms crossed and eyebrows raised, making them squirm even more the longer he failed to say something.

Tam slumped back against the wall comfortably, still smiling, though he closed his eyes to start laughing.

It wouldn't have been a proper Ashowan event if there weren't at least some absurdity.

"B-but—"

"No buts! Honestly, Antony! I told you, of all days, today really isn't the day for pranks!" Kat said, her volume casual, if her tone was more than a bit incredulous. She had already removed the mantle from her shoulders as she spoke to her eldest son in a quiet corridor without anyone nearby to overhear.

"W-we thought you'd find it funny!"

"And I *do*! You're making me regret not dressing Harold up for the day I was crowned princess, but… he should have been left outside."

Antony started to sniffle, and his head dropped.

Kat didn't hide her look of anguish at her son's tears. She slowly knelt down in front of him.

"Listen, my little *ryshka*, I know this is one of those times when you genuinely thought you were doing a kind thing. Personally? I think this is wonderful, but Harold—as lovely as he is—isn't able to understand that eating a noblewoman's dress is frowned upon. Someone could have been hurt if Harold got frightened. And what is it people with the Ashowan blood do?" Kat asked gently.

"P-protect people."

"That's right. Remember, we have to consider what might hurt others. I understand it's hard to tell sometimes, but especially when there is a crowd, you need to ask an adult if it's a good idea."

"Someone like Ass Fuks?"

"He is only thirteen. He isn't an adult. You can ask Les Fuks, though, or your Uncle Tam!"

"What am I getting roped into?"

Both Antony and Kat looked up to see Tamlin Ashowan striding over to them.

Antony hastily wiped away his tears. "Mam was saying that if we have an idea that involves a crowd, we should ask you if it's safe."

Tam stared at his sister sardonically. "You're making me be the voice of reason to *your* children?"

Antony started to cry again.

Kat's stare turned uncharacteristically angry. "I just meant that if they wanted to plan a *surprise* for a crowd for their father or myself, they should ask you!"

Chastened, Tam flinched apologetically before looking back to Antony. "Sorry, monster, absolutely you can ask me in the future. Though I will be away for the next while, so maybe ask someone else, like… erm…"

"You honestly need more friends," Kat remarked with a sigh while standing.

"There are a lot of people he could ask! I'm just trying to think about who is going to be around him in the future once you move to Sorlia," Tam defended while patting his nephew's shoulder affectionately.

Kat rolled her eyes as, upon mention of their move, Antony burst into fresh tears and hugged his mother's legs.

Tam bit his tongue guiltily. He knew the eventual move was a touchy subject for the boys.

"You're really helping me out today," Kat informed her brother sarcastically.

Tam sighed. "And here I was coming to share the good news that Harold is happily grazing outside, and food is starting to be served."

Kat perked up brightly at the idea of feeding the bottomless pit she called a stomach, but was distracted from saying anything on the matter as a tail twitch drew her sight downward to where Pina, her muted calico familiar with a darling freckle upon her pink nose, was wrapping herself around Antony. He crouched and hugged her as she nuzzled his tear-soaked face worriedly.

The familiar to the queen of Daxaria was as famously cute as Kraken, Finlay Ashowan's own fluffy black cat familiar, was brilliant.

"Thanks for helping out, Pina." Kat addressed her familiar sincerely, though she craned her neck to look around her brother.

"Is Sir Cleophus visiting for the coronation?" Tam guessed.

"Yeah, he arrived this morning. I'm surprised he let Pina out of his sight on the first day he's here…"

"PRINCESS!"

The telling roar of the Troivackian knight echoed up to the siblings. His pet name for the cat being Princess had only made things wildly confusing when Kat had, until that very day, also been a princess.

Cleophus was… enormous. He was also utterly terrifying, and rarely spoke more than two sentences unless it was to, or about, Pina. He technically was serving Troivack as a diplomat while spending great lengths of time in Daxaria. Otherwise Cleophus would have abandoned his duties should Pina so much as meow in any meaningful way.

The boulder-sized knight appeared at the end of the hall and started making his way up to the trio.

Antony casually reached out and clutched his mother's pant leg.

When Cleophus's booming steps halted in front of the new queen of Daxaria, he gave a quick incline before lowering himself to Pina.

Antony took the opportunity to slip behind his mother entirely.

Cleophus held out his hand to the cat, who, while fully grown, had retained her small snout, meaning when she slept, she had a tendency to snore. It was a trait that had in fact earned her an even greater loyal following. She also tended to let out snorting sighs, which she did when Cleophus happened to scare the very same little boy she had been trying to comfort.

Frowning, the knight was caught between concern and adoration.

"Sir Cleophus, while I appreciate, as always, your concern for my familiar, we are having a bit of a family discussion right now," Kat said while gently reaching behind herself to pat her son on the back.

Cleophus's gaze momentarily hardened until Pina turned away from him and once again made her way over to Antony to brush against his legs.

All at once the ferocious knight looked like an abandoned child. He rose and at last issued a proper bow to Kat.

"My apologies, Your Majesty. Lady Dana brought her dogs so I was concerned."

Kat gave her best understanding smile, and Tam did what he did best and discreetly backed away from the conversation. While he had nothing personal against the knight, he also did not envy his sister having to draw boundaries with the fanatical man…

Antony stared after his uncle longingly.

Tam gave a strained smile toward him, unable to think of a way to get his nephew out of the situation. Kat had obviously been in the middle of trying to teach her son an important life lesson, and he really had no place imposing.

Though of the various mischievous acts the princes had pulled, this one had at least been well intentioned.

"Ah, Antony!" Tam called out, his conscience unable to let him escape alone.

The young boy perked up.

"I need to go tell your father and brothers about the food being ready. Mind showing me where they went?"

Kat put her hands on her hips and stared at her brother wide-eyed, as though wordlessly asking, *Seriously? You're leaving me completely alone here?*

Tam gave a half shrug as Antony bolted for his uncle like a desperate soldier toward his own fortress with an army chasing him. The two wasted no time in putting a significant distance between themselves and Kat and Cleophus.

Having successfully escaped both his mother's lecture and the ferocious atmosphere that always lingered around Sir Cleophus, Antony let out a breath, almost doubling over in relief once they rounded the next corner.

"Thanks, Uncle Tam!"

"You owe me." Tam raised an eyebrow at his nephew. "If I weren't leaving tomorrow morning, you best believe I would've left you there."

"Pfft, no you wouldn't."

Tam chuckled. Antony sounded exactly like his mother. "Oh? If you keep up that ungrateful attitude in the future, I just might!"

Antony let out an exaggerated moan. "Fiiiine. I owe you!"

Tam nodded, satisfied.

"Are you really going to stay for the whole reception?" Antony wondered aloud interestedly.

It was in fact quite well known how seldom Tam attended official events. Even more seldom were the times he stayed for their entirety.

Tam sighed. "I think your grandmother would have me dragged by horses if I left early."

Antony smiled excitedly and gave a small skip.

"Why do you even want me there? We both know you're going to leave me to go cause trouble with your brothers and the other children." Tam slowed his pace to help Antony keep up.

"Not this time!"

"Oh?"

"Yep! Because I'll be king one day! So I should speak with the vessels!"

Tam stopped in his tracks. "Do you mean vassals?"

"Yeah!"

Uneasiness brewed in Tam's gut. Kat and Eric had not told their sons about the problem of Antony inheriting the throne with him potentially being a witch.

As he peered down into Antony's face, and the boy beamed up at him, Tam could feel his former anger at the coven resurface.

Antony sensed the shift in his uncle and tilted his head, curious. "Everything okay, Uncle Tam?"

Blinking away his dark feelings, Tam smiled down at the young boy's face. "Sure. Just wondering what magic you're going to have one day."

Speculation over such a wonderful event had Antony's face splitting into a brilliant smile.

"I think I'm going to be an earth witch! But Charlie thinks I'll be a mutated witch just like you, an' Mam, an' Grandda…"

The uncle and nephew made their way back down the corridor, each completely forgetting about the rather exuberant celebration awaiting them as they delved into thrilling speculations in Antony's case, and hardening resolve in Tam's.

Gods help me, we better convince that bloody coven to let him be king.

CHAPTER 10

AN ASSISTANT'S ASSISTANCE

Grasping two goblets by their stems from a table so overloaded with food and drink that it was a wonder it didn't buckle, Eli did her best to dodge and weave through the throng of nobility back to where the lord she served waited. Or rather, *hid from* the young unmarried ladies who had been eyeing him the way hungry house cats would a plump mouse.

Keeping her head bowed, Eli was able to deftly make her way back, the scents of Troivackian moonshine, red wine, perfume, and sweat all mingling together. It certainly did smell like a rousing good party.

It reminded Eli of her days back in the Zinferan court. In Troivack, most parties were conducted with great dignity and seriousness, and didn't have the exuberance of the Daxarian court, nor the frivolous luxury of the Zinferan.

Eli looked to the thrones before she could stop herself. Her heart dropped when she once again imagined someone from long ago with alarming clarity...

Chin... Why am I thinking about you now after all these years?

A knight who was already laughing far louder than was necessary tumbled into Eli, knocking her back and sloshing drinks all over her and the couple she ended up crashing into. The older lord and lady squawked in alarm.

Eli pivoted nimbly, already bowing before the couple had righted themselves. "Apologies, my lord, my lady."

"By the Gods, be careful!" the woman trilled while looking in dismay at her stained, bright-orange silk skirt.

"I am sincerely sorry, it seems the party is—"

The woman waved off Eli's words and straightened herself. "I'll send the bill for the cost of the dress to house Ashowan." She'd already lost interest in the assistant.

A deep-rooted ire shook Eli. Before the lady could notice this, her husband did, and he flinched as though sensing some greater power around Eli simmering in the air.

"My lady." Eli smiled, her teeth flashing, and then without bothering to look behind herself, she effortlessly grabbed the knight who'd bumped into her. He was standing right at her back, guffawing with other partygoers. She yanked him forward with surprising strength. "This here is the man who caused the situation. Please send the bill to him. Good evening."

The noblewoman and the knight blinked at each other in confusion. Eli pressed the two half-filled goblets into the knight's hands and stalked back into the crowd, her cheeks still warm from anger.

By the time she reached Lord Tamlin's side, she didn't have to look at him to know he had seen the whole thing. She was sure he was going to say something glib, and if he did, she was already waiting to snap at him to tell him she'd be happy to ditch his cowardly arse there.

"You almost lost control."

Eli's eyes snapped to him. "Pardon?"

"Your magic." Tam's voice was quiet, without an ounce of teasing in it. "I saw the way that lord reacted when you looked at his wife."

Her heart quickened, but she pretended to still be annoyed and not display her panic. "I might have been somewhat terse with the noblewoman. If you prefer, I can return and offer that you, my employer, pay for the dress."

"That is not what I'm getting at. And I'm not asking you about your magic, either. I just need to know what sets it off. I'll avoid placing you in situations in the future where that might happen." Tam lunged swiftly toward a servant carrying a tray of full goblets and managed to pluck up two cups without making the man stop, though the contents in the cups were different; one with red wine the other moonshine.

Eli felt a foreign emotion rise in her throat. When was the last time someone had tried to help her without forcing her to do something?

"I like things to be fair," she heard herself say, then instantly pinched her mouth shut again. Why the hell had she even told him that? Of course he'd have follow-up questions!

"Ah. So you are fine when the exchange is straightforward, and reward or punishment is assigned properly? Business interactions, like when you accept shipments of moonshine or categorize inventory are fine then? Alright. I won't send you to negotiations where you'll be at a disadvantage."

"No, I—" Eli found herself at a loss.

Her first reaction was to tell him that she would accept whatever task he needed her to perform, or that she was perfectly capable of managing her magic and emotions. She didn't get the chance, though, as he handed her the goblet of wine.

"If you want my cup of moonshine you'd better say so now. I'm going to need a few of these to last to the end of this."

Eli squared her toes to face Tam, her mouth opening. Then closing.

She wanted to thank him, but not in a heartfelt way… more like a coworker? An equal?

Instead what came out of her mouth was. "My lord, everyone says you are quiet and do not speak often, but you're actually quite chatty."

Tam snorted as he drank from his goblet and had to cover his nose as the burning moonshine threatened to come out his nostrils.

Coughing, the future duke struggled to right himself. Eli gave him a wary pat on the back.

Tam lifted his dark eyes glistening with humor. "You know… I'm baffled how anyone found you easy to overlook. Nearly every word out of your mouth is insulting."

"Being called chatty is insulting?" Eli countered defensively.

"Did you mean it as a compliment?" Tam gave his chest a final thump for good measure before going to take another drink. He didn't seem to care whether she had intended to taunt him or not.

But again, the assistant didn't get a chance to respond, because two noblewomen descended upon them.

"Lord Tam," the first woman said with a curtsy, her smile hidden behind her lacy fan. She had shining auburn hair that curled at the ends and bright-green eyes, and though her mustard-yellow dress was a few years out of fashion, it was of superior quality.

"Lord Tam, are you having a nice evening?" The second woman had long chestnut-brown hair that she had partially tied back. She wore a modest plum-colored dress and kept her hands gently clasped in front of her skirts. Standing next to the auburn-haired woman—who was draped with so many pearls, she must have rattled when she walked—she almost looked as though she were of commoner origins.

"Good evening," Tam returned tightly.

Eli shuffled a foot, desperately wishing to flee, but a sharp jerk of Tam's head in her direction froze her in place.

"Congratulations to you and your family with regard to our new queen, Lord Tam! I am Lady Josephine Wrights, and this is Lady Ivette Davenshire. We are here from Sorlia," the brunette explained kindly, her warm brown eyes soft as she spoke.

"Thank you." Tam took in a very quiet breath before turning to Eli, who nearly recoiled when the two noblewomen did the same thing.

"Eli, you were just telling me about something quite interesting. What was that again…?"

Any pretense of good feelings toward Tamlin Ashowan dissipated faster than a drop of water on hot coals as Eli was reminded of the primary reason he had forced her to attend the blessed event.

"I'm sorry, my lord, I've completely forgotten. Pardon me, ladies, I must go take care of something very important for my l—"

Eli turned and tried to flee, but Tam was quick. He seized the back of her collar and held her back. Reluctantly, she rejoined the discussion.

"No, no. Don't worry. As your *lord* I think it is perfectly fine that you stay! Now. What was that *very* interesting thing you were talking about?" Tam asked through a pained smile and flashing eyes directed at Eli. The two noblewomen behind him shared looks mixed of uncertainty and irritation.

"We were talking about how it's time you found yourself a wife."

Eli knew she shouldn't have done it. She *knew* she shouldn't have thrown Tamlin Ashowan under the metaphorical carriage. Good Gods. He had been perfectly decent! He was helping her and being far more considerate than she deserved!

So his murderous expression was entirely justified.

Behind him, Ladies Josephine and Ivette beamed.

"I think you have misspoken, Eli, we were talking about *you* getting married," Tam declared a little too loudly. "You see, Lady Josephine, Lady Ivette, there seems to be quite a damning rumor going around that Eli here has five children already!"

"Ah…" Lady Ivette replied slowly, her excitement snubbed.

"I must confess…" Josephine addressed Eli, the docility in her eyes dwindling. "I have heard some strange things myself. Namely that you are the son of Mr. Reese Flint."

Eli bowed graciously. "I am afraid that is not entirely true, either."

"Are you truly in a hurry to marry? You can't be older than twenty! Lord Tam here is twenty-eight, and *he* isn't even betrothed to anyone." Lady Ivette lowered her fan to reveal a broad mouth and square jaw.

"Well, that is because I'm committed to bachelorhood." Tam inclined himself politely to them, his eyes becoming increasingly fixated on the floor.

Eli had noticed him looking up more often of late, but seeing him almost fold in on himself now, away from the women, made her wonder again what his magic was… She reached over and patted him on the back. "While I think Lord Tam should still marry, his lordship is only thinking of the future of the woman he would wed. To be a part of such a curse—ah. Pardon me. I was not supposed to speak of it…" Eli feigned an apologetic expression.

The two noblewomen looked at each other, the reaction in their eyes somewhere between disturbed horror and hungry curiosity.

"Whatever could be so—"

Eli held up a hand, silencing Lady Ivette, while she kept her other hand on Tam's back. She could feel how still he'd grown.

"I'm sorry, I really have said too much already. My lord, would you like some fresh air?"

Tam gave Eli a remarkably convincing sad smile and lowered his head toward the door.

They managed to make their way through the crowd, the blaring colors and music, the laughter and loud conversations. Once they broke free into the corridor, the cool air was both shocking and refreshing.

Tam and Eli walked away from the party until at last they reached the front of the castle, where no one else had bothered to venture as the night's festivities were really just beginning.

Feeling rather proud of herself for getting them out of the situation, Eli was surprised when Tam rounded on her, looking concerned rather than pleased.

"Eli... I know you were trying to help, but you just made my life very difficult."

"How? It deterred those women, didn't it?"

"Remember how the coven is already concerned about how I could harm people? You think they aren't going to be alarmed about a possible curse? Curses are one of the reasons that witches were hunted here in Daxaria in the not-so-distant past. They are never taken lightly."

"But everyone suspects something like that anyway!"

"We have always been very clear that my reservations about my magic have nothing to do with curses. I'm probably going to have to have a meeting about this before we leave to clear it up…" Tam sighed and started rubbing the back of his neck. "May as well go find Mr. Howard now. The sooner he knows to book something with the coven leader, the better. Morgan is already drowning in paperwork…"

"I'm sorry." Eli dropped her face and clasped her hands contritely in front of herself.

"I understand… I do. After attempting to abandon me, you were trying to make it up. I also know you did not grow up here in Daxaria, so you might not have learned about our history. It's alright. I'll handle it. Let's just find Mr. Howard, and then go back to the reception, hm?"

Eli was feeling more uncomfortable than she had in her entire life.

She had never been given any leniency when she'd made a mistake. Not by her parents. Not by her tutors. Not by the Troivackian king. Not even by Chin… Yet here was a stranger, being considerate, protecting her, and just being overall so… so…

"Come on. Don't worry about it." Tam patted her shoulder before striding past her, back down the corridor, his hands finding their way into the pockets of his black trousers. He'd already made it a good way down the corridor before Eli was able to will her feet to move again.

She sprinted after Tam, tugging on the back of his long black coat. Honestly, it fit him about as well as a sheet despite the fine fabric.

When he turned around, his face partially illuminated by a nearby torch on the wall, Eli couldn't quite bring herself to look directly at him. She already felt completely at a loss as to how to convey her thoughts. All because... He was the most lovely person she had ever met.

"What *is* wrong with you?" she blurted. She didn't have to look to know his face had hardened, so she plundered on. "You're nice. Generally. You have a decent sense of humor. You're wonderful with children, you're handsome—"

"Handsome?" Tam laughed, but Eli ignored him.

"You seem like you'd at least have a group of close friends, so... so why don't you? Why are you alone?"

Tam bent forward until the top of his head was in line with her own. His dark eyes bore into her face until she finally looked at him.

He didn't seem angry... but he didn't look happy, either. It was a rather indescribable expression, really. But then he said, "Why are *you* smart, funny, pretty, and isolating yourself?"

Eli flinched.

She hadn't been called pretty since—

A thump in a nearby closet drew both Tam and Eli's attention.

Frowning, Tam carefully reached for the door handle... Pulled it open, and...

His jaw dropped.

"Hannah?" Tam spluttered as his father's lifelong friend, the head of housekeeping for the castle, hid her disrobed state behind the man she was with... a man whose identity left Tam at a complete loss of words.

Eli tilted her head and eyed Tam and the man, confused as to why neither of them were closing the door to give the couple privacy. So what if the king's assistant, Mr. Kevin Howard, was in a clandestine relationship with the woman named Hannah who was the head of housekeeping? Neither of them were married anyway!

CHAPTER 11

AN ERRANT ESCAPE

Tam sat staring dazedly out at the courtyard, Mr. Howard at his side. Hannah had already left to resume her duties for the reception, and Eli waited back in the corridor out of earshot.

"Tamlin, I'd like to think we've become good friends throughout the years. You… you are diligent about your work, and we've always had good rapport together. So if you could—"

"How long?" Tam interrupted the assistant with a deceptively light tone.

"Now, Tam, there isn't really a reason for me to share that with you."

The young lord turned and stared.

Mr. Howard cleared his throat and looked away. "I don't exactly keep track, but maybe a decade…?"

"A *decade?*"

"SSHH!" Mr. Howard hushed frantically while eyeing their surroundings worriedly. "Please, it is a private matter! I'm only telling you because you and I have done good work together over the years, and I know you tend to keep things to yourself!"

"Hannah's like a sister to my father," Tam reminded him weakly.

"I'm aware, but again, it isn't. His. Business. We aren't a couple. And we have no designs to get married, in case you're wondering. This is simply an—an arrangement that works for us, given our chosen lifestyles!"

"You both think and do nothing but work?" Tam supplied while once again looking away.

"Yes. Exactly."

Tam closed his eyes and dropped his chin to his chest. "Mr. Howard, as you said, I do like to keep to myself, and I know I'm like my mother in that I tend to not cause... *excitement* in the way my father and sister do, but how can I not—"

"This is Hannah's preference as much as my own, and I will expect you to respect us both." Mr. Howard's tone was firm, and there was a glint of seriousness in his eyes more severe than usual.

Tam closed his mouth and took in a deep breath through his nose. Then he opened his eyes again. "You're right. Absolutely. And now that you are retiring, I suspect it won't continue—Never mind. I don't want to know." Tam waved off the rest of his words despite it seeming as though Mr. Howard was going to say something on the matter. "I'll have to tease you both, and if my teasing makes you reveal it yourselves I take no responsibility."

The assistant narrowed his eyes. Then, after considering that it was a game of mental fortitude, decided he could handle the younger Ashowan's antics. "I can accept that."

Tam barely hid a smile before remembering the original purpose of seeking out the former king's assistant. "Oh. Also... My new assistant over there? Accidentally insinuated to a couple of noblewomen that I'm cursed."

"*What?* After all we went through assuring the coven that was *not* the case?" Mr. Howard burst out in a far more typical manner.

"Sh—*He* didn't mean to. Eli has been in Troivack the past seven or eight years, and before that, Gods know where. He had no reason to know about Daxaria's history with curses, so I'm thinking we stay on top of this and have a quick meeting with Louise Riddel before I depart for Xava so it isn't a big deal."

Mr. Howard let out a groan. "Here I thought I'd finally get to rest properly in the morning..."

"Sorry. But I have a feeling the king's current assistant is already too deep in his cups to take on the task."

Mr. Howard sighed, wordlessly accepting that Tam was correct. "See what you can do about informing Eli about the situation with the coven. I know he heard a bit during that meeting. Sorry that things aren't looking to be going well with your inheriting the dukedom," the assistant added sincerely.

Tam's mood instantly darkened. "About that... Are they really going to refuse to permit Antony to inherit the throne if he is a witch?"

Mr. Howard's expression turned stony, then sad. "It is being handled very carefully. I'm sure you know that your sister, Her Majesty, is not at all pleased with this. If it were up to her, she would say all manner of things to the coven before insisting Antony should inherit the throne, but I will confess... I can see it building a greater divide if witches not only have the powers of the Gods, but also rule the kingdom. It can breed a great deal of contempt and unrest."

Tam considered this view. Mr. Howard was a cautious man, and he had lived through enough controversy to speak from experience.

"I understand. Though I think the boys need to start being told about what is going on." Tam paused as a new idea struck him. "What if we introduce a vote? If the people of Daxaria are made aware of the situation, a vote could help gauge their feelings on the matter."

"It's a reasonable idea, though if I'm to be blunt, it would open up the monarchy to criticism and subject your nephews to a great deal of hardship."

Tam's frustration cracked under the heavy weight of reason.

The matter of a succession really was a headache to sort out...

"What do the covens of Lobahl and Zinfera believe?" Tam didn't bother bringing up the Coven of Aguas in Troivack, as they tended to defer to Daxaria's coven as a result of being heavily persecuted up until seven years ago when Queen Alina Devark started supporting them.

Mr. Howard's eyebrows lifted. "Now, that is a wise idea. Perhaps the Giong Coven in Zinfera and the Ibida Coven in Lobahl have insight into this dilemma. Why don't you discuss this idea with Louise Riddel tomorrow. You'll be going to Zinfera regardless, so you may as well see if they have any texts or insight." Mr. Howard's work-centered mind visibly took over his thoughts as he continued. "You'll have to wait until the end of your time in Zinfera to ask, so as to not alert anyone beforehand that you are there. After hearing from the Giong Coven, you can decide if you think it's worthwhile to visit Lobahl as well."

Tam unsuccessfully tried not to grimace at the idea of spending even more time away from the comforts of home. Then again, if it meant finding an answer for Antony, and solidifying his own position so he could offer his sister and her sons support, then perhaps an extra year abroad would be worth it.

"Would Lobahl even accept my visit? I think I've only ever met one nobleman who was welcomed into the kingdom. Though I suppose it's more likely given that Lobahl has become more communicative in recent years..."

Mr. Howard leaned back and folded his arms as the evening chill started to find its way through his thick coat. "There is a chance that they will permit it, given that it pertains to the changing world and wanting to uphold the sanctity of the purpose of witches. Again, a question to ask Louise Riddel in the morning."

Tam felt drained just thinking about all the work that would need to go into such an endeavor. He hadn't even made it to the late-night snack time...

Pressing himself to his feet, Tam glanced back down at his father's assistant and said, "You know... I can't help but wonder how the knights that used to serve in the kitchen with Hannah would feel about your relationship. I mean... Captain Taylor may be getting on in years, but he's still quite strong..."

Mr. Howard shrank down at the mere notion as Tam strode away.

The fact that the head of housekeeping was close friends with not only two dukes and the captain of Daxaria's military, but also two knights with large families whose sons adored Hannah, was a sharp reminder that the assistant best be on his toes at all times. These close sibling-esque relationships made these men all incredibly sensitive to any possible harm that could befall Hannah, regardless of her age. And the notion that she was having such an intimate relationship with a man who not only was more powerful than her, but had no intentions of committing to her, would most likely warrant all kinds of strong reactions...

Tam approached the coronation reception purposefully.

Eli fell into step beside him, her footfalls impressively silent.

"New plan, Eli. We're getting out of here. I don't know about you, but I'm ready for a glass of wine in my own chair in front of the fire with one of my books. You're welcome to stay if you like, but—"

"I'll have a cup of tea instead of wine, but I would like that a great deal."

Tam shot a conspiratorial smile at her. "Great. Now... I didn't want to have to go this route, but we'll have to have a pretty drastic reason for leaving, so be prepared. Things are going to move quickly."

"What is it you are going to do, my lord?" Eli asked, unable to hide the hesitation in her tone.

Tam faced the nearing glow of the banquet hall. "I'm going to call on my last resort."

"My lord, are you certain that it is absolutely necessary? Surely in a few hours—"

"I know that what we just learned about Mr. Howard doesn't mean the same thing to you as it does to me, but... my father is *very* protective. Especially of Hannah. And he has far too much fun tormenting the king's assistant as it is. I'll be honest—it's beyond tempting to tell him, just to see what will happen. So I have to do two things."

The pair stopped a short way in front of the doors. "The first? I have to make Hannah be the one to tell my father. The second? I need an excellent reason to leave after that news breaks."

"I'm not sure I understand your plan, my lord. What even *is* your last resort...?"

Inside the packed banquet hall, everyone they laid eyes on save for the servants was absolutely knackered. "We don't have much time," Tam said.

Eli looked at Tam, confused, until she noticed he was staring straight ahead, and so she followed his eyeline...

To the three princes. Who somehow were standing together in a line, already nodding their understanding at their uncle when he jerked his chin upward.

Then, with the seriousness of soldiers marching to battle, they dispersed through the crowd.

Eli slowly turned back to Tam. "Do you know what they are going to do?"

At least the future duke had the decency to look grim when he answered with, "I don't. That's why they are a last resort. Whatever they do will be a success, but I never can ask how, or what. I just have to accept the consequences." Tam then made his way through the crowd to a discreet corner of the room. Eli stuck close, unsure where they were going, given that she was not blessed with his height.

However, when they stopped in front of the duke and duchess, Eli was left once again baffled.

Finlay and Annika were dressed elegantly for the occasion, with Fin wearing a dark-emerald coat and black tunic, while his wife wore a black dress with silvery embroidery, and emerald jewelry draped over her chest and dangling from her earlobes. They appeared to be in the middle of a rather *intimate* conversation... as though the duke had just been about to kiss the wife he famously adored.

"Da, Mum, are you aware that the boys are still here?"

The duke and duchess pulled apart at the sound of their son's voice, blinking themselves back to the present.

"Then why doesn't a kind uncle put them to bed?" Annika countered, facing Tam with her chin and eyebrows lifted expectantly.

"You know it isn't my place to say anything!" Tam was suddenly shouting the words, and Eli winced at his side, wondering just what in the Green Man's antlers he was doing that for. An abrupt halting of movement drew her attention to the left, where she saw Hannah in the middle of loading up a steward's tray with fresh goblets of wine.

She locked eyes with Eli, her face tensing before she hurriedly finished her task and then rushed over to Tam.

"While everyone is in here, Gods know what they are doing!" Tam shouted again, and both his father and mother frowned at his peculiar behavior.

Hannah reached them and placed herself directly in between. "Tam! Mind if we have a word?" she insisted with a strained smile.

"Sorry, Hannah, not right now. They need to hear this!"

"Tam, are you feeling alright…?" Fin's hands found his hips as he eyed Hannah and his son with growing suspicion.

"I'm fine! But this needs to be dealt with sooner than later!"

"Tam! By the Gods—it isn't your business who I bed!" Hannah snapped furiously, her eyes flashing.

Despite the music and revelry of the rest of the room, the five people present for Hannah's outburst fell quiet.

"What does your romantic life have to do with our grandsons being put to bed?" Fin wondered dazedly from behind Hannah.

The head of housekeeping's furious expression froze, then slowly thawed to pure bloodthirst when she realized how Tam had lured her into revealing her secret.

"You arse," she bit out.

"I don't know what you're talking about," Tam murmured back. "Though you have teased me quite often yourself. Remember, it was you who outed me about the office wall incident, *and* who was a key figure in spreading the rumor that I was in love with Queen Alina for a *whole year*. Everyone still thinks I pine for her."

"They were going to figure out eventually that you did something to an entire wall!" Hannah could only defend the one point, as the latter was rather true...

"What is going on?" Annika demanded sharply from behind Hannah.

"Ah, Hannah was misunderstanding our discussion," he explained with a shrug.

"What did you think Tam was talking about?" Fin's blue eyes dropped to the back of Hannah's head.

She cringed. "You don't need to worry about it, Fin. I'm a grown woman and I can handle myself."

Fin didn't look away from Hannah, but he addressed his son. "Taaam? What did you see exactly?"

"I saw what I shouldn't have! But I—" Tam was shouting again, and Eli was about to tell him to knock it off herself when Mr. Howard crashed into the discussion, seizing Tam's shoulder.

"You bloody traitor!"

Annika's jaw dropped.

Fin stared dumbly at the assistant, then back at Hannah.

"You... You two... Are..."

"For the record, Kevin, I wasn't the one who outed you. You just couldn't handle my teasing," Tam informed the assistant lightly, who gulped.

Fin's eyes practically crackled.

Hannah glared over her shoulder at Tam. "I'll get you for this, Tammy. Mark my words."

"Is something burning?" Eli spoke suddenly while wrinkling her nose.

Startled into remembering that she was there, everyone stared at Eli, and then the first shout echoed out.

"LORD TAM! YOUR HAIR IS ON FIRE!"

Jolting in alarm, Tam whirled around, though in doing so the flames spread and one licked his neck, making him yelp.

In the next instant, a bucket's worth of water doused him, putting him out entirely.

The room fell collectively silent, and once he'd wiped the water from his face, Tam looked down just in time to see his three nephews darting back into the fray.

The stench of burnt hair filled the room.

Once he had overcome the shock of being aflame and then drenched, Tam returned his attention to his parents. With a sigh, he said, "I told you they should be in bed. Now… I think I'm going to go home to treat this burn and see how much hair I still have left. Eli, shall we?"

Hannah, Mr. Howard, Fin, and Annika couldn't bring themselves to speak as Tam made his way out of the reception, dripping wet, and wounded… but victorious.

They reached the front of the castle in record time, and sent for a carriage. Eli eventually managed to speak. "Are you… alright… my lord?"

Tam let out a breath as he examined his long black hair—more ash than hair at that point. "Fine for now, though I'll be waking up one of the maids to cut my hair tonight when we get back. Sorry you have to wait for that cup of tea a little longer," he added with genuine sentiment.

Eli studied her employer once more without bothering to pretend she wasn't.

"Honestly, it wasn't as bad as it could have been. Though it was painfully obvious I planned the whole thing, it was bold enough they couldn't stop my leaving. I'm relatively *certain* Hannah is going to break one of my bones, though."

"My lord, to be blunt, you are *very* weird."

"I told you I was, didn't I?"

"It's much worse than you led me to believe."

Tam chuckled. "Well… sorry. You're stuck with a very strange person as your employer for a little while. Hopefully you won't hold it against me."

Eli didn't respond, her true thoughts unknown.

So Tam allowed silence to take over. He had to confess to himself that in a strange way, another nice thing about Eli being his assistant was that Tam had someone who could be an accomplice to his occasional bout of mischievousness. In the past it had always been himself in a supporting role for his sister's pranks and wild tendencies. Then she had gotten married and it hadn't been the same.

This growing affection for his assistant meant his mother had been right about it being good for him having someone at his side…

Which Tam found a touch bloody annoying to admit.

CHAPTER 12

A SIBLING'S SCOLDING

Tam stared at his reflection and let out a disgruntled sigh.

It was the morning after the coronation, and after a long, remarkably undisturbed sleep, the future duke took stock of his new appearance in the light of day.

For a number of reasons, he had kept his hair long since he was fourteen.

For one, it helped obscure his sight and subsequently his magic from acting up. For another, it wasn't a popular style, and so it had done a wonderful job of deterring the first wave of young women who might become interested in him.

As noblewomen had aged and married around him, however, and news of his inheriting the dukedom spread, he had started to look incredibly appealing, regardless of his efforts—though the rumors that circulated about his courtship with the current queen of Troivack back when she was a princess of Daxaria had briefly helped prolong his ineligibility. Many people wondered how Alina could have chosen a gruff man like Brendan Devark over him, and therefore assumed something was terribly wrong with Tamlin Ashowan.

Tam had known his hair wasn't going to be as effective a shield as it once had been now that the day he might inherit his father's titles was closer, so he wasn't feeling too terrible about having to have it cut the previous night. Still, seeing himself without it felt... exposing.

His high cheekbones were visible, as were his almond-shaped catlike eyes, his mouth—full, but shaped like his mother's—his nose, long like his father's... He ran his hand through hair, now only a few inches long, pushing it back away from his face before he accidentally grazed the burn on the back of neck.

Flinching, Tam was just making a mental note to keep a jar of salve on him when the door to his chamber opened. Given that there hadn't been a knock beforehand, it could only be one particular person.

Kat.

She stared at him, her golden eyes glinting, and without a trace of mirth in her face. She wore brown trousers and a white tunic, as was her usual, though she wore her hair braided and pinned in a low bun, which was *not* her norm.

Kat closed the door quietly behind herself, which was all the more disturbing. She stepped over and stopped before her brother, folding her arms.

"What the hell, Tam?"

"I didn't tell them to set me on fire."

Kat didn't say anything.

Which continued to make the situation increasingly unnerving. Kat rarely managed her emotions when it came to him, and she most definitely wasn't the shy type who'd hold back on calling someone out or cussing at them.

"Why did you do that to Hannah?"

Tam blinked. "If you saw Mr. Howard and Hannah together, would you have kept that to yourself?"

"Hannah has been a good friend to us. Yes, I would've."

"She didn't have to reveal it. She could've just trusted me."

"Why would she trust you?" Kat asked coldly.

Tam frowned. "Why wouldn't she?"

"Because she doesn't know you. No one does. Not even me. Not really, and you *wanted* her to reveal it. You goaded her on and were an arsehole about it. I thought you were the more mature one between the two of us."

It was the first time Kat had ever shamed Tam so calmly, and as guilt seized him, he found himself momentarily unable to speak.

"You're right. I'll apologize to Hannah."

"You still haven't answered. Why'd you do it? Did you honestly think it would be funny to laugh at something so personal getting outed so publicly?"

"Everyone is plenty fine sharing my own personal business and having a laugh or telling me what I should do. I'll admit I was in the wrong, but I don't think it's right that my own boundaries get disrespected and I'm expected to just shrug it off. Like when I'd said I wasn't romantically interested in Alina, and yet you all continued to spread the rumor that I *was*. Even when she was betrothed, you all kept going on about it."

Kat raised an eyebrow, unimpressed. "We do it because we care. And that rumor most likely chased away women you didn't want to court anyway! So why was it a big deal? What you did last night wasn't teasing, it was vindictive."

"You think it's fun to be pitied by everyone? And that rumor has made it so I can never be proper friends with Alina ever again! Everyone talks about my every move, and judges my every word, and says what they wish about me. You and everyone else do it because I'm easy to look down on—and I didn't out Hannah to be vindictive, by the way. I did it because I wasn't thinking it'd be that serious. They're adults, it isn't a big deal what they are doing. But yes, I agree I was an idiot and shouldn't have been so cavalier with their secret."

The Daxarian queen's eyes narrowed, then she turned around and stalked toward the door.

Tam didn't call after her, instead looking toward his coat—he'd need it when he went to the castle for his meeting with the coven leader.

"Da already talked to Louise Riddel, and she's aware that Eli's comment about a curse was a slip of the tongue. You just head to Xava as planned to avoid anyone in Daxaria finding out and alerting the court or coven in Zinfera that you're on your way."

Tam squared himself toward his sister, even though she kept her back to him. "Kat, I honestly might have had enough of Daxaria. If I don't come back, keep an eye on Mum and Da."

The queen didn't fully turn around, but she did meet her brother's gaze.

"I hope you grow up, Tam. And finally stop being such a coward. Just because you learned how to do paperwork hasn't changed that, and now you're dragging my boys into acting as your shield and excuse to run away the way I used to. So if you want to stay away? Go ahead. You have my blessing."

"Yesterday you told me how glad you were I'd still be here while you rule."

"Yesterday you hadn't hurt my friend and endangered my children." Kat's tone was emotionless. "If you weren't my brother, you don't want to know what I would do to you."

"I never knowingly put them in danger. I seriously never thought they would take it that far. Kat, you need to at least believe that about me. Make whatever assumptions you will about the rest of my flaws, but I would never put those boys in harm's way. I'd do anything for them."

Kat continued gazing at her brother, and as she did so an ounce of her anger seemed to subside.

She didn't have to say anything. Tam could tell in her face she knew beyond a shadow of a doubt how he felt about her boys.

"Did you take a carriage or ride here?" Tam asked while retrieving his cream-colored coat and pulling it on. "I still have to go to the castle to talk to Hannah before leaving anyway."

"Rode here," Kat retorted tersely.

"Right. I'll take the carriage. I'll make it up to Hannah, Kat. I promise."

The queen's hands clenched at her sides, and she at last chose to face him directly instead of storming out. "I know you will. You're *acting* like an arse. You haven't completely turned into one just yet. But Tam, I *am* worried you're turning into a bitter old man the more you push people away."

Tam bit back his usual responses to such concerns and for a moment considered his sister's sincere worries. Of everyone in his life, he had always felt closest with her—his twin.

"Kat, you used to have trouble letting people in. You would only admit stuff to me, so… How did you get past that?"

The queen's face softened and she looked up at the ceiling thoughtfully. "Eric wore me down? No. That's not it. I guess… I kept being placed in vulnerable situations, and I couldn't get off with my usual tricks. When I was immature, during the consequences, I started to see how closing myself off was hurting people I care about, not protecting them like I wanted to. And when I let myself be open to them? I got stronger, too. Don't get me wrong, I'm still not the most forthcoming, but I've found a balance."

Listening intently, Tam nodded along, even though there were already too many differences between his own troubles with being a part of the world and his sister's old ones for her reflections to be of much help to him.

"I know you're different from me. You're hiding because you're scared of your magic. Whereas I had my own reasons. Though I do find it curious that you only started acting out when that new assistant of yours joined you. Is Eli a bad influence?" Kat wondered, in an only slightly jesting tone.

Tam snorted. "I'm in a bad mood because of the coven, and my pride has taken a lot of beatings. Eli has just happens to be nearby while it takes place."

Kat gave a half shrug as Tam made his way to her side.

"I *am* sorry about last night, Kat. I really hope the boys are alright."

She sighed. "They are. The mischievous goodhearted monsters are just worried about your *juvenile* arse."

Tam grinned. "I'll write them as often as I can while I'm away."

"You better."

Tam reached out and opened the door for his sister, gesturing her through, but the Daxarian queen hesitated as she regarded Tam evenly again.

"Are you serious about not wanting to be in Daxaria?"

Tam lowered his eyes, his slight smile turning sad. "I might be. Everyone here already has their impressions of me, and it'd be nice not to already have everyone assume things because of our father, or you."

"Or because of certain rumors that **someone** started all on their own?" Kat mused dryly.

"They already were thinking those kinds of things anyway. I just wanted confirmation."

"Why?"

Tam let out a defeated chuckle and reached up to rub the back of his neck as he pondered the answer, only to accidentally agitate his burn and jolt as a result, which forced him to drop his hand. "I guess I was hoping I'd changed their idea of me over the past seven years. Turns out, first impressions are hard to shake."

"You and I have that in common at least. Maybe this trip is exactly the opportunity you need to reinvent yourself!" Kat speculated cheerily while patting her brother on the back.

Tam tilted his head, the familiar churn of anxiety burbling in his belly. "I hope so."

"You may be a coward, but you're smart. I'll give you that. So if I figured out how to make the best of my own quirks? You can, too." Kat exited the chamber into the hallway and headed toward the staircase with her brother close behind.

In the past they'd hurled hurtful words at each other out of anger, justified or not, and then not spoken for days, but that was just the way siblings were. Now they tried not to let the hardships of life come between them. If one or both were in the wrong, they owned up to it.

It was a silent agreement they seemed to have developed in light of the birth of Katarina's children, though only Tam knew the reason for it.

Night had already fallen by the time Tam finished apologizing to Hannah and Mr. Howard. After that ordeal, he had gotten reamed out again by his parents, and a colorful bruise on his arm from Hannah still throbbed and reminded him not to lapse into inconsiderate behavior again.

Tam yawned as the carriage rocked its way down the road out of Austice.

His parents were in the carriage just ahead. Once he departed, they were going to begin a tour of the Daxarian offices they'd established for the Coven of Wittica.

This meant he and Eli rode alone.

All in all, it'd been a terrible day, and Tam knew he had deserved it. At least he had received confirmation from Louise Riddel that she would also be interested to hear other covens' thoughts on witches taking positions of power in the kingdom.

Kat had asked him earlier why he had done what he'd done to Hannah. It *was* out of character to act so recklessly. He truly hadn't done it to get back at Hannah for telling on him about the office wall incident, or for her key role in spreading the rumors about himself and the Troivackian queen all those years ago…

Tam stared at Eli's sleeping face.

Luckily, Eli hadn't been privy to this morning's embarrassing events, and it had been during his father's reprimand that it had dawned on Tam why he had done such a thing.

He'd always been overlooked and taken lightly. Treated as though he were broken or an afterthought to barely consider…

But to have someone work closely with him and see how little power he had? How ineffective he was? For a stranger like Eli to see and spend time with him in the company of his other family members in his own home—which had almost never happened—and then witness how those who knew him best truly saw him, had Tam feeling awful. Pointless. And it had brought forward a repressed thought from long ago that had made him act rashly. Which hurt good people and made him feel even worse.

Tam closed his eyes and did his best to take a deep breath.

While he wished his sister's optimistic thoughts would prove true and that he'd be able to overcome his troubles—or at least earn a new reputation for himself and successfully live up to the Ashowan name—he was sincerely doubtful. As a result, the idea of starting over in a foreign land where there were no expectations of him other than the ones he'd been sent with, and he had no one to fail at protecting, started to sound idyllic.

Besides, it wasn't like anyone expected him to accomplish much in Zinfera anyway.

CHAPTER 13

A FOND FAREWELL

Tam leaned against a tower of crates waiting to be loaded onto the ship he and Eli were supposed to board. It had been a gray, drizzly day, and it was already late afternoon. Despite the matured day, the captain insisted they could sail by evening and he'd prefer to do so rather than wait for the morning. So even though the daylight was already starting to wane, they were to leave shortly.

During Tam's wait, Fin made his way over to his son, hands in his pockets, and then he, too, slumped against the crates. Kraken was at the duke's side. Fin's fluffy familiar had grown a gray semicircle of fur around his face, making him look like a wizened old beastie; white fluff sprouted up through the rest of his fur, making patches of his magnificent black coat look ashy.

Emperor Kraken was getting on in years, but, in fairness, he was twenty-nine, which was significantly longer than most cats got to live, and his prolonged life was most likely due to Fin's own curse of slow aging.

"I sent a note to Jiho letting him know you'll be in Zinfera soon. I know you can't visit him while gathering information, but he's there if you need help, and he has sent guides to meet you when you arrive."

"Thank you," Tam returned with a slow nod.

"I'm hoping this goes without saying, but… if you do find the dragon that people are talking about? Please don't try to take it on by yourself."

Tam bit his tongue before replying. "I get it."

Fin looked at his son with a sad half smile. "Tam, it isn't that I don't think you're a capable person. You trained diligently with a sword, with daggers, and even with that Zinferan combat teacher we hired years ago. I know you can take care of yourself. I'm just saying, please spare your old da more stress. We're going to sort things out with the coven, and you're going to be duke, and everything will be alright. You don't have anything to prove."

"I do for myself." Tam locked eyes with his father, taking Fin aback with the intense emotion that sat heavy in his gaze. "I need to step out of my comfort zone and away from everything I've known. I feel like a spoiled brat who's never really made his own mark on anything." He turned away.

Fin smiled as he looked forward. "I get it."

Tam raised an eyebrow and glanced back at his father, who continued.

"I felt exactly the same way before I took the job at the castle in Austice. All I was doing was living in a cottage your grandmother paid for, cooking for her or her patients… None of it was a life I built. Despite having been told my whole life that my magic wouldn't ever amount to much, something in me just said I could do so much more."

"Did you think you'd be doing *this* much more?"

"We both know the answer to that. I can't wait to retire," Fin chuckled. "But… I *have* accomplished a lot that I am proud of, and while it was your mother who pushed me into this lofty position of duke, it would never have happened if I hadn't taken a chance on uprooting my life and starting a new adventure. I have no regrets about moving away. If I hadn't? Well… I'd have missed everything."

Tam listened to his father. He wasn't exactly surprised; he did recognize some similarities to his own present feelings… Though everything he had heard about his da in the past indicated that Fin had been far more confident in both himself and his magic when he had moved to the castle all those years ago, unlike Tam.

Kraken bonked his head against Tam's leg, prompting him to pick up the fluffy familiar and scratch his cheek.

"Is Kraken going to retire when you do?"

The familiar let out a short chirp in between purrs.

Fin grinned. "He says an emperor rules for life. So I don't believe he will."

As he scratched Kraken's salt-and-pepper fluff, Tam turned his mind to his tasks in Zinfera...

Find a dragon. Figure out the state of the kingdom with the emperor on death's doorstep, how powerful was the concubine Soo Hebin, and countless other possibilities... Odds were high he might have to intervene here and there, though he wasn't sure how yet.

"Did you ever say hello to Alina and Brendan?" Fin asked softly.

Tam raised his eyebrows without humor and with a great amount of exasperation. "No, and it's because His Majesty isn't a fan of mine and I'm just avoiding an awkward situation. I'm not avoiding Alina because of any kind of romantic feelings."

Fin pursed his mouth.

No one ever fully believed Tam no matter how much he protested, even when Hannah had come clean about being the main source of this misinformation years ago.

If it *had* been in any way true, though, he would be a lot more bothered about it being a well-circulated rumor.

Kraken let out another chirp, making Fin look down at his familiar, who cracked open his green eyes.

"Kraken says you never were that interested in Alina... So I guess you really do mean it."

Anger stirred in Tam's chest, and, sensing this, Kraken squirmed to be let down.

"Now the word of a *cat* means more than whatever I have to say?" Tam rounded on his father, who pushed off from the crates.

"That's not it. You talk so rarely, Tam. It's hard to get a read on you sometimes."

"Were the words *I have no interest in Alina* not enough?"

Fin held up his hands in surrender. "You're right. I'm sorry. I didn't mean to disregard you."

Shaking his head, Tam looked toward the gangplank of the ship, where Eli was already making her way aboard.

"I think you're right, Da. I do need this trip. I'm not liking who I'm becoming the longer I'm here, and I think it's doing more harm than good all around."

Fin paused, watching his son's face. Tam was a handsome man, but no one had really been able to tell, as he had always hid behind his hair. Seeing his bare face, the house witch could clearly see for himself just how much Tam was struggling to come into his own.

Fin reached out to lay a hand on his son's shoulder. "I wish nothing but the best for you, Tam. I love you more than you'll ever know, and if you find that where you belong is far away from your family…? I understand. But please remember how loved you are, and that we are always here for you."

Tam stilled. When he met his father's eyes, his shoulders relaxed as his agitation visibly ebbed. Most likely due to him not wanting to leave on a sour note. "I love you, too, Da. Thank you."

The two men embraced, and when they pulled apart, Tam even managed to give a half smile to his father before they both faced different directions to walk away. However, Fin turned back to Tam suddenly with a finger raised.

"Ah, one last thing… If you happen to fall in love with someone and want to get married… Mind making sure your mother and I can attend? I didn't know I'd have to make the request, but after your sister—"

At the mention of his sister's scandalous marriage to their future king seven years ago while in a foreign land, Tam at last laughed. "Don't worry. I'll *only* invite you, Mum, and my nephews. Kat never even apologized to me that I couldn't attend her own nuptials!"

Fin grinned at the jest and nodded. "Right. Well… Go say goodbye to your mum, and stay safe. No matter what is going on, remember you can always find your way home."

Tam paused, then smiled again and waved over his shoulder as he headed over to bid farewell to his mother.

With the ship clear of the harbor, and sailing south toward Zinfera, Fin let out a long breath and looked down at his wife in the golden glow of the setting sun that had appeared through the rainy weather in the final moments of the day.

Annika Ashowan was staring after the ship, wearing a knowing smile.

"Do you think he's figured it out?" the house witch wondered while slipping his hands into his pockets.

"If he hasn't, I'm going to have to train him all over again, but I'm confident he knows. Otherwise, he wouldn't have been hiding my glasses from me since Eli started working for him."

Fin grinned. "Tam really did a bang-up job hiding her. I don't think Harris caught a glimpse of her even once!"

"That may have been more Eli's doing than Tam's. I had to warn her in great detail about Lord Harris and his wife…" Annika shook her head as she thought about their chaotic friends.

"How long until Eli stops pretending she's a man, do you think?" Fin wondered as the couple turned and took their time strolling back to their carriage.

"Not long. We were polite about it, and His Majesty Prince Eric was too busy to properly consider that she isn't a young man, but once she and Tam start traveling, more people will notice."

"Did His Majesty King Brendan Devark have any other information about Eli that he was willing to share?"

Annika shook her head. "The Troivackian king thinks quite highly of Eli, so he didn't reveal anything. Though he conceded she was a woman when I pointed out how obvious it was."

Fin bobbed his head as he listened. "And you think she and Tam are going to fall in love?"

Annika froze in her tracks and stared up at her husband, wide-eyed.

"I'd like to think I've learned a thing or two about the way you work, love." Fin's smile was slow and teasing. "You brought up marriage to Tam. Put it in his head… You even got those lords to pester him about marrying their daughters to really make it pronounced. Then you put a woman who is as secretive as he is, if not more so, by his side. You think they're a good match because of their similar natures."

Annika folded her arms and tilted her chin up at her husband. "And what if I said I just thought he could use a good assistant and friend?"

Fin bent down so that his nose was a mere inch from his wife's. "You want granddaughters. I'm not buying it."

Unable to stop the blush that Fin was bringing to her face despite nearly three decades of marriage, she did the only thing she could think to do to stop him tormenting her...

She kissed him. And the duke was all too happy to go along with his wife changing the direction of their conversation.

Back in Austice, the king and queen of Daxaria and the king and queen of Troivack shared a quiet evening catching up and reminiscing over cups of moonshine and wine. There was a nip to the evening air that gave the women an ideal reason to cozy up to their husbands. Though it was more of a reason for Eric, as his wife's magic ensured she was toasty regardless of the cold weather.

"Tam's left by now then?" Alina asked, her cheeks rosy from warmth and drink as she rested her head on Brendan Devark's left shoulder.

"Probably," Kat responded lightly while stretching out her legs to rest them on the low table between the sofas. "He'll send a letter when he arrives in Zinfera, and then we should only receive news once a month or so."

Alina twisted her mouth, her hazel eyes falling thoughtfully to the cup in her hand.

"I hope our boys haven't scared your two sons," Eric added with an apologetic grimace toward his sister.

Brendan took in a very long, slow breath as he stared at the Daxarian king bluntly. "Your children are terrors. I would keep them separated until they are better behaved."

Both Kat and Eric stilled and gradually righted themselves. "Our boys are goodhearted, and they are still young. It's important to have fun as children. In fact, it's the most important thing that they do. It's why we work to keep the kingdom safe. So that children don't have to carry the weight of the world," Eric returned with an edge in his voice.

"There is a very stark difference between having a fun childhood and setting people on fire," Alina pointed out as she lifted herself from her husband's shoulder, her expression serious.

"And we punished them for taking it that far," Kat interjected, her golden eyes glimmering. "I didn't become disciplined until I was in my twenties, and things worked out. Now, we wanted a nice evening together since you both will be heading back to Troivack, so I suggest we don't talk about our children."

Brendan bowed his head in assent, as did Alina.

It was true: Through the years, there had been many fights about their different parenting styles, and so they had learned that it was best to conversationally step away from the subject when emotions were getting a mite too heated.

"Do you really think there is a dragon in Zinfera?" Alina changed the topic smoothly, though the relaxed atmosphere did not return to the room as the terrifying idea of an ancient beast settled over them.

"Gods, if there is? It'll feel like the whole issue with the first witch and the devil is starting again…" Kat chuckled grimly before taking a drink from her cup.

"To be honest," Eric started carefully, "with Tam leaving for such a long time, it made me think how similar the situation is to when you and I left for Troivack,"

Alina's eyes snapped to her brother. "I was thinking the same thing."

Kat winced. "No! Don't say that! Tam travels all the time for the dukedom; this doesn't have to be like that at all! I'm sure everything is—"

A knock on the door cut off the Daxarian queen's last words.

"Come in," Eric called out, a frown already creasing his brow as they all considered the late hour.

Mr. Kevin Howard burst in with Morgan Linsey, the new king's assistant, at his side. "Your Majesties, we just received a missive from Troivack."

Brendan and Alina were on their feet in an instant, while Kat and Eric joined them.

Mr. Howard swallowed as he stepped into the room and Morgan closed the door behind them. The man's face was pale, and his voice warbled as his hand clutched the missive. "It's the first witch… She's escaped."

Silence filled the room, until Katarina broke it by bursting out, "Gods*dammit!*"

While the Troivackian king and queen still hadn't spoken, they shared a very similar sentiment.

It seemed the first witch wasn't through causing problems for them just yet.

CHAPTER 14

A BUNDLE OF BAFFLEMENT

The first morning of their voyage, after a less-than-ideal sleep the night before, Tam leaned over the railing, willing with every ounce of strength and self-control he possessed not to throw up for a third time since breakfast. At least it was a sunny day without a cloud in sight, and despite their boat being farther out on the Alcide Sea, the air was moderately warm.

"My lord, I've brought you a weak ginger tea. It should help settle your stomach."

Eli stood behind her employer, cup in hand, wearing a simple white tunic and long button-down black vest over brown trousers.

Unable to answer right away, Tam slowly turned around, his eyes downcast and his complexion touched with fresh green hues. He accepted the cup that Eli pressed into his hands and sipped from it gratefully as the boat continued to gracefully climb and descend each wave.

"Perhaps work would help to take your mind off the boat," Eli suggested, her hands clasped behind her back.

Tam shook his head. "I can't work belowdecks," he rasped before clearing his throat, prompting him to take another sip of tea.

"Her Grace informed me that you normally train in the morning with her. Would you like to train with me on deck, my lord?"

Tam's eyes flitted upward to his assistant, who was regarding him perfectly seriously. He managed to straighten himself, set the teacup down in a shallow crate that held only a rope, and tilt his head curiously at her.

"Do *you* know how to wield a sword? Or knives?"

Eli shrugged ambiguously. "I can manage."

A mysterious smile lit Tam's face, which did succeed in quelling the olive shades around his forehead. "See, when my sister learned the sword, it was a rather remarkable thing because she was the first woman to have done so. I heard that one of her friends, Sir Hugo Cas, remained behind to teach a group of women in Troivack. But given that you most definitely are *not* a woman"—Eli's polite expression fell flat in irritation at his obvious reference to her gender—"who would have taught you to wield a sword or knives? Were they aware of your… true state?" Tam finished airily, while folding his arms.

"I haven't been trained with a sword or knives, but I can manage well enough," Eli responded carefully. "I am hard to hit, my lord."

Tam's eyebrows twitched at the thought of anyone trying to hit Eli. She was quite slim and petite… He wondered if it was because she purposely ate little so as to appear more androgynous.

Giving his head a shake, he brought his mind out of his growing concern for his assistant and instead stared at her somberly. "I appreciate the offer, but I really am more competent with weapons than I may seem."

Eli raised an eyebrow, peered at Tam up and down, then shrugged.

Tam stared at her with a mixture of disbelief and vague incredulousness at her blatant appraisal of himself. While the future duke did vaguely recall hearing that Eli had once been tasked with attempting to assassinate Eric Reyes (albeit against her will), he had always assumed she had only been considered for the job because of something to do with her magic.

"We can try," Tam conceded thoughtfully. "Do you need knives of your own?" He reached behind himself and procured two daggers.

Though she seemed momentarily caught off guard by the sudden appearance of the blades, Eli blinked several times with a frown as though confused about how she had not noticed he had those on his person. "No. I won't try to attack, I'll just dodge."

The lord and his assistant eyed each other calculatingly—Eli appeared to be watching Tam in case he made a move, and Tam stared due to his increasing curiosity about her.

Feigning an airy countenance, Tam abruptly lunged, and Eli flinched in surprise.

The blade had stopped a breath away from her right ear.

"You didn't dodge," Tam observed sternly, with concern rather than condescension.

"You weren't aiming for me, you were aiming over my shoulder." Eli subtly widened her stance. "I will concede, though, that was faster than what I was expecting."

Tam noted the way she scrutinized his build again, her eyes sharp.

There were just as many reasons he habitually wore clothes that didn't fit him as there were for him having long hair.

They hid him.

His assistant was likely becoming rapidly aware that Tamlin Ashowan was significantly fitter than he seemed.

Tam pulled back his left blade, and in another instant, he had the one in his right hand flipped and cutting toward Eli's middle.

She moved out of the way, but feeling the cold edge of his other dagger against the pulsing vein of her neck, her eyes widened.

Tam watched the realization wash over her: He wasn't just competent with knives… he was frighteningly deadly.

She swallowed, lowered her gaze, and took a quick breath.

Tam was about to ask if she was alright and if they should stop when she gave a firm nod. "I apologize for underestimating you, my lord. I will take you more seriously here on out."

The earnestness and keenness in her face told Tam that something had shifted in her. His instincts prickled, and a knowing smile lifted the corners of his mouth.

So her magic *did* have something to do with her confidence in defending herself.

Despite the peculiar expression Tam gave her, Eli remained focused, poised and ready for his next attack…

Which was a good thing, because the blade that had been resting against her neck flipped again and was about to puncture her appendix. Meanwhile the other was about to gut her. She leapt back, landing lightly on her feet.

Tam's grin widened before he then dove low toward her right side. His right hand aimed for the inside of her left thigh, while he utilized his greater size to wrap his left arm around her back, aiming to slip the blade between her ribs to puncture a lung. However, Eli shocked him by backflipping over his arm. As a result, the blade aimed at her thigh met dead air, and while the tip of the knife in his left hand scratched her vest, she got away unscathed—and even came close to kicking him in the face. If he hadn't reacted in time, she most definitely would have.

When she sprang back from her hands onto her feet nimbly, Tam let out an impressed laugh.

This time he didn't give Eli the chance to steady herself as he slid forward fluidly, crowding her space, his right arm angling the blade upward toward her heart, his left once again wrapping around her shoulders to pin her in place. Eli ducked under his arm and away from the right knife, putting her to his left.

She could have had the advantage in an attack of her own, but in the time it had taken her to get out of his way, Tam had already switched the direction of the knife in his left hand, like a compass finding its mark. Luckily she had gained enough distance that when he jabbed, she merely leapt to her right. Circling closer to Tam's back, she made him turn to keep his eyes on her.

In a twisting motion, Tam stabbed with his left and sliced with his right. The move would have pierced Eli's belly and cut her throat had she not doubled over and, in a short hop, spun her legs out, pulling her torso away. Which placed her out of his reach again.

Tam didn't waste a single breath watching or waiting for Eli to stop moving as he descended upon her, thrusting his blades toward her abdomen and throat again. The speed of the attack threw her off the rhythm that Tam had been following beforehand. As a result, when she darted backward, she wasn't as graceful, and it only took one quick, long step from Tam to pin her against the railing overlooking the stern of the ship, his left hand pressing the flat of his blade to her throat, his right at an angle near her middle. The knives were pointing in opposite directions, so if she tried to jump left or right, she'd be cut either way.

Eli's breath visibly caught in her throat as she gazed up into Tam's calm eyes. His breath was as even as ever, but... he was close to her. *Very* close. They were practically toe-to-toe.

A strong urge welled up in Tam as he stared down at her... a feeling he hadn't had in a very long time. It wiped his mind perfectly blank as the intensity of the moment seized them.

Tam wanted to be even closer. He didn't want to look away from her eyes that were the hue of fresh cinnamon...

It wasn't until he felt a particularly large lurch from the sea beneath the ship that Tam snapped back to his senses.

He heard a rush of air escape Eli's mouth, and he wasn't entirely certain why that sound intensified the desire to hold her against himself, but it took greater effort than he would have estimated to step back from her.

Once he was at a safe distance, Tam nodded, lowered his arms, and sheathed his blades. "Not bad."

Eli's hands fidgeted at her sides as she inclined herself to him in gratitude for his fair assessment of her abilities, avoiding his stare rather pointedly as she did so.

"You're remarkably fast yourself, my lord." Her voice sounded tight and awkward.

Tam bowed in thanks. When he straightened back up, he noted how Eli remained standing stiffly in place, her chin lowered as though hiding her expression. He opened his mouth to apologize for making her uncomfortable, but was interrupted.

"OYY! YOUR LORDSHIP! WE FOUND A RAT THAT SAYS HE KNOWS YOU!"

The shout from a sailor summoned both Eli's and Tam's attention. They crossed to the top of the stairs leading from the poop deck down to the main deck, but they couldn't see the cause of the commotion below them because five or more members of the crew had crowded around whatever it was.

With his brows lowered, Tam made his way quickly down to the excitement with Eli following close behind.

Reaching the sailors, he tapped their backs to alert them to his presence. Though it took some time for things to settle, they eventually parted enough for him to see a young boy being restrained by three sailors. The child wore a dirty gray tunic, a battered brown leather vest that was far too big for him, trousers that were too small, and woven shoes.

While the boy struggled, he didn't speak or shout, and instead grunted against the holds of the sailors.

"Let him go. He can't run off anywhere," Tam ordered with an edge in his voice. The sailors didn't look pleased, but did as commanded.

Tam peered down at the top of the child's head and inwardly sighed. The boy's hair was covered in what looked like dried white paint, which was most likely how he had been discovered aboard—some of the sailors had been touching up crates that held ropes, pulleys, and other items that they might need at night and would need to find easily.

It wasn't the first time someone tried to approach a member of the Ashowan family asking for help, or wanting to serve the dukedom. And while Tam and his family were always happy to do what they could, Tam was away from the connections and resources he could use to help a child in need. He couldn't even risk reaching out to anyone once he landed in Zinfera as it could alert the Zinferan emperor and his court to his presence.

"What's your name?" Tam asked the child quietly.

The boy wiped his nose with the back of his wrist, his chin pressed against his chest. Tam noticed that he was clutching a folded letter.

"I don't know yet," the boy croaked. Then with his slim shoulders still hunched, he brandished the missive at Tam. The future duke was already worrying about what he could possibly do with the boy other than try sending him back with the ship to Daxaria after he and Eli were dropped off in Zinfera… an option Tam wasn't fond of, given the way the sailors were already cursing the child as some of them went over to clean up the mess of splattered paint.

Taking the letter, Tam unfolded it and began reading.

He felt the blood drain from his face.

The letter was from a woman he had known… quite *intimately*… a little over seven years ago.

Rosaline Evans ran a tavern he frequented when traveling. She had shared information with him while he inspected the offices and schools in the city of Rollom back in Daxaria, and collected intel from the brothels his family owned; he had stayed at her establishment during his visits. He had liked her a great deal, but ultimately, she preferred to live an independent life, and Tam had agreed that they were better parting ways.

Except, according to the letter... it hadn't been as clean an ending as he had thought.

Tam gaped at the top of the child's head, his body numb and his mouth slack.

"Can I..." Tam rasped the words, uncertain what he was even going to say as his heartbeat tripled in speed.

"Is everything alright, my lord?" Eli stepped forward curiously, eyeing the child and then her employer, who was quite obviously shocked to his core.

Tam didn't even register having heard her as he, on shaking legs, gradually lowered himself to a crouch in front of the boy. "Can you please look at me?"

The poor child trembled violently, and tears still dripped off his nose onto the boards of the deck... But when he lifted his face, it was Eli's turn to jolt back in alarm.

Tam gaped, utterly dumbfounded, into a pale face that was remarkably like his own. The same brown eyes, the same pale skin. Belatedly, he realized the true color of the boy's long hair—at least the parts that weren't covered in paint—was black.

The boy's lip quivered as he continued to stare back at the future duke, who was utterly speechless.

Of all the surprises Tam had speculated he might come across during his trip to Zinfera...

Being faced with his illegitimate son had never occurred to him.

CHAPTER 15

COLOSSAL CONSIDERATIONS

Dear Lord Tamlin Ashowan,

Hopefully you remember me even though it has been a few years since we last spoke. My name is Rosaline Evans. I am the owner of the tavern and inn you frequented, the Rosey Glass.

The child that delivered this message, well... There is no easy way to say this.

He is your son.

I learned about him two months after we last spoke, but because you had never given me your real name, I did not know how to inform you.

It wasn't until my brother, Liam, discovered you when you were in Rollom with your father inspecting the coven schools that we learned your true identity.

I've debated for months whether I could part with our son, but I'm ashamed to admit that I have not been the best of mothers. At my brother's urging, I never gave the child a name, as Liam believes it is a father's right, and it is important in order for the father to form a bond... Even though I never knew if I'd find you again.

Our son looks just like you. He's quiet, like you are, and always seems to be thinking carefully. He doesn't smile often, but he is polite, and will not give you any trouble. From the bottom of my heart I believe that you can provide him a better life than I ever will, and I think he needs you. I think you need him, too, to be honest.

When my brother and I heard you were going to perform inspections again with your father, I sent our boy to meet you. I've done the best I could for him until now, but please, please accept him. While he seems like he can bear the weight of the world with ease, I know he is a scared child that needs his father. And a mother's love, as great as it is, can't fill that void of another parent.

I wish you my best,
Rosaline Evans

Seated at the small desk in Eli's cabin, Tam reread the letter for a fifth time, then tossed it onto the desk.

Tam had dazedly seen that the boy was fed, and that a bath had been drawn for him in his own cabin. The child had insisted he didn't need any help bathing, and so Tam had retreated to his assistant's cabin to try to wrap his head around the situation.

Eli stood with her arms folded, leaning against the door, watching her employer.

"You have something you'd like to say?" Tam asked, finally lifting his somber gaze to hers.

She stared back at him, devoid of emotion, and Tam felt a flicker of anger in his chest at seeing the coldness that had appeared in her countenance.

"Not at all, my lord."

Tam's voice sharpened. "I'd rather you not hide your true opinion."

Eli swallowed but didn't cower at his apparent displeasure. "Were you ignoring the mother of your child to the point she had no choice but to send him to you?"

"No. I had a relationship with her while I was using a different name. I occasionally had to travel without alerting the local nobility or the coven. So she had no way to contact me after we concluded our… relationship."

"You didn't think to check in, just in case?"

"She is the kind of no-nonsense woman who didn't want a clingy ex-lover. She's busy running her business, and her brother made it perfectly clear I shouldn't return."

Tam could tell that Eli felt her moral high ground was starting to crumble. She pushed herself off the door as she struggled to settle into the conversation.

"What are you going to do about him?"

Tam raised an eyebrow, then rested his elbows on the tops of his thighs, his hands loosely clasped while he stared up at her. Despite his position being lower than hers, Eli shrank under the intensity of his gaze.

"It's a little more complicated than I'd like with him being here. For one, I can't just send him back to Daxaria alone, and I'm concerned for his safety while we're in Zinfera."

A flicker of softness passed through Eli's eyes as he spoke.

"Then there is the obvious question: Is he the devil?"

Eli jerked back in shock, and her eyes widened. "What?"

"How much were you told about the events of the war in Troivack?"

"Well, I… That is… That is private information belonging to the crown—"

Tam closed his eyes with a sigh. "You know about the devil and the first witch. Good. Then you most likely also know that the devil was supposed to be reborn shortly after Her Majesty killed him. Seven years ago."

Eli gaped at Tam.

He was right… And it *was* true… She had remembered the king and queen of Troivack discussing how much the devil had resembled Tamlin Ashowan…

"I thought the devil respawned from the ashes of his past corpses. How would he have been able to get this former love interest of yours involved?" Eli wondered aloud, betraying how well informed she was of the whole situation.

"The devil would, I imagine, have connections…" Tam added, lowering his gaze, his moment of intensity dissipating.

"During questioning, the first witch claimed that she had disposed of many of the devil's connections and contacts, and she seemed rather confident on the point," Eli recalled carefully.

Tam gave a humorless chuckle and lifted his face once more. "So you think that the boy really is my son?"

Eli shook her head. "I do not know for certain, given your astute point about him potentially being the missing devil, but he does look remarkably like you."

Tam eyed his assistant a little longer, weighing whether or not she was sincere. But he eventually reminded himself that her thoughts weren't his business, so he stood. "Regardless of the possibility, until we know for certain one way or another, I'm going to treat him as though he is my.... my own. But we are going to be extraordinarily careful about revealing any information around him. Our time in Zinfera was supposed to be relatively low-risk, mostly gathering information; if we *do* interfere, it is to be as discreetly as possible. At present, I'll think more on whether I'll send him back or take him with us once we dock in Ori."

"Pardon my saying so, my lord, but you are underestimating how dangerous the Torit Desert is. No one is safe traveling through. Let alone a child."

Tam grimaced. "You tell me then. Which is safer? Sending him back alone to Daxaria, or bringing him along? I'm deferring to you on this, Eli, because you know Zinfera best." Tam's hands found his pockets as he waited on her opinion.

A blush crept up Eli's face as she suddenly remembered earlier that day, when Tamlin had her pressed against the rail at the stern of the ship... How, rather than feeling frightened or panicked, she had felt drawn to her employer. His solid strength had been an odd comfort as opposed to a threat.

She lowered her eyes, unable to look at him while forming her answer. On the one hand, sending a child back with strangers was terribly risky, even if Tam revealed that the boy was his son. There were pirates, slave traders; even the weather was a danger.

On the other hand, bandits roamed the desert, and the elements could kill them as well. Not to mention the talk of a dragon being sighted at the other end of the kingdom. Still, Lord Tam would be there, and his family had their own connections. Besides, if the child *was* the devil reborn, it'd be best to keep him close.

"I suppose he should join us," Eli agreed at last.

Tam jerked his chin down. "Alright."

Her employer then moved to step around Eli, making her entire body flush with awareness once more, causing her to shrink away from him. Tam paused, his brows twitching in concern.

Not wanting to address the dragon in the room, Eli quickly blurted, "What will you name him?"

Caught entirely off guard by the question that was almost shouted at him, Tam balked. "Er… I… I was going to ask his opinion on that. To be blunt, that detail made me particularly suspicious about his story… Though when I remembered Rosaline's brother Liam, it did kind of make sense. He was wildly controlling at times, and most likely wasn't all that kind to the boy. Rosaline is a strong woman, but when it comes to her younger brother, she lets him sway her and doesn't address his anger. Anyway. You don't need to hear about that." Tam seemed to blink away the memories as he reached for the cabin door. "I'll talk to the boy and see what names he likes."

"My lord?"

Tam glanced over his shoulder. Eli was fidgeting as she always did when she was uncomfortable and attention was directed at her.

"I… I believe you are commendable for handling this as well as you have," she said, making Tam straighten in surprise. "I believe it is an assistant's duty to provide both criticism and praise to their employers, as they see them in ways that no one else does."

A soft smile curved Tam's mouth, right as she stole a glance to see his reaction. "You sound like you're the one in charge here. You're doing a fine job yourself, Eli."

"At least with everything going on, your seasickness has eased off!" she burst out awkwardly.

Tam wondered if her straightforward nature made her completely unable to handle teasing. Then turned his mind back to her point and felt his lightened expression dwindle. "Oh, I still feel like hanging over the rails, but I just don't have time to right now."

"Most people can't control seasickness," Eli pointed out.

"Most people don't find out they have a seven-year-old son in the middle of the sea, either."

With a final wave over his shoulder, Tam exited the cabin to go face the child who might be his son… or the son of the Gods—the child responsible for the evil of all mankind.

Either possibility brought with it a world of complications, though if Tam were honest with himself…? He couldn't help but already consider the boy his own. It was hard to think otherwise when he had never seen the devil in person. Besides, it really was remarkable how much he and the boy looked alike.

As Tam walked through the narrow galley of the ship toward his own quarters, he idly thought how excited his nephew Antony would be about having a cousin near his own age.

In fact, all three of the boys would be over-the-moon excited to have another person to play with.

When Tam caught himself smiling while imagining this future meeting, he felt his heart jolt in alarm. Was he already deluding himself into thinking that he was fit to be a father?

He couldn't even handle crowded rooms for an entire evening! And what if his powers got the best of him again, only this time, instead of an entire wall and desk being the victims, it was his own son?

Tam's gut churned.

Rosaline had said she thought their child would be better off with him, but she didn't know how little people thought of the future duke… To bring in an illegitimate child and subject him to even more judgment than would be the norm in such cases…?

Tam arrived at the cabin door and hesitated.

His heart skipped several beats, and a cold sweat started to prickle along his back.

Amazingly, his magic wasn't adding to his problems in that moment, but who was to say if that would last?

Tam reached up and patted his chest, where he could feel the pendant under his tunic. The one he kept hidden from sight, but that brought him immeasurable comfort.

Closing his eyes, Tam did his best to shelve his fears.

If the child was his, then it was reasonable to assume that he was frightened and uncertain about his future. And he would of course deserve kindness, patience, and room to feel however he needed to in that moment. Tam's own insecurities needed to wait.

So, reaching for the door handle, Tam faced his new responsibilities while also making the firm decision to press the possibility of the boy being the devil to the back of his mind. Even if there was a strong likelihood this *was* the son of the Gods? If there was the tiniest of chances that was not the case, Tam was not going to risk scaring a child who had done nothing wrong.

Tam opened the door and stepped in, albeit he did have one final thought before focusing on whatever scene would greet him.

Gods… My parents thought Kat eloping when she was out of the country was bad… Coming back home with a new illegitimate grandson might even have her beat for outrageous surprises…

CHAPTER 16

AN UNINTENTIONAL UNVEILING

Tam entered his cabin, paused, then closed the door as quietly as possible behind himself.

It wasn't the most spacious of rooms—any extravagant boats pulling into the harbor in Zinfera would've attracted a lot of attention—but there was still a built-in bed with the headboard on the same wall as the door, enough room for a set of low shelves along the back wall, and a round table that could comfortably seat three to four people. A window on the port side of the room let in the evening sun as they sailed south; now, in early afternoon, the warm light had only just begun to creep along the weathered boards of the room.

His son was standing by the window next to the foot of Tam's bed, his black hair damp from his bath, and he was wearing the white tunic that Tam had laid out for him, despite it being too large. The child was holding the brass sextant Katarina had bought for Tam back during her time in Troivack, and the future lord watched as the boy turned the tool over carefully in his hands, admiring its interesting shapes and the way it gleamed in the light.

Because the boy's back was to him, Tam couldn't see the look in his eyes. If they were keen and understanding, it could indicate a wisdom beyond his years... hinting at perhaps a Godly parentage. But if it were childish innocence, perhaps...

The boy stilled, then turned around abruptly and jolted in alarm at the sight of Tam, dropping the sextant with a loud clatter.

"I'm sorry!" he shouted, panicked. Dropping to his knees, he picked it up frantically, his hands trembling.

Tam strode over and held out his hand.

With his head already hanging, the child carefully handed the instrument to its owner.

Lifting the sextant up and peering through the eyepiece, Tam found it was intact, though even if it had cracked, it wouldn't have been the first time. Asher had done almost exactly the same thing to it the year before.

Looking back down at the boy, Tam lowered the instrument. "It isn't broken. It's alright. Though in the future, please ask before touching things."

"Y-yes, my lord. I-I'm sorry, m-my lord!" The child's words warbled, and his shaking grew more noticeable.

Tam took in a slow breath as he lowered himself down to a knee.

"I'm not upset," he explained, softly but firmly. "I just happen to own things that could be dangerous if not handled with the proper care."

The boy nodded hastily.

"Now, you mentioned that you didn't have a name, and your mother's letter confirmed this. So... Is there a name you yourself like?"

The topic change seemed to succeed in stopping the boy's quivering, though his hands moved in front of himself and he began to pick at his thumbnails.

Tam's heart twisted.

Rosaline had the same habit when nervous.

"I-I-I want you to pick one!"

Silence rested between them for a time before Tam spoke again. "Really? Even if I wanted to name you something silly? Like Artichoke?"

The child was so stunned he temporarily forgot his shyness and stared directly at Tam, and even though the fear in his dark eyes made it seem as though he was going to immediately look away again, the gentle smile on Tam's face made the boy freeze. He, for whatever reason, looked surprised.

"If you… If you think that…" He swallowed. "If you think that's the right name for me… then that's… that's fine."

Everything about the child's tone and body language screamed the opposite of his words.

"Oh, really? Have you ever heard of the former earl, Lord Dick Fuks and his son Les? Or about his grandson, Ass?"

Despite his nerves, a brief laugh escaped the boy's mouth, though he quickly pressed his lips together.

Which was a good thing, as thoughtful alarm struck Tam. The boy's astonished laugh was like that of Katarina Reyes, Tam's sister's, the Daxarian queen…

Am I imagining things? Trying to find proof he is my son and not the devil…?

"Tell you what, I won't name you something funny, but you have to tell me the truth if you do or don't like one. Deal?"

Smiling, the boy looked up again, albeit shyly. "Okay."

"Alright… Here is what I'm thinking. Tonight, you and I are going to do something together. It's something I don't do with anyone else other than my family."

Unable to resist the allure of a secret activity, the child leaned closer.

"We are going to use this sextant, to find constellations. Maybe as we do that, we'll find a name for you. What do you think about that?"

The child's wide excited eyes dropped to the instrument, which in turn brought another smile to Tam's face.

"I… I like that idea," the boy said.

"Wonderful. Now, there is one other very important thing I need to ask you."

The child's shoulders hunched in preparation of hearing some sort of somber request. Gods knew what it was he was expecting…

"I need to ask you to stop calling me 'my lord.' On this ship, you can call me Tam. Are you comfortable with that?" The future duke received a shy nod in response.

"Alright, I'm going to go do some work with my assistant. Are you able to read? I don't have many books that you may be interested in, but I do have one about the legends of the constellations."

The small face tensed. "I… *can* read, but… not very well." His cheeks burned.

Tam mentally kicked himself. Of course his son hadn't had a lot of opportunity to read. Rosaline was busy day and night running her business. She hadn't owned many books back when Tam knew her, either.

"Not a problem. I'll buy you as many books as you like in the future. For now, though, how about… erm…"

"You don't need to worry about me, my lo—T-Tam. I-I can just sit quietly in the corner."

Tam frowned but decided not to comment on the boy's behavior. He had known Rosaline to be a stern, independent woman, but her son's reactions were those of an abused child.

"Who did you spend most of your day with, if you don't mind my asking…?" Tam asked, though he already felt like he had a good answer.

"M-my Uncle Liam."

Tam gritted his teeth. He should have guessed as much earlier. Obviously, Liam's harshness had also prevented Rosaline from naming her own son. Tam felt a mixture of rage and disappointment. He had thought Rosaline was a fair, just woman, even if she was blinded by her affection for her brother at times.

To think that her opinion of her brother outweighed her love for her child?

Tam did his best to remind himself that this young boy could still be the reincarnation of the devil, in which case this might all be an act. But… the boy was convincing. There was no trace of deception in his words or face.

And in the event that it *was* the truth, that Tam had sired a son… then he could not come from a moral high ground when it came to rearing children.

As a result, Tam forced himself not to say anything that could possibly make the lad become defensive.

"Tell you what, do you like to draw?"

A wary nod was his response.

"Perfect. I would appreciate it if you could draw some pictures for me, and if you feel like writing, I would love to read about what kinds of things you like. Your favorite color, your favorite food, your birthday… All of those things." As Tam spoke, he made his way over to the round oak table and pulled a fresh stack of paper in front of the chair, along with an inkwell and quill.

The cabin floor rocked beneath their feet as the nameless boy watched Tam work.

When he'd finished, Tam turned and smiled while gesturing to the chair. "I can see about a cup of tea being made for you. Do you like tea?"

The child began to fidget with his thumbnails again. "Can't I stay with you?"

Guilt seized Tam's heart.

Of course someone so young and in such a frightening situation would want to stick by the person who had been kind to him... and also happened to be their father.

"Why not? I'll handle my work in here, but I hope you won't mind that I'll be reading, and I may have to go out for some fresh air often. To be honest, I get seasick a lot." Tam added the last part in a conspiratorial whisper.

"I know." The boy smiled sheepishly. "I watched you this morning from my hiding place."

Tam put his hands on his hips and rolled his eyes to the ceiling. "Damn. I guess it wasn't as big a secret as I'd hoped."

The boy laughed. His brown eyes were bright and warm as he stared at Tam with open admiration.

Excusing himself to go tell Eli the change of plans, and see about getting a few cups of tea for the three of them to sip around the table, Tam left the cabin feeling as though things were going tentatively well. Though he knew a lone conversation couldn't be what determined how everything would unfold, he was clinging to whatever positives he could.

At Eli's cabin, Tam knocked on the door. He didn't hear a response, and so he turned to check above deck to see if she had simply gone up to get some fresh air. Suddenly the ship tilted. Tam was thrown into the wall beside the door, and from within the cabin, he heard a loud thump that sounded like a body hitting the floor, followed by a groan.

Concern seizing him, Tam threw open the door, his body tensed in preparation for whatever he might find, except...

There was Eli.

Without a tunic or vest.

Her chest was mostly covered by bindings, but there was a long swath of cloth that lay over her lap undone from the rest of her wrappings.

She was slumped against her desk, clutching the back of her head, her face scrunched up. Evidently the lurch of the deck beneath her feet had sent her careening back, to the point of stumbling and thwacking her skull soundly.

Tam figured this out while he stared rather dumbly at her... though something that was far less passive started to rise in his being. Something akin to protectiveness and perhaps a tinge of the same compelling feeling he had experienced earlier when he'd stood close to her at the stern of the ship against the railing...

While the future duke remained frozen in place, Eli, still clutching the back of her head, slowly opened her eyes.

When they met Tam's, it was her turn to go still.

Her stare widened a fraction, as though she could see the mysterious well of feelings coming up in her employer.

But then a cool draft swept across her middle. She looked down at her bare stomach and remembered what she'd been in the middle of doing when she'd fallen and hit her head.

Thanks to living with the infamous house witch who cooked meals that tasted beyond anyone's expectations, she'd found she had to loosen her bindings more regularly.

Eli's eyes darted back up at the same time Tam began to come back to his senses. He was opening his mouth to begin apologizing when the sound of small feet pounding down the corridor interrupted him, making him turn in time to see his son careening toward his side.

"Tam, I'm so sorry! The—the ink! It spilled everywhere when the ship—" The child skidded to a halt, then looked into the cabin where Eli still sat on the floor.

He stared at her. Then back up at Tam.

"I didn't know Eli was a girl."

Tam instantly cringed as he dove for the door handle, fumbled, and at last yanked the door shut just in time for Eli to drop her face to her hands.

Still in a state of confusion, Tam continued staring at the closed door while his son peered up at his stunned profile.

"Should I call her Miss Eli? I'm sorry, I didn't know..." The child was utterly unaware of the secret he had just discovered.

"Ah... about that... Come on, let's go back to my cabin and... We need to have a quick chat about Eli." Tam gently grasped his son's shoulders and steered him back toward his own cabin while trying to pull his thoughts together.

"O-okay." The boy looked over his shoulder uncertainly. "But is she your betrothed or something...? Why were you there when she was getting dressed?"

The sound of footsteps belonging to the crew thudded down the stairs behind Tam, prompting him to gently cover his son's mouth as he moved them even more quickly back to the cabin.

While Tam had always prided himself at being exceptionally good at hiding his nonsense in almost every area of his life (a skill his father had never seemed to master), he was starting to wonder if maybe the inability to stay discreet or stay out of trouble was an affliction that developed with age.

CHAPTER 17

STARSTRUCK STORIES

E li climbed the stairs to the top deck, her employer's son at her side.

She hadn't looked at him or said a word to the boy since he had discovered her secret. This was out of fear that the child wouldn't be able to stop asking her questions about why she would hide her gender.

As it was, the boy hadn't breathed a word, though Eli wasn't certain that that was any better. She was constantly tense, waiting for it to begin. Even though she assumed Tam must have said something, she knew people's curiosities often got the better of them.

"Oh."

Eli jumped at the lone word the boy uttered, then realized why he had: Tam was sitting at a small round table on the deck, with two other chairs pulled up to it. Under the light of a large brass lantern containing three burning candles, they could see that the table was laden with tea and cakes.

The future duke sat with his back to them, a book in his lap as he gazed up at the sky, a far-off glint in his eyes, and a smile on his face. Eli couldn't take her eyes off Tam's profile at that moment. The gentle rise and fall of the ship beneath their boots, the brilliant starry sky above them... There was something about the moment that struck her.

A gentle tug on Eli's hand snapped her out of her thoughts.

"He's waiting for us," the boy whispered, excitement etched in every inch of his face.

She blinked past her distracted moment, gave a tight-lipped smile, and proceeded to the table.

"Good evening, Lord Tam." Eli bowed.

Tam looked over his shoulder with a smile and rose to gesture toward the other two chairs. "Hello to you both. Sorry I had to leave you for a few hours—I had to brush up on some of my constellations."

More like you are struggling to wrap your head around either being a father or being close to the devil, Eli thought.

She couldn't really blame her employer for needing to take time to process his present circumstances. Very few people would handle things half as well as he was.

Once the trio had seated themselves, Eli picked up the teapot and started pouring out whatever her employer had brewed, though her arched eyebrow conveyed her dubiousness.

Tam grinned knowingly. "I selected a rooibos tea. I know it's more forgiving for oafs like myself who aren't as refined with their tastes."

Eli's face flushed as the familiar scent of the tea wafted up to her. Only...

"Rooibos isn't *really* a tea and— Is there dried orange in this?" she asked with interest.

"Yes, there is," Tam returned with a smile. "And yes, rooibos tea is not like black tea, or herbal teas—"

"It's more of an infusion than a tea. Rooibos tea comes from Lobahl, though I've never tried any that had orange mixed in," Eli expounded thoughtfully.

"That would be because this is from my father's friend, Mr. Jelani. He is an earth witch and he loves to see what food combinations my da can come up with using the fruits and plants he grows from his home in Lobahl," Tam explained while slipping some buttery cookies onto a plate and placing them in front of the boy—who'd been listening attentively until he was faced with a cup of warm tea and treats.

Eli didn't respond. She wrapped her slim fingers around her cup and allowed the comforting warmth to send goosebumps up her arms as the sea breeze tried to chill her. Lifting the cup, she sipped it tentatively… then perked up.

"Aside from the fact you over-steeped this, it has quite a lovely flavor!"

Tam grinned as he turned his attention to the boy, who slurped it dubiously.

"I thought so, too. My father always pairs it with lighter-flavored snacks. Scones, and butter or nut cookies make for a nice bedtime snack with the tea." Tam picked up a cookie and sat back.

After polishing off most of the cookies and tea, the trio were feeling quite content with their sated states. Tam set his book on the table, opened it to a page he had bookmarked with a red ribbon—the spine creaking and the pages rustling—and then reached down to his side where his sextant sat in an open case.

"Now, the first constellation I'm going to be showing you today," Tam began with a glance at his son, "is the Three Fish."

Both the dark-haired child and Eli stared blankly back at him, but Tam didn't mind. He lifted the sextant to his right eye and peered southeast of the ship.

"Now, with all constellations, there are stories."

"Why?" the child blurted abruptly, his eagerness getting the better of him.

"To make it more fun to remember which stars are where. You see, stars help sailors and travelers on land navigate where they are going. You need to remember what they look like, and so people made up stories to help them. However…" Tam said with a wink, "there are some who think the Gods used the stars to show us the history of our world."

Eli and the boy leaned closer, entranced.

"Whether you choose to believe that or not is entirely up to you, but more people think that way than you know. Astrology hasn't been explored much in any of the kingdoms in the past two hundred years or so, but around a hundred years ago, a Troivackian scholar decided that we shouldn't lose these stories—he sincerely believed that the Gods had given us these stars for a reason. So he traveled every kingdom—"

"Even Lobahl?" the boy interrupted with wide-eyed wonder.

Tam nodded. "*Especially Lobahl.* You see, Lobahl is far more advanced than any other kingdom, and many of their beliefs involve the stars."

"How do you know that Lobahl is more advanced or their beliefs about the stars?" Eli wondered aloud, her curiosity getting the better of her.

"My father's friend, Mr. Jelani. I wheedled a few stories out of him with the help of his two children. Though the both of you need to keep that information a secret. Alright?"

While the boy smiled, Eli's gaze darted uncertainly to her employer. Tam felt he knew the source of her unease. Should he really be sharing *any* kind of secret with the possible devil? But Tam pushed the concern aside.

"Now, the story of the Three Fish is one of the oldest, yet not many people have heard it."

Tam held out the sextant to the boy and pointed southeast. "Do you see the grouping of stars that looks like three whirls connected? Almost like a windmill without its base?"

The boy squinted, his mouth pursing and twisting until at last it split back into a smile. "I think so!"

"Excellent. Those three whirls signify the three times of day in which one of the fish swims in the Goddess's pool. And depending on which fish is swimming, the divine properties of the water change. In the morning, the fish that sees the past, present, and future swims. It is said that the Goddess and Green Man drink from the pool when this fish swims in order to see all that has been, that is, and that will be. The second fish arrives after the high sun while the first fish returns to the underground streams to rest. The second fish knows magic innately, like witches do, but it also knows how to summon magic with the language mages use."

The boy lowered the sextant and stared at Tam earnestly, his bum on the edge of his seat.

"The Goddess and Green Man use the water this fish swims in when they create a new witch. It is only during this time that the crystals lining the bottom of this sacred pool can be plucked out."

"Are those the mage crystals?" Eli, too, had shifted closer, her teacup still clasped in her hands.

Tam tilted his head in acknowledgment. "They are indeed. In this tale, witches were *made* with the water. The first mage was given a vial of the water to drink, and then after begging the Green Man, was also gifted one woven bag filled with crystals. That is how he learned the language of magic. He wrote down this language for others to learn as well, though they can only summon magic from the Goddess's pool through their crystals."

The helmsman steering the ship handed the wheel off to his crewmate then, and for a moment the sails fluttered.

Despite the interruption, neither Eli nor the young boy had lost focus for even an instant. Tam took another sip of his tea and continued.

"The third and final fish… is the chaos fish."

Eli let out a giggle.

It was so uncharacteristically feminine of her that it made Tam laugh a little while she cleared her throat awkwardly.

"What's a chaos fish?" Obviously, the poor child couldn't handle any delays getting between himself and the answers.

"The chaos fish… well, she swims at night, and it is said that when the balance of the world is in danger, the Gods create chosen beings to be molded with its waters," Tam explained while leaning forward in his seat to rest his elbows on his knees, bringing him closer to his son.

"Have they ever given the water to someone to drink like they did with the magic midday fish?" Eli pondered aloud.

"Some Lobahlans think so; however, the Troivackian astrologer I mentioned before? He doesn't believe that is the case, nor does he really think that the Gods create beings with the water—that would be cruel in its own way. What he hypothesized in his work was that whenever the world needed a change, the Gods would simply fling a cup of water over us, and thunderstorms, tidal waves, or earthquakes would reset what had grown uneven."

"What do *you* think, Tam?" the boy implored, hanging off every word that fell from his father's mouth.

Tam leaned back in his seat pensively. "I think… the Gods decided to use chaos water to make my father's and sister's familiars, Kraken and Pina. I mean, I'm sure even you know about those two, right?"

The child nodded with a laugh visibly bubbling up his throat, but then his shoulders suddenly slumped forward. "I like the story a lot, but…"

"But?" Tam prompted gently.

"There weren't any names in it."

Tam jolted in surprise, then was awash in fresh guilt.

The poor boy had to be eager for a name, and here he had dragged on a story without any.

"What was the name of the Troivackian astrologer?" Eli interjected, her hint obvious.

"Ah, it was Luca Bilgin..." Tam looked down at the child's crestfallen expression, warmth spreading in his chest. "Luca."

The child looked dazedly up at his father.

"What do you think of being called Luca?" Tam's voice was gentle, and he did his best to hide his preference in his tone in case the boy had an aversion to it.

"I... I like it a lot." The child broke into an excited smile, and tears started to fill his eyes in the glow of the candlelight. "Luca! *My* name is *Luca!*" His hands curled into fists as he then lowered his head. "Thank you, Tam... Thank you so much!"

Mortified in every sense of the word that his own son should bow to him, Tam reached out and gently clasped Luca's shoulders. "Don't ever bow to me. I'm sorry I made you wait before finding you a name."

Wiping his eyes with his sleeve, Luca shook his head. "I-it doesn't matter! I now have a name, a-and that's all I care about!"

Tam smiled and gently rubbed the top of the boy's head. "I'm glad you're happy with your name, Luca. How about we finish our tea for the evening, and tomorrow night, I'll tell you a new story about a different constellation."

With tears still overflowing, Luca nodded, and Tam embraced his son for the first time since they'd met.

Eli watched from her seat, feeling alarmingly overwhelmed with emotion at the touching scene, but also because anxiety brewed in her gut. While Luca had done absolutely nothing to be suspicious of, behaving every bit the way a normal seven-year-old would in such awkward circumstances, she couldn't quite free herself of the suspicion that the devil was somehow tied to him.

And if so?

Her heart ached terribly as she stared at her employer's face while he held the boy in his arms...

She had a feeling it would destroy Tam's heart. After all, it was plain to see that despite his better judgment, in the span of a day, Tam had already started to love the child that he had named.

CHAPTER 18

A BOUNDARY BEND

An arrow pierced through the imp's eye, and he released his hostage. Meanwhile, the golem was overwhelmed with familiars, stumbling about the perimeter of the castle trying to battle against the mighty Kraken and the elusive Pina—"

Eli interrupted Tam's vivid retelling of Troivack's civil battle, which his family, with their familiars, had been instrumental in winning. "You forgot to mention Reggie the raccoon's contribution."

She seemed adamant that Tam shouldn't overlook Reggie the raccoon, who was quite famous in his own right. The beastie was unfathomably large yet somehow healthy, and was a familiar to a Troivackian witch who had aided the king's army in the war.

Tam let out a long sigh.

He had never seen Reggie the raccoon, but he had most certainly heard about him in great detail—too much detail at times—through the years from his father, sister, and brother-in-law. He didn't understand the fascination with the rotund beastie from the tales he'd heard. It was a large raccoon. So what?

Their vessel was two-thirds of the way through the journey to Zinfera, and every night since the first, Tam, Eli, and Luca had sat on the deck with tea (that Eli insisted on brewing), snacks, and the sextant as Tam told the fantastical stories of the stars or—on a night like this, with the clouds above blocking the moonlit sky—legendary tales of the Ashowan family.

Tam had discovered during the voyage that he was an exceptional storyteller, and it wasn't long before Eli and Luca eagerly joined him for their evenings together, appearing to enjoy that time above any other time of the day.

"Which are imps and golems again?" Luca's legs swung to and fro while he sat at the edge of his chair as was his norm when listening to his father speak. The past few nights, they had in particular been discussing the ancient beasts that had been summoned from the Forest of the Afterlife to aid the first witch, daughter of the Gods, in banishing the devil to another realm and taking power in the Troivackian kingdom.

"Imps are the ancient beasts associated with water. They are *seven feet tall* and usually have purple, black, or blue hair. Their eyes are similar colors, and they have three spinning pupils in each one," Tam explained, pointing at his own eye and drawing circles to illustrate his point. "My father's familiar says that they can turn into sea creatures in water, and they wield their element as well as the most powerful water witches."

"And golems are the giant rock men tied to earth power? Taller than some keeps?" Luca recalled.

"That's right. They don't talk much, and I'm sure you've heard about the stone golem that is loyal to the new Daxarian queen's familiar. He stands off the shore of Austice and guards the harbor," Tam confirmed.

Luca nodded along, though a line had formed between his eyebrows as he sifted through the information.

"Sirins are associated with air magic. They fly; they have pointy teeth, white or gray hair, and red, blue, or even white eyes. They can sing the most beautiful song you've ever heard, or scream and drive you mad," the future duke said.

Luca shuddered at the imagery just as a particularly biting wind whisked through the trio.

"As for the last of the ancient beasts associated with the elements… dragons. Dragons are giant lizards that burp fire," Tam concluded bluntly, making Luca laugh. "We know the least about them, as they rarely show themselves, but they are associated with the fire element, and are thought to have superior wisdom."

The group fell into an amicable silence. Tam leaned back in his seat, his hands folded over his belly as he stared out over the inky sea.

"Tam?" Luca asked suddenly.

"Mm?"

"My Uncle Liam said you're a witch…"

Tam's easygoing expression tensed.

"I heard one of the crew members say that Eli's a witch, too."

Tam and Eli looked at each other, hardness entering their eyes as Luca continued speaking.

"What… kind of witches are you?" the boy finished, though he was looking increasingly uncertain. The tension in the air was as taut as a harp string.

Neither Tam nor Eli answered at first, instead gazing at each other in wordless communication.

"Luca… Eli and I aren't like most witches," Tam began carefully. "Neither of us likes to talk about our magic. No one knows what mine is, and Eli… Eli does not like her magic. I understand why you are curious, but, in the future please do not ask about it."

"But wh—"

Tam raised his eyebrows as he stared firmly at his son. He hoped the expression in his face showed Luca that while he wasn't angry, he was not going to budge on the point.

Luca, looking horribly chastened, gulped, and started fidgeting with his thumbnail.

Burning shame scorched Tam's chest. The boy hadn't fidgeted in days.

Despite starting to squirm, Luca still went on to ask, "Wh-what if I'm a witch, though? What if it's like *your* magic?"

Tam felt his heart drop to his stomach at the thought that Luca might inherit his magic. Luckily, he swiftly came back to his senses.

"It has never happened that mutated witches have children with the exact same abilities. So you aren't in danger of that, and you most likely would've already noticed some kind of magic by now. It's not very often that magic arrives any later than at seven years old."

"So you're a mutated witch?" Luca latched onto the tidbit hopefully.

Tam straightened at the question, and his gaze sharpened, making the boy shrink back.

"Luca, how about you go to bed now?" Eli changed the subject smoothly, already sensing that the situation was about to escalate.

"O-okay," the child stammered before nervously sliding to his feet.

As he did so, Tam took the opportunity to mask his emotions and resume a more relaxed posture. "Have a good night, Luca. I'll see you in the morning."

The boy gave a shy wave but couldn't bring himself to meet Tam's eyes as he made his way back to their cabin, where Tam had hung a hammock for him.

Once Eli and Tam were alone, the assistant looked expectantly at her employer.

He stared back unimpressed.

"Weren't you the one saying I needed to exercise more caution around Luca?" Tam pointed out coolly. "Was that line of questioning Luca was pursuing not something to be wary about?"

"They're normal questions for a child to ask, my lord. Especially one who hasn't grown up around a lot of witches," Eli replied calmly.

"Luca normally doesn't push boundaries when they're set. That was strange."

"Or it's a sign he is getting more comfortable with you."

Tam let out an irritated breath. "How should I have handled that, then?"

"A lot of people know you're a mutated witch. You could have confirmed that and let it be. Furthermore… if Luca *is* the devil, it isn't a bad thing for him to start showing his agenda."

The future duke didn't respond immediately, instead turning the argument over in his mind while he gazed back out over the water.

"My lord, I know I've said this a few times, but we still don't know if he is the devil or—"

"I know. But there is still the chance he isn't, and if not…?" Tam shook his head, at a loss at how to proceed.

Eli sighed. "If you would be so kind as to indulge me, my lord, but how about we switch sides of our arguments. Why did you get so upset about your own son asking about your magic? He has every right to be afraid when it's clear you yourself are terrified."

Instantly Tam recoiled as a spectrum of emotions struck him in response to his assistant's observation. But he suddenly froze, and his gaze locked on something in the water.

"My lord?" Eli frowned, then followed his line of sight. She paled upon recognizing the dark shapes in the water.

A loud bell clanged from the helmsman before Tam or his assistant could say another word.

"PIRATES!" the captain roared while emerging from belowdecks, the brass buttons on his emerald coat still undone as he dashed up to the helmsman.

Tam rose from his seat and, without looking, reached over to the lantern, opened its door, and with his left hand pinched out each flame on the candles.

"Eli, you are going to go to my cabin, and you are going to stay there with Luca until I come get you. There will be two passwords. If I say that everything is clear, that means someone is holding me at knifepoint, and you are to hide Luca immediately. If I say everything is fine, it's safe. Understood?"

The assistant bobbed her head.

When Tam was finally able to tear his eyes away from the longboats that had crept up alongside the ship, he discovered that despite the imminent threat, Eli appeared perfectly calm.

He lowered his gaze in thanks, and she turned to see to his orders. Inside his pockets, Tam's hands curled into fists as his magic started tearing urgently at his chest.

He swallowed with difficulty and closed his eyes.

This was precisely what he had worried would happen while he was trapped on a boat: a situation arising where he might lose control over his magic. Not only would there be witnesses, but someone could get caught up in his power while he could do nothing to help.

"Captain Pinnel, the pirates are just bobbing around the ship while their own vessel comes to our side. We've got Basque and Torrie on either side of the deck prepared to fire off the crossbows at them, but we don't want to waste resources."

"They're waiting to dispose of anyone that jumps into the water..." the captain rumbled ferociously as he stared at the longboats.

"Why are you letting the pirate captain aboard our ship for negotiations when they are planning on killing all of us?" Declan, the first mate, had his dark-brown eyes intent on his superior.

The captain, a fit man in his early forties, stared at the pirate's ship that was pulling up alongside their own. "Lord Tamlin Ashowan said it would be fine if we did."

"What?" The first mate turned to face Captain Pinnel abruptly.

"He said he would defer to me, but he believed he could manage the negotiation as long as we didn't reveal who he was."

"He is a pampered noble!" the first mate declared angrily. "He is well known for being adept at paperwork but useless everywhere else! He is not capable like the rest of his family!"

"Have you seen him train with his assistant?" the captain asked softly, his eyes gleaming when they rested on Declan.

"No, I haven't," the first mate confessed. "Why? Did you see his magic?"

"No… but he can handle himself far better than you think. I only watched for a short while before he noticed me and stopped, but truthfully? I sincerely doubt anyone in the Ashowan family is useless."

"You're gambling our crew's lives with barely any—"

The sound of a gangplank slamming down on their deck prevented Declan from making another furious comment. The two men turned toward it in time to see the Zinferan pirate captain sauntering across the gangplank, seemingly without a care in the world, the yellow plume in his hat matching the yellow of his baggy pants. He wore a well-made black coat that he had obviously stolen from a much larger nobleman, and a crisp white tunic that signified he was a rather wealthy pirate—and of course, no one missed the curved sword on his hip.

He had long black hair threaded with white, his face hidden by his hat, though a silver hoop in his right earlobe flashed in the faint light of torches and lanterns.

"Where is Ashowan?" Declan asked abruptly as he glanced around the ship deck, expecting to find the future duke standing, wearing his usual black vest and pants, hands in pockets, waiting.

Instead, he was nowhere to be seen.

The captain said nothing, but there was a peculiar calm about him… almost as though he knew something Declan didn't.

One of the Daxarian crew members approached the Zinferan pirate as he stepped aboard with five more of his men at his back.

"Did you tell Roberts to greet them?" Declan couldn't take his sights off the deck as the scene unfolded.

"I didn't." Captain Pinnel craned his neck to see that his crew member was gesturing toward the bow of the ship, still looking remarkably unperturbed.

"Why would Lord Tam want to meet with the man up there?" Declan wondered with growing exasperation.

Captain Pinnel paused, tilted his head, then glanced over to the port side of his boat as he listened to shouts and orders to move the longboats, drawing a smile from the captain's mouth.

"By the Gods, he guessed right."

Declan looked at the captain, puzzled.

"Lord Tam just forced two of the boats to have to move to keep an eye on the pirate captain. We have fewer eyes on *us* on this end of the ship. Declan, start quietly letting the men know that my cabin is empty. If they happen to have any of those steel spears around, they should be able to add some… renovations to the pirate ship beside us from my window."

Momentarily stunned by the turn of events, the first mate gave a quiet chuckle before saying, "Yes, sir."

Apparently, the next head of the Ashowan family had a trick or two up his sleeve after all.

CHAPTER 19

A PIVOTAL PARLAY

Tam stood at the bow of the ship, the sea breeze cool when it brushed along the back of his bare neck, a sensation he was still getting used to after cutting his hair. His hands were tucked into his pockets, and he leaned against the railing, feigning a casual air as the Zinferan pirate captain strutted the rest of the way over to him.

"Good evening, sir," the pirate called out in mocking tones. "I am Captain Kwon." He tilted his head, a smug smile on his face, revealing a gold eyetooth that glinted in the lantern light.

"I am Mr. Voll. I'm a scholar who is hoping to revive the study of astrology in Daxaria. I was hoping I might persuade you that there is nothing of value on this ship aside from the men." Tam bowed his head.

Captain Kwon ran his tongue over his golden tooth, the short goatee around his mouth shifting in the light to reveal that the hairs were spackled with white.

"That might be believable if you weren't looking so…" He eyed Tam up and down. "Calm. Or if the Gondol harbormaster had received notice of your arrival."

"We aren't going to Gondol. We're sailing around the south of Zinfera and docking in Junya. As the oldest city in Zinfera, it is more likely to have ancient texts on the constellations." Tam lied easily about their destination while mixing in a bit of truth about the city. "And I'm not overly worried because, as I said, there isn't really anything here to steal."

"Well, I don't know about that. This is a fine boat." Captain Kwon looked around with an appraising eye.

"You'd spread your crew thin sailing two ships," Tam stated bluntly.

Captain Kwon's slanted eyes drifted back to Tam, and after a moment of silent evaluation, he scoffed. "See, there's that superior attitude that tells me you aren't just some scholar, and I don't like being lied to in my waters. Now, how about you let me know who you really are, or—"

The pirate pulled his sword, and Tam could tell by the way he gracefully angled his feet that he was damn good at using it.

"—I'll kill everyone on this ship and take whatever I find. It won't be hard to steer a ship to Ori and sell it off anyway. People aren't asking a lot of questions since the creature has been lurking around."

"Creature?" Tam frowned.

Captain Kwon began stretching the wrist of his sword hand, making the blade lazily weave closer to Tam.

"Ah, you haven't heard about ships disappearing around Zinfera? Gone without a trace. No survivors. The only reason anyone knows the disappearances aren't due to *liberal* sailors such as ourselves, is that a young deckhand happened to see it one day from a merchant ship. After he alerted his captain, well… Every spyglass was spoken for."

Tam felt his heart skip several beats. "What did it—"

With a quick jolt, Captain Kwon's sword tip dove forward, stopping abruptly an inch from Tam's left eye.

Tam had seized the rail behind him, prepared to launch himself off the back. His magic surged in his being and felt like it was trying to tear his skin away from his muscles.

The captain smirked, and he'd just opened his mouth, undoubtedly to make a sarcastic, heartless retort, when a flicker by the lantern to Tam's right drew his attention. When his eyes swiveled to it, he discovered black wisps streaked with silver in the light, fluttering from Tam's skin.

"What—"

It was Tam's turn to interrupt Captain Kwon. His left forearm came up in a flash while the captain was distracted, knocking the blade aside. Before the pirate could recover, Tam had shot his heel into the man's lean gut.

There were shouts from the pirate ship, and boots pounded on its deck like a coming storm… But the captain held up his hand to halt the ruckus and slowly rose to stand straight once more, his eyes intent on Tam. "You aren't a normal human, are you?"

Tam's magic was making his brain feel like it was crawling with ants. "You should go back to your ship and say there is nothing of value here." The future duke's voice came out a rasp. He didn't dare move.

The power was leaking from him against his will.

The pirate captain tried to smile with his former bravado but failed horribly. The grip on his sword turned unsteady. "I'm not leaving until I get something of value from this ship."

Tam locked eyes with the captain. "You don't value your own life?"

He paled. "This Daxarian crew can't hold up against—"

"I don't need the crew to deal with you." Tam knew it was dangerous to take a step closer to the captain. Knew he was hanging on to his magic by a thread… but he needed to wrap things up quickly. He needed to go to a small, safe room and get his magic to stop trying to consume him and everything around him.

The captain made the grave error then of interpreting Tam's desperate gaze to mean that *he* actually had the upper hand.

Unbeknownst to Captain Kwon, over his shoulder, Tam had noticed someone emerging from belowdecks…

Luca.

Eli was scrambling up behind him.

The boy must have thought he could help. He had probably heard the earlier commotion on the boat beside them and thought the fighting had started.

The five men whom the pirate captain had boarded with all turned to Luca and Eli, raising their swords.

Tam's control dissolved.

"Men!" the pirate captain roared, intending to follow up the call with orders… until he discovered that his sword was on the ground. He could only watch as Tam, eyes filled with obsidian black, and silver smoky tendrils fanned out from his body, seemed to wipe away the world around him with darkness. How had he moved so quickly…?

Captain Kwon soiled himself, and then he was thrown overboard before he could even process what was happening.

Tam swallowed with difficulty, still battling against the power that was spilling over.

The pendant underneath his shirt glowed when he started to utter guttural words and turned toward the stairs to the main deck where five of the captain's men waited. He pulled out his two knives from behind him, murmuring under his breath, making the glowing crystal under his shirt gleam brighter and brighter.

By the time the pirates had reached his deck, Tam had successfully battled back the darkness that poured from him. Yet when he fixed his attention on the first two pirates, their murderous expressions turned fearful.

He approached, fluidly flipping a blade in his hand. They tried to lunge at him but found they were too slow, and quickly they, too, joined their captain in the cold waters of the Alcide Sea—alive, thankfully.

The next two happened to be more seasoned. When Tam's gaze turned toward them climbing the stairs, they were taken aback but recovered in an instant.

Sheathing his blades once more, Tam gripped either side of the railing at the top of the stairs and swung his legs up. When the pirate in front tried to slice one leg off just below the knee, Tam kicked his blade aside with his left boot heel and smashed the man's chin with his right, sending him tumbling back into his fellow pirate.

Tam glanced over to where he had last seen Eli and Luca and was relieved to see that his assistant had somehow managed to shove Luca back belowdecks. But then Tam saw Eli staring up at a pirate who easily had a hundred-pound advantage on her. Tam leapt over the pirates that were still recovering at the bottom of the stairs and sprinted toward her.

But he couldn't reach Eli before more of the pirates had stormed the gangplank. Luckily, some of the crew on Tam's ship had sprung into action. But unluckily, it had become clear to the pirates that Tam was the biggest threat.

Three of them appeared in front of Tam. Faced with three obstacles with poor hygiene blocking him from Eli, he withdrew one of his blades again. He wanted to avoid killing as much as possible…

"Gods… it's the devil…" one of the pirates in front of him gasped while his two accomplices shared nervous glances.

"Get off this ship." Tam couldn't tell what he looked like in that moment, but if pirates were calling him the devil, there was a chance he could get them to flee without having to fight them.

Sadly, the seasoned sea dogs were determined to uphold their dignity as pirates, and so with gritted teeth, they lunged toward Tam with their curved swords.

Luckily for Tam, neither of them was quite as skilled as their captain. He was able to step out of their reach, his eyes darting to Eli just in time to see her duck out of the path of a pirate's sword, followed by Captain Pinnel's arrival to save her.

However the time it took Tam to see this had distracted him, and he failed to dodge a slash toward his middle. He felt the awful, stinging pain of a slice across his abdomen.

Stumbling back, his free hand seizing his wounded gut, Tam saw the sword swinging back toward him a second time, but was able to avoid it and plunge his knife into his assailant's kidney.

The pirate crumpled onto his side, taking Tam's blade with him, and giving the two other pirate crew members a better opportunity to strike him.

Fortunately, Tam had been trained for just such circumstances. He lowered his head, leapt over the body of the man he had just stabbed, and rammed his shoulder into the nearest pirate, toppling the two together much as he had the men on the stairs.

By now Declan had appeared and was able to give the killing blow to the pirate that had fallen. But the one Tam had shouldered had already recovered; he now drew a knife from his boot, shot upward, and thrust the blade toward Tam's throat.

Seeing this, Tam seized the pirate's arm with his left hand then elbowed back with his right, breaking the pirate's nose.

Declan ran the final man through right in time for them to hear shouts from the pirate ship beside them that they were already steering away from.

"WE'RE TAKING ON WATER!"

Tam released a breath of relief when he saw that the pirate ship had already moved far enough away that no one could jump or throw hooks to reach them. After a quick scan around himself, he realized that all the other pirates aboard had been dispatched by the crew, though there was a Daxarian man Tam had seen managing the sails of his own ship who was lying quite still near the railing where the gangplank was...

Closing his eyes in both pain and dismay, the future duke tried to steady the world around him as it began to spin.

Then it occurred to him that the first mate wasn't saying anything despite his passenger being quite obviously injured. Opening his eyes again, Tam squinted at Declan, who flinched in response.

If he hadn't been focused on the throbbing pain radiating from his middle, Tam would've felt his stomach churn at the fear in the man's eyes.

He decided that was something he could worry about later. With a nod of wary thanks to the first mate, Tam took shuffling steps toward the stairs that would take him belowdecks. He wanted to check on Eli and Luca, and then maybe see about stitching his wound.

The stickiness of his blood and its metallic smell grew stronger in Tam's nose, and while it was far from his favorite scent, he was at least somewhat used to it. With a shaking right hand, he seized the railing and started to descend.

"My lord! My lord, I brought bandages, a needle, and thread! I put Luca back in your cabin—I'm so sorry he came abovedeck, he heard the commotion and got worried about you and—" Eli had rushed up the stairs to his side, but when she noticed the blood staining his shirt she abruptly stopped talking.

Tam halted on the second step and leaned his head against the wooden wall. He shook his head slowly, then immediately regretted it as nausea began to build.

"Not... your fault... You're fine? He's fine?"

"Yes, my lord," Eli assured him with a firm nod, though she was looking a mite shaken.

"Good... Good. Let's go to your cabin. I don't want Luca seeing this..." Tam swallowed and then resumed his journey back down the stairs, wondering if he was going to vomit or faint first.

"My lord, I... Luca did not see it, but I... I saw something when you faced the captain... It was like everything around you and him went black. Was that—"

"I don't ask about your magic, you don't ask about mine," Tam managed as he touched down on the corridor that would take him to Eli's cabin.

"I-I wasn't sure if it was your magic. My apologies, my lord... I was confused. Especially when it seemed like that necklace you're wearing was glowing like a mage crystal."

Tam halted and looked at Eli.

Surprisingly, she didn't flinch.

"If we're asking questions now, does *your* magic somehow make you lighter on your feet?"

Eli pressed her lips shut, and Tam, having expected this reaction, proceeded forward to her cabin. He just wanted to get the pain of stitches over with so he could go to bed. Hopefully, he'd have some time tomorrow to rest and think about tonight's events.

Unbeknownst to Tam, the surviving pirate crew and even the men of the vessel he rode were all busy discussing his mysterious dark power, and how it must mean that he had to be none other than the devil, son of the Gods, creator of evil. The Daxarian crew sailing with Tam wouldn't dream of asking if this assumption were true or not, and so all decided to give the nobleman a wide berth for the rest of their journey to Zinfera.

CHAPTER 20

A STRAIGHTFORWARD STITCHING

Sitting on the edge of Eli's bed, Tam did his best to pretend that sweat wasn't beading along his hairline.

He knew that what was about to happen was going to hurt. So while he waited for Eli to retrieve the bottle of moonshine that was absolutely necessary at that moment, he tried thinking about anything other than getting stitched up on a rocking boat by an assistant who most likely hadn't sewn closed that many people, particularly not at sea.

For one thing, Captain Kwon of the pirates they had just evaded had mentioned a creature that was sinking boats along Zinfera's northern border.

Was it the dragon?

None of the Daxarian crew members had said anything.

I'll ask around the harbor when we arrive. We'll rest for a couple of days and stock up on supplies for crossing the desert. Mum said our guides will meet us at the docks. Hopefully they don't quit when they find out Luca is with us...

The cabin door opened a crack and Eli slipped in, the bottle of moonshine, thankfully, in hand.

"Alright, my lord, we should hurry. Luca is getting restless the longer you are away."

Tam nodded, not bothering to muster the strength to speak. He stripped off his torn black vest, followed by his tunic.

In his injured state, he barely registered that Eli's eyes went round and her cheeks started to burn as she took in his bare torso. She probably wasn't used to the sight of blood. Well… it wasn't like there was any other option. So as unfortunate as the present reality was, there was no escaping it.

As she had suspected during their training, Tamlin Ashowan had a build that he kept well hidden. Now, though, Eli no longer needed to speculate about his physique. There was some bulk in his arms and shoulders, but the rest of him was lean muscle.

Tam tossed his bloody clothes onto the cabin deck. "Sorry about the mess." He lifted his chin and stared at Eli, who was startled by the wave of tingling that rushed through her.

She was spared from him noticing her flustered state when he reached desperately for the moonshine in her hands. Though it took her another moment to realize what he was doing… in a spell of madness, she'd briefly thought he was trying to hold her hand.

Awkwardly, Eli thrust the bottle at her employer. He gratefully took it, uncorked it, and gulped down the liquor like it was water.

"M-my lord? You said that was to clean the wound!"

Tam lowered the bottle to stare at her, a flush already appearing in his cheeks. "You think I'm going to sit perfectly still while you jab me with a needle twenty or more times in a row without anything for the pain?"

"Some men do!" she blurted before noticing that she had accidentally insinuated that he was weaker than some men.

Tam seemed to take no offense, but he did raise his eyebrows and give a quiet chuckle.

He blinked leisurely then spoke. "I'm willing to bet that if these men you know had the option to take some moonshine when they were injured, they would. And if I were to lose that bet? I still don't see why I should suffer pointlessly because someone else is willing to. Now, would you prefer me to lie down on the bed or the floor?"

Eli swallowed.

It was probably just because Tam knew she was a woman that she felt so uncomfortable. Still, the idea of him lying half naked on her bed was making it very hard not to squirm, and so she jerked her chin downward.

"Floor. It looks like they cut you straight across so it'll be easier to reach over you," she explained.

Tam nodded and, with a rumble in the back of his throat, eased himself off the edge of the bed with its dull-blue wool coverlet, and onto the floor.

Eli sidled over to her desk, plucked up the needle and thread, and slipped the needle through the flame of her lantern to sterilize it. "You're lucky—it doesn't look like they punctured any important organs," she noted conversationally.

"True enough. Though I'm starting to think my family is cursed when it comes to boats and traveling. My sister had her own incident when she was sailing to Troivack, and then she got stabbed a few times while there... And now here I am, almost gutted by pirates."

"Did your sister discover she had an illegitimate child as well?" Eli questioned drolly, hoping to distract herself from Tamlin Ashowan's muscular torso.

"No... Though she did have a scandalous marriage."

"I remember." Eli threaded the needle.

"Do you miss Troivack?" Tam asked abruptly.

Eli scoffed. "Why yes, of course I miss enforced labor while being under investigation for crimes against the Daxarian and Troivackian crowns."

Tam stared at the ceiling of the cabin, wincing at his insensitive question. Then Eli sloshed the remaining moonshine on his wound, and he flinched for a whole new reason.

"Gods*dammit* that's— Shit." Tam clenched his fists at his sides as he tried to take deep breaths through his nose.

Eli refused to look at his face from then on. The less distracted she was, the sooner she could finish. And so without waiting for the evident throbbing pain from the moonshine to stop, she set to work closing the wound.

"Zinfera!" Tam gasped out. "Tell me about Zinfera!"

Due to her attention being focused on her task at hand, Eli actually answered before calculating her words.

"Zinfera... If there is a corner of that kingdom where its people aren't selfish or self-serving, I'd be shocked. I wasn't born into a poor family by any stretch of the imagination, but they still sold me off to the emperor to acquire even more prestige and wealth."

Tam's body relaxed as he listened.

"What did you think about the Zinferan food?"

"The food was... food. I didn't think much about it." Eli squinted, unsure if she was looking at a wide spot of injury, or if it was just that blood had smeared more heavily in that area. "The tea is the only thing I truly miss about it."

"Was your family... involved in the tea trade...?" Tam wondered with a faint grunt as Eli worked closer toward the space below his navel.

"They weren't until after I was sold off. They actually invested in rooibos distribution. Not many Zinferans thought it would be successful, because rooibos technically comes from Lobahl like I mentioned a while ago."

"How old... were you?" Tam bit down on his tongue until he drew blood as the cold needle went through him.

"When they handed me over to Chin? Eight."

"Chin?"

"The emperor's mother, Chin Taejo. She was the one who insisted that the emperor adopt me."

"That must've been hard," Tam said slowly. He wondered if she realized she had just revealed that rather than being a mere servant at the emperor's palace, she had been one of the adopted children... He decided not to draw attention to the fact in an effort to keep her talking.

Especially as this profound discovery was distracting him magnificently from the pain he was in.

Eli's mouth twitched, her mood turning brittle. "It was a blessing in a way that I left my mother and father's home. I was happier with Chin than I was with them."

"You lived with the emperor's mother? Instead of the other children?"

"The emperor's adopted children are usually sponsored by other concubines or officials in his court. Most of those people jump at the chance to back these children, since it means they can increase their odds of having someone they can control inheriting the throne,."

"But no concubines were interested in you? Was it because your family aren't nobility?"

"No. They are nobles. But my mother complained about my magic to their peers and anyone else who would listen, and it influenced everyone's opinions of me."

Tam's gaze slid from the ceiling to Eli's profile. He could see the weary irritation in the set of her mouth. "I take it that when the emperor's mother died a few years ago, you were abducted and sold off?"

Eli knotted the end of the thread and looked around for a knife. When she didn't find one, she shrugged and set to biting off the ends of the thread. It put her mouth a breath away from Tam's abdomen, and he was suddenly in a whole new world of discomfort.

In order to alleviate his troubling symptom of distress, he closed his eyes firmly and started thinking of Lord Dick Fuks striding nude around the castle in Daxaria.

Finished with her task, Eli leaned back on her haunches, though Tam could still feel the goosebumps near his hip where she had hovered moments before.

"It took a few months after Chin died, but yes. Without Chin looking out for me or managing the emperor's concubines, I was abducted by people working for one of the more influential women. They intended to have me die slowly in slavery, but... well..."

"You used magic?" Tam guessed without moving. He wondered if the conversation would proceed naturally if he just kept lying there.

"Yes. And the slave traders figured out I could be useful."

"How is it you met Eric Reyes?" Tam wondered, his mind turning to his brother-in-law, the Daxarian king. What was his history with Eli, when he himself had been mysteriously missing for four years?

"He was abducted for ransom a year into my stint with the traders. It was thanks to him I was freed for a while." Eli let out a long steadying breath. "My lord, I've shared a good amount about myself. I'd say I've earned a few answers."

Tam's eyes snapped to her poised expression. So she had shared some of her secrets intentionally to leverage him. He pushed himself up with a subtle groan of pain, then eased back to lean against the planks of the cabin wall. "I never agreed to that exchange."

"You're a fair man," Eli argued, clearly nervous that he wouldn't allow her underhanded negotiation to pass.

And if it weren't for the moonshine that was making Tam's head feel fuzzy, he might not have. "You should know better than anyone that when it comes to survival, things aren't always fair."

At the flash of hurt and anger that moved through Eli's eyes, Tam yielded a few breaths faster than he had planned. "Fine. My magic... Part of the reason I don't talk about it is that I don't understand it myself. But if I say as much to any of my family members or the coven, they'll suggest experimenting—and I do not want to try *anything* with my ability. What happened today was because I couldn't control it."

"Then your power is that you... emit darkness? Or night?" Eli speculated with a frown.

Tam's head flopped forward. "I disappear, and anything I happen to touch or am near goes with me."

Silence flattened the air between the pair.

"Where do you disappear to exactly...?"

"No idea. It's nothing but blackness. I don't even have a body if it completely overtakes me. I have no sense of time, place... anything. It's just me, but lost in a void."

Eli tried to imagine what he was describing. Being in absolute black nothingness...

"Why do you have a mage crystal?" she plunged on, though she hadn't fully wrapped her head around his previous answer.

Tam looked at her dumbly, then back down at his chest. "It helps me not disappear when my magic starts getting the best of me. Kind of like... well, the stars. It's something I can hang on to and keep an eye on to make my way back. I've always found constellations and their stories interesting. They're comforting because they tell you where you are when everything is gone. I got the idea about using a mage crystal years ago after I had an... an outburst. It took me a long time to convince the mage school to give me one, and I had to do a lot to earn it, but I got it in the end."

"Was the outburst the time you made an entire wall and desk full of important paperwork disappear?"

Tam stared at Eli blankly. "Who told you about that?"

"Her Majesty Queen Alina heard about it from Her Grace your mother, when some important documents regarding the coffee trade went missing—"

"And *you* found out because you were working alongside Likon, most likely to draft whatever paperwork needed to be re-sent," Tam surmised with a grunt of irritation. He closed his eyes.

"By the way…" Eli hedged, already angling her tone so she could maybe yank free one more answer from her employer—even though she had just been told secrets that *no one* else knew about Tamlin Ashowan. "Are you aware that your eyes turn black with your magic? Are you able to see when that is happening? Or is it like when Her Majesty your sister is overcome with her own abilities? Not that I've seen her use her power, but I've heard multiple accounts about what it's like when she does."

Tam's attention snapped back up in alarm at the description of his eyes during his magic incident.

Apparently, he *hadn't* been aware of that. And unfortunately, the question broke his streak of direct responses.

He looked around the cabin. "You wouldn't happen to have a tunic that fits me in here, would you?"

Not bothering to mask her disappointment, Eli stood. "No, my lord, but I'll go get you one. I'll let Luca know you're on your way back to him."

"Thanks." Tam reached for the bottle of moonshine and took another mouthful while Eli slipped out of the cabin.

Tam stared blindly ahead of himself, his head light and his body throbbing in pain, but warm from drink.

He already regretted revealing the truth about his magic.

Why the hell had he confided in Eli? He barely knew her, and she could be a spy for someone. She could have made up her entire backstory! Besides, if she let it slip about his power? The Coven of Wittica would be breaking down his father's door, demanding more information about his abilities while insisting it was just to ensure he wasn't a threat...

Anxiety wormed its way through the throbbing in his gut and the alcohol.

Why had he lost control of his power when faced with the pirates to begin with? He had been in far worse situations thanks to his secretive line of work with his mother. Had it just been because he was trapped with nowhere to go in the middle of the sea?

Or was it that he now had a child? He wouldn't have been so sloppy during the fight and gotten hurt if he hadn't been watching out for Luca and Eli...

Tam allowed his head to thump back against the cabin wall.

He hadn't even arrived in Zinfera, and already everything had spun far out of his control.

Maybe I should've been more understanding of Kat growing up... Things really do just happen sometimes.

CHAPTER 21

CURIOUS QUESTIONS

Tam staggered away from Eli's cabin back to his own, but as the ship started to rock more noticeably beneath his feet, he wondered if perhaps he should have accepted her help getting there. By the time he finally reached the end of the passage and rested his hand on the door handle, he was forced to swallow down bile that burned the back of his throat. He hoped the sheen of sweat over his forehead wasn't too noticeable in the dim light of the lanterns.

His mental preparations were interrupted, however, when the door to his cabin swung open on its own. There stood Luca, breathing hard, tears already falling down his face.

Tam blinked down at him, caught by surprise, but when the child saw his father standing before him, he burst out into fresh sobs.

Instantly forgetting about his pain and nausea, Tam hurriedly stepped forward, knelt, and hugged Luca, angling his wound away from the embrace. He could feel the boy's tears soaking through his tunic as he held him, and he could smell the wind in Luca's tangled black hair from having spent most of his day outdoors.

"I'm alright," Tam murmured with a grand attempt at sounding comforting.

Luca still couldn't bring himself to speak, and so Tam didn't release him. He simply allowed his son to cry as long as he wished, though the longer it carried on, the more uncomfortable Tam's right knee became. Soon it was wobbling on the wooden planks of the deck.

Just as he was about to gently tell his son he really needed to lie or sit down, Luca pulled away, hastily wiping his tears from his face with the sleeve of his tunic.

"S-sorry for crying, Tam," the boy managed while sniffling.

Tam tousled his hair and gave a half smile he hoped didn't betray any of the pain he was in… or the fact that he was moderately inebriated.

"You have nothing to be sorry about. It was frightening. Even I wasn't sure what would happen."

Luca's hands gripped his own pant legs as his brows stroked downward to a frown. "Why didn't the captain take care of them on his own?"

Tam pushed himself back up to a standing position, doing his best to make his expression appear pensive rather than anguished from the action.

"That's because I'm a lord, and as the highest-ranking person on this ship, I should be responsible for everyone. Especially because I'm the whole reason they're here."

"My Uncle Liam said you don't have a title yet, but that you'll be a duke one day," the boy recalled offhandedly.

Tam pursed his lips while guiding Luca to the table and chairs in his cabin. "The firstborn sons in noble families are still lords. They don't have official titles until they inherit, but… There you have it. And I might just be a viscount. Not a duke."

"Why's that?" Luca plunked himself down across from Tam while giving his nose another cursory wipe with the back of his sleeve.

"Mm, that's a bit complicated to explain right now." Tam's head was already hurting, making his thoughts sluggish, thanks to his need for sleep. Despite this, he knew he had to address one particular thing before going to bed. "Luca, in the future, I need you to swear to me that you'll listen if I or Eli tells you to stay put. You could have been hurt today, or seen things you shouldn't have."

At this, Luca's shoulders widened. He locked eyes with his father. "A man doesn't back down from a fight."

Tam didn't respond straight away.

Instead, he pondered this reaction...

He thought back to Rosaline's brother, Liam... He had been all about appearing strong and being the most powerful person in a room, so it did make sense that he would have hammered in a principle like that one.

Regardless, it was a bad lesson to enforce on a child.

And so he looked at his son levelly and said, "Promise me, Luca. Or I'll have to find a way to send you back to Daxaria without me. I'm sorry, but I can't have you putting yourself in danger. I'll be too worried. Then again, maybe you'd prefer going back. I can arrange for you to be received by my father, Duke Finlay Ashowan, and he will take care of you until I return."

As Tam spoke, he wearily rubbed his left eye as his mind stumbled through everything he would need to do to give Luca safe passage home. Perhaps he would send Eli back with him. That wouldn't be an issue, either; she would probably prefer staying out of the kingdom that had given her nothing but pain...

Then the sound of Luca's rapid breaths through his nose reached Tam's ears and registered in his clouded mind.

Looking up, Tam saw that Luca's eyes were shining once more with tears.

"I'm sorry," Luca croaked, his hands fidgeting under the table. "I-I promise I won't get in the way again—I'm sorry I-I-I didn't listen, I'll be better, I promise, I'll—"

Tam stood, even though it made the sharp agony bite hard into his flesh, rounded the table, and crouched down to be eye level with his son. He was relatively certain he broke a stitch doing it, but he didn't care.

"I want to be with you, Luca. I only just got to meet you, and I've loved having our nightly meetings where we get to stargaze. But that also means I hate the thought of something happening to you. You scared me today more than you could ever imagine when I saw you come upstairs while those pirates were aboard."

Luca didn't stop fidgeting or stave off a fresh wave of tears, but at least his anguished expression had eased a little. "I thought you were gonna die today," he confessed, his nose already dripping again, prompting Tam to reach over with the sleeve of his own tunic and wipe Luca's face.

"I'm not going to die today, and I don't plan on dying tomorrow, either, and most important, I don't want *you* dying today, tomorrow, next month, or even in twenty years. You have to live until you're a hunched-over old man. The kind of old man that farts without knowing it, and even if he did? He wouldn't care."

At this, Luca let out a burbling laugh.

Tam smiled. Fart jokes always went over well with his nephews; he was glad it seemed to be the same for Luca.

"So you promise to listen if I tell you to hide?"

Luca's mouth flattened and he looked down with obvious displeasure. "Okay."

"Thank you." Tam squeezed Luca's upper left arm. "It'd be a shame to not get to spend as much time as possible together, don't you think?"

All the troubled feelings that had moved across Luca's face during their conversation melted away. A corner of his mouth lifted, just a bit, as if he weren't sure he was allowed to grin.

Seeing this, Tam smiled broadly and said, "How about we go to sleep for tonight. Tomorrow… what do you think about cutting your hair?"

Luca paused, staring at him. "My… my mother said my eyes scared people."

Tam had to fight off his alarmed reaction, but once again he forced himself not to comment on Luca's upbringing. "Well, they don't scare me. Or Eli. We all have brown eyes. Isn't that interesting?"

"My mother had dark-blue eyes."

Nodding, Tam stood back up. "That she did. I remember when I met her, they reminded me of dark sapphires."

Luca leaned forward. "She says you had a nice voice and she didn't expect it."

Tam chuckled while also subtly gesturing Luca toward his hammock. "She wouldn't have been the first person to say that about me."

"Did you love her?" While Luca may have asked the question in a casual tone, the fragility in his face told Tam it was anything but. And so he prayed to the Goddess that his drunken mind could come up with an appropriate response.

"I… I really liked Rosaline. And I think she really liked me, but your mother is very committed to running her business—as she should be! She's wonderful at it, and I was young at the time, and she was a bit older, and it just wasn't meant to be more."

Luca climbed into his hammock, an earnest glint in his eyes. "If she wasn't as focused on her business, would you two have loved each other then?"

Tam felt his insides curling and writhing. He wished his son had known the same happy, wholesome upbringing he had experienced growing up. "I'm not sure, Luca, but I will say… regardless of how we ended, I'm glad you exist."

Luca froze. Foreign emotionlessness took him over as he stared blankly at Tam.

"Luca…? Luca, are you alright?"

Just as abruptly as it had come on, the spell ended. Luca blinked and stared up at Tam with his usual nervous adoration.

"Yeah, everything's fine… Do you think there'll be any more pirates, though?"

Tam chuckled. "I sure hope not. Let's cross our fingers that we have a peaceful time through the rest of our trip."

"Eli says crossing our fingers isn't good because it confuses fate on whether it should give you good or bad luck."

Tam balked. "As in… She thinks fate is a person…?"

Luca shrugged. "I don't know, but she got upset about it when I said the same thing! Also!" Luca dropped his voice to a whisper. "Aren't we supposed to keep saying Eli's a boy?"

Fighting off a smile, Tam nodded and lowered his voice to match Luca's. "Yes. You're absolutely right."

"Why does she want to pretend to be a boy, though?" Luca whispered even more quietly.

"She feels safer pretending to be a man than being a woman."

"Oh…" Luca paused thoughtfully, then nodded to himself. "Are you and Eli in love?"

Tam's eyes bulged and his mouth went taught in surprise. "No we are not. Why do you ask?" he forced out calmly.

"Because you are always together, you keep secrets for each other… and… and you smile more when she's around."

This observation succeeded in stunning the future duke. Fortunately for him, Luca was already turning over in his hammock, preparing to go to sleep. When Tam eventually returned to his senses enough to notice he was standing staring at the cabin wall, he moved to his own bed, snuffing out the candles and lanterns on the way, his thoughts fluttering around aimlessly.

The longer Tam found himself on the ship with Eli and Luca, the more mysteries cropped up.

What creature was terrorizing Zinfera's ships? What had happened to Luca earlier that had him react so bizarrely when Tam had said he was happy he existed? Why was Luca so fixated on love? And lastly… Why in the world *was* Tam finding himself smiling more and more around Eli?

Lying down without bothering to turn down the covers, Tam stared at the ceiling above, then laughed as it struck him: *Maybe I'm getting a little more interested in Eli because I know she's a woman, and maybe it's because I haven't been this close to someone… well… ever.*

Tam closed his eyes and fought off a louder laugh.

Or I might be getting a crush because I'm in a lot of new situations and need someone to rely on. Or because I've been thinking about marriage a lot more with Luca being around. It makes sense that it'd happen, but… I'm sure I'll get over it.

CHAPTER 22

FAMILY FRIENDS

By the time Tam's ship pulled into Ori harbor, he was well aware that his confrontation with the pirates had sparked a new reputation for himself.

Sadly, it was not one he liked any better than the old one as a mentally unwell, possibly blind, cursed, or scared-of-his-own-shadow lord.

No, unfortunately, everyone that had borne witness to his fight with the pirates that fateful night had instead concluded...

That Tam was the devil.

Even the captain barely managed to appear cordial and unruffled in the future duke's presence.

Luca, who thankfully hadn't witnessed Tam's leaking magic, noticed the way everyone but himself and Eli were treating his father. He had asked both of them why this was, and Tam had explained that everyone was simply worried that the pirates would come find them again.

But Tam could see the uncertainty in Luca's eyes at that answer.

At the very least, Luca was aware that it seemed to be a sensitive topic. Amazingly, he was able to stop himself from asking questions.

Eli and Tam stood, both leaning against the railing of the ship as its cargo was unloaded onto the dock. Luca had gone to the upper deck to marvel at the harbor town from a better vantage point.

"My lord, we should leave as quickly as possible before the rumors about you spread throughout Zinfera," Eli murmured to her employer while eyeing the sailors as they hauled out Tam's trunks filled with books.

"And we will. I doubt Luca is ever going to see Ori again, so might as well let him take his time looking out."

"There's nothing much to look at," Eli commented irritably under her breath while turning her face toward the sea that sparkled in the early-afternoon sun.

Tam lifted an eyebrow. "Are you going to be alright being back home?"

Eli's jaw clenched and unclenched. "It's been years. People have probably already forgotten about me."

"I doubt that." Tam gave a snort of disbelief and pushed off from the railing to go holler at Luca, unaware of the stricken look Eli was giving his back.

The trio gradually made their way down the gangplank to the dock, taking in their surroundings as the harbormaster spoke with the ship's captain.

Ori was small, and it wasn't what most would call an attractive town. While the roofs of the buildings with their curved shapes and peaked roofs had the classic Zinferan tiles, the walls were layered in thick coats of dust and salt from the sea, as were the pillars that marked the end of the dock, originally painted bright red, with whirling black designs.

Beyond Ori lay leagues of desert that Tam, standing in the thick, roasting heat, was in no way looking forward to traversing.

"Your mother mentioned that our guides are well known to your family," Eli recalled while already craning her neck to look along the rocky beach for anyone waving to them.

"Yes. She tried to keep it a secret, but they're from Lord Ryu's family and—"

"Lord Ryu?" Eli spun around abruptly. "Is he going to be here?"

Both Tam and Luca halted in their tracks, wearing identical startled expressions.

"Er... no. I believe he was sending his sons. Bong and Jeong," Tam explained.

His assistant swallowed, visibly trying to calm herself.

"Do you happen to know... Lord Jiho Ryu...?" Tam ventured delicately.

Eli's eyes darted down to Luca, then back to Tam.

Ah. She knew him when she was a princess in the emperor's court, Tam interpreted seamlessly.

"Well, Bong and Jeong should be here already waiting for us at the local inn. I can ask some of the crew where we can find—" Tam stopped, frowning at something over Eli's head, then leaned to peer around his assistant. Luca did the exact same thing in the opposite direction; a puzzled Eli followed suit.

There, coming down the dock, were two Zinferan men.

Both had their black hair tied in buns atop their heads. One was wearing a teal silk coat with white lapels tied closed at his waist, while the other wore a royal-blue coat. Both had on white, loose pants that fluttered in the wind as the men leapfrogged over each other.

The man in the teal coat was giggling exuberantly as the one in royal-blue launched himself over his companion's back. The sailors filing down the dock gave them a wide berth and bewildered stares.

"What in the—"

Eli's words were cut off as the man in the blue coat spotted them and straightened. "TAMLIN!" he shouted with a bright grin, his white teeth flashing... Until the young man behind him leapt at his back, unaware that there was not a lovely little frog in front of him, but a tall obstacle.

An obstacle that was pitched forward by his companion headbutting his spine.

The two men lay in a heap on the dock seven feet from where Tam and Eli stood.

Luca was laughing.

Eli, on the other hand, didn't hide her concern. "My lord, are these men… our guides?"

"Tamlin!" The man in the blue coat hollered up once more, though it was mixed with a grunt as he tried to right himself. "I'm… Bong!"

The Zinferan in the teal coat lifted his hand from his face-plant at Bong's back. "Jeong!" he shouted, though the introduction was muffled. He pushed himself off his brother while trying to stretch his nose that was red from the impact.

Freed, Bong leapt to his feet energetically, his short goatee spreading with his smile as he bowed and held out his hand. "It is an honor to finally meet you! My father has spoken endlessly about your family!"

Tam, caught between amusement and wariness, slowly reached out and shook Bong's offered palm.

Bong, with his well-defined cheekbones and pointed chin, was a delicate kind of handsome, with a smile filled with unbridled happiness.

Behind him, his brother finished tapping his nose experimentally as though feeling for a break in it.

"This will be a wonderful opportunity for us to get to know each other better, Tam! We're here to take yo-oooouuu... Why is there a little version of you here?" Bong was pointing at Tam when he started speaking, however his finger slid over to Luca when he suddenly noticed the boy, who blinked and went cross-eyed while staring down Bong's digit. "We heard about your lovely assistant..." Bong continued in confusion.

Jeong lunged past his brother and grabbed Eli's hand, plucking it up and kissing it. "Marvelous to meet you."

She stared at him, openly horrified, prompting Tam to gently grasp her wrist with one hand, place his other palm on Jeong's forehead, and shove him away.

Tam knew Eli was probably reeling behind him at being recognized as a woman, and also at the untoward greeting, but he kept his gaze locked with Bong.

"This is my son, Luca. And this here is Eli—"

Bong clapped his hands together. "Your wife! My apologies for my brother, Lady Eli! Here in Ori there aren't many women you don't pay to share company with—" Bong bowed to Tam's assistant while rambling, until Tam cleared his throat loudly, interrupting him.

"Eli is my assistant. Not my wife."

Both Bong and Jeong regarded each other, eyes narrowed thoughtfully.

"So... She's the mother of your son... and your assistant. By the Goddess, are things ever different in Daxaria!" Bong shook his head in wonder while Eli's ears and cheeks burned red. Luca grinned up at her and apparently decided to emulate his father in being a bit of a mischievous arse: He grasped her hand as though to confirm the Ryu brothers' speculations.

"No, no... she's just my assistant. Luca's mother... is not joining us on this trip," Tam explained vaguely. He was hoping to divert the conversation onto a preferred topic such as where they were staying, or how they planned to survive the desert, but both Bong and Jeong were still struggling with the introductions.

"Wait—so you are... single?" Jeong asked while aiming a hopeful smile in Eli's direction.

The assistant shifted backward, her brows lowering—she didn't seem to notice that she was holding Luca's hand.

Tam sidestepped between her and Jeong. "She is my assistant, nothing more." The firmness in his tone, as well as his movements, deterred Jeong from any further advances.

Bong smiled affably. "Very well... Congratulations on your marriage back in Daxaria, though! My father will toast to the good health of your—"

"I'm not married."

"Oh my." Jeong and Bong lifted their hands to their chests at the same moment—rather than looking judgmental, they appeared pleasantly enthralled at the notion of a scandal.

"Shall we go to the inn to discuss when we are departing?" Tam's eyes were hard, but neither of the Ryu men looked chastened or worried.

"Absolutely, Tam! Would you like to leapfrog back? Because of the bounce of these planks, you get spectacular height to your jumps!" Bong clapped a hand on Tam's shoulder and thumped the dock beneath his black boot as proof.

At first, the future duke opened his mouth to say no, but then he paused with a hint of a smile.

"You know... *Luca*, I'm sure you would enjoy trying it!" Tam swung around and stared at his son, whose eyes widened at being put on the spot. Luca looked at Tam in wordless wonder as to why his father would do such a thing, but Tam glanced down at his son's hand, still clasping Eli's, as explanation. Realizing his crafty act had been caught, Luca blushed and hung his head in acceptance while letting go of Eli's hand at last.

"Come along, little Tam! Or, sorry, what was your name again?" Jeong crouched down into a frog position expectantly.

As the game resumed, the Ryu brothers hopping over each other with Luca in between asking all sorts of questions, Eli and Tam loitered behind.

"They knew I was a woman instantly... I need to cut my hair," Eli whispered more to herself than Tam.

He looked down at her with a sympathetic shine in his eyes. "Pretending to be a boy might have been something that worked when you were younger, but I think you're better off owning the fact you are a woman. The choice is up to you, though."

Eli lifted her face to stare grimly at the Zinferan shore as they walked, her dread visibly growing. "It'll spark rumors about you, my lord."

"For one, I'll remind you I am not traveling as a lord, but as a scholar, and for another, even if my identity is found out, I think my traveling with a woman will be overshadowed significantly by Luca's existence."

Eli's uneasy expression faded as she stared up at Tam. "Why did you tell them the details of his birth?"

Tam shrugged. "It wouldn't be hard to find out that I lied, and it could make a lot of things more complicated later on. If I lied and said I was married, my parents would hear about that and I'd have chaos waiting for me at home. If I lied and said he wasn't my son... That'd hurt Luca."

Eli fell silent in the face of such reasonable answers.

"Besides, I don't know about you, but *I'm* personally more worried about dying of thirst in a desert with you and Luca." Tam touched his chest and made his eyes comically wide when he stared at Eli, trying to counter her grim mood.

"Is it the company you're worried about dying around, or the thirst part?"

"That depends. Are Bong and Jeong perfectly hydrated when they ask me invasive, personal questions as I'm dying?"

At last, Eli cracked a smile, which made Tam smile back. He let out a breath he didn't realize he had been holding.

"What do you reckon... three weeks in the Torit Desert?"

"That's if we don't run into problems. It'll be hard on Luca." Eli lifted her chin in the direction of the boy, whose infectious laugh could be heard echoing back to them.

Tam sighed. He thought about his idea the night he had fought with the pirates...

Sending Eli and Luca back together would definitely put his mind at ease while he investigated matters in Zinfera, but... He subtly stole a glance at Eli's profile as they walked. She had a funny bounce in her everyday walk, Tam had come to learn. As if she exerted more effort in springing upward than in propelling herself forward.

He felt the fluttery sensation in his chest that he'd noticed occurring from time to time as a result of his crush. He shook his head. There were more important things to do or think about—though he didn't have the audacity to lie to himself and say her presence wasn't making the entire trip a lot more pleasant and fun, regardless of a surprise son, pirates, and gaining a reputation as the devil.

Eli stepped over the bench and seated herself beside Tam, her attention hovering around the bartender, who was giving her an equally suspicious stare.

She had just come from ensuring that Luca was in bed, along with organizing Tam's own room at the inn where they were to stay for the night. In the morning, they were going to find proper footwear and clothes for Luca and Tam in order to blend in better; afterward, they would set off in a carriage on the treacherous desert road known for its alarming number of bandits: The nice ones simply lightened you of your valuables, the more nefarious ones kidnapped and sold people, and the worst kind killed you and took whatever they pleased afterward.

"We are going to take you on a detour from the original plan," Bong began once Eli had settled herself, even if she seemed not yet mentally present for the meeting among herself, Bong, Jeong, and Tam.

"I don't have time for detours," Tam cut in. "Detours are risky. I need information on the person your father told you about, and I need to tour the mountains on the other side of the kingdom."

"Yes, and while I agree that traversing the Torit Desert and sledding down dunes could be a good time," Bong countered, sounding perfectly serious, "you are going to find more about your... *person*... in Junya. Rumor has it she wants to make Junya the capital of Zinfera again once she manages to wrestle a certain child of hers into a position I don't need to name," Bong continued with remarkable insight. "If she's already begun taking action, then those she trusts the most will be in Junya. It's better than talking to those towns under her thumb in the desert, and you will have more people to converse with about the... mountain... occupant."

When Bong's brother looked at him in confusion, he added a suspicious cough while uttering the word, "Dragon."

"More people can recognize me in Junya," Tam argued back, leaning his forearms on the table and lowering his voice.

Bong grinned and looked at his brother.

Despite having met the Ryu brothers only that afternoon, Tam and Eli tensed with the knowledge that it wasn't a good thing when they looked at each other like that.

"To be honest, you already have the perfect disguise."

"Someone who looks partially Troivackian claiming to be a scholar is still going to stick out—" Tam interjected, but Jeong was too excited to bother hearing the future duke's perfectly reasonable argument.

Jeong looked at Eli with glittering eyes. "Not if you're there because your wife's family is sponsoring your research!"

Both Eli and Tam turned to breathing stone figures.

"Are you… suggesting…" Tam started, already cringing as Jeong practically vibrated in his seat with delight.

"You, Eli, and Luca can be a happy family! You've been raising your family in Daxaria, but your wife's family is funding your research in Zinfera! It means you can research the dragon or meet who you need to without suspicion. And *you*, Miss Assistant, can inquire about Junya becoming the capital, as you would be very interested to hear about how Zinfera has been changing!"

Tam didn't bother hiding his frustration. "I'm not forcing my assistant to do that. Besides—"

"I'll do it. It does make sense. It's safer to travel with Luca, we can learn more, and we don't have to worry about dying in the desert. We can stay put in Junya for two months. Do you already know where we can acquire accommodations in Junya? There will be the assumption we're staying with my family."

Jeong waved off Eli's worry. "Just say they live in the capital, or Haeson, and you're joining them later. Junya is best known for their astronomy records, which explains why you aren't staying with your parents while your scholarly husband studies!"

"They also have great *astrology* books," Tam added, though his voice sounded like it came from a distance as he processed the dramatic shift in plans.

"What's the difference again?" Jeong wondered aloud while looking to the ceiling, his round, clean-shaven face illuminated in the lantern light.

Eli clarified before her employer could. "Astronomy is the positioning and rotation of the world, sun, moon, and stars. Astrology is the stories associated with the stars."

Both Tam and Eli seemed more than a little determined to not look directly at each other.

"With your assistant on board, it sounds like we have a new plan!" Bong concluded brightly, leaning back in his seat.

The future duke audibly swallowed.

"Now all that's left will be to tell your son, Luca, in the morning," Jeong chattered. "Do you think he'll mind?"

Tam had no idea.

Nor did he know if he himself minded. And *that* particular elusive answer was making his palms already start to sweat.

CHAPTER 23

A DISTRACTING DISGUISE

"So? What do you think?" Jeong's expression was bright and eager as he clutched Luca's slim shoulders.

The boy's dark eyes were fixated thoughtfully on the wooden floorboards of the inn where they'd spent their first night in Zinfera. Jeong had just finished explaining his plan: having Tam and Eli pose as a married couple, with Luca as their son. Tam sat off on his own in a corner, poring over a Zinferan map so that he could best understand the new route they would be taking to Junya rather than crossing the wide Torit Desert.

The future duke was far enough away that he couldn't overhear the conversation, and it most likely was for the better. While he'd mentioned that he planned to talk to Luca about their revised travel plans, he would not have been able to explain the plan with the same enthusiasm as Jeong.

And in response to Jeong's exuberant delivery method, Luca cracked a smile. "Does that mean I get to call Tam 'Father'?"

"Of course! It'd be strange if you called him anything else! You'll have to call Eli 'Mother' as well—hopefully that doesn't bother you!" Jeong responded sunnily.

Luca hesitated, his smile fading.

Jeong, seeing this, changed his mood swiftly to match. "Oh Goddess! I'm terribly sorry! You must miss her! I'm sure we can—"

Blinking rapidly, Luca gave his head a firm shake. "No, it's fine. I... I want to."

Jeong winced and started to inch back from Luca as he noticed the gleam of tears in the boy's eyes.

"Would... Would you like a dumpling? It's hard to be sad with a dumpling! Here!" Jeong reached over to the table where he had been eating breakfast before Luca came downstairs and shoved two dumplings into his cheeks, making his round face bulge like a chipmunk's.

"THee? Har' ta b' thad!" Jeong waved his hands demonstratively, and Luca couldn't help but giggle in the face of such absurdity.

"Everything alright here?" Tam's voice sounded behind Jeong, making him jump.

The Zinferan was unable to respond as he struggled to finish consuming the dumplings.

Seeing this and raising his eyebrows in amusement, Tam didn't bother waiting for a coherent answer from Jeong; he just turned to Luca who, by that time, looked right as rain.

"Luca, mind joining me outside? I have to go over a few things before we leave today. I ordered breakfast for you, so it should be ready for you once we return."

Luca nodded tentatively, and so his father reached out and gently guided him toward the door, though the boy still stole a glance over his shoulder at Jeong and gave his best conspiratorial wink. Jeong responded by giving him two thumbs-up with as much of a grin as his bulging cheeks could spare.

"You really don't mind having to be involved with this...?" Tam asked his son carefully as the pair stood just outside the inn. Despite being no more than a foot or two from the thick wooden door with its black grate window, the father and son were already on the hem of the morning traffic of the port town, though the clientele that filed by them were not of the clean or refined walks of life.

Luca wrinkled his nose as one particularly odorous fellow stumbled past, clothes tattered, his jutting jaw revealing more teeth missing than remaining.

"I-I'm fine with it. But I... I can really call you... 'Father'?"

Tam stiffened, his shoulders broadening. "No."

The tears were instantaneous, and so Luca directed his gaze to the tips of his crude, woven shoes.

"Being called 'Father' sounds far too awkward. I call my own father 'Da,' so that might be odd as well... 'Dad' works. What do you think?"

Luca's face snapped upward, and for the second time that morning Tam jolted in surprise.

"Wh— Oh... Shit. I'm sorry, Luca! I should have clarified sooner!"

"N-no! I'm stupid for crying!" Luca breathed angrily before wiping his eyes on his right sleeve. "I don't cry like this! Not all the time! It's—it's really, really *stupid!*"

Tam rubbed his hand over his face in vexation at his own blunder. "No, Luca, I'm the stupid one. You're getting dragged across a kingdom with your estranged father whom you've never gotten to meet until a few weeks ago, and you're now getting involved in matters I can't even fully explain. The fact that all you're doing is occasionally crying is... both incredible and worrisome from my point of view."

"S-sorry."

"Don't be, Luca. *I'm* sorry. Again. The reason I didn't want you calling me 'Dad' or 'Father' before was—"

"THERE'S BONG'S CARRIAGE!" Jeong exploded from the inn, his left cheek still stuffed full, and another dumpling in his right hand that he expertly shoved into Luca's mouth while pointing at the black peaked carriage approaching them.

Tam turned around to see the vehicle approach, the two horses stomping to a stop and casting clouds of dust up into hot morning air.

Bong opened the door and bounded out of the carriage with a bright smile.

"We got everything for the trip for a young Mr. Luca." He bowed to the boy, who was struggling to chew through the dumpling, and produced a pair of black leather boots.

"Fank oo!"

"Do not mention it, Mr. Luca," Bong responded happily while stepping to the side. "But I also have the great privilege of introducing you to your *wife*, Tam!"

Tam had just opened his mouth to object to the theatrics when Bong swept out his arm and Eli removed herself from the carriage, looking wildly grumpy.

She wore an icy blue top that tied to the side, with pink flowers embroidered near the shoulders, along with a long, full white skirt that Tam instantly thought should be nowhere near the dirty road. Her short hair had been slicked back with water and perhaps a hint of hair oil, but a silver hairpin with a dainty white flower rested near her right ear.

Tam was struck speechless. She had even painted lines on her eyelids and a flattering blush on her lips.

Luca gaped at Eli as well.

Despite having a face full of food, Luca smiled. The smile grew when he glanced up at his father and saw how red his ears were.

"Goddess's Pool, did you ever make her lovely!" Jeong said.

His brother grinned proudly in response. "I thought so! Turns out our sister *does* have excellent taste after all. I never would've thought listening to her talk about trends would result in me learning anything!"

Meanwhile, Luca, having swallowed his dumpling, kept peering up at his father. Tam continued gaping at Eli, who by that time was blushing herself.

"Isn't she pretty?" Luca pressed quietly.

Tam cleared his throat and managed to spare a glance at his son. "Er. Yes. Yes, Eli you look… quite nice."

"Do you think he's ever had to compliment a woman before?" Jeong whispered loudly to his brother.

"Not one he wasn't related to," Bong returned, his whisper even less subtle.

Both Tam and Eli turned to stare at their Zinferan guides wearing flat looks.

The brothers merely smiled, as though they hadn't intended their conversation to be overheard.

"Well! Shall we let mini-Tam change into the clothes we got him and start our journey toward Junya?" Bong moved over to Luca and, without waiting for an answer, ushered him back into the inn, leaving Tam and Eli alone in the street.

Tam cleared his throat. "You do look—"

"My lord, it is unnecessary." Eli dismissed his attempts to improve on his compliment, then held out her hand to him.

Tam stared at it, completely befuddled.

When he did at last reach out his palm to her, she huffed. "Your left hand."

Tam still had no idea what was happening until his assistant shoved a gold band over his wedding finger. Then he noticed that she was already wearing one.

Eli still had not yet been able to meet her employer's eyes, and when she turned to the inn doors, it seemed she didn't intend to say anything else to him, either.

"Eli?"

She looked back, and it was plain to see that while she was trying to appear as composed as usual, there was discomfort and vulnerability storming beneath her mask.

Tam understood all too well how to handle the situation.

"Do you think you can finish packing my books, but leave out the maps and the letters that my father shared with me from Lord Jiho Ryu? I want to review what he has said in the past about the state of Junya while we travel today."

Lowering her chin obediently, her shoulders relaxing, she responded, "Yes, my lord."

"Thank you, Eli. For… all of this. You're a loyal assistant, and dedicated to your employer. I'm sure you won't have any problems in the future finding work with any magistrate you wish to learn under."

Eli bowed again. "Of course, my lord."

Was there a hint of a smile on her mouth just then?

Tam gave a quiet laugh as he reached for the door handle. At least they both understood that nothing had really changed between them. Even if they were pretending to be married.

When he opened the door, however, he found their way blocked by Jeong and Bong, who had quite obviously been listening to the entire conversation through the grate.

The brothers remained comically frozen. That is, until Jeong looked to Bong and said, "You know, I don't hear any termites in this door. The innkeeper has nothing to worry about!"

"That's truly excellent news for the man! I'll go share this with him while I pay our bill!" Bong cleared his throat and hurried over to the innkeeper, who had just set a plate filled with rice, kimchi, and a rolled omelet in front of Luca. He stared at the foreign fare uncertainly.

"Yes! Wonderful thinking!" Jeong rushed after his brother.

Tam closed his eyes while taking in a very long, slow breath.

He was having a hard time reconciling the wise, calm Jiho Ryu with sons that were so carefree and energetic.

"Do you think they are going to be like this the entire time we are here in Zinfera?" the future duke wondered aloud with a subtle note of good humor, and a more pronounced level of exhaustion.

"I'm inclined to think so, my lord. Oh... I... I forgot to tell you." Eli's voice was oddly high-pitched.

Tam looked down at her. He could sense several sets of eyes swivel toward her from the dim shadows of the inn, as well, disturbingly.

"Because I now look like this..." Eli said haltingly, "you probably should call me by my name."

Tam turned to fully face her so abruptly that she staggered back a half step.

"Eli, you really don't have to if you don't want to. We can make up another—"

"Elisara."

Tam's mouth hung open, as he had been in the middle of speaking, but he closed it... Then casually folded his arms across his chest.

"Elliesara? Ellie?"

"Less *e* sound. More of an *eh*, and— You're making fun of me, aren't you?"

Tam held up his hands in surrender. "I would never. I was just thinking it's a very Daxarian-sounding name. How about I call you Ellie when using an alias?"

Eli's eyes narrowed as though she didn't quite believe his innocent deflection. But she must have been tired from having to wake up early and go shopping at Bong's unrelenting insistence, and so she let the matter go without any further accusations and stalked over to where Luca sat, joining him on the bench.

Tam saw the way she gracefully maneuvered the skirt, how her back had straightened, and how her movements became gentler... it was as though the instant she had put on those clothes, some unconscious part of her remembered how to act.

Closing the inn door behind himself, Tam was distracted from his drifting thoughts by the glint from the ring on his finger. His stomach somersaulted.

Opening his palm, he stared at the gold band. It was a strange, uncomfortable sensation. But at least when he was busy talking with Eli, he hadn't noticed it.

Lifting his attention to both Luca's and Eli's backs, Tam felt a larger emotion stirring… one that sparked more anxiety than he had ever known in his life, and as a result, he started to feel that damnable surge of magic in his being. It pulled at him, making his movements feel leaden, as it tried to summon him into the black void he feared terribly. He had to lower his eyes as he focused on every step carrying him over to Eli and Luca, hoping that the feeling would not last long.

CHAPTER 24

PERFECTING PLANS

"If human trafficking is involved, wouldn't Soo Hebin want to keep the capital in Gondol, the hub of the slave trade?" Tam asked Bong, who sat with his hands clasped loosely over his flat belly.

Eli answered on behalf of the Ryu brothers as she kept her gaze on the letters exchanged between Finlay Ashowan and Jiho Ryu. "She's most likely hoping not to rely on the trafficking to maintain control, as well as trying to gain loyalty from the lords in Junya who have remained neutral on who they support to be the next ruler of Zinfera. Many of them would love the chance to improve their own investments, and Junya becoming the capital once more? Would undoubtedly do that."

Tam considered this information for a moment before continuing his questioning. "Which lords specifically could Soo Hebin be trying to win over? Any that would be surprising?"

Jeong replied, in a rare show of seriousness, "Kim, Soon, Bak, and Guk, to name a few. That isn't including the low-level untitled officials."

"None of those lords care about human trafficking?" Tam interjected. "Even after Troivack cut their trade, in light of the case with Duke Iones, where they discovered hundreds of people he had illegally acquired from Zinfera?" Tam didn't disguise his disgruntlement, keeping his arms folded while the carriage jostled them.

Bong responded with a sad shake of his head as the arid land outside the window raced by on his right. "Lord Kim definitely does not approve, and Lords Soon and Bak are uncomfortable with it but won't speak out. And Lord Guk is a greedy soul; he doesn't care as long as it benefits him. He probably has been a helping hand to Soo Hebin smuggling people in and out,"

"How can we convince Lords Soon and Bak to take a stand against her? What is it they in particular would gain from Junya becoming the capital again?" Tam queried.

"Lord Soon has a good amount of real estate in Junya that hasn't performed as well as he'd hoped, but with Junya becoming the capital, the value of the land would triple. As for Bak… it's hard to figure out how to sway him either way, as he is in the tea trade. He would be more heavily taxed for exporting his goods if Junya were to be the capital again, but his profits within the city due to the increase in demand for his high-end leaves could overcome those losses—*if* he secures a deal with the next emperor. Which I imagine is the angle Soo Hebin is going to take when she broaches what her son, Jum, could accomplish on the throne," Bong concluded.

"The easiest solution would be for us to cripple Lord Soon's and Lord Bak's power," Tam reasoned before letting out a sigh. "But they don't sound absolutely evil. Would it be possible that Kim could persuade them?"

"He's…" Bong searched for the right words to describe the nobleman.

"Prudish," Eli supplied bluntly. "He's a member of the Acker religion, and it hasn't boded well for him among several of the other nobles. Most of them have a friend or loved one who prefers the same gender, and so he has alienated himself in a lot of ways,"

Tam cringed.

The religion of Acker had been founded by a Daxarian woman named Valerie Acker. Those that followed the religion believed that homosexuality to be a sin, and witches to be no better than the devil. Only the Gods who understood the universe in its entirety were worthy enough to indulge in both sexes.

Years later, it came to light that Valerie herself had been abandoned by her husband, a witch, for another man. Upon discovering that this religion was illogical and spiteful in origin, it swiftly lost its popularity with its followers in Daxaria. During its peak popularity, it had spread to Zinfera. The Zinferan scholars, however, believed she was correct when it came to homosexuality not being meant for mortals. When it came to witches, they were of the mind that those with magic were only a step below the Gods themselves, and therefore were capable of favoring both genders in their romantic lives. Despite changing a large component of the Acker religion's basis, the Zinferans continued to call it 'Acker'. Though even with this change, very few people still followed the religion.

"What if we simply make an example out of Guk?" Tam speculated, earning a look of wariness from Bong and Jeong.

"How would you do that…?" Jeong dared to wonder aloud, though he was already eyeing Luca, who was staring dazedly out the carriage window from his spot on the carriage bench between Eli and Tam.

"What is Guk's business?" Tam asked instead of answering.

"Lord Sang Guk has a diverse portfolio of investments," Eli began, her gaze drifting to an empty space on the plum-colored upholstery of the bench across from her where Bong and Jeong were seated. "It isn't easy tampering with his means of income. He's a smart man, with ships importing wine from Daxaria, farms near the capital, and some real estate in Gondol. He also breeds horses. So… food, land, transportation, and luxury. He even buys debts, and I wouldn't be surprised if the people who have no hope of earning enough to pay the interest or the debt itself off find themselves forced to work for him for free. And who knows what kind of connections he has, now that he has been a part of the human trafficking." The assistant lowered the pages in her hand, the set of her jaw revealing her anger.

"Unfortunate," Tam agreed. "I guess that just means I'll have to be more base in my approach to dealing with him."

Eli looked at him, a fleeting inclination to discourage her employer notably passing through her eyes before she managed to begrudgingly ask, "What do you mean?"

"Get to him through those he's close to, or… simply attack him outright."

The carriage fell silent.

Jeong slowly reached over and covered Luca's ears.

"Tam, are you... are you suggesting harming Lord Guk?"

"Yes, but I was trying to be vague for Luca."

"That was far less vague than you thought it was," Eli informed her employer glibly.

Jeong spoke out in a quiet, high-pitched voice. "Goddess, I thought you Ashowans were wholesome!"

"That would be my father. I don't have his charm."

"You can be charming when you want to be," Eli rebutted.

Tam raised an eyebrow at her. "I suppose being dour can have its charms, but I just meant I don't have his ability to charm people into becoming better."

"You find Tam charming?" Bong looked at Eli interestedly.

"Bong! Focus!" Surprisingly this outburst came from Jeong. "Luca is about to hear that his father wants to K-I-L-L people!"

"He can spell," Tam pointed out dryly. "And for the record, it is only my last resort."

"Tam!" By this point, Jeong had his arm fully wrapped around Luca's head and was smothering the poor lad against his chest. "You aren't setting a very good example!"

Tam looked to the ceiling of the carriage, caught between wanting to save Luca as the boy struggled in Jeong's arms, and changing the topic all together. "Would you like to hear about my non-lethal plan, to start?"

In the end, it was Eli who gently pried Luca from Jeong's hold. The boy's hair was sticking up at funny angles, and one of his eyebrows was standing upright.

"Yes!" Jeong sniffed while straightening his coat and ignoring the incredulous look Luca was giving him while Eli tried to fix his hair.

"We make him paranoid—he'll wonder if he's losing his mind. We make him act so outlandishly that either his wife leaves him and divides his assets, or his businesses fall to pieces and no one is willing to work with him."

"I have several follow-up questions," Jeong declared, his skepticism obvious.

"How would you make him paranoid?" Eli wondered.

"You expect to do that in just a few months?" Luca was the one who asked the last question, and Tam had the decency to look a mite guilty about saying such things in front of a child.

"I'd aim to create three incidents with his behavior that are beyond explanation or excuse. Eli, you mentioned earlier that his wife lives in the capital, right?"

"Yes…?"

"We make him have an incident in front of a party or two filled with nobles. Word will spread to the capital. Lady Guk gets humiliated, and Soo Hebin gets concerned that she is sinking her efforts into the wrong person. She'll refocus on winning over one of the other two men to her cause, but ideally by then we'll have warded them off. To help deter people from helping, we can even add into the rumor mill that whatever is wrong with Guk is contagious." Tam paused thoughtfully. "If we succeed, Soo Hebin will be forced to continue dabbling in the risky business of human trafficking. Her son won't gain any more supporters in his fight for the throne, and she'll waste resources in the meantime. I'll make contact with Lord Kim and ensure he isn't interested in supporting Soo Hebin, just to be sure there isn't an overwhelming number of people interested in cozying up to the concubine."

The inhabitants of the carriage remained silent for a time as they pondered this new plan.

"Can't you just try baking cookies? At least once?" Jeong pleaded after wading through the information with a headache-induced frown.

"You want me to bake cookies to… solve all of this?" Tam stared flatly at Jeong.

"What about poison cookies?" Luca wondered while looking up at his father.

Tam proceeded to avoid everyone's eyes, which had pointedly moved to him.

"Not to kill them!" Luca clarified bashfully. "Just make them sick…"

Tam started nodding. "Entirely possible! Other than dosing some moonshine and wine, I've never really tried food tampering—my father gets really sensitive about it."

"*I wonder why!*" Jeong exclaimed, his tone a near squeak by that point.

"Eli, with you posing as my wife, we could induce his incidents with laced baked goods you bring him. Or you give them to me, and I'll get him to eat them."

"How would you make Lord Guk eat the cookies…?" Bong questioned while idly patting his younger brother's back.

"I'd observe his behavior for a few days and figure it out, but I have a few options."

"The initial obstacle will be getting close to Lord Guk and Lord Kim. You can do it in three ways—" Eli started.

Tam held up his hand. "I won't have any problem with it. If he's a follower of Acker, he's going to want to talk about the Gods at great length, and I can get close to him with my studies of the stars."

"How are you getting close to Lord Guk then? Are you going to kidnap him? Throw him down in a deep hole?" Jeong cast out dramatically while flopping back in his seat.

Tam cleared his throat, then very carefully reached over and covered Luca's ears again.

"My family owns a few brothels and taverns with your father in Zinfera. Did you honestly forget?"

Jeong's face fell. He looked at Bong. "Right. We *do* own those, don't we…?"

Bong laughed, and Tam let his hands fall away from Luca's ears.

"What if they don't go to brothels?" Luca asked, revealing that there had been no point to covering his ears at all.

Tam dropped his head and hands, feeling a fresh wave of parental shame.

"Then that means they most likely are part of the other social groups that play chess, sample ine teas, or gamble," Eli answered. "Those should be relatively easy to access with my knowledge of tea and chess. My lord, do you gamble at all…?" Eli regarded Tam, her previous unease over the state of royal affairs evolving into focused determination.

"I have. I'm terrible."

"That would make you popular with the lords, then," she pointed out.

"I may be of assistance there," Bong volunteered.

"You're good at gambling?" Tam's assistant looked at the eldest Ryu brother with interest.

Bong merely laughed in response.

Tam and Eli regarded Jeong, who at least was smiling again, as he giggled to himself. "We're known for being a lot of fun. Please leave the frivolous activities to us."

Luca, Tam, and Eli glanced at one another then back at the Ryu brothers, who continued twittering mysteriously.

"Right…" Tam trailed off. "Do you two know which brothels we could visit to find some drugs then?"

The two Zinferan men did cease laughing at this question, though surprisingly they still smiled.

"Of course. We don't go to them often for that very reason, but we know about them."

Tam nodded. "Alright. Then we have a plan."

Bong stretched his arms above his head then cradled his head in his hands. "Excellent. No one dies, and we rescue Zinfera from corruption. I like this new venture, as opposed to simply gathering information. I have a good feeling about our time together this coming year!"

Tam stared down the sword whose tip was touching the bobble in his throat. The hot midday sun bore down on him as the rush of the Ho River surged beneath the stone bridge he stood on.

"Didn't you hear me? I said give me your valuables!"

Glancing down at the bandit's torn light-brown pants, then his thin dirty face and frantic eyes, Tam leaned over slightly to his right where Jeong stood with his pudgy hands in the air, breathing rapidly. "Remind me to explain to your brother what a jinx is when this is over."

Jeong whimpered.

"You should look more fearful," Eli whispered from his other side, Luca safely hidden behind her.

In a bored fashion, Tam spared a brief look at the other three men standing in front of their carriage. "Why exactly?"

"Because your son and wife are in danger right now, my lord," Eli informed her employer through gritted teeth.

Tam stared at the man who held him at sword point, who was also trembling ferociously. "Eli… you know I will panic if I need to—"

"Do I, though?" She turned on him angrily.

Tam regarded the bandit's twitchy state again, as the man licked his lips and looked at his friends, who stood in front of the carriage.

"Pardon me, sir," Tam began.

The man cowered at Tam's voice, making the future duke's suspicions grow... However, there'd be more time to figure out what that was about later.

"I said, give me your valuables!" the bandit shouted up at Tam's face, though he had backed up enough that Tam no longer could feel the tip of the sword.

"I understand what you asked me, but I was wondering if you recall that we had another person in the carriage with us."

Alarm and distress at this news snapped the bandit's attention to the opposite side of Jeong, where Bong had been standing when he'd been first forced out.

And that was all the opening Tam needed to kick the man in the groin and send him to his knees, his sword clattering down beside him.

"See? Perfectly fine," Tam pointed out to Eli, who still looked irritated.

"What about the other three men?" she snapped back.

A commotion behind Tam prompted Jeong and Eli to peer around the horses, but Tam merely beckoned Luca to himself as he opened the carriage door and ushered him back inside. "Did Bong finish up, Jeong?" he called over his shoulder.

"Not quite! He... Oh, yes. There he is. All finished!" Jeong turned around, looking his usual cherub self.

Which was a stark contrast with Eli's less-than-impressed expression.

Tam closed the door behind Luca and smiled pleasantly down at her, making her roll her eyes.

"Luca, stay in the carriage. We need to ask these men a few questions."

"Okay!"

Jeong whirled around as Tam ambled over to the bandit he had kicked, and picked up his sword. "You aren't going to kill them, are you?" Jeong asked, panic tinging his voice.

Tam held his arms out and shot Jeong a *seriously?* expression before jerking his chin in Luca's direction. The carriage curtain windows were open.

Jeong let out a groan of annoyance, shaking his head while wrenching open the carriage door for himself. But before he climbed in, he leaned over to Eli and said, "I understand that he's handsome, but you have a very strange taste in men."

CHAPTER 25

REVEALING RANKINGS

"Now, Tam... dear, reasonable Tam. Think about what your father would do, there is no need—"

"I really don't know why you're so concerned about *my* violent tendencies when it was *your* brother who just beat these men into the road." The future duke gave Jeong a significantly more blunt retort than he had in the carriage prior to the robbery attempt.

"My brother wasn't the first one to jump to murdering a person, that's why!"

"I said it was a last resort!" Tam defended himself irritably before turning away from Jeong with a long sigh.

The group of four men who had tried to take the carriage knelt on the road in front of Jeong, Tam, and Eli. The apparent bandits' swords were safely stowed in a secret compartment under the seat Bong and Jeong had been occupying in the carriage.

By the time Bong gave a bow of his head to confirm everything was fine in the vehicle with both the weapons and Luca, Tam was more than ready to get the questioning started.

"None of you," he began while sweeping his finger through the air at them, "are real bandits. None of you have held a sword in your life, and you're more terrified of us than we are of you."

Jeong looked back and forth from the men on the ground to the future duke, his round face dumbfounded. Eli blinked and raised an eyebrow, but otherwise didn't react as dramatically.

Bong merely watched the men as though he, too, had come to the same conclusion.

"My question is this. Is it that you're all desperate to feed your families? Or did you target this carriage specifically?" Tam's hand fell back to his side as he awaited their answer.

However, none came. The bandits kept their eyes and chins lowered.

Tam said nothing as he continued studying them in their stoic silence, until he eventually crouched down in front of them. "We can either strip you and leave you by the edge of the road while we ride on to the next town and report you, or you can tell us the truth, and we might be more forgiving." Tam's tone was even, but not necessarily kind.

The man who'd pressed a sword to Tam's throat was still visibly quaking, and he was the first to slip a glance at his fellow bandits as though asking permission to speak.

"You have until I count to five to let me know what you've decided. One... two..."

"Forgive me, sir!" the bandit leader cried, falling forward so that his forehead could press against the road. "We were forced out of our village! W-we had no other options—"

"Who gave you the swords?" Bong asked softly.

The bandit fell silent again.

"Three... four..." Tam continued, his volume rising with each number.

"The traders!" the bandit burst out, his voice breaking. "T-they said they wouldn't take our women and children if we worked for them."

It was Tam's side of the road that quieted then.

The future duke barely resisted looking at Eli to gauge how she was reacting to the news.

"Do you happen to know any names of these traders?" Bong spoke up, and while he still sounded gentle, there was an edge to his words.

"Who else?" one of the bandits on the ground uttered darkly while lifting his face to stare at the nobles. "The one who is friends with Lord Yangban."

Tam watched Bong's reaction to the news. The steeliness that entered into his face was wildly at odds with his usual happy self.

The Zinferan nobleman peered down at the bandits, his thoughts unknown, and just as Tam was about to suggest he finish the interrogation alone, Bong turned and strode to the carriage while calling over his shoulder, "I will give you all silver. You will pay the traders, and when they leave, you will take your families, and you will flee to Haeson. You will report to the magistrate there that you are to work for the Ryu family."

All the bandits looked up with a start. "R-Ryu… family…?" the bandit who had been the first to speak asked faintly. "S-sir, are you…"

"I am a servant of the Ryu family. However, I am capable of hiring men to work for their fishing businesses. You will tell the magistrate that Daeba sent you." Bong stated the lie stiffly.

The bandits gaped at Bong's back, too stunned to move as this information sank in. By the time Bong returned with a small satchel that clinked with coin, two of the men began to cry, though they didn't make a sound as they gazed up reverently at Bong.

"Thank you, sir," rasped the bandit who had revealed which traders were responsible for their present fate.

The four men, from their knees, all bowed to Bong, who laid the silver in front of them.

"Pardon us, but we must be on our way," was all Bong said to them. He returned to the carriage.

Tam could tell something had greatly disturbed the Zinferan nobleman. He, Eli, and Jeong followed Bong back to the vehicle, climbed in, and alerted their driver that they were ready to resume their journey.

Bong didn't speak at all or look at the group when the carriage lurched into movement. Sensing that he wasn't quite ready to explain what had him uncharacteristically serious, Tam turned his attention to Luca.

"You're sure you're alright?" Tam asked quietly.

Luca nodded. "It was a bit scary… But I guess I have to get used to that, right?"

"Of course not!" Jeong jumped in fiercely. "That is not at all what you should get used to! We will get to Junya, and you are going to spend your time like any child should! Playing games! Eating! Maybe a bit of studying... Tam, have you thought about hiring Luca a tutor to continue his studies?" Jeong directed at the future duke earnestly.

Tam opened his mouth, but no sound came out.

Right... Tutors...

They would be in Zinfera for months; it'd make sense that Luca would study. It'd probably help him when they went back to Daxaria as well.

"My lord, I can see to arranging for a tutor or two for Luca once we reach Junya," Eli volunteered.

Turning to his assistant, Tam was just about to issue his thanks when he noticed the tension in Eli's face.

His gaze flitted back to Bong, still staring out the window. Tam resolved to ask for details about this trader later on. He had heard about Soo Hebin's cousin during the council meetings, but judging from Eli's reaction, she must have crossed paths personally with Lord Yangban directly at one point or another.

But what grudge did Bong have?

That night, they set up camp at a break point where several other travelers were settled in beside the Ho River. After Luca had been put to sleep in Tam's tent with a lantern lit to keep him warm, Tam sought out Bong and Eli—only to find that Bong had retired abnormally early for the night, and Eli...

Tam found Eli sitting on a flat rock beside the river, the brilliant starry sky spreading its cloak over the desert land and exhibiting its unapologetic beauty for any lonely souls to confide in.

The air had cooled considerably since that afternoon, as Tam had been warned would happen when traveling in the desert. And so when he approached Eli, who sat in nothing but the clothes that Bong had purchased for her that very morning—but felt like a week ago—he carried with him a blanket.

Dropping it over her shoulders, Tam plunked himself down a few feet away without a word.

"Thank you," she said awkwardly.

Tam nodded vaguely. "If you get sick, we'll have to figure out where to find a physician. Better you stay warm."

"People don't instantly get sick just because they get a little cold," Eli countered stubbornly, though she still pulled the dark-green blanket around herself.

Tam shrugged. "Maybe. Maybe not. Why take a chance when you don't have to?"

His assistant let out a loud breath through her nose while returning her attention to the river that rushed by. Sounds of the other travelers talking and laughing wafted over to them.

"I take it you know the traders and Lord Yangban better than most people?"

Eli swallowed. "Yes."

"I see." Tam paused. "Is there anything I should know about either of them?"

"Lord Yangban is the one who first started working with the traders to help build their power. He's one of the greatest supports to Soo Hebin."

Tam feigned a casual, receptive air to the news. "Why didn't Jeong or Bong mention his importance when citing the influential lords we had to sway?"

"Because there is no swaying him. And he's most likely in Gondol right now anyway. He wants Junya as the capital because he knows it will weaken the power of those that support other concubines—he's most likely the one who gave Soo Hebin the idea to begin with, to help her gain power in His Excellency's court. The trader he works with who oversees everything is named Captain Woo. He's... He's the one I spent time with when I was first taken," Eli explained ambiguously.

"Is there anyone, or any combination of people, powerful enough to destroy both Lord Yangban and Captain Woo?"

Eli's upper lip curled disdainfully. "The court is a mess right now, and I haven't been a part of it in years, so I haven't a clue."

Tam pondered this while gazing up at the Goddess's Pool constellation. "Alright. So Lord Yangban is another possible threat while we are in Junya?"

Eli nodded. "If he's in Junya instead of Gondol, he'll recognize me if I see him."

"And I'm guessing he and Lord Guk get along well?"

"Surprisingly, no. They compete with each other for power in Junya. It's one of the reasons Lord Guk could theoretically still be swayed to go against the change. That said, if they both stand to gain a lot by working together, they might."

"Hm… And I thought hearing about Troivack's court problems was a headache. This isn't even all of the palace's affairs."

Eli closed her eyes. "That's right."

Hearing the tight irritation in Eli's voice, Tam felt disgruntlement sprout in his chest. He tapped a finger slowly against the stone they sat on.

"How highly ranked is Lord Yangban?"

"Fourth."

Tam winced.

In Zinfera, as opposed to marquis, duke, or other titles, the nobility knew where they were in the pecking order based on twelve ranks assigned to them either by the emperor himself, or by family inheritance—rankings that the emperor could change if he wished.

Those ranked at least fifth could attend court and weigh in on official matters prior to public announcements. Those ranked fourth, tended to be distantly related to the royal family, could live at court and have access to some of the more exclusive palace buildings and parties. If not directly related to the royal family, fourth-ranked individuals had daughters who had married into it.

Second and third ranks were related to the royal family as parents, half siblings, or lower-ranked princes and princesses. And first-ranked individuals were either close in line to inheriting the throne, or already on it. The higher a person's rank, the more difficult it'd be for a lower rank to oppose their power. But allied with someone of higher rank, even a fourth rank had a chance to overpower, say, a second or third.

Tam pressed his luck with another question. "Technically, by the Zinferan standard, I am ranked between second and fourth in Daxaria. What was your ranking before you were taken?" he asked, well aware he was requesting more information than Eli might be comfortable sharing at the moment…

"I was in the first rank."

Tam's head whipped around. If he had been in the midst of taking a drink, he would've spit it out. "Pardon?"

Eli's grip on the blanket around her shoulders tightened. "I was favored by Lady Chin. I was ranked first."

"Even though you were adopted?" Tam asked bluntly, his astonishment overcoming his sense of manners and restraint.

Eli bobbed her head wearily.

"Then the entire reason you have been scared of returning, and why they want you dead..."

"Yes. Soo Hebin saw me as a legitimate threat, but I wasn't. I had no ambition to take over the throne, and furthermore, last I heard, the emperor hadn't ever broached the subject with the coven here in Zinfera. So really, I was given the first rank because his mother insisted. He never was going to name me empress."

Tam found himself at a loss for words.

His mild-mannered—though occasionally disgruntled—assistant... had been named as a highly viable heir to the Zinferan throne.

"Why the hell did you come back here?"

At last, Eli turned to look at Tam, her eyes rife with pain and anger. "If I'd stayed in Daxaria, someone would've found out the truth and then they'd be obligated to tell your king. The only reason I was overlooked in Troivack was because everyone was too busy learning about the extent of Duke Icarus's crimes, and not many Zinferans wanted to go to Troivack in the first place. Which meant no one knew me there. Well, aside from Duke Icarus, who must have heard from the traders who I was."

"Then he found out you had been kidnapped... knew about your abilities... and figured you would be useful," Tam said, piecing together Eli's history. "Why are you so certain that if you stayed behind in Daxaria, someone would've remembered you?"

Eli fidgeted, then, reaching some sort of defeated conclusion, gave a bitter laugh. "Because I'm related to a close family friend of yours."

Tam had felt like he was making progress with wrapping his head around Eli's royal lineage, but now his thoughts collapsed back into a baffled heap.

He blinked, sitting up straighter and leaning forward to stare at his assistant's face, his mind already racing. "What? You are? Who?"

Somberly, Eli gazed back at her employer, prepared to reveal yet another well-guarded secret to a man she had known for only a few weeks...

"I'm related to Lord Oscar Harris. Duke Iones."

Tam's jaw dropped.

"My mother is Marigold Nam. Formerly Marigold Iones. Lord Harris's half sister."

CHAPTER 26

BEDTIME BONDING

After hearing the astonishing news of Eli's parentage, Tam excused himself to retrieve a bottle of moonshine and two cups.

As he passed by Jeong, who was seated around the fire with five other travelers, the inebriated fellow exclaimed very loudly that he was capable of spitting fire. Tam briefly slowed down to assess whether Jeong was in need of an intervention.

However, when Jeong spotted him, the boisterous Zinferan called out to him first. "Ta—Mr. Voll!" seeming to belatedly remember Tam's alias. "Where are you off to?"

"Just having a drink," Tam retorted while inching away.

Unfortunately, Jeong noticed the second cup Tam was holding, and instantly his face broadened with a grin. "Aaah, Mr. Voll, it's wonderful you and your *wife* still enjoy sitting and having a drink together! Isn't it heartwarming, Song?" Jeong nudged one of the other travelers seated beside him. "This friend of mine and his wife are *inseparable*."

Tam stared at Jeong's smug, glassy eyes for a long beat, and during that beat he decided that the next morning he was going to find two pans and beat them together to wake Jeong up.

Just as he was about to turn and resume his journey back to Eli's spot on the rock, his revenge plan set, the fluttering of a skirt drew his attention, and he found that Eli had instead returned to the camp.

"I'm tired. I think I'll head to bed," she informed her employer quietly.

He was about to say of course she should get a good night's sleep when Jeong decided that he also needed to be a part of the conversation.

"Mr. and Mrs. Voll! Heading to bed after all? Don't worry! I set up your sleeping rolls in the tent with Luca, so you're aaaall ready!"

The slowness with which Tam and Eli rounded on the Zinferan left lots of time for Jeong to repent and maybe feel a little guilty for what he had allegedly done.

But when they both faced him, glaring daggers, it was evident he was feeling nothing but the highest form of glee.

"My lord…" Eli ground out while trying to keep her voice down. "Is he serious?"

Tam didn't respond. He slipped his head into his tent and, squinting in the low light, peered at Luca's sleeping form close to the lantern. Gradually, as his eyes adjusted, he did indeed see two bedrolls side by side.

When he pulled his head back out, he didn't need to say anything. It was apparent that Eli saw the answer on his face.

"I'll speak to him about this tomorrow morning," Tam murmured as an apology. "Right now if I say or do anything, it'll seem strange to the other travelers."

Unable to meet her employer's look of concern, Eli ducked into the tent without another word.

Tam returned his attention to Jeong, who was giving him the thumbs-up while the rest of the men he drank with all turned and shot Tam encouraging smiles.

The future duke looked to the sky once more and wondered how it was possible that there was someone in the world who apparently loved tormenting him more than his sister did.

Stepping into his tent, Tam found that Eli was already dragging a trunk to place between her bed roll and his.

"I'm sorry. I obviously had no—"

"I understand, my lord. Thank you for agreeing to talk with Jeong in the morning," Eli interrupted briskly as she worked.

"Er... I was going to say I can just leave and fall asleep by the fire outside instead. I can say I'm just there for a drink."

"It's fine," Eli snipped.

Despite not having the most well-rounded of social experiences growing up, Tam knew better than to believe someone when they said *I'm fine* in the tone Eli had just used.

"It's alright, Eli, I'm not going to make you—"

"It's fine! It's probably safer this way!"

The extent of Tam's wisdom on how best to navigate the situation had been exceeded.

"So you... *want* me to stay...?"

"It's fine!"

"You keep saying that, but it really doesn't sound—"

A muffled moan followed by the rustling movement of Luca rolling over in his sleep interrupted Tam.

Once Tam and Eli had waited long enough to ensure that Luca truly was asleep, Eli returned her attention to climbing into her bedding.

Moving uncertainly, Tam lowered himself down to a single knee and half crawled, half slid over to his own bedroll.

After he'd situated himself and lay staring up at the tent ceiling, he realized that his heart was pounding.

It was loud... and it was fast... Was it always that fast?

Eli spoke quietly into the dark. "Why are you risking getting involved in Zinfera's politics? His Highness really only wanted us to gather information."

An excited rush from his stomach surged through Tam as she spoke. *Godsdammit, this crush is something. Maybe it's because I keep learning more about her and it's all so... different? Surprising?*

"My lord?"

"Ah." Tam coughed. "I'm interfering more because I only promised to do nothing if I found the dragon, which I haven't. And even if I report everything we've learned so far, there is too much uncertainty for it to be useful information. If I can influence events a little, I can report more, and besides... it's kind of expected that my family would do some amount of meddling."

Eli seemed to accept this answer, as she made no response, and the two fell into a moderately more amicable silence.

Then a question occurred to Tam. "Do you happen to know why Bong reacted the way he did earlier?"

"Not really... He might just be disturbed by what is happening in his kingdom. I didn't even know that the traders were coming far enough inland to take over villages closer to Junya... It really does show how unstable Zinfera has become," Eli theorized.

The night air was starting to chill the tip of Tam's nose. He knew that if he turned onto his side and pulled the blanket up over it, he'd be warm through and through in no time, but he was reluctant to stop talking with Eli.

"Have you ever met Lord Harris?"

"Once. A long time ago... back before I was adopted by the emperor."

"I didn't know he'd ever gone to Zinfera."

"He didn't. We went to Sorlia. We visited briefly. Back after my brother was born, my father paid for my mother to spend a summer there. As a thank-you of sorts."

"You have a brother?" Tam turned his head, expecting to see Eli's profile, but instead he found himself staring into the scratched leather of the trunk.

"I do. Chul. And then I have two sisters. Chul will be... twenty now," Eli recalled after taking a moment to think about it.

Tam found himself at a loss for words.

To think she had an entire family that wasn't in poverty. They were nobles. And they had simply handed her off.

"They sent you away... just because you were a witch?"

Eli didn't reply for a long time, and when she did, all she said was, "Good night, my lord."

And Tam could tell that while she was trying to sound polite and unbothered, her family's betrayal had hurt her horribly. He could sense it in the heavy air following her firm ending of the conversation.

That same unpleasant agitation Tam had felt earlier when talking with Eli down by the river started wrenching his insides, making the future duke feel more awake.

Gods... if my father heard this, I'm relatively certain he'd offer me up on a silver platter to officially make her part of our family...

The thought brought Tam a measure of giddiness, prompting him to give his head a shake.

As if I should even be thinking about that. I need to first figure out how the hell to father a seven-year-old.

Despite this very down-to-earth thought, Tam found that the rest of the night was a fitful one. His mind raced with everything he had learned about his assistant, and he kept wondering how he could help her build, at long last, the happy life she deserved, while also being a good father to a child who might be the devil.

The rest of the journey to Junya was, thankfully, uneventful. The day following the robbery attempt, Bong was back to his usual self—particularly after witnessing Tam wake his brother by bashing together two steel pans he had borrowed from another group of travelers.

The younger Ryu brother took the impromptu wake-up call in stride and bore his scolding from Tam later looking perfectly contrite.

That said, from that night onward, the sleeping arrangements never changed. It really did make the most sense for Tam and Eli to be in the same tent to avoid anyone becoming suspicious. Though Tam didn't allow himself to think about what would happen when there was an actual home to sleep in, where beds would become a factor...

As the carriage began passing more trees and rice fields, and fewer patches of ungroomed land, the city gate came into view. A large bell hung over the road, and massive trees that had been stripped of their bark made the pillars. A ribbon of white plaster walls wrapped around the north side of Junya and continued all the way down to the sea on the south side of the city.

"I rented us a home in a respectable area. Not the most expensive or popular, but it'll only have residential traffic, which will help things stay private," Bong explained, jolting Luca awake—the poor boy had fallen asleep leaning against Tam's shoulder.

"How did you find this residence on such short notice?" Tam asked, pretending not to be aware of the patch of drool on his shirtsleeve that Luca was only just spotting and starting to blush about.

Jeong jumped into the dialogue while perking up when the city wall could be seen from the window. "One of my sister's former tutors lives there, but my father invited her to our estate to visit recently, so she agreed to let us use her house. Luckily I was able to receive her message of confirmation at the last small town we stopped at."

Tam nodded. "We'll settle in for tonight, and tomorrow I'll go to the records library to introduce myself and request information about the stars. According to your father, Lord Kim loves knowing about everyone and everything, and he often spends time at the library, so I'm sure he'll approach me quickly. After the library, I'll hang around a few of the tea shops you told me about and start to become familiar with the area. Eli, you're fine organizing a tutor for Luca?"

Eli was in the middle of bowing her head dutifully in response when Luca turned abruptly to Tam.

"I-I don't need school! I... I'll just go with you to study the stars!"

"I'm afraid we can't do that, Luca. I have to do more than just research constellations. Besides, if you want to help, it's best to learn lots of things so you know what to do in all kinds of scenarios!" Tam encouraged brightly. "I know it might seem like a lot at first, but trust me, once you start learning, you'll find out you have all kinds of interests and things you love that otherwise you'd have no idea about."

"But—"

"Luca, I'm sorry, but this is nonnegotiable." Tam cut off the boy firmly while reaching up to muss his hair.

As it turned out, Luca's hair grew incredibly quickly, and so it was already almost the same length it had been weeks before when he'd first appeared on the ship. But at least he looked better fed, and his long hair was cared for as it should have been.

Turning to his best ally, Luca tried to plead his case. "Jeong, don't you think that—"

"Sorry, Luca." Jeong shook his head. "It was my idea, remember? You know I'm on your side, but on this matter, your father is right. You need an education."

It was the first time Tam had ever seen Luca scowl, and rather than feeling angry or exasperated by it, he was biting back a laugh.

Tam looked at Eli, who was watching Luca with equal astonishment.

"I promise I'll find you a great teacher," she reassured calmly.

"My mother said I was already smart enough…" Luca said under his breath, his heel tapping the back of the carriage bench in irritation.

"You can be smart without being knowledgeable," Eli argued back. "Don't you want to understand what your father does so you can help him?"

Luca sulked in silence.

The adults shared knowing looks, just as the sounds of Zinferan guards questioning their driver reached their ears.

Reaching over, Jeong tapped Luca's knee. "Cheer up! This afternoon I'll take you for the street vendor snacks! I've been to Daxaria, and I can say with certainty that their snacks can't compare even a little bit with what Zinfera sells! You like dumplings, yes?"

Luca seemed to sense that he was being bribed and distracted, but he gave a reluctant nod.

"Wonderful!" Jeong enthused. "Now what about dumplings filled with berries and cream?"

Luca sat perfectly straight. "Berries and cream? You aren't fooling me?"

"I would never!" Jeong slapped a hand on his chest in mock indignation. "I haven't even mentioned the flavored whipped creams!"

Luca's jaw dropped open, and as was becoming the norm on the trip, everyone's mood started to lighten when they had the excellent distraction of a child getting to experience the wider world for the first time.

It gave them all a sunny disposition as they passed under Junya's great bell, even though they knew the coming months would bring no small amount of stress and excessive work.

Ah, well. Maybe they would all make a point of having tea with Luca to remember the simpler pleasures of life.

CHAPTER 27

ROLES REVIEW

The stone streets of Junya were lined primarily with cherry trees, already budding with the progression of spring, though the plum trees sprinkled about were much closer to opening their flowers. The curved, peaked tile roofs were coated in a metallic paint that burned bronze under the sun and brightened the entire world. Whitewashed walls with thick wooden beams made up most of the homes Tam and his traveling companions could see from their carriage—though as they passed some of the more luxurious shops and homes, they noticed rounded, painted pillars of bright reds, greens, and blues. As musical chimes tinkled against the breezes, low stone garden walls revealed front yards where neighbors talked, shared tea, or sampled fermented foods and homemade liquors or wine.

It felt like a fantastical world out of a dream!

Luca watched the scenery with his jaw agape, his eyes round as he observed women dressed similarly to Eli with their beautiful and colorful silk skirts passing by.

"Do you notice the people wearing orange?" Jeong asked while smiling fondly at Luca's reaction to one of the largest cities in Zinfera.

Luca blinked himself back to reality, then swept his eyes through the throng of people that flowed along the sides of the road.

"Yes?"

"Those people are important servants of lords. It gives them priority in shops so that they can conduct their business more quickly. If anyone is discovered wearing orange that is not employed with a noble house? They will be fined. And if they are doing it with the intent of preferential treatment—in other words, fraud—they could even be charged and jailed."

Luca looked back at Jeong fearfully.

Tam leaned forward, arms crossed. He had slid to the middle of the bench in order to give Luca the better seat by the window. "Just don't wear orange. You'll be fine."

Luca gulped.

"If you see any women wearing white like our lovely Eli here? That means they are either incredibly wealthy, or nobility. So be especially careful around them," Jeong warned.

Luca looked even more stressed, so Tam interjected, "Most noblewomen will be traveling in carriages, so it won't come up often."

Jeong tilted his head from side to side. "Better to know these things early on."

Tam sighed. Jeong wasn't wrong, but he had been enjoying seeing his son's excitement…

Bong jumped into the conversation, smiling at Luca. "In a month, there will be a blossom festival here in Junya. The streets fill with lanterns, performers, and vendors, there is dancing, and games… It'll be wonderful fun."

The boy nodded, but his face remained wary.

At least Jeong didn't bring up any other warnings that would make Luca worry even more. They made a right turn around a particularly large ginkgo tree and ascended a quiet street. The beautiful homes here were not as ostentatious or massive as others they'd seen on their journey through the city. Here, the trees shaded the street and the yards were tidy. Best of all, there were only a couple of people milling about the road.

The carriage stopped, and Tam and Eli peered out with mutual curiosity. On either side of the narrow road were two lovely, traditional Zinferan-styled homes.

"That is where we will be staying." Bong smiled and gestured with his chin out the window to his left. The steadfast driver who'd taken them through the desert without a word of complaint popped up to open the carriage door.

Luca sprang out immediately, followed by the rest of the carriage occupants, though they exited with more decorum—particularly Eli, who was handed down from the carriage by Tam. Another new normality in their lives that she had eventually stopped blushing over.

The house was a single floor, with a higher surrounding wall than most other homes on the street. Two large wooden doors to the courtyard had been propped open by two terra-cotta pots with fresh green sprouts pushing through their soil. There was a beautiful plum tree in the middle of the yard, and the house itself boasted a red roof and trusses, wooden walls, and sliding doors; a planked porch wrapped around the three sides of the home facing the courtyard. The charming, inviting house was framed by manicured gardens at the ends of the porch, with rain barrels and covered pots lined up efficiently along the side walls.

The travelers all stood together peering happily at their destination. Tam looked down at Luca. "What do you think?"

"It's a strange-looking house, but... it's where we get to live together, right... Dad?"

Tam felt his world stop and all the air squeezed from his lungs. "Yes. We will live here together." Tam grasped Luca's shoulder, and the boy wrapped his arms around Tam's waist to hug him tightly.

Tam swallowed and felt a firm lump form in his throat. He felt happy beyond words.

Was that normal?

His own father had always said that being a parent was one of his greatest joys in life... but Tam had thought maybe the sentiment was only so potent thanks to Finlay Ashowan being a house witch.

A sniffle sounded beside Luca, where Jeong stood.

Everyone turned to see the man pulling a handkerchief from his pocket to dab teary eyes. "The pollen this time of year is quite... something."

"As is the beautiful moment between Tam and his son," Bong contributed helpfully.

Jeong's shoulders began to quiver as he covered his mouth with his hankie to theoretically stop any blubbering sound he might start making.

Not wanting to make Luca feel awkward, the future duke turned to Eli. "Any thoughts on your end?"

However, when his gaze rested on his assistant, Tam found her staring toward the neighboring wall where two older women stood watching them. Realizing they'd been spotted, the women quickly huddled and continued to whisper to each other animatedly.

"We'll have to be careful. This looks like a street filled with well-meaning, curious neighbors," Eli informed her employer quietly.

Tam nodded. "We can use it to our advantage to establish ourselves… Anyway. Shall we go inside to unpack before finding some dinner? Perhaps we'll even purchase some fresh tea for you."

Eli perked up and hopefulness filled her eyes, making Tam smile.

Until Jeong blew his nose with a loud, prolonged honk.

"Right, in we go, everyone." Tam herded Luca through the doors of their temporary home with his hands resting on his son's shoulders.

Though Tam would soon have to handle the rather delicate matter of how and where he and Eli would be sleeping.

As it turned out, the house was managed by a quiet older woman by the name of Haewon. She supervised one maid and a cook, whom Bong had hired for the duration of their stay.

Haewon had a kind, round face with a small chin and an age spot on her left cheek, but the manner with which she carried herself was elegantly beautiful. She wore her hair in a low bun with not a wisp out of place, but the prim hairstyle didn't make her appear severe.

After Haewon showed Luca to his room and Bong and Jeong to theirs, she stopped at the final door, pulling it open to reveal a bed built low to the floor. "Your room, Mr. and Mrs. Voll."

Tam didn't know it was physically possible to instantaneously sweat as much as he did in that moment. Eli stood just in front of him, frozen. Haewon bowed her head, then excused herself.

"Godsdammit. I knew this would happen... I'll sleep on the floor. There is a screen there we can put between—"

"If she comes into the room at night, or the maid does to light the candles, they'll see. Just sleep in the bed." Remarkably, Eli sounded perfectly calm.

She proceeded into the room. Their driver could be heard coming down the hall to deliver their luggage. Tam was left wondering if he was experiencing a second puberty, given how flustered he felt.

As the rest of their belongings were brought in, he managed to step inside to investigate with pointed interest a painting on the wall featuring a pond and pergola.

Once that task was finished, and the door with its paper covering slid shut, he turned back to his assistant, feeling as though all the blood in his body was rushing either to his face or southward. In their previous bedtime situation, Luca had been there in the tent, so things hadn't felt so... intimate.

However, Eli apparently wanted to give her employer a heart attack, since when Tam laid eyes on her again, he found she was removing her shirt.

"Woah, wha—What? Pardon me—ah, sorry, what are you doing?" Tam shielded his eyes and looked away.

Eli blinked at him, the corners of her lips twitching. "My lord, pardon me saying this, but it's hard to believe you have a child, when you act so... coy."

Tam didn't comment on the subtle slight. "What are you doing?" he repeated instead.

"I'm wearing a white tunic underneath. We need to finish writing your thesis on the constellation Gatral Dragon to show the record keeper of Junya, and I'm not getting ink on silk." She squared herself to him. "My lord, we will need to adapt to behaving as a couple. I understand it is unpleasant for you, but I am a professional, and I promise you don't need to worry about treating me as—"

"It isn't unpleasant." Tam almost cringed at his outburst, but his tongue continued working regardless. "And I'm going to treat you with the respect you deserve."

"I am not deserving of the respect of nobility. Forget what I told you about my past. In Daxaria, all I am is a lowly assistant. With no title. So, please, my lord. You are making me feel... uncomfortable."

Tam slowly faced Eli, his bashfulness fading as he studied her expression.

He noticed how she shifted under his gaze; how she couldn't help but fidget a little with the powder-blue shirt in her hand. "You feel like if you are seen and held up on a pedestal there is a greater chance you will be hurt."

Eli reared back as though he had slapped her, but he continued nonetheless.

"You're trying to convince me you aren't worth anything, because you think if I see you as someone worthwhile, I'll use you, or people will come and tear you down. Or both."

"I *am* powerless, my lord. I *am* worthless."

"Not as a human you aren't. It doesn't matter if you lack power, wealth, or support. You're a thinking, feeling being. I will treat you with respect. When have I ever said you can't say no? When have I said your comfort and boundaries should be ignored? If I have crossed them at any point and you want to leave my employ right now, go ahead. I will pay you a handsome severance. I'm almost certain I've said this before." Tam moved closer to Eli, and he could see her wide-eyed hesitation as he neared.

"My lord, I just mean if… if you keep treating me like a woman rather than simply an assistant, there could be a misunderstanding, or it could be unnecessarily stressful for you. This is a unique situation, and if we have to keep boundaries in mind at all times, it could make things more difficult or inefficient."

"Common decency is not something that should be trumped by efficiency."

Eli opened her mouth to argue again, but Tam was inches away from her, and her breath caught in her throat as he pressed on.

"And what kind of misunderstanding are you worried will happen between us?"

Tam knew he shouldn't have asked that question. Why was he risking making things even more tense? How the hell would he respond if she said what she was implying more directly? He was going to be crossing boundaries he had just been preaching about!

I'm an idiot, I'm an idiot, Godsdammit I'm a massive *idiot…*

Eli gripped the shirt in her hand even more tightly, then slowly lowered it to her side.

"My lord, please… stop."

Tam blinked and leaned back.

"I haven't lived as a woman in more than a decade. I don't feel like myself when you keep treating me as one both in public and behind closed doors. It is bad enough that I even have to pretend to be a mother in public—I don't know what a good mother should look like. So please, when we are alone, treat me as a man."

The heated well of pure unreasonable instinct disappeared, and Tam could feel disgust flood his insides.

Now I'm an arse and an idiot... Where's Kat hitting me when I really need it?

"My apologies, Eli." Tam dropped his gaze. "I will do my best to respect your wishes. Though I will still look away when you are undressing in any capacity—please accept this shortcoming of mine, but I can't help but feel conscious of it. Again, I apologize."

Tam gave a bow of his head—but he was still standing near enough that the bow brought him even closer to her. He caught a faint scent—a perfume that smelled of citrus and something else he couldn't identify.

He righted himself and left the room as quickly as possible.

Eli sank shakily down onto the bed. She was grateful Tam hadn't seemed to notice how deeply she was blushing, or the fact that her knees had buckled a little when he had been close enough for her to feel the heat from his face near her own. As much as she had claimed she wanted him to ignore the fact that she was a woman, she had to admit that she had said such things to convince herself just as much as Tam. It would be ridiculous to feel anything like lust, or Gods forbid, romantic interest between them.

Tamlin Ashowan would never be interested in me. He's just trying to do what's right. That's it. There is nothing more. And just like he shouldn't feel tense around me, I shouldn't feel such foolish emotions, either.

CHAPTER 28

A TIMELY TEA TALK

Acker-following Lord Kim tended to frequent the library that famously held the most texts related to the study of the stars. It was where he would review complaints filed by his tenants, and where he also drafted reports on his many opinions on the laws of Junya and Zinfera.

The reason for this was that the library had offices at the back of the building that could be rented out to sponsored scholars, or nobility. And the library was a particularly popular place to study, as it wasn't far from the seaside. Zinfera's multiple small islands dotted the distant waters, adding a scenic view from the library's front doors. It was also an ideal location with its close proximity to the stylish shops on the main road.

The library was three stories tall—one of the tallest in Junya. Its floors and pillars were made of dark-stained wood, with whitewashed walls and lightly papered sliding doors dividing the rooms, much as in the house where Tam was staying with his companions.

On the first floor, shelves lined the walls. Rows of long tables ran down the middle of the room, benches tucked underneath. The building smelled of books and pine-scented wood polish.

Tam instantly loved it.

Approaching the official who sat behind a large desk carved with dragons and laurels, Tam clutched to his chest the thick manuscript he had spent the night crafting as his thesis, hoping he appeared timid and uncertain.

"Pardon me, sir?" he called out.

The official had a long, straight, salt-and-pepper beard touching his chest; he wore a tall black hat. He didn't so much as glance in Tam's direction.

"Excuse me?" Tam tried again.

The official turned the page of the large volume in front of him.

Tam had worked with many types of difficult people in his time gathering information for his mother and the crown of Daxaria, and even though he was in a foreign land now, he still knew how to handle people.

"I'm here to request the records for the Gatral Dragon constellation?"

The official, again, gave no sign of having heard the request.

Tam smiled, sighed, and then stepped around the desk, as if to go rummaging about on his own.

A long cane appeared, coming down with a crack in front of him.

It was roughly the reaction he had been anticipating. Still wearing a polite smile, Tam turned to the official. Despite wielding the cane, the man hadn't looked up from his book.

Tam again squared himself to the desk, noting the number of Zinferan men that either ignored him entirely or only bothered to spare him a brief look of annoyance as they continued to pore over their own studies.

"I am new to Zinfera," Tam began. "My wife is from here, and her family has sponsored us so that I might continue working on my thesis. Is there something I need to do or have in order to see these records?"

"Name?"

"Voll."

"Your wife's maiden name?"

Tam tilted his head. "Goe."

At long last the official lifted his eyes that were framed with deep wrinkles to Tam. "There are no Goes in Junya."

"They reside in Haeson and Gondol, but everyone knows Junya has the best records of the stars," Tam replied with his most innocent smile.

The official was not impressed. "You should stay with your wife's family if they are funding your studies."

Tam quickly recalled how important the hierarchy of family was in Zinferan society. "We have traveled with her cousins. Her father wishes us to join them in Haeson in another month or two."

The official sniffed disapprovingly before turning back to his book, his wiry eyebrows raised.

Tam waited patiently.

The official turned another page then called out. "Po, records on the Gatral Dragon. Case twenty-three, shelf four."

A younger man who had been seated nearby with an inventory ledger in front of him sprang up and took off down the left side of the room.

If anyone thought this was odd, they didn't show it.

"Thank you." Tam bowed his head.

The official said nothing.

Stepping toward where the young man had disappeared, Tam pretended to be eyeing the room as any foreigner would: with undisguised interest, while also pointedly not gaping at the people.

That didn't mean he didn't take note of everyone there…

No one was dressed in a manner befitting a lord who could be Lord Kim, but then again, neither was he. Tam wore a simple Zinferan wrap-style black shirt, along with his boots and trousers from Daxaria.

The young Zinferan man named Po led Tam to the very back left corner of the room. There he pulled out four books, handed them to Tam briskly, and hurried back to his seat closer to the front doors.

Tam stared down at the texts, made a show of shrugging and looking pleased, then sat down and started working in the quiet room, with no sounds other than pages turning and quills scratching around him.

By the time Tam was closing the last book, the sky outside the front doors had dimmed and he was the only patron left in the library—aside from the official who had been guarding the door, who appeared quite abruptly beside Tam.

"We are closing. Leave."

Tam stood up, forcing himself to be clumsy as he did so. "Of course! My apologies! I get too involved in my studies and—"

The official was already walking away.

Tam sighed with a smile, his eyes fluttering closed as he stretched his neck.

"Dongu is a brilliant man, but unless you are made of paper and ink, he will have very little interest in you."

The voice that sounded at Tam's side would have surprised him had he not heard the subtle nasal breaths moments beforehand. He turned to find a stout Zinferan man with a closely trimmed goatee and a long royal-blue silk coat watching him with a twinkle in his eyes.

"My name is Lord Kim," he said with a smile.

Tam blinked, gave a convincing gasp of astonishment, and bowed. "My lord! My apologies! I had no idea! I—"

Lord Kim chuckled. "Not to worry. I have a room in the back, and I don't usually herald my presence. I noticed you are quite a serious scholar, and you are very clearly not from our shores. I confess that I am curious about you and your studies. Would you mind having a cup of tea with me, Mister…?"

Tam pressed his hand over his heart and bowed again, making sure that while proper, the gesture was a bit sloppy so as to not betray his own nobility.

"Mr. Voll! And of course! I'd be honored! My wife is used to me forgetting the time, but I don't want to get back too late—our son loves to hear about my studies before bedtime."

Lord Kim's smile broadened. "A scholar and a committed family man! The first round of tea is on me, hm?" The Zinferan nobleman clapped a hand on Tam's back, steering him toward the doors where Dongu waited, his nose wrinkling in displeasure at their slow departure.

"Have a good evening," Tam said, bowing to the official who, as expected, said nothing, instead slamming the doors behind Lord Kim and Tam hard enough to make the handle rings bang.

"Did I offend him?" Tam asked with feigned worry.

"Oh no, no, dear boy. He doesn't like anyone. Now, tell me, what kind of tea would you care to have this evening? Black tea? Fruit tea? Milk tea...?"

"I'd best have a citrus. If I drink black tea I'll be up all night and won't be able to get a full day to study tomorrow."

Lord Kim laughed again and gestured at a quaint store with its windows already aglow, just up the road in the same direction as Tam's guest home. Its pillars were painted a mint green, and its sign gleamed with gold lettering: Lang Tea.

Inside, the shop featured low tables, all crowded with men. In the center of each table sat a painted porcelain pot over a small lit flame. Tam watched as Lord Kim waved to a man behind the counter, who hurried over.

"My room upstairs," Lord Kim informed the teahouse attendant quietly.

The attendant bowed, but shot a curious glance in Tam's direction, prompting the future duke to smile in thanks.

"You're tall... I'm sorry to say that it really does not help you blend in, and not everyone is happy to see foreigners in the kingdom these days. Particularly those from... Troivack?" Lord Kim ventured as he followed the attendant. A staircase led them up to a balcony encircling the ground-floor room, with private rooms built off it; different-colored round lanterns hung between the rooms.

"I'm from Daxaria," Tam clarified while hunching his shoulders.

"Ah, that is better. Though you don't look too much like a Daxarian."

"I had a Troivackian grandparent," Tam said truthfully. Duchess Annika Ashowan's mother *had* been Daxarian herself; but Tam's grandfather was Troivackian.

"I see. How is it you happened to meet your wife?" Lord Kim asked as they headed toward what appeared to be the largest room. It sat open and three women wearing fine, jade-colored tops and orange skirts stood in a line along the wall, waiting for them to enter.

"Is this teahouse yours, by chance...?" Tam ventured after remembering what Jeong had said about the color orange and those who wore it.

Lord Kim looked over his shoulder at Tam, his eyes sparkling. "What a quick mind you have. Yes, it is. Please come in and sit."

Tam bobbed his head in thanks and entered. Lord Kim finished giving the women their tea orders.

Once the door had slid shut and the lord took his place by the table, Tam joined him in sitting cross-legged on the floor. A beautiful painting of a woman in a red dress standing on the shoreline took up most of the wall behind Lord Kim, drawing Tam's eyes. The rest of the room was decorated in white and shades of brown.

"Ah, it is a beautiful piece, is it not? This was quite a popular style back when Grand Lady Chin Taejo first earned the favor of the emperor at the time. Have you heard of the mother of our emperor?"

Tam nodded, his eyes still fixed on the red dress.

"A fearless woman not to be trifled with… It is a pity that Zinfera has fallen on such uncertain times." Lord Kim shook his head. "But enough of such thoughts. You were reading about the constellation of Gatral. You aren't one of those foolhardy men who think they can find a dragon and a golden treasure hoard, are you?"

Tam held up his hands. "Not at all! When I was a boy, I found some old books in our family's library about the stars. Ever since, I have been dreaming of the day I could come and study the texts here in Zinfera. Gatral just happens to be the constellation that interests me presently."

Lord Kim nodded along. "That reminds me, young man, you never mentioned how it is you met a fine Zinferan woman?"

Tam looked at the table bashfully. "My… my brother-in-law introduced us. I am often reserved in nature, and our families happened to know each other, and, well… we've practically been inseparable since the day we met."

Lord Kim laughed good-naturedly as the door to their room slid open. In shuffled the three serving women, their faces tilted toward the floor as they set the table and poured the tea. Lord Kim and Tam waited quietly until they were once again alone.

"How long have the two of you been married?" Lord Kim persisted.

Tam, making sure to keep smiling, answered, "My lord, you must have so many more important things in your life to worry about than my own marriage. Have you always lived in Junya? Forgive me if that was impertinent!" He bowed so deeply that his hair grazed the table.

Lord Kim sighed, and reached for a teacup painted with delicate cherry blossoms. "I apologize, Mr. Voll. It must seem I am prying into your life unnecessarily. As I said earlier, we seldom get many visiting foreigners. I have been living in Junya many years, though I did spend a bit of time in Haeson in the early days of my own marriage. I find Junya to still be a traditional place, and one steeped in Zinfera's history. I do hope you discover the charm of this city during your stay."

"I'm already enjoying it a great deal." Tam picked up his own cup, sipped tentatively, and perked up. "I should bring Eli here. She would be able to tell me all about this tea."

Had he just said that out loud?

"Eli?" Lord Kim pressed leaning forward.

"Ah. *Ellie*. My wife. She is exceptionally knowledgeable about tea," Tam clarified. Though he mentally kicked himself for not using his assistant's alias.

"Your wife sounds like a quality woman. If you are interested, I'd be happy to have her come to my teahouse. I may even bring my own wife should she rejoin me here in the city—our eldest daughter has children of her own and requested my wife's help for a time."

"We would be honored, sir!" Tam gushed.

Lord Kim chortled, pleased.

As they fell into other topics regarding popular stores and politics of Junya, Tam took another sip of tea. The citrus scent reminded him of his exchange with Eli the night before, when she had ensured that a very clear boundary remained between them. As a result, Tam had taken a very long walk around the side streets of Junya, trying to clear the emotions clouding his mind. Then he had returned and insisted on writing the thesis at the low kitchen table, sending Eli to bed alone.

He had realized at some point during the previous night as he worked that he was toeing a far more dangerous line than a simple crush on his assistant, and so he had been grateful that he had an excuse to be elsewhere.

While everything else was going along splendidly with his new plan to assess what was happening in Junya and finding Lords Guk and Kim, the matter of him falling into a one-sided infatuation with Eli was not helping his peace of mind in the least.

Hopefully Eli was able to find Luca a good teacher today. Then maybe I can stay in Luca's room with him, saying I'm helping him study and learning to stick to a good schedule for school without suspicion. That is the best-case scenario... I think.

CHAPTER 29

THE FALL AND FOLLOW-THROUGH

Returning home from the teahouse, Tam's steps stalled in front of the courtyard doors of the guest house as he remembered the awkward state of his relationship with Eli.

Gods, what the hell do I say to her? "Sorry I'm acting like a hormonal child rather than a respectable employer"? *Do I just come out and tell her the reason I'm being an arsehat and refusing to sleep in the same bed? No. Godsdammit, no.* "Hey, Eli, remember how you were worried about misunderstanding me? Well, there isn't a misunderstanding. You're fantastic. And I'm having the best time of my life being here in Zinfera with you."

Tam rubbed his eyes. "When… did I become such a twit?"

"Mr. Voll! Mr. Voll! Heeey, Mr. Voll!"

Before he even turned toward the slurred shout sounding from the darkness down the street, Tam knew that Bong and Jeong were approaching.

He waited until they were beside him before asking, "Did you find Lord Guk?"

"We did!" Bong said with a grin. "He is very well known at three particular brothels. We introduced ourselves and got invited to his party. It's in three days, at his home here in Junya,"

"Mr. Voll!" Jeong burst out unexpectedly.

Tam stared at Jeong who, thanks to the lit torches by the front doors, he could see was alternately closing his eyes as he struggled to see only one of Tam.

"Yes?"

"When's the first incident supposed to be?" Jeong managed in a loud whisper.

Tam pursed his mouth and turned to Bong, but Bong looked like he was asleep on his feet, so instead Tam opened the front doors. He could have this conversation when the Ryu brothers were a little less soused.

But when the trio of men took stock of the courtyard, they saw before them Eli, Haewon, and two older Zinferan women they'd never met. Eli wore a white top with a dark-emerald skirt. A shawl was draped around her shoulders despite the balmy temperature of the night.

One of the unknown women gently elbowed Eli in the back.

Tam, frozen in confusion, watched Eli's uncomfortable expression and her inability to meet his eyes.

"You all are home late. And... you missed dinner."

Tam blinked. Then he glanced at the other women present, then back at Eli, who looked like she wanted the earth to open up and swallow her whole.

"Luca... missed you at bedtime."

A loud hiccup sounded from Jeong. "Mr. Vooooll! How could you?" he slurred indignantly.

Tam's lips flattened as he fought against a sigh.

"Yeah! Mr. Voll! Luca... is a *growing*... boy!" Bong added from his position at Tam's side—an only temporary position, since he proceeded to faint face down. Tam stared at Bong's back long enough to ensure he was breathing and then returned his attention to Eli. At least the unhelpful interruptions from the Ryu men had bought him enough time to get the gist of what was happening.

The two women must be neighbors who had shown up nosily wanting to meet him, and they'd insisted on staying until he was home. No doubt they'd repeatedly told Eli how furious she should be with a no-good husband who kept his loving wife and son waiting.

The solution to this awkward situation came to Tam a little too readily (he couldn't quite fault the logic... though he would later admit it may have been biased). Crossing the courtyard to Eli, he reached out and gently grasped her hands, ducking his head closer to her. That same heart-stopping smell hit him—citrus and some other floral he couldn't quite pinpoint.

"I'm sorry I'm late. You know how I get while studying, and then I happened to have tea with a kind lord who was curious about what had me so busy. I bought you some of the tea we had... Would you like to go inside and have some now?"

Eli had looked utterly mortified when Tam initially grasped her hands, but at the mention of tea he saw a glint of interest.

"Pardon me, Ms. Haewon and...?" Tam looked pointedly at the neighbor women. The one wearing a rose-colored shawl had her hand to her chest, while the other, who wore a royal-blue shawl, still scowled in his direction. Tam wasn't surprised when she cleared her throat pointedly.

This managed to snap Eli out of her trance. She turned to Jeong. "You are drunk, go inside and stop making a scene."

That much at least sounded natural coming from her, but then she stared back up at Tam and he damn near had to kiss her.

"These are our neighbors, Lu and Sosa."

Tam nodded politely to the two women. Blue-shawled Sosa raised an eyebrow at him, while pink-wearing Lu watched him dazedly.

"It is lovely to meet you both. But if you wouldn't mind, I would like to go inside with my wife and maybe check on our son."

"You don't look like a scholar," Lu blurted suddenly.

Tam tilted his head as he started to realize just what the older woman was getting at.

"Looks aren't everything," Sosa scoffed. "He shows up late and tells his wife she should know how he is and to just put up with it! How is that right? Don't you agree, Haewon?"

The housekeeper didn't answer, for which Tam was grateful. He moved around Eli to face the two neighbors, slipping his hands atop her shoulders. "While I appreciate you commenting on my shortcomings," he said a mite dryly, "I will ask that you please leave the premises for the evening. It's late, and

I would like to hear from my wife herself about her day. Good evening." Tam slid his hands from Eli's shoulders and once again grasped her hand, leading her into the house, not wanting to look back at her as he led her down the hall to their room.

Only when they were safely behind the closed door did he let go of her hand and place some distance between them.

"I apologize for the untoward touching," he said swiftly, not quite able to meet her eyes.

"It's fine, my lord. As I said before, I understand what our jobs are. Touching is inevitable."

Tam decided not to drag out the conversation. "I take it those neighbors are the local gossips?"

Eli sighed, and at last the future duke felt it safe to look up. "They are. Annoying but informative. Apparently, Lord Guk's wife is adamant that Junya should become a capital again. Even though she isn't here, she is in constant communication with the household staff."

Tam blinked. "That is incredibly useful information. Thank you."

Eli cleared her throat. "You mentioned having tea with a lord. Was it Kim?"

Tam nodded. "It was, and he invited both you and me to his teahouse. I figured you wouldn't mind," he added with a grin.

Fidgeting, Eli busied her hands by starting to untie her white top. "I don't. But I care about more than just tea, you know— Oh. I'm sorry, my lord." She had just noticed that Tam had turned around so that his back was to her as she undressed.

"Eli, I have to ask, but... just as you aren't certain how I could father a child, I am equally clueless how you did not reveal you were a woman for so long given that *you keep casually undressing in front of me.*"

There was a beat of silence. Tam had no idea if his words had upset his assistant. But then he heard it.

The gentle, whimsical laugh.

Before he could stop himself, he turned around and saw her smiling. Her eyes were closed, her teeth flashed... She seemed to glow...

That was when he knew.

Somehow, someway, he had gone and wound up in love.

Despite all his reasonings and best efforts.

He'd fallen for his assistant.

Completely.

Tam sat at the breakfast table the following morning, sipping his coffee and avoiding looking in Eli's direction while Haewon set the table.

He had managed to escape sleeping in the same bed with Eli, again by giving a barely coherent excuse that he'd sleep in the sitting room so that their housekeeper Haewon and the local gossips would think Eli had given him an earful for his tardiness. Of course, this was to ensure no one thought he was disrespectful of his wife, or that she was a pushover.

But he doubted he'd be able to keep avoiding sharing a bed with her for long.

A stack of papers appeared in front of him, forcing his mind back to the present. Morning light warmed the dining room with a hazy gold hue as street sounds and birdsong drifted in through the open sliding door.

"What's this?" Tam asked, looking over the papers, his eyebrows twitching toward a frown.

"The information on the tutors I looked into for Luca," Eli retorted in clipped tones that prompted Tam to spare a glance in her direction.

She didn't look at him.

Tam lifted his face toward Haewon, but the woman didn't let on a thing as she finished setting down the teapot.

So after she left the room, he took the opportunity to lean closer to Eli.

"Are you pretending to be angry with me because of yesterday...? Or are you actually angry with me?"

"I'm not angry, my lord," Eli bit out, her eyes flying up to his face a little too sharply.

Tam leaned back in surprise.

All I did yesterday after making her laugh was go sleep out here... Did I do something else...?

The future duke was opening his mouth to ask more questions when in stumbled Jeong, clutching his head and moaning. "I should have said no to the sweet wine... Never say yes to the sweet wine," he muttered.

"Where's Bong?" Tam wondered aloud, though he suspected the eldest Ryu brother was still unconscious.

"He's outside meditating," Jeong answered in a manner far grumpier than anything Tam had ever heard from him. "In three days we have the party at Lord Guk's residence, which is the perfect place for the kind of… event… you were thinking of." Gesturing to Eli, he added, "Bong will take you shopping for a dress."

"I can take her," Tam volunteered a little too quickly. "It'll be better for us to be seen together."

Jeong was too hungover to even bother teasing him.

"I can go on my own, my lord. I—" Eli's firm insistence was interrupted by Luca entering the room, still yawning. Then he spotted Tam and brightened. "Morning, Dad!" he called in sunny greeting.

Tam smiled back at him. "Good morning. How did you sleep?"

"I slept alright. It's a bit hard because it's a new place and… it's weird having a room all to myself."

Tam perked up. This was exactly the excuse he needed to sleep in a different room than Eli!

However, Jeong clapped a hand on Luca's shoulder as the boy sat down beside him and said, "You can bunk with Bong and myself. He usually can't sleep anyway, so I'm often alone in the room while he sits outside or reads elsewhere."

Luca nodded, looking more than a little disappointed, as though he, too, had hoped Tam would be sleeping in his room.

"As I was saying, my lord, I can go alone—"

Eli was cut off yet again by the return of Haewon, who placed a plate in front of Luca before quietly leaving.

"You need to stop calling me 'my lord,'" Tam whispered seriously. "Just call me Joe. That's what I'm going to tell people once we get on a first-name basis. 'Tam' is too notable a name given my mixed heritage."

"Actually, you should use a pet name, like 'dear' or 'love' or 'my everything,'" Jeong contributed without his usual buoyancy as he reached for the rice on the table.

Eli's mouth remained screwed shut, but Tam could see by the way her jaw moved that she was angry as hell. And so when she stood up from the low table abruptly and stalked out of the dining room, it didn't take him long to follow.

Concerned about what was going on with Eli, he almost failed to see Jeong shoot Luca a knowing smile before he left.

Having no idea what he should do, Tam caught up to Eli just before she reached their room. Regardless, he tapped her on her shoulder and made her swing around so quickly that it caught him off guard.

She stared at him expectantly, her head tilted, and her nostrils flaring ever so slightly.

"Why're you angry…?" Tam managed.

"I'm not angry, my lord, I—"

"Stop." Tam waved a hand, expertly controlling his expression. "And I said to stop calling me 'my lord.' I said it back in Daxaria, too, come to think of it."

Tam noted the way her right hand fidgeted, then gripped her burgundy skirt.

"Is it because Jeong took the teasing too far…? You seemed upset before he got there, so was it something I did?"

"No!" Eli exclaimed, though her volume had risen, which told Tam he was onto something.

"So I *have* done something…? Was it because I forgot to give you the tea I said I bought? I have it just in the other room if you—"

Eli turned and started storming off again, but Tam grasped her arm.

"Eli, you know I'm sinfully awkward. I'm not going to know unless you tell me."

"Nothing. Is. *Wrong.* You are just being irritating!"

Eli tried to leave again, but this time Tam took three ground eating steps and shot an arm out in front of her. He happened to be quite close to her as he was doing this…

"Yes. I am irritating. And I am terrible at pretending you are not a woman. I've apologized and I've stayed away from you to try to be more considerate and distant so I make fewer errors. Is there anything else I can be doing for you?"

Eli leaned back against the wooden panel behind her, her face not all that far from Tam's hand. Her cheeks were pink and she couldn't seem to lift her eyes.

Tam felt himself starting a losing battle.

"Eli, please? Can you look at me and tell me what I did?" Tam's voice had quieted, and he had to struggle to keep from moving any closer to her.

"You didn't sleep beside me. And you're avoiding me, and you're just... You're not... You just..." she stammered as she became more and more frustrated.

Her words sent a mind-numbing rush through Tam. His self-resolve was crumbling.

"You want me to sleep beside you?" His voice was hoarse.

Eli's fidgeting worsened and she licked her lips while seemingly trying to figure out how to explain what she meant. Tam knew she was blissfully unaware that she was destroying any hope of coherent thought from her employer. "I just... I've actually been sleeping well with you beside me, and I... I have never slept well. Not since I was a child, and I don't know why. I hate that I trust you. I don't trust you, I mean, but I-I-I find you reasonable, and—"

Tam lowered his face to hers, and at last she lifted her eyes to his. Then they widened in surprise and a small breath left her mouth.

"Eli... Do you know why I might not be sleeping beside you anymore?" While Tam kept his tone patient, the tension in his body betrayed him.

"You... you don't find me appealing like that, and you don't want me—"

Tam kissed her.

His hand flexed against the wall, while his other found her waist as he relished the heady sensation of kissing the particular, grumpy woman he'd fallen for. Surprisingly, despite the staggering power of Tam's emotions, his magic was silent.

He pressed into her. He could feel her hands gripping the bottom of his tunic and found himself thinking how near their room was, when she made a small sound.

He broke off the kiss, his breath rough as he stared down into her eyes. His arm, still braced beside her, quivered.

"Eli, I need you to tell me to stop or keep going, but whichever it is, have mercy and say it quickly."

She swallowed, and her lips parted, but no sound came out, and Tam decided then and there the woman was a bloody master of torture.

But he waited... He waited and hoped to the Gods he hadn't gone and just made a terrible arse of himself.

CHAPTER 30

THE WAY TO WANT

Tam, with every bit of self-restraint he possessed, waited, suspending his previous activity of kissing Eli senseless. But with every breath he scraped together, his next step became more obvious. Though he somewhat begrudged his mental faculties for bringing it to light.

Pressing himself off the wall, Tam took a step back, leaving Eli slumped there on her own, her expression still dazed.

"Pardon me, I'll... I'll step outside for a while. You don't need to say anything if you don't want to, and I won't do something like that again. If you want to ask for an apology, that will be as much of an answer as I'll need. I hope you'll understand my avoidance in the future."

Then he turned and walked away. Even though his feet felt leaden and his heart was racing, he forced himself to put as much distance as possible from his assistant, and left the house entirely. He managed to stop in the courtyard beside Bong who sat with his legs crossed and his eyes closed, facing the plum tree. He didn't announce his arrival, just took a steadying breath and focused on the sound of the warm breeze rustling the budding tree, and the songs of the birds...

"Everything alright, Tam?" Bong asked peacefully.

"Maybe. I hope so, anyway. But..." Tam let out an agitated sigh. "I don't know why I don't seem to be as cautious and collected as I usually am."

Despite his eyes still being closed, Bong smiled. "Have you ever wanted something for yourself, Tam?"

The future duke stilled, then squared himself to Bong. "Of course I have. Who hasn't? It's why I have more books than shelf space."

Bong finally looked over at Tam, a calm knowingness settled around his features.

"You've never wanted something that required you to open yourself up, or that meant a lot to you."

Tam frowned. That didn't sound right...

"I used to be like you in a lot of ways," Bong continued. "I believed I had to do everything in my power to live up to my father, or even to surpass him. I had the honor of our family to uphold, and I will one day have to manage everything." The Zinferan sighed. "Since childhood, I have keenly felt how little time I had to learn and improve. It seemed an impossible goal." Bong's eyes drifted thoughtfully down to the ground. "And then one day when I was twenty-three, after years of studying endlessly, pushing myself to a breaking point time and time again, I was running to one class or another, and I saw children in the street playing a game with a leather ball. They were so... free. I realized that's what I wanted right then, in perfect clarity. I wanted to feel happy and unburdened. For the first time in my life, I found something to burn for that was only for myself. And so I had to think for a long time about what a happy, free life looked like. For once not caring how others believed it should be."

Unable to speak, Tam listened, identifying in many ways with what Bong was saying, only... he *hadn't* figured out what he wanted. He didn't know what he wanted his life and future to be, only what he wanted to live up to.

"Luca finding you now was, I think, quite by the hair of the Goddess. Fated. Children in general are wonderful reminders to enjoy the beautiful, simple things in life. Like a warm spring day outside." Bong smiled and looked up at Tam, though he had to squint against the sun. "I also think you are working out how to provide a happy life for him, as a good father should, but you have no idea, *because* you have not made a happy life for yourself, Tam. But now that you are trying to? You're going to find yourself making all kinds of exceptions to situations you previously may have handled more cautiously and capably."

Tam slowly seated himself beside Bong. "I'm worried I'm making another person uncomfortable with what I want."

"Eli would have said something. She is quite good at being blunt."

All pretense that it wasn't his assistant Tam was talking about was swiftly abandoned.

"She's in a tough situation, and I'm in a position of power over her." Tam shook his head at himself.

"From what I can tell, you've made it clear she is welcome to tell you where she stands with you. Your fault lies in not telling her what meaning *she* has in your life."

"I think she's got the picture," Tam replied, aiming the comment more at himself than Bong.

However, the Zinferan raised an interested eyebrow and glanced over his shoulder back to the house. "Are you aware she suffers from significant trauma?"

Tam cringed. "I am. Which makes me even worse."

"Your self-hatred is a waste of time." Bong closed his eyes again. "Make yourself clear to her, and then adhere to whatever she wishes to do. As you have been. She may need more time to recover from her past before she can even entertain the thought of a wholesome relationship. Assuming, of course, that that's what you want."

Tam gnawed on his tongue.

He was in love with Eli, absolutely, but… what if they simply were happier living their own lives?

Just because you loved someone didn't mean you had to marry them.

"I'm already tired of moping and agonizing over this." Tam reached up and rubbed the back of his neck. "She knows how I feel now, and that's that. Thank you for helping me figure myself out, Bong."

The Zinferan bowed his head gracefully.

Tam grinned down at the Zinferan and then recalled him passed out face-first in the dirt the night before. "Honestly, after your escapades last night, I thought you'd be in significantly more pain today."

"I have spent a great deal of time out here trying my best not to vomit."

Tam nodded. "That makes sense. Would you like to come inside for breakfast?"

"I can't move yet."

"Still might vomit?"

"Yes."

Tam's smile widened. "Would you like me to get you some water?"

"That would be appreciated."

Laughing, Tam clapped a hand on Bong's shoulder, earning the quietest of whimpers from the man before Tam stood up and turned back to the house.

He really was living a strange life: kissing his assistant one instant, in inner turmoil the next, and then perfectly at peace again with his present, all before breakfast.

Upon reentering the dining room, Tam found Luca and Jeong in deep conversation. "Sorry about leaving like that," he announced, drawing their attention to himself.

Luca and Jeong looked up at the same time, curious.

"Is Eli alright?" Jeong asked worriedly.

"I think so. Though she might want to go shopping with Bong after all. She'll let us know." Tam reached over and plucked up the papers that his assistant had handed him previously, with information about the various tutors they might be able to hire for Luca.

"Luca, what did you do yesterday?" Tam inquired as his son slowly started to inch closer to him.

"Oh, I... I helped Eli unpack your books, and we talked about what I might like studying."

Tam gave an encouraging smile to Luca then returned his attention to the tutors.

"Dad?"

"Hm?"

"Can I... go shopping with you if... if you and Eli are going?"

Tam looked up, momentarily stunned. "Is there something you need?"

"N-no."

Tam glanced with an arched brow at Jeong, whose attention was completely captured by his cup of tea.

"I just... want to spend time with you," Luca finished vulnerably.

Tam paused, then reached over and rested his hand on Luca's head. "How about, even if Eli wants to go shopping with Bong, you and I go out, hm?"

Luca's entire face lit up.

Tam smiled, ruffled Luca's recently cut hair, and returned his attention to the tutors.

All was peaceful until both Eli and Bong stepped into the room.

Eli seated herself beside Jeong where Luca had previously been sitting, which wasn't the farthest she could sit from Tam, but it wasn't exactly close, either.

"I think I'll go shopping with Bong today," she informed everyone evenly, though she didn't look in Tam's direction.

Tam masked his emotions as best he could and addressed Luca. "Guess that means it'll just be you and me."

Luca smiled, his right cheek filled with the dumpling he had just shoved into his mouth.

Tam then proceeded to grasp the glass coffee container from the middle of the table, while Bong downed several cups of water.

"Sorry I wasn't able to bring that out to you quicker," he called out.

"It is fine. I didn't give you much time."

Tam reached for the cup of coffee he had abandoned earlier to add fresh brew to it, but he caught Eli staring at him discreetly and froze.

She looked away immediately.

While Tam's heart started to sink, he noticed that she actually happened to be blushing.

He wasn't entirely certain why, but... maybe it wasn't a bad sign.

Tam and Luca spent their day browsing the various vendor booths on the street. And once Tam had spent a good amount of money on the various snacks that Luca was interested in trying, he found himself relaxing in a way he hadn't in a long time. He wondered why his magic wasn't acting up, but whatever the reason for it, it was a blissful reprieve.

Staring up at the clear blue sky, Tam let out a breath that seemed to take with it years of tension.

He was outside on a lovely day. No one was cringing away from him or whispering behind their hands, he already was right on schedule with making contact with the lords, he was gathering information, and...

He was getting to know Luca.

His son who did not like eating fish. In any capacity. Which was tricky when Junya was a seaside city.

Tam also learned that Luca liked the color red, and that he was really quick on his feet as he dodged and wove through the crowds between stalls.

Luca was conscious of people, but uninterested. His eyes followed food, toys, and even the buildings with their unique designs...

"Luca?" Tam summoned his son back to his side after he'd started to get a little farther ahead.

Once the boy was back, still chewing on a chicken skewer, Tam asked the question that had occurred to him. "Did you have any friends in Daxaria? Back when you were living at the tavern?"

Luca paused, his carefree expression turning serious and hesitant.

"Not... really. I was either helping Mother clean the tavern, or helping my uncle keep track of inventory."

"Hm." Tam frowned.

"Jeong's my friend now!" Luca reminded him with forced energy

"That he is, as is Bong, and Eli... But you should have friends your own age, too."

His mouth twisting to the side, Luca looked disappointed.

"Is there a reason you don't want friends your own age?" Tam pressed.

Luca busied himself with finishing off his chicken skewer and disposing of the garbage in a nearby street brazier while Tam waited.

Eventually Luca answered. "I'm different from other kids. I don't know." He shrugged, but there was a nervousness around him as he shoved his hands in his pockets. A move that looked a lot like Tam's.

"Different how?" Tam persisted.

"Well, I just..." Luca stopped, his chin lowering to his chest. "I have weird dreams, and... I can't focus sometimes. I only talk to adults, I don't know any games, and I didn't have a dad, and... I'm just different."

"You have a dad now, and it's fine to get distracted. It happens to everyone," Tam assured him, while also subtly directing their journey down a quieter side street.

"But I... I sometimes feel like a different person when the distraction happens."

Tam felt his insides turn to ice. "How do you mean, Luca?"

There must have been something in his tone that frightened the boy, as he stopped in his tracks and shuffled backward uncertainly. "I don't know exactly... I just—sometimes it's like I've heard things before, or I feel some way because I've seen something, and it doesn't make sense. Or I suddenly think I remember something that didn't happen..."

Tam ushered Luca to the side of the road where no one else walked and crouched down. Fear was crawling up his belly. "Luca, what kinds of things do you remember?"

The boy's distress worsened. "I don't know! Scary things, and they are like my dreams so I don't know if they are memories or, or—"

Tam saw the tears in Luca's eyes and without being able to help himself he pulled Luca in to hug him. "It's okay, Luca. I promise. I promise everything is alright. It... It is really important you tell me as much as you can about this."

"Why, though? Mother said I shouldn't! It scares people!"

"Because I... I might be able to help." Tam knew he was lying, but how could he tell Luca the truth? What even *was* the truth?

Was Luca the devil? He genuinely didn't seem evil, or conniving...

Could it mean that he simply didn't remember he was the devil?

Tam pulled away and did his best to put his own concerns aside to focus on Luca as the boy said, "I dream about... about big creatures. And I dream about people. Some of them are scary, and some I think are witches," Luca's voice warbled.

Tam listened seriously, though nothing of what he heard really helped shed any light one way or another. He opened his mouth to console Luca, only...

He spotted something in the corner of his eye, and turned with Luca at the same time to see...

Eli. Strolling down the street by herself. She had on a white shirt and a pale-pink skirt. Her back was straight, her expression neutral...

She looked beautiful.

But that wasn't what caught Tam's eye.

There were two men following her.

"Where the hell is Bong?" Tam stood up. "Luca, you stay right here. If anyone approaches you and tries to move you, you scream."

"Okay!" Luca replied firmly, his previous moment of vulnerability forgotten as he, too, gauged the danger his father's assistant was in.

And that was it. Tam rushed off in pursuit, his long strides easily closing the distance, though the two men pursuing Eli were gaining on her as well.

Seeing this, Tam felt his magic surge.

It was as though after all the peace it had given him recently, it was returning with a roar. He scrambled internally to maintain control, but he couldn't stop. He couldn't fail to protect Eli.

He kept walking, even though he was relatively certain he noticed one or two people leap back from him in surprise…

He didn't want to know what he looked like. Though he strongly suspected his eyes had turned black, just like Eli had described back on the ship when facing off with the pirates.

It didn't matter. He just wanted to get Eli and Luca to safety. Hopefully, whatever happened, whatever amount of magic he wasn't able to contain, it wouldn't swallow him whole once and for all.

CHAPTER 31

A DISTRESSING DEPARTURE

Eli lowered her chin elegantly toward the vendor who accepted the payment for her new dress from Bong, and then allowed them to drift down the sunny, bustling street. The fine weather had everyone outside and in fine spirits, though Eli herself was feeling far from fine.

Bong interrupted her thoughts as he took the carefully wrapped parcel from the vendor with a grateful bow. "That should be everything you need for the party."

"Thank you," Eli managed, though her voice sounded tight.

Bong didn't comment, just passed the package to Haewon who had joined them to see to any of their needs.

The pair walked on, leaving the housekeeper behind. Bong trudged, lacking his usual light step, his complexion still not quite right after the rousing good evening he'd had sussing out Lord Guk in the brothels.

"Shall we return to the house, Mrs. Voll?"

Eli jerked to a halt and gave Bong a disgruntled glance at the use of her alias before continuing on. The abrupt reaction seemed to startle Bong, visibly making him green a little as a result. He took a moment to breathe deeply, settle his stomach, then hurried to catch up to Eli.

"Is there a reason you have been ill at ease since this morning?"

"No."

Bong nodded amiably, and didn't comment on her short retort for at least another storefront or two.

"I had an interesting conversation with Tam while I was meditating out in the courtyard this morning."

"Do you mean when you were too hungover to walk?" Eli's clipped tones didn't faze Bong.

"I happened to be doing both of those things."

"Of course, my lord."

Bong sighed and stared at Eli's serene face. "I see you feel better now that you have the upper hand."

Her serenity twitched back to irritation.

"Tell you what… I will share a few thoughts I gleaned from the future duke, hm?"

Eli didn't say anything in response.

"Tam is aware you have a troubling history, and he is also aware he is in a state of great upheaval what with lovely little Luca's presence."

Bong paused as he paid for two cups of water and some chilled dumplings from a nearby stall, handing one of each to Eli and sipping from his own cup. "Good Goddess… My brother says there is nothing better than spicy food when hungover, but I say cold foods are the best for quelling the heated storms inside."

"That's a very poetic description of the consequences for overindulging."

Ignoring her, Bong returned to his original speech while also inclining himself toward a pretty older woman dressed in pale pinks and blues that passed by him. "Tam is not entirely his own person just yet, and so you both have a way to grow, and intentions therefore won't always be clear. His feelings in the romantic sense are quite sincere, but he of course wishes only to make sure you know you are respected."

When Eli still didn't contribute to the conversation, Bong took a little more liberty.

"I believe it is best that you are aware of the situation so you might understand Tam's actions and thoughts as he figures things out. Though I'm curious if you know your own mind on this particular matter."

"That is not your business, my lord."

"Of course not, I am simply willing to share my own thoughts. It *is* important that we all work well with one another during this time here in Zinfera. Especially if we are going to be meddling rather than simply... listening."

"My lord." Eli turned to face Bong, who had just finished his dumpling and set down his empty cup of water on a barrel outside an eatery. "If everyone simply follows the plan, then there is no need to delve into any personal matters."

"Pardon me saying this, but that's ridiculous."

"What?"

Bong smiled warmly. "Any plan that involves humans is bound to be imperfect. That is why no matter what large-scale endeavor people undertake, we are advised to plan for human error. And what is it that makes us human? Emotions."

"I thought it was higher consciousness and thought."

"That too." Bong chuckled. "You've studied philosophy. That is unusual for someone of no rank or title."

Eli stormed off once more, leaving Bong to once again rush to catch up.

"I do not bring these things up to have you tell me your inner thoughts. I bring them up to help you gain perspective on yourself."

"My lord?" Eli turned around sharply once more, her voice louder, and Bong cringed at the sudden assault on his headache. "Stop speaking to me like you are a seventy-year-old man. We are near the same age. I might even be older."

"I feel quite old today. Does that help?" Bong leaned forward, his brow arched seriously.

"No, it does not."

"Ah." Bong nodded. "Are you afraid to turn Tam down? Or are you afraid to start a relationship with a man who already has far too much control over your life?"

Eli looked as though the wind had been knocked out of her.

"Go away." The words came out a whisper, but she could feel her movements affected by a frantic energy as she stared at Bong.

"Eli, I—"

"For the love of the Gods, no one listens to me! Am I-I-I to be a bloody pawn at all times? Do I really have absolutely no power? Why? What have I ever done to deserve this? I've worked, and I've worked, and I do my best to accommodate, and everyone just wants more! They want things I don't have, and because I don't have them? I am punished! If I am not what they expect me to be, I am also punished!"

"I understand that—"

"You understand absolutely nothing. All I want… is to work. And I will do my job *damn* well, but why do people think they are owed more than that?" Eli was crying. Her nose was running, her voice hoarse and choked, but she did not relent. "You, Lord Bong, who were born into privilege, might understand heavy responsibility and having to make tough decisions that affect others—oh yes. I've served a king. I already know what is involved in being a leader! But you have never had your dignity dragged through the mud for another person's amusement. You've not had your life tossed around as though you were nothing. Like a thing. You've never been at the mercy of the world and wanting to die, with *no one* on your side, and you claw and you fight, and you drag yourself out of those hells, only to find not much has really changed at all. It doesn't matter what you do, or who you're with; people want more. I don't want to share my feelings. They are mine! Can't they just stay mine?"

Bong's look of sadness and pain on Eli's behalf in no way placated her.

"Go to hell, my lord. Don't ever try to push me to do or feel or question anything. You are not a friend to me. You are a friend to Lord Tam."

"Is Lord Tam a friend to you?"

"No," Eli bit back. "No. He isn't a friend. He… he… Never mind. I'm going for a walk. Do not follow me."

She had *wanted* to say Tam was like everyone else. He was just an employer, and she *wished* she could say for the point of winning the argument that he treated her as though she were inconsequential, so why should he be more to her?

But he didn't treat her that way.

No. He, more than anyone she had ever met, had *always* honored whatever she wanted. The only time when he didn't? When he didn't want to risk hurting her. He had ignored her wish for them to sleep beside each other, because he apparently was attracted to her and didn't think that was something he should continue.

He had respected her from the day they met. Even now, when he wanted something from her, he added distance to ensure she stayed as comfortable as possible.

Eli kept her teary face lowered. She didn't know if Bong was behind her or not, and she frankly didn't care whether he was. She pulled free a silk handkerchief from her skirt and blew her nose, though as she cleaned her face, she noticed the glint of the wedding band on her hand…

I wonder when he started to be attracted to me. Probably being stuck in a carriage for days on end with only men didn't help, but… Developing amorous feelings because of lust doesn't seem like Tam. Then again, he does have an illegitimate child, so maybe it is exactly what he is like.

Eli was deep in thought when an unpleasant churn in her stomach and a prickling along the back of her neck alerted her that something was off.

Pausing briefly, she pretended to be interested in some framed mirrors for sale just off the street, and as she did so, she spotted the two men following her.

Of course. Of course that is what happens the instant I try to take time for myself.

Noticing two streets she could detour onto up ahead, Eli did her best to keep an eye out for any signs of respectable stores or taverns, even though she knew she was on the frayed edges of the upscale area of Junya. Eventually she spotted the *Side Street Tavern*, and aimed there. If she could flag down the owner, she could have a carriage sent for, and taverns typically had hired muscled "helpers" to handle any unsavory characters.

Eli had just taken the second left down the street, her panic rising, when she sensed something new.

Something familiar. Comforting. Relief washed over her.

Tam was nearby.

She didn't need to look over her shoulder or listen for his footsteps, which were as quiet as her own. She simply knew.

"Excuse me," an unfamiliar voice called behind her.

She tensed but kept walking.

"Are you Elisara Nam?"

She stopped and spoke over her shoulder. "I don't know who you are talking about. Please leave me alone."

"We were hired by Chul Nam to find his sister, Elisara Nam. Are you... certain you are not her?"

Eli took her time turning around. Facing the two men, she found them wearing matching periwinkle shirts with black pants and boots. The one who had called out was a little older than his companion, with wrinkles creasing the skin under his eyes. The taller one was unable to mask his excitement as he stared at Eli, and she felt herself want to cringe away from them, when...

"I don't know who you are, but get the hell away from my wife."

The two men jumped and swung around to find Tamlin Ashowan looming behind them at the mouth of the shaded street they stood on, with tall walls boxing them in.

Tam stared at them, his eyes filled with pure blackness. The two men took large steps backward.

"Mr. V— my dear one!" Eli called out awkwardly as she rushed forward past the two strangers. It was better that the two men didn't learn any details about them—even if the last name Voll was made up. "Thank the Gods you found me! I tried to find the spot where you wanted to meet for lunch with our son, but I got lost."

Tam continued to stare at the men, but his eyes regained some of their whites as Eli spoke. "Where is your escort?" he rumbled.

"I... I wanted to be alone—"

"Leave us!" Tam barked at the supposed investigators, who were starting to edge toward the couple once more. The sharp ring of Tam's voice sent them bolting away fearfully.

Once they were out of sight, Eli let out a breath, her shoulders sagging forward. "Thank you, my lord. I'm sorry I— My lord?"

When Tam rounded back, to her, his eyes were once again consumed with darkness.

"Eli, get the hell away from me," he ordered, his tone a mix of frightened and insistent.

But she didn't.

"My lord, what about your crystal? I'm sure you can—"

Tam stumbled past her toward the back of the street, alone. Dark, silvery wisps were emanating from his body, and the toes of his boots scraped against the stones.

"My lor— Tam! Tam, it's alright. You don't need your magic to—" Eli's words were cut off by an anguished grunt from Tam. His shoulders curled, and the misty tendrils consumed him entirely until...

He was gone.

Eli stared in shock at the place where he had been standing. Where the blackness and silvery magic had just been... but there was nothing.

It was as though Tamlin Ashowan had just... dissolved.

CHAPTER 32

A ROUGH REELING

Eli's legs didn't want to move. She had stayed on that side street, looking around every nook, cranny, and store in the vicinity. She whispered, calling Tam's name over and over, until her throat dried up and she couldn't speak in hushed tones anymore without coughing.

What was she supposed to do? What could *she* do?

Tam had said he disappeared into a void when his magic overtook him. So where exactly was the void? Did he just turn into nothing? Did he go to the Forest of the Afterlife?

She debated using her magic. Could it even be helpful in this situation?

People will see me use it, though, she told herself as she glanced back at the crowded main road of Junya a short distance away.

Surprisingly, the tavern that the day's events had taken place in front of had been closed most of the day... A fortuitous thing as it turned out.

Maybe if I come back after dark and use my magic. Maybe then I—

"Eli?"

Swinging around, Eli found herself staring at Luca, who looked pale and frightened.

Right. Hadn't Tam gone shopping with him? Where had he been the whole time?

"Luca!" she cried out. "Is everything alright? Where were you?"

"I-I was just around the corner of the next street over. Dad said… he said not to move until he came back, but it's been so long, and he was going after the men who were following you. Where is he?"

"Oh… Well…" Eli glanced over her shoulder a final time, hoping to find her employer standing there again. "I… don't know. He scared off the men following me, but I… uh—"

"Eli! Luca! Thank the Goddess I found you!" Bong darted over to the pair from the street.

"Bong! Did you happen to bring the carriage?" Eli asked quickly, hoping that Luca wouldn't ask her again where his father was.

"Wha— Yes, I did, but what is—"

"Luca, please go to the carriage," Eli ordered without sparing him another look as she continued to peer desperately around the street.

Luca looked like he wanted to argue, but having been out all day, he was exhausted, and no doubt waiting in the sun had taken its toll as well. He dragged his feet to the carriage without any argument.

"Is something wrong?" Bong asked slowly.

"Yes. Everything. Tam just disappeared, and there were two men who were following me who say they were hired by my brother, and I don't know what to do. My lord, do you know any witches who could maybe—"

"Eli, I am not certain I am understanding what you are saying."

"Tam disappeared. His magic… I know he doesn't want me to talk about it, but he just vanishes, and I don't know where he is, and *he* doesn't know where he is, and I just… He's gone. He came to help me because he got worried, and he's gone."

Bong blinked rapidly and opened his mouth to say something, then closed it again when he realized he had no response, despite his two attempts.

"Does he do this often?" he wondered aloud for his third try, while watching Eli lift a potted plant and look under it.

"No! He usually stops it from getting this far! But then I came along, and… Good Gods, why do these things keep happening? Why in the world do things keep going *wrong!*" Eli shouted angrily. Whirling back around, she spotted a crate that she dove for and peered under.

"I don't believe our dear Tam can fit underneath the crates," Bong reasoned gently.

"Do you have a better idea of where he is then?" Eli demanded, chucking down the crate.

Bong moved carefully over to Eli. "What is everything you know about Tam's power?"

"I already told you everything!"

"So he has no control over where he goes once he disappears?"

"No."

"What has happened in the past when he has returned?"

"I have no idea! Please, can we just go back and get in touch with Zinfera's coven?" Eli insisted, peering up at Bong desperately.

"It would be days until we heard anything, and all requests like this one go through the emperor. It would alert everyone to Tam's presence, and then Daxaria's coven would be summoned as well." Bong held up his hands. "I believe we should try to wait and give Tam more time. Given your explanation, it's entirely possible he'll reappear here. I'll pay the staff of the stores on the main road to keep watch for him, alright?"

Eli looked like she wanted to object, but as she stared into Bong's concerned yet calm face, the fight left her.

"It is not your fault," Bong informed her quietly.

"It is. It is my fault that I didn't just go shopping with Tam in the first place. It's my fault that I… I was followed, and that I—"

Bong laid a hand on Eli's shoulder. "Let's go back to the house. There's nothing we can do here, and it is getting late."

"How can you not be worried?" Eli snapped, her defeat swiftly turning into a fiery accusation.

Bong didn't react to her mood change. "I *am* worried. But the longer we are outside talking about it, the more risk we create. We need to manage the situation and regroup as best we can. I'm sure that is what Tam wants."

"Tam wants to get out of the void," Eli informed Bong coolly.

Bong's lips flattened, then relaxed. "What would you like us to do right now?"

Eli stared at Bong, emotion starting to close her throat.

Sure, the situation was bad… but she'd been in worse. Why was she so upset? She normally was fantastic at being resourceful and figuring out what to do. There was no reason to be afraid really. She was in no imminent danger.

She lowered her eyes. *I need to stop being like soggy tea leaves. Like a useless lump. I'm better than this. We need Tam back or our plans aren't going to work. Tonight, I'll return here and use my magic to try to find him. If I can't find him after a few days, I'll force Bong to write to the coven. Or we can ask around for any other witches living in the city.*

Nodding to herself, Eli started walking to the carriage, completely ignoring Bong. She'd figure things out. And even if Tamlin Ashowan had disappeared for good, she'd survive.

She'd always survive.

It was the same, vast, black nothingness it had been before.

Tam felt as though he were trembling the same way he had as a child. He tried to scream…

And he did.

The fact that he could hear his own shout echoing out into the distance startled him into stumbling back…

Stumbling.

He looked down.

There were his hands.

His feet.

He was in his body!

Relief washed over Tam as he grasped his forearms and found them solid under his touch.

The last time he had been in the void had been seven years ago, and that time he didn't have a body…

This was significantly better.

Tam turned around, looked up, looked down... only to find there was nothing under his feet. He wasn't even sure how he could see his hands and legs. It seemed like the light was coming from above, but every time he looked up, the source shifted.

"Hello?" he shouted out, and listened to his voice echo once more. "If I echo, that means my voice is bouncing off something solid," he explained to himself.

He took a few tentative steps. It was wildly disconcerting—he didn't feel like he was moving, and yet his muscles worked in his thighs as if he had crossed some kind of distance. Closing his eyes, Tam pinched the bridge of his nose.

The two times he had disappeared in the past, he was gone for half a day at most... he hoped that that was all it would be this time as well. He was sure he'd frightened Eli. And Luca. Gods, Luca would be especially terrified.

Tam felt his anxiety mounting. He turned his attention back to trying to walk, his arms held out, wondering if he could feel anything. But after what seemed like half an afternoon went by and nothing changed, he stopped.

Gradually he lowered himself to sit on the mass of nothing surrounding him.

"I hope Eli's alright. And Luca... What if Eli doesn't see Luca, or he waits on the street without anyone finding him?" Fresh panic washed over him, prompting him to jump back up. "IF THERE IS ANYONE THERE! PLEASE GET ME OUT! PLEASE! I NEED TO GO BACK!"

Tam felt familiar dread worm its way through his heart.

He'd been able to stay calm far longer than he ever had in the past thanks to the fact that this time he at least was in his own body...

Wait. My body. Every time I've vanished before, my body has disappeared with me. Why is it here now? What is different now?

His mind raced. Was it that he was older? Had his magic grown stronger? Why would it be stronger? Did Luca have something to do with it?

He frowned. Then he did something he had avoided since the first time his magic had manifested: He turned his attention inward and examined his power. Tam allowed it to flow freely through him, even though it made his vision turn black again, making him lose sight of his body once more.

He let out a yelp as chaos filled his senses.

He heard sounds... so many sounds whirling around him. Voices, animals, music, things banging, crying, laughter...

But that wasn't all. He could smell things. He could smell smoke, cold night air; he could smell fish cooking and incense burning…

He tried to free himself from the onslaught, except something else was happening.

He started to *feel* things. The brush of a cold stone under his left fingers, the uneven road beneath his feet… Then it changed and he seemed to be touching the inside of a wooden coffin, then a clay one. What was happening?

Tam felt like he was being strangled by stimulation. He started shouting, unable to think clearly…

When a violent yank dragged him to the ground.

What the hell was happening now?

The sensations overwhelming Tam lessened bit by bit. When he was able to focus again on the tug he was feeling, it happened again.

It was as if a rope had been knotted inside his chest, and it was pulling him.

Tam was dragged again, and again…

When he finally flipped onto his back, he stared down at his chest, not sure what he should expect to see.

Perhaps the mage crystal that had refused to work for him in the void was acting up?

No.

Tam's eyes widened.

There was a glowing, red thread coming out of his chest.

And every time it went taut, he was dragged.

Tam started to hear sounds again. Someone rummaging about.

Looking around, he saw nothing. The thread attached to his chest seemed to drift off and disappear into the void.

Reaching for it, Tam watched as the line once again went taut, only this time…

Something jerked on the other end. Tam saw the wavering line in the distance become as tense as a violin string, and he had the keen sense that someone, or something, was on the other side.

The question was, who, or *what* was it?

Holding firm, Tam rose to his feet once more and shuffled forward, making sure to not let go of the line for an instant. At least he had this thread of hope he could, quite literally, hang on to.

Please Eli, Luca… I hope you're alright.

"Welcome to Zinfera, Your Magnificence." The hooded figure knelt on the dock in the mist and dull lantern light.

Handed down from the ship by a young man with sandy-brown hair and brown eyes, a woman approached her greeter.

"It's been some time. Tell me, has there been any word about my brother, the devil?"

"No, Your Magnificence. However, by the time we reach the palace in Gondol, there may be news."

The woman tilted her chin and smiled. Her olive skin and black hair were pristine, but the coldness in her dark eyes made her appear more terrifying than attractive.

"Very well. I look forward to meeting with that concubine again. She was most gracious in funding my escape."

"Of course, Your Magnificence. Shall we?"

The woman laughed. Surprisingly, it didn't sound as cutting as her smile indicated it could be.

"Come, Ansar. It's been years, but you have been loyal. Call me Aradia. I doubt many people know the true name of the first witch, so it should be safe to use, don't you think?" She held out a gloved hand to the hooded figure.

He rose, took the hand and kissed the back, then peered up at the daughter of the Gods reverently.

"As you wish, Aradia."

CHAPTER 33

GALLING GUIDANCE

Tam felt sweat drip down the side of his head as he continued to hold the red thread, which had once again gone taut.

He had no idea how long it had been since he'd entered the void, but he knew it was longer than he'd ever been there before.

Shouldn't there be a limit to the length of time I can be in here? I'm using magic, and all magic has limits…

Tam readjusted his grip on the thread again. The magical line that was tied to something deep in his being had come and gone since he'd been in the void. He wondered if he should simply let it drag him, but he wanted to understand what the hell it was to begin with.

Lobahlans think that it is the hair of the Goddess when they see a red thread. That it connects them to their fate. Even Kat says she sees or senses something like this with her magic when she is bolstering people. But not a lone thread; she says there are several.

Though the devil apparently was tied to her with a red thread.

Am I tied to the devil?

Tam grunted as his muscles strained. He felt his grip weakening.

And then, just when he was about to let himself be yanked forward again, the thread disappeared.

Collapsing to his knees, Tam panted heavily, his hands red and swollen from holding on for so long…

"Why am I still in here?" he shouted upward desperately. "People need me out there!"

His throat parched, Tam dropped his chin to his chest and closed his eyes in frustration.

"Why do you think people need you?"

Tam jolted in shock.

The voice had come from behind him, making him roll instinctively to face the newcomer in a better position to defend or attack.

But he found himself staring at a simple, harmless, older man.

He was bald on top of his head, with a few short white hairs prickling the sides; he had a droopy nose and a long, wrinkled chin. The man definitely didn't appear threatening at a glance. He wasn't very tall, and he wore humble clothes: a tattered tan vest, a white shirt, dark-brown pants, a red kerchief around his neck. But his bright, ethereal shining blue eyes were something else entirely. They weren't warm—or necessarily kind— but they were sharper than any sword's edge.

"Who are you?" Tam rasped.

The man tilted his head, studying Tam with an interested expression. "I am a friend and enemy to all. You must be Tamlin Ashowan."

Tam's hands shook, and his legs felt weak. Yet he couldn't look away from the man.

"You've been here awhile. That means you must've found them."

"Found who?" Tam summoned the last vestiges of his strength and stood tall once more, allowing him to gaze down at the peculiar man.

The stranger did not answer, he only continued looking at Tam in that unnatural way, with a white light moving behind his eyes that instantly made Tam say:

"You've been to the Forest of the Afterlife. Your eyes are like my da's."

The man smiled, the first glimpse of friendliness in him. But Tam remained wary.

"Yes. I've met your father. He's a funny sort. I look forward to seeing him again."

Tam swallowed. "You aren't... You aren't human."

The man shook his head in confirmation.

"Are you one of the Gods...?"

The man crossed his arms patiently, though his smile faded. "In a way. I came into existence with them, and I will disappear one day with them as well."

Tam knew who the man was. It was on the tip of his tongue, but the realization was making it harder to speak...

"I am death's carriage driver. Or simply Death, if you will."

Tam felt his face go pale. "Am I dying?"

The carriage driver shook his head once more. "Do you see my cart with me?"

The answer did nothing to settle Tam's nerves. "What are you doing here then?"

"Do you know where 'here' is?" Death asked with a chuckle.

Tam's hands moved to his pockets. "Not really."

Death nodded. "This is a place of everything... and nothing. You've probably heard noises and found some smells, as well as felt things around you. It's also a place where there is nothing. Nothing but you—and me at present."

"Why does a place of nothing exist?" Emotions swelled in Tam as for the first time in his life, he learned more of this void that haunted his dreams.

"Sometimes lost souls need time to rest in a nothing place. It is not unlike the Grove of Sorrows where those who lived a terrible life will spend time repenting their actions after dying."

"I come here because of my magic... Is that my ability? To travel to a nothing place?"

"In a manner of speaking. There is more to it than that." Death smiled again, more to himself than Tam as he started to pace. "You've been struggling with your magic pulling you here for some time."

Tam watched Death move but remained rooted to his spot. "I have. It's been hell."

Death laughed at that. "You have no idea about hell."

"Isn't it reliving your own worst days over and over again until you understand what you did wrong? Isn't that what happens in the Grove of Sorrows?" the future duke speculated with a frown.

"That is hell, yes… But you haven't had to do that, have you? You simply rest here for a while."

"Why do I get dragged here?" Tam could hear his heartbeat in his ears.

Was he really going to get all the answers to his magic? Without having to subject himself to testing and Gods knew what else…?

"If not here, where do you want to be?" Death returned instead of giving a direct answer.

Tam couldn't even bring himself to reply for a moment—the question incited outright fury. "Out in the world where my friends and family are! Where my son is! People are counting on me and— Godsdammit, I wanted to do things right! I wanted to be able to do things alone, and not have this happen for once!"

Death stared calmly up at Tam. "Do you really?"

"What?"

"Do you really want to be out there?"

"Of course I do! Of course I—"

Death held up his hand then continued his pacing while gazing around the void pleasantly. "Tell me, do you feel absolutely certain, without a shadow of a doubt, that you want to be back where you were?"

Tam opened his mouth to loose another tirade, but his voice died in his throat as realization dawned on him.

Every time he struggled with his magic… he had wanted to disappear.

To hide from people for one reason or another. Whether it was an awkward public event with his parents or an uncomfortable one-on-one encounter, he would focus on the floor to stop feeling overwhelmed by everything around him.

The very first day he disappeared into the void, he had been playing hide-and-seek with Kat. She had always been able to find him, and as a result, she'd taunt him endlessly. Tam had wanted to disappear then. He hadn't even wanted to play. He had just wanted to sit in the shade with a book and some snacks, and not be teased… And then he'd simply appeared in the void.

The only time he could say that he didn't want to disappear had been this time. Right after he had scared off those men that were following Eli. His brows twitched to a frown.

"I really don't want to be here right now. I want to be back with everyone."

"Oh? You want to be back alone with the woman who seems to have rejected your advances? In the street after you saved her? After she saw your black eyes and would have to take care of you or pity you?"

An awful feeling spread through Tam's chest.

"But—but Luca…"

"Ah. That child. That child you are afraid of loving because of what he may be, and yet you love all the same."

Tam's eyes snapped up. "Is Luca the devil?"

Death stopped pacing, but he didn't turn around to look at Tam, whose gaze bore into Death's frail back.

"That answer shouldn't matter."

Tam strode over and faced Death, his eyes flashing. "That's ridiculous. The devil has tortured and hurt people. He has done horrible things, and might be plotting to do even worse. Wasn't it the Gods who told my father that Kat or myself would help a being they care about?"

"They never said that being was the devil," Death pointed out, unbothered by Tam's impassioned questioning.

"Then is it the first witch? Or yourself that one of us will help?"

Death didn't respond at first as he stared at Tam, his ethereal eyes unblinking. "Is there anything you aren't afraid of?"

Tam chewed the side of his tongue before he looked away. He could tell that he wasn't going to get a straight answer.

"So I should just live impulsively like my sister? Love a child who could be the devil, despite what might happen down the road?"

Again, Death did not offer a response.

"How do I get out of here? I just decide I don't want to be?"

"That helps… But have you decided where you would *like* to be?"

Tam paused. "How much time has passed outside of this void?"

Death shrugged ambiguously. Tam wanted to grab him by the lapels and shake him into being less infuriating, but knew this would be futile.

Instead, he reached up and rubbed the back of his neck while letting out an aggravated breath.

"Why did I never see you in the void before? Or my own body?"

Death smiled but said nothing. Then he turned and started walking away.

"What am I supposed to do now?"

"You're a smart man, Tamlin Ashowan. You'll figure it out."

Taking two long steps with the intention of sprinting after Death, Tam found that he wasn't able to. At some point, he had blinked, and Death had disappeared as though he'd never been there at all.

"Dammit… Dammit… Dammit…" Tam doubled over.

After allowing himself to agonize over his situation for another few moments, however, he pushed himself back up straight.

"Given what he told me, I need to want to be back with everyone. Completely." Tam closed his eyes and tried to envision the house he, Eli, Luca, Bong, and Jeong were staying in, but the instant he imagined it he felt anxiety gnaw at his gut.

He already had an inkling what his assistant would say to him about their kiss. She had started to trust him, and she wanted to sleep beside him because she most likely had been living in unsafe places for years… She had been trying to say she felt safe with him, and he'd gone and betrayed her.

Knowing Eli, she wouldn't even be angry with him. She'd merely apologize for not being able to return his feelings (when she most definitely did not need to), and that would be the end of it.

Tam recoiled even at the thought of that awful conversation.

Giving his head a shake, he refocused onto Luca who was thoughtful and kind, and who obviously idolized Tam when he shouldn't. Luca who was just a little boy in a situation no child should have to be in.

Tam lowered himself to the ground with a long exhale.

It was going to be a lot harder than he'd realized to sincerely convince himself how much he wanted to face his troubles. The whole incident with the men following Eli had been the catalyst, but the events leading up to it had already primed Tam's magic to explode—like kindling to a flame. Yes, he did want to be responsible, fair, and good when facing life's trials. But the part of him that wanted to scurry away and hide in a room with his books lingered.

"Gods... I really am such a coward."

CHAPTER 34

A DESOLATE DUO

Eli finished tying her black shirt with quick, tight movements. The smell of the freshly lit fire in the room gently coaxed her not to rush out into the night, as the promise of a cozy, quiet room all to herself beckoned with all the inviting comfort of a mother's voice to her newborn.

The comforter on the low wooden bed had been fluffed and warmed in the sun that day. It was a wonderful weighty thing, and Eli hadn't been able to enjoy such a luxury since she was a child.

But she was only getting a taste of such luxury thanks to the very man she needed to go find.

The crescent moon had almost crested the peak of the night sky, and the air was colder than it had been the past few evenings.

She was wearing black pants that she had managed to stow away from the keen eyes of Ms. Haewon, and while her hair was growing rapidly, it was still too short to fully tie back. Luckily, she managed to keep it out of her face successfully with a thick black ribbon she tied like a band to hold her bangs back.

Everything was set, but while turning toward the ground-level balcony that she intended to leap over to escape the house unnoticed, Eli halted in her tracks at the sound of the door being slid slowly open.

Her heart leapt to her throat as she expected Tam to appear...

Only it was Luca instead.

At dinner, he'd asked where his father was and had been told only that Tam would be away studying for a while, but he'd come back as soon as possible. It had been obvious that the boy had wanted to ask more, but despite his young age, even he had noticed the grim atmosphere that hung over Jeong, Bong, and Eli.

Eli had barely eaten the entire meal.

Bong and Jeong still left that evening, and though they didn't say what they were doing, Eli knew Bong was going to continue to make an impression on the local nobility and build a reputation, while Jeong would look more for Tam.

But Jeong had returned not long ago, and if Eli strained to listen, she could already hear the Zinferan man's snores echoing down the halls.

Despite the deepness of the night, Luca proceeded into the room, and closed the door behind himself. Then, in the dull glow of the firelight, he saw Eli awake and dressed.

"Where are you going?" he asked fearfully.

"I'm going to see your father." Eli faced the child and answered quietly, already listening to see if Bong or Jeong were aware that Luca had snuck out of bed.

Luca stepped forward. "Can I go with you?"

Eli shook her head. "I am sorry, Luca, but your father would want you to stay safe. I'll be back soon."

"Is... Is my dad lost?"

In the faint light, the assistant could see the tears glistening in the boy's eyes.

"He isn't studying... is he?" Luca whispered.

While she debated lying to Luca again, a foreign ache in her chest stopped her. Until she reminded herself Tam would most likely ask her to try to be honest, but not to the point of revealing anything worrisome.

"I don't know. He might be."

Luca blinked quickly, forcing his tears back. "Can I wait here until you get back?"

While she wanted to say no, Eli discovered her compassion had entered a rapid growth spurt. "Fine. But sleep in the meantime. Your tutor is going to start lessons with you tomorrow."

Luca's face wrinkled, making him look more like his usual self.

"Do you promise, Luca?" Eli folded her hands behind her back as she waited sternly.

"Yes... I promise."

Satisfied with his word, she turned on her heel and strode toward the balcony door.

"Eli?"

She stopped and looked back over her shoulder.

"You won't leave me, too... right?" Luca looked shy, but the way he set his chin showed her he was determined to hear her answer.

Eli let out a breath, her eyes moving to the floor before facing the child again.

"One day I probably will, but not today. Most likely in a year."

"Why can't we all stay together?" Luca was unable to keep his true emotions from his face any longer.

"No one stays together forever. Not even families." Eli was unaware there was a streak of pain and bitterness in her tone.

"But... why not stay together as long as possible?"

A funny old memory was stirring in Eli's mind. One where she was screaming at her mother, begging her to not make her leave for the palace, insisting that she wanted to stay home. And then her mother had turned away from her without a word as the emperor's men grabbed her arms and hauled her away.

Eli had escaped the lavish inn where she had been dropped off by her father only that one time. She never tried again.

The day she had been officially made a princess, she'd been unaware it was happening. She had simply thought she was on a fun outing with her father, and had naively started to think that her parents were going to forgive her for what she'd done in her mother's quarters when her magic had surfaced...

Eli shoved the memory aside. "Life isn't kind, and everyone is doing what they believe is best to survive. Being together and relying on people, family or not, is hard."

"My dad is kind."

Unable to say otherwise, Eli nodded. "He is."

"And I won't leave *you*," Luca promised. "You're—you're my mom now. I mean, I have a mother back home, too, and I know with you it's pretend, but still. Even if you are my dad's assistant, you talk to me a lot nicer than my mother did anyway." Luca looked away. The hurt in his young eyes rattled Eli to her core. She knew where such a look came from: rejection and apathy from someone you loved more than anything.

Some small instinct told Eli that the right thing to do was to hug Luca, but that was for someone who was willing to love others and rely on them.

"I'll be going now. Get under the blankets. It's cold tonight," was the only stiff farewell she could manage, and so she slipped out into the night, trying to pull her thoughts from her horrible past and onto the present.

The moon had lowered in the sky, and a bird or two chirped in question as a sprinkling of stars started to fade while Eli snuck back into her room.

It had been a frustrating night.

For one, it had been years since she'd used her magic, and letting it loose once more was very disconcerting. She counted herself lucky she hadn't really felt an urge to use it. She'd never had the troubles Tam evidently did, or the way his sister was rumored to.

That said, it had twinged a few times since Tam had been missing.

Eli blamed the fact that she was so focused on finding a witch just like herself, which automatically made her think about magic.

But she now doubted that using her magic would make much difference in finding Tam. When she used her magic in the street where he'd vanished, she could sense him, but she could also sense that he wasn't quite in their world anymore.

Then his presence would suddenly disappear. Eli would wait silently, and sometimes he would flicker back, but no matter how hard she looked or flexed her abilities, she was left clueless and frantic, trying to find some shred of Tamlin Ashowan.

Undressing herself quickly and slipping back into her shift, Eli crawled into bed and almost yelped when she felt the small body there.

Then she recalled she had told Luca he could wait in the bed. With her hand still clamped on her mouth, she stared down at him.

He looked so helpless.

His mouth was open, his face slack, and his dark lashes sharp in contrast against his pale cheeks…

Eli finished climbing into bed beside him, and lay staring at him.

"I'm sorry I can't be a better mother figure for you, Luca," she whispered. "I just… didn't have a good mom either."

Swallowing down the lump that had formed as she spoke, Eli cleared her throat and turned onto her back to hopefully get a bit of sleep.

Surprisingly it was easy to slip into oblivion for the start of the sunrise. But even more surprising was when Ms. Haewon came in later to wake her up, she found that Luca's hand had been holding her own as they'd slept deeply beside each other. It made Eli's heart twinge, and oddly, when she sat up to resume her daily tasks, she found it harder to let go of Luca's hand than she thought it would be.

The night of Lord Guk's party, Eli continued scrawling down her summary of the day's events, her eyes heavy as she struggled to stay awake. The evening wind rustled the plum tree and slid across the back of her neck, making her reach up and gently scratch the spot. She had started logging everything that happened while Tam was gone. That way it would be easier for him to catch up once he returned.

Eli had been forced through a day of skin care and massages in preparation for the party. Of course, Jeong and Bong were of no help when she had insisted she didn't need it. Really, she just wanted to keep trying to track down another witch in Junya to help search for Tam.

Three days had passed without any sign of the future duke. Despite this, every day, Jeong and Bong scoured Junya for him, and at night, Eli snuck out and looked for him herself using her magic.

Unfortunately, she had yet another motive driving her dogged attempts to track down her employer: She couldn't stand it if one day she had to tell Luca that Tam wouldn't be coming home.

And so she'd dreaded going to a party, of all things, *and* seeing Luca's slim shoulders sag as he was left alone once more.

While his initial foray into formal lessons and homework wasn't really helping his spirits much, remarkably he didn't seem to be holding this against Eli. Which she was grateful for, though she'd never admit to it.

She couldn't quite explain what had changed between them in those three days since Tam had vanished, but she did know that she had come to expect returning to her room to find Luca asleep under the feather-stuffed duvet. If he had one foot sticking out from under the blanket, she would make sure to get it tucked back into the cozy warmth. One night she gently rested her shin against his toes because they felt cold.

"Eli?"

She jumped. Had she been sleeping sitting up?

Blinking rapidly, Eli realized the last sentence she had written made no sense, and so she cursed softly to herself.

"Eli."

She startled a second time, and then belatedly recalled that someone had to be with her to be calling her name.

Looking over her shoulder, she saw Bong and Ms. Haewon. She was not obtuse or sleep-deprived enough to miss their disapproving expressions.

"You should try to sleep before we go tonight," Bong suggested softly.

Eli made a disgruntled noise that she knew was unlike her usual polite self. Haewon shifted backward subtly.

"Fine. I also won't stay long at the party. Just until we make the proper introductions." Secretly Eli intended to slip out again to keep searching for Tam later on.

As she stood, Bong waved away Haewon and fixed his somber gaze on her. "I know you've been going out every night to look for Tam."

Eli schooled her expression as best she could with burning eyes.

"You need to take better care of yourself. I know you're worried about Tam—"

"Pardon me, my lord, but I should go sleep." Cutting Bong off curtly, Eli excused herself.

Nothing had really improved between them since Eli's outburst the other day when shopping.

Not needing yet another reason to stress, she abandoned any troubling thoughts of the rift between herself and Bong as she entered her room and hungrily eyed the fluffed blankets. Without bothering to change out of her day dress, Eli crawled onto the bed and fell unconscious almost instantly.

As always since her employer had gone missing, her dreams were filled with blackness and images of Tam wandering and calling out in the vast empty space. Sometimes he was talking to a peasant man, sometimes he was pulling on something, sweat pouring down his face as he struggled.

Seeing him in this dark world alone, Eli jerked and tossed in her sleep. This time a certain boy wasn't there to hold her hand through the dreams. And so, as her frustration rose, from the depths of her subconscious she uttered, "Tam… come home."

CHAPTER 35

A WICKEDLY LATE WITCH

Unlike all the other times Tam had reappeared back into the world, he didn't find himself in the same spot where he had disappeared.

No.

He was in the room he shared with Eli back at the house.

Tam sank to his knees with a shiver.

What the hell had happened…?

He'd been struggling to get out of the blasted void, and trying to convince himself that he was ready to face his problems. That damn red thread suddenly felt like a chain and hauled him out of the void. He had tried to fight it, but in the end he'd had very little strength left to resist.

Rubbing his face as he struggled to adapt to being around colors and light again, Tam could feel that he was slick with sweat. His body involuntarily trembling, he tried to focus on his breaths to settle his nerves after the jarring sensation of leaving the void so abruptly.

Outside he could hear the sounds of the night: the fluttering of bat wings, the hum of bugs.

"D-Dad?"

Tam dropped his hands, and his gaze shot upward to see Luca sitting up sleepily in his and Eli's bed.

Luca's eyes went round as he stared at his father, but then as he registered that Tam was actually there and it was not all a dream, he scrambled across the covers.

"DAD!" Luca flung himself at Tam.

His slim arms clutched Tam tightly, his desperation and relief seeping into Tam's bones, washing away his shock. He returned Luca's embrace, slowly stroking the boy's head.

"Luca," he rasped. "How… How long have I been gone?"

While the child pulled free of the hug, he didn't release Tam's shirtsleeves. "Th-three days. Mom—Eli—she's at the party with… with Jeong and Bong."

"Dammit," Tam cursed. "Luca, I need to go see them right away. I'm so sorry, but I'll be back tonight, and—"

"Eli went out every night looking for you! She's so tired, Dad!" Luca whispered.

Gods… He really had made a bloody mess of everything.

"I'll go get her, and I'll make sure she doesn't get out of bed for three days. Sound good? I'll even make her eat in bed."

Luca nodded seriously.

"Have you…" Tam trailed off for a moment, unsure if it was a bad idea to ask the question. "Have you been sleeping in our room since I've been gone?"

Lowering his chin as though he were about to be reprimanded, Luca nodded again. "I… I knew you'd come here when you got back, and I… I wanted to make sure I saw you."

Tam's heart swelled. "I'm glad I got to see you right when I got back, Luca."

The boy smiled nervously.

"But I do have to get to Eli and the others, alright? So go back to sleep, and we'll have a nice breakfast together."

"Okay, Dad."

Tam ruffled Luca's hair again for good measure, making the boy smile more genuinely, then stood, calm once more. He pulled on the very last reserves of his strength and stamina to keep going.

He wasn't even sure what it was that Luca had done to restore his sense of self, but at the moment, he couldn't spend any time working that out. He needed to order a bath and change into appropriate clothes as quickly as possible. He'd make up some story to explain how he got into the house without anyone noticing, and then he'd hire a hackney to get him to the party.

Tonight was important, and he had been making everyone worry for far too long.

And if Eli really had been exhausting herself day in and day out looking for him?

Resolve solidified in Tam's being.

Whether she loves me or not, I'm going to take damn good care of that woman.

Eli had thought she would enter Lord Guk's party and do as she always did: find a place along the wall and stay there. She would position herself not too far from the food table, or the door, and observe the goings-on around her. Usually, she was able to learn a lot about the guests simply by watching the way they interacted and the snippets of conversations she was able to eavesdrop on.

As it turned out, tonight her typical method was shot to hell.

The second the doors opened and her presence was announced alongside Bong and Jeong, she found herself the subject of everyone's attention.

Lord Guk owned a lavish home, and on a warm night such as this, he had spared no expense in decorating his gardens with lanterns, even hiring musicians to play as the guests intermingled among shrubs and trees that were just starting to flower in delicate white and pink blossoms. Fountains dotted the courtyard space, complemented by nearby golden swan statues—evidently a symbol of the noble house of Guk.

This meant that even Lord Guk's guests were adorned in expensive fabrics and jewelry.

Eli had assumed that because she had chosen a modest gold hairpin with white flowers, plain gold earrings, rings, and a bracelet, she would be the most unassuming one attending.

She had forgotten, however, that the wealthy were commonly bored, and with the weather only turning warm more recently? That meant there weren't as many events to preoccupy them. And she was a *very* mysterious newcomer from a foreign land…

"Tell me, Mrs. Voll, where is your husband these days?"

"You look quite tired! It must be so difficult raising your son when your husband studies so intently."

"Were you married in Daxaria, or here in Zinfera? Do you think you'll move here permanently?"

By halfway through the party, Eli hadn't been able to move more than five feet from where she had first been stopped, and her throat was completely parched.

Bong and Jeong had taken turns remaining by her side. Often, they were not addressed, as many of the guests who wished to speak to Eli were in fact women. Furthermore, in the short time they had been in Junya, Jeong and Bong had already made themselves familiar to the nobility attending the party, and so they were less of a novelty. Particularly as they had painted themselves as party-loving hedonists.

Bong's falsified identity as Daeba had been taken well, and Jeong's as Eun wasn't far behind.

However, Eli was on the final, frayed thread of her patience, thanks to her newfound popularity, whereas Bong and Jeong bore their rise to fame spectacularly.

What was irking Eli in particular was that she, Bong, and Jeong were there to force Lord Guk to make an outrageous scene, which was supposed to spark the first wave of destruction to his reputation. They were still going to try, but Bong was nowhere near as adept at such things as Tam had claimed to be.

Furthermore, Bong hadn't been able to get close enough to Lord Guk to tamper with his food or drink. And given that the night had already progressed a good deal, people were inebriated. They wouldn't think much about Lord Guk acting outlandishly.

As Eli basked in the brief moment of silence granted when her latest inquisitor was pulled away by a heaped food platter, Bong pressed a glass of cool water into her hand. She couldn't help but feel like an utter failure. She sighed and took a sip.

"Elisara?"

Turning in alarm at the use of her real name, she found herself staring at a young man she did not know.

Frowning, Eli saw Jeong pull his shoulders back, making himself appear all the larger, and subtly more threatening.

"I beg your pardon, but my name is Ellie. Mrs. Ellie Voll, sir...?" Eli gave a polite but frosty smile as she waited for the person to speak.

But she very suddenly recalled the men who had been following her the day Tam had disappeared. She hadn't had time to really think about it since then, but now she could feel panic welling up in her.

The young man looked to be in his early twenties, was clean-shaven, and had his black hair slicked back, even though it was long enough to touch the tops of his ears. He had high cheekbones, pale skin, and.... Eli kept staring with growing suspicion. He was wearing a bright-red coat with gold trim and pants to match. A snowy silk shirt was buttoned to his throat, and his fingers were adorned in gold rings... The straight lines of his coat were more Daxarian than Zinferan.

He was starting to seem familiar.

The young man looked around nervously as he shuffled forward.

"That's close enough," Jeong called out softly, but the glint in his eyes had the young man freezing in place.

"Elisara, it's me. I... I'm Chul?"

Eli's eyes went wide, and she felt like she was going to be sick.

"Is this your... Is this your husband?" Chul cleared his throat and looked up at Jeong, who had an eyebrow raised.

"No. No..." Eli cleared her throat before turning and gulping down the rest of her drink. "I think you are mistak—"

"AH! There she is!" A loud, bawdy voice from her right side interrupted Eli right as she was about to insist to her younger brother, the boy she hadn't seen since she was eight years old, that she was not his big sister.

Torn between gratitude and annoyance, Eli looked over in time to see none other than the party's host, Lord Guk, approaching her.

He was a wide man and not particularly tall, but his eyes were keen and intelligent. His hair and beard were long, and he was dressed almost as flashily as Chul in a lime-green silk coat and matching pants, both embroidered with gold.

"I have not had the *pleasure* of meeting my most interesting guest of the evening!" Lord Guk seized Eli's hand without waiting to see if she would accept the gesture, planting a wet kiss on her knuckles. "Pity your husband couldn't join us this evening, but his loss is my gain!"

Eli forced a smile and hoped it didn't look as pained as it felt. "Lord Guk, thank you for inviting me to your wonderful home."

She curtsied as much as her dress would allow her.

"Of course! Your cousins said you could use a night away from the house. I must say, I can't believe your husband would leave as remarkable a woman as yourself alone on such an occasion!"

Eli felt her right cheek start to twitch from the strain of forcing her smile to remain in place. "My husband is very diligent with his work."

"Of course, of course! I'd love to hear more about his studies when I get the privilege of meeting him." Lord Guk smiled, and despite his being older and not in the finest shape, the smile was charming. Still, when his gaze roved over Eli's face, there was a gleam of knowingness in his eyes. As though he could tell she was forcing herself to be pleasant...

Eli wanted to cringe away. She hated it when people could smile so fondly yet be so awful underneath.

"Your cousins here were telling me that your husband is interested in studying the constellations to learn about dragons, or something to that effect, hm?" Lord Guk persisted, not seeming to care that Eli was hardly a participant in the conversation. "I happen to have a very good friend here who would love to pick his mind about it. He has great interest in the alleged dragon sightings by Gondol... Lord Yangban! Ah! There he is!"

Eli's knees buckled.

Her magic just about tore out of her in a way it hadn't ever before as blind terror filled her.

She needed to run away. She could *not* see Lord Yangban, or he'd recognize her instantly. He was the one who had orchestrated her abduction from the palace all those years ago!

"No need to trouble yourself on our behalf, Lord Guk," Jeong said, jumping in. "Say, I haven't had a rematch with you at cards since the first night we met!"

Jeong's words fell on deaf ears. He seemed to sense something was very wrong with Eli, and when he noticed that Lord Guk wasn't going to surrender her company easily, he began looking around for Bong, only to realize that things were even more complicated than they'd thought.

"Ah, Lord Yangban is speaking with your other cousin, it seems. I'm sure he'll come over soon. Now, I hope you don't mind my asking, but your hair is quite short. Is there a particular reason for that?" Lord Guk leaned closer, either unaware or unbothered that his guest had become a new statue in his garden.

"Excuse me, I need to refresh myself…" Eli started backing away, only belatedly remembering that her brother was still standing behind her, waiting to talk to her.

She was trapped. If she went inside claiming she needed to relieve herself, her brother would wait until she was on her way back to talk to her again, and if she rejoined the conversation with Lord Guk, Lord Yangban would be upon them in an instant. If she tried to leave the party, they wouldn't have accomplished anything!

Her heart raced. On trembling legs, she tried to move back again.

What the hell could she do?

And that was when she bumped into something very firm. Or rather… someone.

Warm hands clasped her upper arms, and the smell of frankincense and peppermint filled her nose…

Her entire body flushed with relief.

"Sorry I'm late—Lord Guk? My name is Mr. Joe Voll. I'm this beautiful woman's husband."

Tamlin Ashowan was back.

CHAPTER 36

A HARD HOMECOMING

Tam leapt out of the hired hackney in front of Lord Guk's home.

As with most houses and estates in Junya, Lord Guk's home was directly off the street, its front steps leading to the doors of the outer wall of the estate where just beyond were the courtyard and gardens. Lord Guk's home in particular had exceptionally large wooden doors at the entrance to the gardens and courtyard, and red pillars decorated with leaflike green designs outlined in glimmering gold paint stood on either side.

Music and chatter wafted over the white plaster wall to Tam as he approached two guards holding spears who stood in front of the doors.

The guards crossed their spears instantly, blocking his entrance.

"Hi there! My name is Mr. Joe Voll, I-I was invited to this event? My wife and her cousins are already inside." Tam feigned a look of nervousness.

It was never a good idea to show your true self to anyone, no matter their station, when entering into a dangerous situation with a fake identity.

The guards glanced at each other, then back at Tam, not saying a word.

Their lack of verbal reaction reminded the future duke a little of the recordkeeper named Dongu he had had to deal with. The door behind the guards opened, and an older, hunched-over man dressed in an emerald-green coat with a black sash stepped out, clutching a board with parchment pinned on it. He must have heard Tam speaking from just inside the doors.

"Good evening, sir. Please repeat your name for me?" the servant asked in a high-pitched, creaking voice.

"Mr. Voll. Joe Voll. My wife Ellie is already here."

At the mention of Eli's alias, the man perked up. "Why, yes! She is an exquisite woman! She has been the talk of the party all night!"

Tam barely resisted a wince.

Eli must be having a Gods-awful time...

Thankfully, the servant saw no reason to bar Tam from entering the party, particularly when he was allegedly married to the star of the evening, and so the guards permitted him to proceed inside.

The night's festivities were already well under way, so even though Tam should've stood out due to his height and pale skin, he was able to go unnoticed as he got his bearings and slipped to the side wall to study the surroundings.

Overall, everyone attending the party seemed... drunk.

Damn. If Eli and the others are still here, it means they weren't able to drug Lord Guk while everyone was of sound mind... Then again, it could make it seem more of a natural descent into madness.

Tam sighed, nearly triggering a yawn.

While he hadn't seemed to need sleep or food in the void for the three days he had been gone, he now felt like he'd been awake without food or water for at least half a day.

Tam refocused his attention on locating the host of such a debauched party, and found him talking to a woman in a stunning dress, even though it wasn't quite the style that most Zinferan women wore. It combined Troivackian and Zinferan features with its dark brassy shimmer in a velour material that would help stave off any chill in the night air. It was a long plain sheath that rose to a halter at the back, exposing the woman's shoulders and back.

Tam startled when he noticed the short hair of the wearer. Was that Eli?

His heart lurched almost painfully into his throat. He was glad no one was around to see his reaction; it gave him time to come back to his senses.

Which was good because he then noticed the way a young man wearing a bright-red coat was loitering just behind her, and the older man he had already identified as Lord Guk wearing lime green, stood in front of her.

Even though Tam had never met Lord Guk, the way he commanded the room left little room for mistaken identity.

However, the way Eli looked, pinned in between the two men, troubled Tam. He could tell by the tension in her spine that she was uncomfortable, and the unease on Jeong's face told him that his friend wasn't sure how best to get them out of the situation.

Then Lord Guk waved to someone Tam could see from his vantage point, a man talking with Bong, and he saw Eli take a step back.

Something was very, *very* wrong.

Tam moved.

He had to get Eli out of there.

As he passed by more and more of the guests, he could feel eyes and whispers following him as closely as his own shadow, but he didn't care. He normally would've wanted to hide, but now knowing that such a sentiment would send him back to the void, he avoided the thought like a mouse avoided a hungry cat and made Eli his sole focus.

Tam moved quietly past the young man in the red coat, who jolted in surprise when he looked over at Tam and saw the sharp warning glare he was giving.

Then, in an act Tam knew was sparked by a possessive and protective urge, he reached up and gently grasped Eli's arms.

Lord Guk's eyes drifted upward in shock at the size of Tam, who for once wasn't hunching his shoulders to make himself smaller in a crowd, but rather stared down the host.

"Sorry I'm late—Lord Guk? My name is Mr. Joe Voll. I'm this beautiful woman's husband."

Tam didn't look down to see what kind of expression Eli was making, but he could see Jeong beaming while closing his eyes and letting out a blissful sigh of relief.

"Ah! Right! Of course! I was just now saying how odd it was that she should be left unattended at such an event." Lord Guk took a few moments to recover, but he eventually reclaimed his charming smile. "I've been telling Mrs. Voll that you should speak with Lord Yangban over there—he lives in the capital and is very interested in anything related to dragons, what with the rumors flying all over the place. Pun unintended."

Tam smiled, though there wasn't any warmth in the expression. "I would greatly appreciate the opportunity to speak with Lord Yangban in the very near future. I'm sorry to say, however, that part of the reason I was late to the event tonight was that when I went home to change, I learned that our son is feeling unwell. You know how Luca is." Tam said the last part while looking down at Eli, his eyes gentling the instant they locked with hers. "He won't stop asking for you when he gets like that."

Eli wasn't able to speak as she stared up at her employer, and fresh pink warmed her cheeks.

"I'll see you back at the house?" Tam looked at Jeong, who was now openly crying.

Jeong nodded, and when Lord Guk raised an eyebrow at his peculiar emotional display, he said, "I'm just so... distressed to hear about their son's illness. I'm also a bit gassy. It's the clams."

Tam gingerly patted Jeong's shoulder while subtly turning Eli away from Lord Guk and shielding her from both Lord Yangban, who was starting to turn in their direction, and the young man in red.

As they headed toward the entrance, he ushered her off the gravel path where they'd been standing and around a golden statue of a swan to avoid another group of party guests.

"We haven't been able to cause a scene." Eli's voice cracked as she whispered to Tam.

"Are you alright?" he returned softly, ignoring her lament.

Once they passed a large three-tier burbling fountain and were completely alone, Eli pushed his arm off her shoulders and rounded on him, her eyes fixed on his face.

"No! We have a job to do! This is your plan, and we need to see it through!" The ferocity in her voice made Tam hesitate.

He had a hunch she was angry about more than just their plans for Lord Guk going awry, and so he folded his hands in front of himself and waited, all the while both marveling at how beautiful she was, but also how horribly exhausted she looked.

Guilt sank its relentless jaws into his gut.

"Since you're here now," she spat, "why don't you go handle this with Bong and Jeong?"

Tam tilted his head and said nothing. But he also didn't move an inch.

"What?"

Tam's voice was low and even. "I'm sorry for worrying you, Eli."

While he had apologized countless times before to his assistant, this time…?

This time tears sprang to her eyes despite the look of anger she shot him.

She gave a breathy laugh.

"I wasn't worried about you!" she declared, though her voice was starting to crack.

"I know you weren't worried about me. You were worried about your job and how your well-being would be affected. As your employer, it was my shortcoming that led you to have such anxiety. When we return, I want you to take three days off. You'll rest in our room, and you aren't going to do any work. Understood?"

Tam watched as she opened and closed her mouth, three tears falling in quick succession.

"My lord, with all due respect, fuck you."

The words hurt. A lot. But Tam knew he deserved them.

He'd put Eli through hell so far, and she'd only been under his employ for two months.

"Fair enough. If you'd like to return home without me, I will arrange your passage to Daxaria. I do have another way we can be successful this evening, but I think you have more than earned a night off, and I understand you don't want to run into Lord Yangban, so—"

"You understand Godsdamn *nothing*! Stop assuming you know me! You don't know me! Stop apologizing and stop just guessing what I mean or want!"

Tam recoiled slightly, but he carefully avoided the thought of wanting the ground to swallow him up whole, even though it made a knot tighten in his chest.

"Then please tell me what you want. Whatever it is, you'll get it."

"Because you want to bed me?" Eli bit out viciously.

Horror filled Tam, and he didn't hide it in his face for an instant. "No. Because it is the least I can do after everything you've had to put up with. I'd apologize again, but you're a little terrifying right now."

Eli's nose began to run as she continued to fight against the tears that kept falling, reddening her eyes in the process. "Ha! That's ridiculous! What could *I* do to *you*?"

"Everything."

The weight of Tam's response turned her into living stone, but Tam didn't shy away from the truth of it.

Nor did he elaborate.

He knew some of her unleashed anger must've come from her confusion, and another large amount from her bone-dead exhaustion, but in a way it was better she was letting it out.

She had a tendency to hold on to her anger.

"I want you to carry out your new plan, and then I want you to return to the house," Eli ordered once she had regained a measure of composure.

Tam nodded, then turned and strode off toward a covered walkway of the house that lay in the shadows, as the nearest corner would most likely lead to the servants' quarters.

Eli followed him after a moment's hesitation, matching his quiet footfalls.

They reached the next corner of the house, the one that marked the largest part of the courtyard where everyone was mingling.

Tam stopped and reached down into his boot to procure…

A slingshot.

"Wh—"

Eli didn't finish the words as Tam slipped a small, sharp pellet into the pad of the slingshot, lifted it, drew back the pad all the way to his ear, aimed… and released.

Tam watched as his target, Lord Guk, seized the back of his neck in confusion just as he was starting to say something to Lord Yangban. At first the Zinferan nobleman looked around himself curiously; then he pulled his fingers away and studied them. Noticing faint drops of blood, Lord Guk looked around the courtyard again as Tam flattened himself against the wall and waited.

Then after a count of ten breaths, he retreated.

"We should leave now."

"But—"

"I dosed the missile. It would've just felt like a mosquito bite. He's going to start acting quite unlike himself very soon."

"How did you—"

"I had several backup plans for tonight. The slingshot was my last resort, as I knew even if I got searched, I could just say it was Luca's." Tam continued toward the doors without looking to his side, where Eli was struggling to keep up with him due to his longer legs. "I didn't know if I'd have many vantage points to hide with this method, which is why we were going to rely on dosing his cup. This was much easier, though."

"Easier for you, maybe. I can't believe you used a *slingshot*... a child's toy, no less. Not even a real one." Eli laughed weakly in disbelief.

Tam shrugged as they freed themselves from the darkened walkway and crossed the gardens to the front door. "My nephews showed me long ago how effective they are."

He stopped before the doors and bowed to Eli while gesturing her through.

She faltered at the move, but upon noticing the guards and servants hovering a little way down the path, she swallowed and exited the premises without commenting on his behavior.

As the couple descended the front steps, Tam waved to one of the hackneys that sat outside the house waiting expectantly for wealthy, inebriated guests to require their services. He didn't look at Eli, until in grumbling tones she said, "At least this time you didn't have to get set on fire to leave early."

Caught by surprise, Tam burst out laughing.

Even if he knew there were far more horrible conversations and situations he was going to have to suffer through in the near future, in that moment, he was sincerely relieved to be back in the world where his assistant could knock him senseless just with a look, and her grumbling quips could make him laugh more easily than the most talented of jesters.

She may have been mad at him, but it was hard to feel down when she made him so happy.

CHAPTER 37

BREAKING BARRIERS

Tam slid the door to the room shut behind him. Eli had already stomped in ahead of him and was in the middle of removing her earrings.

The future duke didn't say anything as he slipped the black silk coat from his shoulders and started rolling up the sleeves of his white tunic. He knew Eli's bout of silence in the hackney ride home was mostly because she was still reeling from the harried events of the night.

"Who was the man in red that was lurking behind you?" Tam asked innocuously.

Eli whirled around. "Why? Why do you need to know that?"

Tam blinked and stared at her flatly. "Because I need to know everything that's been going on since I've been stuck in a void."

Eli huffed. Turning back to the dresser where she had put down her earrings, she worked on taking off the rest of her jewelry as well.

Tam wondered fleetingly if she'd noticed she'd left the wedding ring on, but decided he didn't want to point it out just yet.

"Did you really go out looking for me every night?"

Eli chucked down the bracelet she had just removed from her wrist with enough force that it might've chipped the wood.

"Who told you that? Luca?"

Tam said nothing, but his frown did deepen. "Eli… is there something you'd like to say?"

Her hands flew to her hips as she stared up at him more intensely and unabashedly than she ever had before. Tam was suddenly finding it rather difficult to think coherently.

"You make complicated plans, and then disappear! You saved me and then vanished into thin air! You… You kissed me! And have been gone for *days*! Everyone was counting on you, but I have no right to be angry with you because it's due to your magic, which you can't control!" Eli made a remarkable combination of a grunt and a hiss and then turned away from him.

"You've been nothing *but* angry since seeing me again," Tam pointed out slowly.

Despite his cautious tone, his assistant still reacted explosively.

"HAVE YOU NOT BEEN LISTENING?"

Tam was so shocked at her shout he stumbled back. He recovered swiftly, but he still couldn't believe she was actually yelling at him.

He realized, then and there, that there was nothing he could say or do, nothing but let her rage at him. He hoped that maybe he wasn't too tired by the end of it to go find something to eat.

"You shouldn't be here in Zinfera! You shouldn't be doing anything important if you're just going to disappear! You should be at home in Daxaria with your books, causing silly little rumors. You should be where you can be safe and just get over your damn pride about it! Because you cause problems when you try to do more! All kinds of problems, and now you have someone who needs you to be a father!"

Tam rescinded the notion that simply taking in Eli's furious words would be a matter of patience; it was more a question of whether he had the emotional fortitude to deal with it.

"Eli. I'm sorry you were placed in a—"

"Stop apologizing!" she breathed while stalking back toward the dresser. "You're a liability, my lord, and you have people who care about you. You can't—" She looked at Tam as she began slipping the halter of her dress over her head, and she must've seen the expression on his face because she stopped talking and moving at the same time.

The tension in the air mounted, and Tam fought not to betray a single thought on his face as he folded his arms over his chest and leaned back against the door.

He stared at her expectantly.

Tam doubted he was the picture of patience and calm.

His jaw was set on edge and he could feel heated emotions brew in him. Another man could have simply been angry about getting torn apart by his assistant. Tam however stared at Eli, hoping she recognized the challenge behind his silence.

What she would continue to do? Berate him, or undress? Could she accept the consequences of either action?

Tam was doing everything he could to turn his insides into iron for her next decision.

Eli swallowed. He watched her do it.

"You… You can't… You shouldn't… Come and go… You have a job to do and—"

"The job is done. I came back in time, and I intend to explain to Luca about how I might disappear from time to time and that he shouldn't worry." Tam's voice was even, and he noticed Eli draw herself straighter upon hearing it.

"He shouldn't worry?" Eli rasped, and Tam could tell it was a sign of renewed rage sparking. "You dissolve into a void, and it terrifies you more than anything else in this world, and you can't find your way out. Of course he should worry! We all should!"

"I don't think I've ever said it terrifies me more than—"

"You don't have to!" Eli snapped.

Tam knew she was stubborn, and when it mixed with her exhaustion, he acknowledged that he shouldn't have been surprised that she'd explode at him.

He closed his eyes.

If he kept staring at her and her bare shoulders, he wasn't going to get a hold of his thoughts, even if he stood there the rest of the night.

He put himself in Eli's position. His mother always said if you wanted to best help or hurt someone, you had to see things from their perspective, and Tam was very firmly in the former category in that moment.

She would've been scared about not being able to poison Lord Guk, and she would've been uncertain of her future if Tam should disappear for good. Of course she wouldn't trust that she'd be safe, even though Bong and Jeong would vouch for what happened. She'd still be the subject of scrutiny, and the Coven of Wittica would most definitely reject her citizenship, barring some very serious intervention from Finlay Ashowan and the new king.

Then she would also have to comfort Luca.

And of course there was the matter of him kissing her.

Not to mention the men following her saying that they were hired by—

"The man in red was your brother, wasn't he?" Tam spoke before thinking.

He should have been working on how to best calm her down, but he found he was unable to stop himself.

Eli paled, and instantly Tam mentally cursed himself for being so careless.

He shook his head and tried to change the topic. "I learned more about my magic while I was in the void. I can manage to avoid it a bit better going forward. Though if I do get trapped there again, I can't say for certain how long I'll be gone. I'll have to think about it more to get a better handle on things."

He waited in the tense hush that followed to see if he had been successful in negating any more anger from his assistant. When she didn't shout or say anything else, he decided to press a little in a different direction.

"You should go to sleep." Tam lifted his chin in the direction of the bed.

"What… Are…" Eli couldn't fully speak.

Tam didn't rush her, and thankfully he felt more in control of himself at that point. The quiet also helped him grasp what state his assistant was in.

He definitely didn't dare let himself broach the topic of how she might or might not feel about their kiss, because he had absolutely no idea, and he wasn't sure he wanted an idea, either.

However, Eli exceeded his non-fixed expectations as she frowned, then blinked. Tears were gathering in her eyes for the second time that night, and his iron core started crumbling. He still managed to hold his tongue and not move, but he felt his stoic expression cracking in light of his worry.

She reached up and pressed the heels of her palms into her eyes, then crouched and released a quiet, breathy sob.

Tam felt his heart rip itself apart.

He walked over to Eli, then lowered himself to be nearly eye level with her. He clasped his own wrist to stop himself from touching her, in case it wasn't something she wanted.

"You made me count on you," Eli said brokenly between weak, shuddering breaths. "Made me think you... You really could handle everything."

The lump that rose in Tam's throat nearly choked him.

"And it's my fault... you disappeared."

Alarm rushed through Tam as he stared wide-eyed at her.

"Wh— No! No, no, no it was *not* your fault! Not for an instant!" Tam's grip on his wrist tightened painfully.

"You... You saw those men following me, and—"

"Gods, Eli. No. Absolutely not. I disappear when I'm being a Godsdamn coward, not when I'm stressed."

Eli lifted her bloodshot eyes to him. Tam's head started to ache from the effort it took not to touch her.

"I go to a place that is connected to everything and nothing. When I get overwhelmed, or I don't want to be somewhere, or... Or maybe I want to make someone else disappear, I suppose. That's when I disappear. You have done nothing wrong. I'm just going through a bit of a late-in-life growth spurt when it comes to interacting with the world."

"I don't understand," Eli whispered.

Tam gave a halfhearted smile. "It's okay. The point is, it is no one's fault but mine. You are right to be concerned and angry. I know you don't want to hear it, but I *am* sorry, Eli. I'm sorry I'm not a better or stronger person that you can count on properly."

"You arse!" Eli's voice rose a fraction. "You're the best person I know, and..." She paused to swallow. "It isn't fair to you that I started relying on you."

Tam let out a frustrated breath of his own. "No. I want you to be able to count on me. I'm going to be better, I promise. I'm just terrible at personal relationships, and... I'm working it out. That's why I'm apologizing all the time. But I really do want you to feel you can trust me, Eli."

"Why?" she asked, looking utterly baffled.

Tam smiled again, his heart warming at her innocent gaze.

Gods help me. How can she be so worldly and yet so clueless?

"Aside from the fact I think life has been far too unfair to you and you deserve better? That you deserve to have someone help you and not want anything in return? Well... I had kind of hoped I'd made myself clear when I kissed you."

Tam watched Eli's eyes go round and her breath stop. For a moment she seemed to react vulnerably to his words, her expression softening, but Tam didn't let his hopes rise. And sure enough, he saw her walls erect themselves once more behind her gaze.

"You want to bed me."

Tam gave a weary chuckle before rubbing his mouth and resting the side of his face in his palm. He'd have to be honest and direct with her if he wanted to resume building any kind of trust with her.

"I want to do that, yes. But it's because I happen to be in love with you."

Tam watched as his words froze Eli's face.

"I don't expect anything from you," he continued. "You don't have to return anything to me, and I know I'm a big enough arse for feeling this way as your employer." Tam paused to sigh then smile. "If you didn't keep trying to take your clothes off in front of me, I'd keep it to myself, but you've left me with no choice. You need to know everything if we are going to work well together."

Silence hung in the air between them. Tam dropped his hand from his face and waited patiently for whatever his assistant's reaction would be. He also resolved to spare her and change the topic if the quiet dragged on too long.

Though thanks to his rushing heartbeat, he wasn't sure he had a great grasp of time.

"You... You really don't want anything from me?" Eli looked like the idea was more than a little foreign to her.

The briefest flicker of a violent urge drifted through the back of Tam's mind as he considered who would have made such a notion strange to her.

"All I want, Eli? Is what you are willing to give."

"What if I don't feel the same and never will?"

"I never expected you would."

"But you kissed me."

Tam winced and looked at the ceiling. "I did. I'm sorry. I won't do it again."

"You aren't going to ask me how I feel about you? Or about the kiss?" Eli asked carefully.

"Do you want me to?"

Eli paused and considered this question. "I liked it."

It was Tam's turn to be stunned. He blinked and his lips twitched as voracious joy rushed through his blood.

"But I don't like anything else."

Tam didn't bother hiding his look of incredulousness. "Holy antlers, Eli. You really aren't afraid of torturing a person."

The assistant made a grumbling noise of frustration that sounded much more like herself.

"I… I like things to be fair—"

"I know you do."

"Shush…. my lord," she added the respectful title when she registered how snappish she had sounded. Clearing her throat, she continued with a more even tone. "I am no one. With nothing but problems, and I would feel like I am beneath you in every way if I were to entertain the idea of…"

Tam raised his eyebrows and he felt a roguish smile claim his face, daring her to finish the thought—even though his insides were a mess of screaming, awkward, excited nerves he was trying to settle.

"If I were to entertain the idea of something more. If you tired of me, you would hold even more power over me than you already do."

"I understand… But I don't think *you* do."

Eli blinked.

"You have far more power over me than I do over you. You see, I know you don't feel quite the same way."

The assistant opened her mouth, but Tam raised a hand. "If I'm getting this right, you do like me, but you don't know in what way yet. That said, if you continue to take that stunning dress off in my presence, I may interpret it to mean you want to bed me."

Eli blushed scarlet.

"I sincerely predicted an outright rejection of my feelings, but you've decided to play an even more dangerous game and give me a bit of hope. So here is what I will say. If you want more? You have to say so. I've made it somewhat clear what I want, and however much you are or aren't willing to give, you are going to have to be the one to initiate or communicate that."

Tam dropped his hand, signaling he was finished speaking.

Fidgeting, Eli dropped her eyes to her lap. "You have terrible taste in women, my lord."

The future duke laughed. "I don't know about that. Pretty, capable, and prefers a quiet night with some tea and books? You seem like the ideal woman."

Eli couldn't meet his eyes, and Tam struggled against the urge to reach over and wipe the tears from her cheeks.

"Will you sleep in bed with me tonight?"

Tam's heart stopped.

Eli lifted her watery gaze to him at last. "I still feel safer and sleep better when you're there."

Unable to speak, thanks to all of his blood rushing away from his brain, Tam cleared his throat and leaned closer to his assistant.

"I will, but Eli?"

"Yes… my lord?"

"You better build one hell of a barrier between us in that bed if all you want is my presence."

Finally catching on to what was being hinted at, Eli managed a faint "Oh."

Her lips stayed parted. Waves of powerful urges flooded through Tam, but he did his best to battle them back.

"Do you need me to leave while you finish taking off that dress?" Tam heard himself ask, his voice gravelly.

So much for controlling himself.

"U-um yes? Yes."

Tam gave a tight-lipped smile at Eli while raising his eyebrows in a teasing albeit affectionate move, and then pushed himself back up to standing even though it physically pained him.

He turned and strode out of the room while doing his utmost to redirect his thoughts to the less dangerous matter of food, while praying to the Gods that he would be able to manage himself better in the coming months.

Even though he knew that would entirely depend on whether or not Eli decided to torment him into utter madness.

CHAPTER 38

A WELL-ROUNDED RETURN

Tam woke with a gasping jolt.

Then he flinched at the bright sunlight filling his vision, regarding the white ceiling while trying to relish each quick breath of fresh air he indulged in.

His mind gradually shifted out of panic.

I'm not in the void anymore. I made it out... Somehow.

Tam reached up and rubbed his eyes, but he didn't do so for long. It was too nice to see the sunlight. Even if it made his eyes ache.

Forcing a slower breath out of his lungs, Tam turned over to his right side, the tension in his shoulders starting to ease away... until he found himself staring at Eli.

Asleep.

Beside him.

Without so much as a pillow between them.

Tam felt his eyes bulge.

She was breathtaking.

Quite literally.

Tam had to remind himself to inhale when he found himself getting light-headed.

He wasn't certain if his dumbfounded state was due to the shock of seeing her, or if he was still readjusting to being back in the world with everyone.

Maybe he'd died and was being given a glimpse of something he had found himself wishing to see during the journey to Junya when Eli had slept just on the other side of him with luggage between them.

Studying her in the present, Tam noted that the dark shadows under her eyes were already improving, but she'd require a little more rest to fully recover.

One question he had wanted to ask the night before was whether or not she had used her magic when she'd looked for him. He could feel a streak of frustration in his chest at the idea that she'd been wandering around the streets of Junya at night without any protection.

Not that Eli would listen to him or take kindly to the implication that she of all people would need or be worth protecting.

Tam let out a sigh, though he smiled.

Stubborn as a mule and single-minded in her work ethic. Gods... I didn't stand a bloody chance. Not when she's cute on top of all that.

Tam flopped back onto his back and allowed himself to enjoy the quiet peacefulness of the morning.

He could smell coffee brewing and eggs frying, and while there was the unfamiliar tangy scent of the foreign sauces and spices that his father didn't use as often back in the keep in Daxaria, that morning felt more like home than... well... home.

Tam slowly slid from the bed, the plush comforter giving off soft crinkling rustles. Dressing himself in his trousers, but leaving his loose sleep shirt on, Tam cast another look at his assistant, his face aching with a smile.

The room was filled with the scent of lemons and florals, and the air was suffused by the glow of the sunshine. Tam pressed the sight firmly into his memory.

It was the best morning of his life.

Gods... If Eli ever does decide to properly seduce me, it might actually kill me with happiness.

Slipping out of the room, Tam padded down the hall and angled left into the dining space to find Jeong, Bong, and Luca already seated at the table that Haewon was just finishing setting.

"Dad!" Luca jumped up from his cushion at the table and shot over to Tam, flinging his arms around Tam's hips.

Wrapping his arms around his son, Tam looked up at Jeong, who was already beaming. Bong smiled, though it didn't quite reach his eyes.

Tam's good mood stalled. Something was wrong.

He gave Bong a quiet nod of acknowledgment.

Jeong, if he noticed, ignored this.

"Welcome back, Mr. Voll." Haewon lowered her chin, her words stiff.

Tam knew he had firmly nailed shut the coffin of his chances of Haewon ever liking him after having disappeared for so long.

"Thank you, Haewon. And thank you for helping my family while I was away."

The housekeeper said nothing else as she bowed and exited the room, leaving them alone.

"Well, well, well. Our quiet, dignified lord made quite the dramatic entrance last night," Jeong chortled as Tam patted Luca on the shoulder then lowered himself to his place at the table. Luca, not wanting to leave his father's side, sat down on his right.

"I'm sorry about being gone for so long." Tam bobbed his head.

Jeong slid a very quick glance at his brother, who was acting completely nonplussed as he sipped his tea.

"We're glad you're back. Eli—she wasn't doing well. Not to mention everything that has been going on." Jeong cleared his throat, his eyes drifting to the top of Luca's head as the boy worked on devouring his bowl of rice topped with eggs and kimchi.

"Yes, how was the rest of the party last night?" Tam asked vaguely while pouring himself a cup of coffee from the tall glass pot in the middle of the table.

Any semblance of good-natured fun in Jeong's face disappeared.

"It went well enough. Our host suddenly started shouting at the golden swan statues around his garden, saying they were laughing at him. He also started screaming into the faces of some of the women…"

Tam smiled humorlessly. "Good."

"At that stage in the evening, most attendees saw it as a drunken escapade, albeit far from acceptable or appropriate."

"We'll see how the lord manages the consequences. If he's overly prideful, it could work in our favor, as he'll act out angrily," Tam explained while filling his own plate with eggs.

He had managed to find some leftover chicken the night before after his talk with Eli, but he was absolutely ravenous for a hot meal right then.

"He might. However, he isn't a foolish man, and with Lord Yangban here, he might instead be on his best behavior," Bong interrupted, his words hard and bitter.

Tam's gaze cut to the elder Ryu son. He had never heard such a tone from him before.

Rather than commenting, he nodded slowly, then said, "By the way, Bong, I haven't had any proper training since arriving in Zinfera. Would you mind indulging me?"

Bong inclined himself in assent.

"Can I watch?" Luca asked excitedly. "My dad's really fast with knives!" He mimed stabbing forward multiple times, his brows furrowed like Tam's.

Bong managed to smile genuinely at the child's obvious pride and enthusiasm.

"Sorry to say, you are going to have to go to your lessons as usual." Tam rested a hand atop his son's hair.

Luca let out a loud moan. "But you just got home! Can't I miss class?"

Tam laughed. "Not a chance. Don't worry, I'll be here all day, and I won't be going back to the library for another day or two."

That succeeded in placating the child, and so the rest of the breakfast passed by peacefully.

As the men rose from the table and Haewon returned to clear away the dishes, Tam sidled up to the housekeeper. "Could you please see to delivering a tray to my wife? She's not going to be leaving our room today under any circumstances."

Haewon's lips pursed, her thoughts unclear, but she tilted her head dutifully and left.

With Luca having scampered off to prepare for his lessons, and Jeong venturing off to bathe, since he had returned too late the night before to do so, Bong and Tam headed to the courtyard.

"Did you and Eli make amends?" Bong ventured casually as they walked.

Tam continued inspecting one of his daggers to see if it needed to be sharpened. "More or less. I'm giving her space."

"That is wise, from what I could tell. Especially with her supposed family nearby… While you were away, she alluded to the fact that they are interested in finding her again for one reason or another. I know less than you do about her past, but it is easy to discern that romance is one of the farthest matters from her mind."

"Might not be as far as you think," Tam murmured more to himself than Bong, but the Zinferan raised an eyebrow in his direction all the same. "Mind telling me what your history is with Lord Yangban?" Tam went on, transitioning the discussion smoothly.

Bong paused as they reached the plum tree, its white flowers blooming prettily.

"He has harmed more people than you could ever imagine. It has been particularly bad in recent years."

He kidnapped a princess who was a strong candidate to be empress and is walking around without any repercussions. It's not hard to guess he feels untouchable.

"My father has tried to save the people he pushes under his thumb and controls with the pirates and traders, but it's like stanching a wound while the dagger still keeps cutting a bigger and bigger hole." Bong paused to let out an angry breath. "The number of people I have tried to comfort after they've lost their loved ones due to his machinations… I have to confess, this goal we are working on, to cripple Lord Guk, is proving to be far harder for me than I anticipated, now that I have to smile at that man who is nothing but a poison in this world."

Tam knew then that if he happened to casually mention what Lord Yangban had done to Eli, there was a very large chance that Bong would be unable to compose himself in the lord's presence ever again.

Hell, even Tam hadn't had to face the man directly yet to see if he could restrain himself.

"Before I leave Zinfera, Lord Yangban will be dead and his power crushed. You have my word."

A rueful half smile lifted Bong's mouth. "If your last name were any other than Ashowan, I'd say it was impossible."

"When there is no higher power to hold someone like him accountable, it doesn't take long for an empire to collapse. I'll be doing my best."

"Well said. Now, before we start to train, I of course have to ask… Where did you go?"

Tam rubbed the back of his neck. He had known it would come up sooner or later; quite honestly, he was shocked it hadn't already.

"My magic takes me to a place that doesn't technically exist. I've been trapped there for a while."

Bong's eyebrows flew upward. "Your magic creates a… a prison?"

"No, it—" Tam stopped.

A prison.

The first witch… The devil…

Was he supposed to send them to the void as though it were a prison?

Power suddenly flushed him, as though he was getting closer to an answer.

"It could be like a prison," the future duke began carefully. He decided not to mention his recent discussion with Death. "But I could leave. I just didn't know how to before. And even though I now know, it isn't simple."

"Where did you reappear? Was it back in the street?" Bong wondered.

"No, I—" Tam stopped again. He hadn't really considered why he had reappeared somewhere else.

Everything had happened so quickly.

Had it been that he'd traveled in the void?

Could he do that? Disappear one place and reappear in another?

Tam remained silent as he thought through this possibility. But he hadn't been the one to pull himself from the void. The red thread had done that, even though he had fought it. He was being pulled by someone or some*thing* he didn't want to meet… and he had wound up in his and Eli's room.

Where Luca had been sleeping.

More and more questions and theories started to pour into Tam's head.

Finally, Bong clapped his hand on his shoulder, jarring him free. "It seems as though you have a great many things to think about. But I confess, I was actually quite happy that you requested to train with me. It might help work out some of my agitation about Lord Yangban."

Tam did his best to finish swimming through his thoughts back to the present. "Ah, sorry. Of course." Giving his head a shake, he squared himself to Bong.

However, he did not anticipate the man instantly pummeling him in his gut without any further ceremony.

Luckily, Tam had been trained in combat by his mother, and while she was a good woman, when it came to combat and training? She was far from gentle.

So despite being winded, Tam seized Bong's shoulder, braced his knee, and tried to flip the Zinferan onto his back.

While Bong was caught off guard by how fast Tam had recovered, he managed to wrench himself free of Tam's grasp and spin off to the future duke's side. Bong's elbow was winding back to jab Tam in the ribs, but Tam peripherally tracked the movement, caught the elbow, dragged Bong forward with it, and elbowed the Zinferan in the chest, knocking Bong back several feet.

Tam turned and cracked his neck while raising his hands and lowering his head.

He didn't bother drawing out the blades stowed at his back.

Bong touched his chest, coughed, then gave an impressed incline of his head toward Tam before reaching up to the tie of his purple silk shirt and shrugging it off to reveal that he was made of pure, lean muscle.

"I knew you were a capable man, Tam. It's expected of anyone who manages brothels. But I'm starting to think you may be a step farther than that and are in fact quite deadly."

Tam gave an innocent quirk of his mouth that turned into a smile, but didn't respond.

Bong widened his stance and lifted his open palms upward. A sparkle of interest lit his eyes. "Shall we?"

Tam ducked, darting forward and swinging out his leg in a long roundabout kick that caught Bong's side. He could hear a fraction of breath crushed out of the Zinferan's lungs.

Stumbling, Bong was still quick to circle back, his hands raised defensively.

Tam felt his mood lift. It'd been a while since he sparred with someone on a similar level as himself for fun. The back of his mind continued to slog through his endless questions about his magic, but the movement was helping hone them.

Who knows? Maybe my magic will be more useful than I originally thought.

CHAPTER 39

THE MIGHT OF THE MEDDLESOME

Soo Hebin lightly outlined the smooth slope of her neck with her fingertips, her oval face tilted in the mirror as she peered at her skin with satisfaction. Despite being in her forties, she looked remarkably young, but that of course was thanks to all of her painstaking efforts. Frankincense, rose oils, creams—only the best.

Lowering her eyes, she rose from the silk cushion of her stool, causing her four ladies' maids to rise from the floor behind her.

"What word have we received from Lord Nam about the silk shipment?"

One of the maids replied, "He said that it is on time, Your Highness, and that there are even some other items on the vessel that will please you."

Soo scoffed, but with a smile. "I'd say he was being impudent, but he does seem to know my taste."

Lifting her chin despite the incredible weight of her bejeweled hair, laden with stiff gels and perfumes, the concubine glided toward the doors of her quarters until a knock stopped her in place.

"Your Highness?" an unfamiliar voice called out. Not that Soo Hebin, mother to the next emperor, really took note of her servants. "A Mr. Julian is here to see you with two guests?"

The corners of Soo Hebin's mouth curved upward. "Already? This day is full of good news. Tell them I will see them now."

The two doors slid open, and in stepped a man with sandy-brown hair, brown eyes, and pale skin. He wore Daxarian clothes: a dirty black coat that had four heavy buckles, dull-black trousers, and underneath, a faded tunic. He bowed to her, and then stepped aside for a man with similar coloring, but one in his late thirties who wore a plum-colored silk coat over a fine cream vest embroidered in gold. The material was without a doubt Zinferan, but the cut and style were Daxarian.

"Your Highness, my name is Ansar," he said calmly with a bow.

When he straightened, he met Soo's gaze, and her expression turned cool. Those below her station were not to meet her eyes. She would have to take it up with this man's mistress. While he may have been her primary contact since the last time the daughter of the Gods had been in her company more than a decade ago, he was not an equal. Even if he was the closest confidant to the first witch.

Speaking of the daughter of the Gods… in swept the final guest, who stood with her hood drawn to shadow her face and did not say a word.

Soo raised an eyebrow, her displeasure growing as she lifted her left hand. "Leave us."

The serving maidens filed out without a word of protest, their slippered feet gently whooshing over the polished dark wooden planks. The doors slid shut once more.

Soo Hebin waited as the figure slowly lowered her hood.

The redheaded woman in front of her was in her early twenties, was quite short, with wide hips and a slim torso, and steely, colorless eyes.

"Glad to see you have arrived without incident," Soo said in greeting, her smile not quite matching her gaze.

"I'm glad to see you succeeded in growing your power," the first witch returned calmly.

"I confess, your ancient beasts were quite helpful. Particularly with convincing the coven to stay out of my affairs."

Tilting her head, Aradia looked toward Ansar. Soo had no idea what the look was supposed to mean, but it was already grating on her nerves.

"I appreciate the lengths you went to in order to help me escape Troivack," the first witch continued. There was an air of superiority in her voice as her gaze roamed over the large room with its white walls, thick wooden beams, painted screens, plush red carpets, gilded mirrors, and exquisite Zinferan paintings.

"Yes, well, I would like your assistance in ensuring my son takes the throne. Daxaria has been far too quiet as of late, and I had a hunch that your escape would help keep them busy."

Aradia didn't respond as she moved farther into the room. "I made sure to change my appearance multiple times on my journey here so you will be free of suspicion."

Soo scoffed. "I don't fear Daxaria's influence. They won't want to risk a war yet, and I've ensured that chaos is reigning here in Zinfera. Even if they wanted to, they would struggle to figure out who is the enemy, and who is innocent."

The first witch continued to study the room, as though inspecting it.

Soo knew better than to lash out at the first witch, and instead looked sharply at the man called Mr. Julian.

"I don't remember you."

At least this one hadn't made eye contact.

"I was recruited by the first witch in Troivack when I served the crown prince of Daxaria more than seven years ago." The stiffness that came into his shoulders made Soo's eyes glitter.

"You mean Eric Reyes? The one who now sits on the Daxarian throne?"

"Yes, Your Highness."

Soo strode over to the young man and lifted his chin with her index knuckle. His eyes seemed innocent, and yet there was a keenness to them—a shiftiness that betrayed his true nature.

"Interesting," Soo murmured.

"I take it there is more you believe I can do for you?" Aradia called out idly as she neared the end of her stroll around the concubine's room.

Once again reminded that the daughter of the Gods was making herself far too comfortable in her quarters, Soo inclined her head regally and turned around. "Yes. Take that dragon of yours and make it stop attacking my ships."

Aradia's eyebrows pulled together. "Wixim has been sinking ships?"

The concubine couldn't hide the twitch in her upper lip. She didn't like repeating herself.

The first witch saw this and held the concubine's eyes, appearing to be entertained, then dragged her gaze over to the corners of the room in thoughtful silence for a moment before daring to laugh. "I see. Well, I can help you with Wixim, of course. However, you will need to help me first."

"I have already helped you."

"Not quite. You paid your debt to me for the ancient beasts, and giving you access to Witch's Brew both for profit and for consumption. I hear the emperor has been declining in health—quite impressive that he lasted so long while being dosed." Aradia rounded the concubine to stand before her with Ansar. "Now you want me to move the dragon, and I'm saying I will require your assistance, though to be perfectly honest, what I'm asking for is beneficial for you as well."

Soo waited, feigning patience.

"The devil is in Zinfera. You will help me locate him, and I have no doubt that if we find him, we'll happen to find an Ashowan or two nearby."

Unable to hide her shock, the concubine widened her eyes. Her mind spun through the implications of arguably the most powerful family in Daxaria getting anywhere near her.

"The devil has not been seen in years. However, amongst the sailors, they talk of a man who wields darkness that can swallow you whole. And he happened to be traveling to Zinfera's shores."

Soo composed herself. "Rumors."

"Perhaps, but it is interesting that they started around the time of my escape. And now you say ships are being attacked by an ancient beast... I'm inclined to think all this *chaos* is starting to bring everyone, and everything, crashing together."

Wordlessly, the concubine moved toward a short, ornate wooden desk near a darkened window.

"I will contact my informants in Lord Jiho Ryu's household and see if he has any visitors, or if he is traveling. That peasant playing dress-up has been the Ashowans' source of information for years," Soo explained. She lowered herself to the white pillow and reached for her ink well.

"I'll need soldiers. Soldiers skilled in stealth and capture," Aradia declared evenly.

Soo Hebin paused.

One day, she would make the daughter of the Gods bow before her and rue the day she ever thought she could dominate her...

"How many?"

... But for now, Soo needed to guarantee her son's ascension to the throne. The first witch was the ticket, and who knew? Maybe if some Ashowans were lured to her, she'd find uses for them, too.

Tam stood quietly with his shoulder pressed against the doorframe as he watched Luca with his tutor.

He could see by his son's slumped shoulders that he wasn't paying attention at all as the stern Zinferan man continued to explain the mathematical equation he had written down on the piece of slate in his hands.

"He's the best tutor in Junya," Eli informed Tam, almost startling her employer into jumping. Almost. Tam had grown used to getting caught off guard by her.

"I read your notes," he said with a nod. "He's smart, but... I think Luca hasn't learned to focus while sitting down. It'll take some time."

The pair continued to watch the lesson until Luca let out a long yawn. Both Tam and Eli wordlessly decided that it was best if they moved back into the house before either of them felt the need to interrupt.

"Jeong and Bong say there is a boat launch ceremony in two days, and both Lord Guk and Yangban will be there," Tam started seriously. "Would you prefer to stay back?"

Eli sighed. "As much as I'd like to say no, it is too risky for me to go."

Tam slid a discreet glance in her direction. "Because your brother most likely will be attending?"

Eli stopped in her tracks and looked up at Tam, her expression hard as stone, until... it cracked.

The future duke hoped he hid his surprise quickly enough to prompt her to keep talking.

"I don't know what he wants or why he's looking for me. I was legally removed from the family. They owe me nothing, and I can ask for nothing." A breath of annoyance rushed out of her nose. "It'd also be problematic for you if I talked and acknowledged him."

"It might be riskier not to at the rate he's pursuing you," Tam pointed out gently.

Eli fell quiet, her brow crinkled in serious thought.

Haewon appeared. "Mr. and Mrs. Voll, there is a young man here to see Mrs. Voll."

Tam and Eli stared, dumbfounded. "Did—Did he give a name?" Eli closed her eyes as though mentally kicking herself for stammering.

"He did not, but he did say he tried to speak with you at the party last evening?" Haewon supplied helpfully.

"Alright, thank you." Eli tried to smile but she didn't succeed, and her eyes were filled with dread.

"Mrs. Voll, shall I tell him to come back another time?"

"He can… He can come in for a cup of tea."

Haewon nodded and smiled encouragingly at Eli. "I'll prepare a pot for the two of you."

"My husband will be there as well," Eli blurted in a rush.

Haewon's lips twitched toward a grimace. Then, remembering herself, she bowed respectfully and left.

Tam looked after the housekeeper, and once he was certain she was no longer within earshot, he shook his head. "Gods, she really hates me."

"I'm sorry."

He turned, startled, toward Eli.

"For making our time here more complicated, I—"

"I disappeared for three days, thanks to my magic. You are the *least* problematic of anyone in this house."

"Bong and Jeong aren't problematic."

"Bong when drunk is a bloody nuisance. He fell asleep in the tree when he got home last night. When Jeong went to help him out, he bruised his shoulder. And speaking of Jeong—do I really need to elaborate on why he is a menace? A lovable one, of course, but do I?"

The last comment chipped free a small smile from the assistant.

"Besides." Tam slipped his hands into his pockets and leaned against the wall behind him, his eyes homed on Eli, who was wearing the powder-blue shirt she looked the most stunning in. "I'm your husband. I need to look out for you."

Eli blushed, started to fidget, then stopped. "I thought you said you'd wait for me to say—"

"I'm just stating facts. It's what a husband does."

"W-while that may be... you are saying it while looking at me like that."

"Like what?" Tam raised his eyebrows innocently.

"Like you really think of yourself as my..." She trailed off, evidently unable to find the words.

"Would you like me to act indifferently?" Tam's voice lowered, but the question was sincere.

He watched her cheeks flush. "Not... Not really. Maybe?"

Tam smiled and lowered his chin. "Message received. Now, we spoke of the devil; let's go face him."

Eli's eyes snapped up in alarm. Tam realized that during his subtle flirtation, she had completely forgotten about their impromptu guest.

"Let's go greet your brother," he clarified, his smile lightening.

"Oh, right. Yes, let's do that! I promise I won't reveal your identity, my lord—I mean Ta—Joe!" Eli turned and hurried ahead of him as voices sounding down the hall drifted back toward them, signaling that Chul Nam was already in the house.

While Tam was worried about how the exchange could affect Eli, he had to silently confess that his mood had been difficult to dampen, especially when he'd noticed a subtle smile from Eli when he first referred to himself as her husband.

Who knows... Maybe if I'm patient, I can say it without it being a lie.

CHAPTER 40

A FAMILIAL FLOURISHING

Tam sat across from the future successor of the Nam household and eyed him with a schooled expression before regarding the man on Chul's right, who had been introduced as Chul's assistant, Yun Shik. Yun was a few years older than Chul, handsome and poised, his features catlike, his hair long.

Yun had been perfectly polite, but there had been a reverence in his eyes when he'd seen Eli, and Tam had barely managed to resist glaring at him as a result. At least Eli hadn't seemed to notice. She had kept her own eyes mostly on the ground during the greetings, and even seated at the dining table, she couldn't seem to look up. Tam was relatively certain she had not once met her brother's gaze.

Funnily enough, Chul was exactly the same way, even while Tam looked him over: The younger man sat staring awkwardly at the table while Haewon continued pouring tea.

This was odd behavior, given the blaring, bright-red coat Chul wore. In Tam's mind, that coat hinted at a louder personality.

Once Haewon had finished pouring tea and quietly exited the room, Tam waited for Chul Nam to start talking.

But he didn't.

And Eli didn't.

Tam focused his attention on Yun, who was gazing with a glint of longing at Eli.

The future duke's index finger started to slowly tap the table, which succeeded in drawing Yun's attention to him. The assistant had a long neck, a long face, and shiny hair swept to the side. He wore a unique indigo-colored shirt and white trousers.

"Forgive me," Tam said, deciding that if he didn't get the ball rolling, they'd be there all day. "The two of you have come on a day when my wife is supposed to be resting, and I can't say I've ever met you before."

Chul's face finally snapped up, and his startled eyes fastened on Eli. "Are you sick?" he asked, his expression taut.

Tam could tell by the shape of his cheeks that there was even more family resemblance than he had originally noticed.

"No, I..." Eli cast a sidelong glance at Tam as though wanting to chastise him, but he ignored her.

He *had* told her to stay in bed all day. When she had joined him in observing Luca earlier, she had just finished bathing.

"I was up late due to the party last night, and my husband insisted I rest today. That is all," Eli finished explaining stiffly, her eyes briefly darting to her brother. "You were introduced last night, sir, as Chul Nam. I'm sorry to say I think you have me mixed up with someone else—"

"El, it's me."

Both Tam and Eli's attention shot to Yun, who was leaning forward earnestly.

"You used to tutor me when we were children. Don't you remember?"

Yun turned to Tam. "Elisara was already ahead of all the other children her age, myself included, and I was the smartest child in Bani until she caught up."

Eli opened and closed her mouth, her eyebrows twitching together.

Tam could tell she was confused, and felt some modicum of relief that while this man remembered her and still thought about her—*ardently*—she hadn't a clue who he was.

Yun blundered on while shaking his head with a chuckle. "You have those two beauty marks behind your left ear, Elisara. I know it is you."

"I sincerely do not know who *you* are, I'm afraid," Eli informed him.

Yun at last appeared to believe her, and his cheeks deepened in color.

"Do you know... me... though?" Chul ventured with cautious optimism.

Eli looked at Tam nervously, but the way he saw it, it was her brother, and he trusted her judgment.

He gave a subtle shrug of his right shoulder, and relished the way she understood him perfectly before she turned to Chul.

"I do. Somewhat. Though you are five years younger than me, and I left when I was eight."

Chul's face brightened with relief. "I've been looking for you for so long! Ever since I turned eighteen and Father gave me properties to manage and a ship to start building my own fortune, I—"

"Why?" Eli interrupted stiffly. "Why have you been looking for me?"

Chul's joyous energy dwindled when he saw Eli's eyes.

"What do you mean, why? You're my sister."

"Did they not tell you what they did?"

Tam noted that she hadn't referred to their parents directly.

"Mother and Father said that you were in the palace doing important work! But I went to Gondol looking for you with Father when I was fifteen, and I couldn't find—"

"Chul, they sold me."

Both Chul and Yun drew back, disbelief stark on their faces.

Eli leaned forward. "Chul... I understand why they tried to shield you from this, but Father and Mother gave me away to Chin Taejo. I was adopted by the emperor."

"What? Why would they—" Despite being an assistant, Yun was the one to speak.

Evidently Yun and Chul had a very equal footing in their partnership, which was raising several questions for Tam.

"I'm a witch and our parents didn't like that," Eli explained tersely. "I was in the palace for eight years, and then I was abducted and sold. I was in Troivack for a time, and then I..." Eli paused, blinking herself back away from the truth as she finished, "I met Joe Voll. My husband. We have our son together, and I want nothing to do with either of the families that handed me off. So forgive me, but I can't say I'm interested in fostering much of a relationship. I just wanted to ask that you stop approaching me or sending people after me."

Yun paled and Chul appeared too stunned to speak.

"I-I had no idea. That… That can't be right! It can't—"

"That is something you can discuss with your parents," Eli said, cutting Chul off firmly. "And if they answer differently, you can choose what you want to believe, but I'd like to finally be happy in my life."

"I… No, I just… You're my sister! And I couldn't believe you never sent a letter, or visited, and Yun, he… He said you're so incredibly smart, and I'm starting to take over more of Father's ventures—he and Mother are wanting to go on another trip to Daxaria, and—"

Tam held up his hand. "So you only wanted to find her because you thought it was strange she wasn't in contact?"

Chul stopped his rant and nodded.

Yun on the other hand was staring rather coldly at Tam, and the future duke didn't have to guess why.

"I'm alright, Chul," Eli started softly. "And thank you. For… For wanting to find me. I'm well. But to me? You are a stranger. I have my own life now."

"You, in particular, are a stranger," Tam added helpfully with a nod toward Yun.

Eli shot him a brief questioning look, evidently having no idea why he had felt the need to add that comment.

The corners of Yun's eyes twitched while Tam held the gaze firmly.

"If you were sold, does that mean your husband bought you?" Yun asked loudly.

Whatever reaction Tam had been expecting to this accusation, it was not the one Eli gave.

"How… *dare* you," she rasped, her eyes flashing with rage. "You have men follow me down an alleyway, frighten me, worry my husband, make me concerned that our *son* is going to be approached, and you have the *gall* to ask if *he* is the one of a questionable character? Of course he didn't purchase me! He's the only one who has ever given me any measure of freedom!"

"Freedom is not something that should be measured," Yun responded somberly.

Eli's hand banged on the table. She rose and pointed to the door. "Get out."

"Elisara, I'm sorry! Yun, apologize!" Chul ordered though it was obvious he wasn't used to issuing any kind of command to his assistant. He turned desperately back to Eli. "Of course I don't want to scare you or make matters difficult! I'm happy that you've found a life for yourself. I-I was so worried, and wondered what happened, and... And I just wanted to tell you that if you ever wanted to come home, you could! Even if I ask Mother and Father about this and they say they don't want to see you, please tell me! Family is supposed to take care of each other, and—"

"I don't know what family raised you, but that isn't what I learned in the Nam household," Eli bit out coldly. "'You are to be beautiful and useful.' That is what it is to be a Nam child. You had to be impressive and add prestige to the house, because that house did not accept anything less than perfection, and if you deviated? You were sent away."

"Elisara, I'm sorry," Chul choked out, tears gathering in his eyes. "Please—"

"Mom?"

Chul was once again stopped from talking as Luca nervously entered the room.

Turning abruptly, Tam gave his son a reassuring smile and gestured him forward.

Chul fell silent, and Yun's eyes bulged.

"Luca," Eli greeted breathily, while blinking herself back into a calmer state and straightening. "Are your lessons finished for lunch?"

The boy nodded while eyeing Chul and Yun uncertainly. "I... I brought this for you." He produced a sprig of small branches covered with white plum blooms.

Eli stared, then eventually reached out and accepted them. "Thank you, Luca. These are beautiful." Her words were awkward and her movements halting, but the way her eyes gentled... Tam could tell she liked the gift.

Flowers. She likes flowers. Tam smiled at Luca proudly.

The boy, not knowing what precisely he had done to earn such a look, smiled back.

"You wouldn't happen to be giving your mother flowers because your tutor has something to say to us, would you?" Tam asked while ruffling his son's hair.

Luca's jolted with shock. "What? No!" he nearly shouted defensively, which hinted that the boy may not have been entirely honest.

Amazingly, a soft laugh sounded behind Tam. He looked back to see Eli unable to help herself from finding the scene funny.

"I think we should leave now. My apologies again, Mrs. Voll." Chul stood, tears falling from his eyes.

Yun stood as well, though there was a sharper edge to his expression. "It is good to present flowers to your mother, though if the plum tree does not keep its flowers, no fruit will come."

Tam was about to tell the man he could leave with his jaw intact if he begged for forgiveness over the implied chastisement, but Eli's response was significantly better than any vengeance he could've doled out on his own. "Those flowers were a gift from my son, and therefore have more value to me than the seven plums that would've come."

Tam noticed the way Luca's eyes shone at Eli's words, and felt his heart swell, though he did worry that Luca was starting to like the idea of being a family a little too much. But he chose to focus instead on the fact that the annoying assistant was still loitering by the door. Tam rose, making sure to draw himself to his full height, an inch or two above Yun. "I'll see you out."

"There's no need—" Yun began.

"Oh no, I insist. Luca, would you kindly go ask Haewon for lunch, and you"—Tam pointed at Eli—"Get. Back. In. Bed. You still look exhausted."

She opened her mouth to protest but Luca leapt in front of her and grabbed her hand. "You have to! And you'll eat lunch there, too, like you did for breakfast!"

Tam didn't wait to hear Eli's response, just clapped a heavy hand on Yun's shoulder and started pushing him out.

And while he did remove his hand once they reached the courtyard, he still walked the two men out the two front doors, closing them behind himself and making Chul and Yun turn to him.

Chul's eyes were red-rimmed, but Yun was positively simmering with anger.

Tam slipped his hands into his pockets but made a point of still standing as tall as possible. "Is there something else you'd like to say?" he asked Yun.

"That child," Yun started, his voice rasping. "She would've only been eighteen, possibly even younger, when she fell pregnant with him."

Tam's face hardened, and he fought against the urge to clarify that Eli didn't give birth to him.

"Elisara Nam is the eldest daughter of the Nam family. A descendant of a Daxarian duke, and a Zinferan lord who—" Yun's righteous rant was cut off by Tam.

"Oh, the Zinferan lord who was nearly bankrupt before his marriage to Marigold Iones?"

Yun's mouth clamped shut, and Chul's eyes snapped up to Tam. "You… You know of us?"

"I happen to have met His Grace Duke Oscar Harris. Marigold Nam's half brother."

"*Lady* Marigold! And your *wife* is Lady Elisara Nam! And yet she is saddled to a mere scholar?" Yun seethed.

Tam didn't bother trying to defend himself, but he did keep his eyes on Yun, who visibly wrestled his atrocious mood and attitude back. He seemed to have some awareness of the scene he was causing.

The man was quite earnest in his admiration for the Nam family. Elisara in particular…

Yun attempted to sound mild, but the ferocity in his expression still betrayed his true emotions. "Mr. Voll, with just us being here, I will ask you, as I know Elisara would never betray a vow or contract, but *did* you force her to marry you?"

"Hardly. It was our friend's idea, and she was more in favor of our marriage than I was at first." Tam watched the way his words made Yun's ears turn red, and relished the fact that it was, in fact, the truth.

"She is exactly where she wants to be, can do whatever she wants, and I will support her—after she rests, of course. I'm discovering that she tends to work herself past her limits," Tam finished, speaking mostly to himself.

"She could've married someone far more powerful, or even ascended to the throne!" Yun exclaimed.

Tam felt a cool smile curl his lips. "And do you think she wants to be the next empress?"

"Of course she would! She's brilliant!"

"Brilliance doesn't mean she wants power. Which is a foreign concept to you, I'm sure."

"She wants to make the world fair," Yun rumbled.

Tam paused.

For someone Eli had no memory of, she certainly had made an impression…

"She does want things fair. She might even want to become a Daxarian magistrate at some point, but we are still working out the legalities with the coven there."

"Can I help?" Chul asked, stepping forward eagerly. The young man seemed the warmhearted type, and Tam genuinely believed that all he wanted was for his sister to be well taken care of and happy.

"I'll let you know, Lord Chul, but thank you."

Chul nodded firmly in response.

Tam offered his hand, and Chul took it.

It was during the handshake that Tam leaned forward and whispered, "Mind Yun. An ambitious, intelligent assistant can make marionettes of even the best of lords."

Chul swallowed and stared up at Tam. There was something behind his innocent wide-eyed stare that struck the future duke…

"Chul, would you like to have a cup of tea or coffee with me tomorrow? Alone?"

While Yun at least had enough sense not to outwardly object, he did square himself to his employer.

"Yes, I… I would appreciate that very much." Chul's eyes darted nervously toward Yun.

"Wonderful. Do you know Lord Kim's establishment? Lang Tea?"

Chul nodded, his watery gaze determined. "I'll find it."

Tam bobbed his head back. "Then I will meet you there."

Releasing Chul's hand, Tam watched as a discreet carriage pulled forward and stopped in front of them.

A footman jumped down and opened the door for Chul, bowing. Once the young lord had climbed into the vehicle and seated himself, Tam called out, "Yun."

The assistant turned, already frowning at the casual summons.

Tam beckoned him forward and laid a hand on his shoulder. "Disparage my son, or upset my wife again? And you will regret it."

Yun laughed. "My family has worked with the Nam household for generations, yet you think you, a mere scholar—"

Tam leaned forward, and for once he didn't fight his magic, allowing his vision to fill with blackness—something he hadn't known how to do prior to his time in the void—and watched Yun shudder in horror. "I'm a man content with my life right now, but if someone upsets Elisara or my son? That will change. Understood?"

Yun grasped the carriage door with a shaking hand and clumsily clambered in.

Tam watched as the carriage pulled away, allowing his eyes to return to normal. He continued to stand outside the house with pride welling inside his chest.

He had threatened someone. And that wasn't a good thing. But… it meant he had something that was his own to protect. Something his family hadn't given him. Even with Jeong and Bong there—two people he had never met before—he actually felt like he belonged.

And even if Eli remained nothing but an assistant to him, she was in his family.

As if sensing his thoughts, Jeong and Bong stepped through the doors behind Tam.

Jeong was fully dressed in a white-lined dark-green shirt tied at his waist, but he was looking far more serious than usual when, with his thick fingers slightly curling at his sides, his cherub face turned to look after Chul's carriage.

Bong had only put a coat back on after their spar that morning, but his bow staff was in hand as he, too, stared after their surprise guests.

"Anything we need to worry about?" Bong asked pointedly.

"We'll see," Tam answered, his tone uncertain.

The future duke could feel the intensity of strength at his sides from the Ryu brothers, and so he rounded back to re-enter the courtyard with the knowledge that the more he noticed the great people he had surrounding him, the more steady he felt.

He needed to warn Chul about Yun, and then hopefully, the Nam lord and his assistant wouldn't meddle in Eli's life anymore.

But in the meantime? He'd have a lovely afternoon with his friends and family, who made him feel like he had, at long last, found his own home.

CHAPTER 41

TURNING A LEAF

"This is ridiculous."

"That's too bad."

"I don't need to stay in bed for—"

"Don't tire yourself out trying to argue with me." Tam rolled up the sleeves of his white tunic while gazing in the full-length wood rimmed mirror.

"My lord—"

"Tam."

"Fine! Tam! There! Tam, I'm bored! There has to be something I can be doing!"

The future duke turned and stared at Eli in silence.

It was the morning after her brother's visit, and she was sitting upright in their bed, wearing a long, cream-colored satin shirt with faint silvery flowers in its print. Were it not for the fan of hair that stuck straight up and waved about in the air with every movement, she would have looked terribly lovely.

Instead she looked hilariously lovely to Tam.

"Don't you have any hobbies?" he asked with genuine curiosity.

"When would I have had time for hobbies?" Eli demanded.

Tam barely resisted smiling. She had become completely unguarded in showing her unbridled irritations with him, and it made him far happier than it should've.

"Well, it sounds like now's a great opportunity to find some." Tam couldn't resist smiling at her exasperation. "And don't go hovering around Luca during his lessons. He'll figure out how to pay attention once they start giving him tests. The tutor will communicate with us if he thinks we need to intervene."

Eli's shoulders slumped forward. "My lo— Tam. Tam, we need to figure out how you can induce another bout of madness for Lord Guk by the blossom festival. If you are around him too obviously, someone could suspect you."

Tam's gaze drifted up to the ceiling. "For the blossom festival, Bong will charm the serving staff and lace Lord Guk's personal stock of mead. I've already decided to switch to a different drug from the first one to make it harder to trace. This one will involve two doses. So even if others around Lord Guk drink the mead, they won't have any side effects. Neither will he until he gets pricked with the other drug."

"What drugs are these...?" Eli wondered while blinking intently, a frown on her face.

"The last time, we used a basic mushroom-infused oil; this time we are using a hearty nutmeg mead. Everyone else will feel like they are in great moods, but when Jeong or Bong shakes hands with Lord Guk, they will transfer marij to him both topically and with a prick to ensure he gets the full effects."

"Marij? Isn't that a common pipe tobacco known for its relaxation properties?"

Tam cleared his throat sheepishly. "Yes, but my mother has managed to see that its more potent oils are harvested. When mixed with nutmeg, it will heighten the hallucinogenic effects while also making Guk less prone to violence. I brought some with me for this trip."

"Won't people be suspicious about Bong and Jeong, given that they were around for the other poisonings? Also, why would your mother do such a thing to pipe tobacco?"

"Well, they... We own brothels, like I've mentioned before. She was just trying to figure out what was being sold to her patrons." Tam coughed innocuously. "And you're right. People might be suspicious of the brothers. Which is why there won't be a big second incident. Only a large third. In the meantime I'll have to break into Lord Guk's home and tamper with his space a bit to help the gossip among the servants for smaller outbursts from him."

Eli rose hastily. "You're breaking into his house? That's far too dangerous to do by yourself!"

Tam shrugged. "I've done it before in significantly better-guarded places."

Eli scoffed. "Is there anything you can't do?"

"Be socially adept?"

She snorted, looking reluctantly amused.

Seeing this, Tam decided to extend his list. "Command a room? Make moving speeches? Eat while keeping my back straight? Be ambitious?"

"You don't think you're ambitious?" This time Eli's laugh wasn't humored so much as it was skeptical.

Tam blinked at her seriously. "I'm doing all this because it's expected of me. Not because I really want to."

Eli's expression turned enigmatic. "What ambitions of your own *do* you have?"

Tam lowered his gaze in thought. "I'm working that out for myself, but the first thing that comes to mind is a peaceful paperwork position, a house where every wall is a bookshelf… A life with more time for my own family in a space of my own."

He hesitated at the words *my own family*, but Eli caught on quickly enough, and blushed.

Tam raised his eyes to hers. "Are there any personal ambitions of your own? Aside from becoming a Daxarian magistrate so that you can make the world a better, fairer place?" Tam folded his arms as he asked the question, his head tilted as he waited to hear her answer.

"I…" Eli trailed off. There was that same hardness in her features that, while not exactly illuminating as to her emotions, did show Tam that to her it was not an easy question.

Her silence and the distress in her eyes prompted Tam to interject carefully, "It's alright. You don't need to tell me."

He turned to the door, already shifting his attention to his tasks for the day, but Eli stepped in front of him, the back hairs on her head fluttering like a peacock's tail feathers, almost making Tam laugh… But given her determined gaze, he could tell that was a bad idea. "When are you planning on breaking into Lord Guk's house?"

"Tonight."

"What? That's too soon!"

Tam reached around her for the door. "We lost too much time with my absence."

"I'll go with you."

Tam's eyes cut to her. "Do *you* have a lot of experience breaking into heavily guarded homes?"

"No, but I could be waiting with the carriage to take you away. Jeong and Bong will be keeping Lord Guk busy tonight, correct?"

Tam let out a breath of agitation. "You have worked enough to earn some time off. I'll—"

"My *lord*," Eli enunciated through her teeth. "I will rest for today, but I will be doing this with you as your assistant tonight."

There was no point in arguing anymore or he'd be late for his appointment to meet with her brother. And given that he had not disclosed he was doing such a thing, he couldn't quite explain to her the importance of his timely departure.

"Fine. But if there is any trouble, you will leave immediately. That's an order for my *assistant*, understood?"

Eli nodded and offered her hand to him as though to shake in agreement.

Chortling, Tam took her warm hand in his own, and noted that while her palms were small, her fingers were long...

He felt that damnable urge to hold her, kiss her... Gods. Everything. He wanted to do everything with her, and she must have seen it in his eyes because she swallowed and stepped aside so he could leave.

"I hope you have a successful day studying."

"Thank you," Tam returned, sounding a bit more gruff than he meant to.

Luckily, Eli didn't seem to notice, as she was focused on averting her gaze and fidgeting.

Giving his head a shake, Tam managed to return his thoughts to the matter of Chul Nam's assistant, Yun, who was more than a little obsessed with Eli. This shift of focus made picking up his feet that felt chained with weights a little easier—though Tam didn't have the gall to lie to himself and say he wasn't sorely tempted to linger a little longer in the room with Eli, and her hilarious hair.

Lang Tea, as it turned out, was busy every moment of every day.

With its serving staff trained better than any other in Junya on the proper way to prepare the wide selection of teas they offered, and the bright, friendly atmosphere, it wasn't hard to understand why. Fortunately, Tam had been wise enough to book a private room for his discussion with Eli's brother.

For their meeting, Tam had made a point of dressing simply in Daxarian clothes.

While he wouldn't have made the choice if he were meeting with Yun as well, when he considered the gentle nature of Chul Nam, he had a hunch he'd need to appear more approachable and harmless.

One's wardrobe is like their armor. It will subtly set the tone for your daily battles, his mother had always counseled. And while his sister, Kat, had made a point of ignoring the advice, Tam had leaned into it.

"Name?" a pretty teahouse server asked, pulling Tam's mind to the present as he stepped up to the glowing oak podium that had previously been blocked from view by a couple that were waiting to be seated.

"Voll. Joe Voll. I'm meeting a friend."

The hostess peered at the scroll in front of her, then nodded. "Your guest is already here. Please follow me."

Tam smiled politely and walked with her to the stairs.

One extravagant detail of the building that Tam had not noticed during his first visit with Lord Kim (as it had been nighttime when he had been there), was the slanted ceiling that climbed to a paneled point and was made of glass. It flooded the space with sunlight that cast the plants on the walls in a magical glow and illuminated the beautiful swirling steam from the various tea pots and cups, and the tasty snacks on the tables before the patrons.

Tam marveled at the sight, and found himself once again thinking that he needed to make a point of bringing Eli there. He also found himself feeling a twinge of envy over having a sturdy roof made of glass. It would make stargazing during winter far more comfortable...

"Here you are, Mr. Voll." The hostess gestured Tam toward a sliding door. Standing just outside this door was Yun, looking wildly unhappy.

"You're late to meet Lord Nam," the assistant informed him curtly.

"I was delayed while tending to my wife," Tam returned breezily.

Yun's eyes narrowed fractionally. Apparently, the assistant was trying to stay in better control of his emotions this time.

Ah well. Tam simply took pleasure in being able to refer to Eli as his wife. Even if it was pretend.

Ignoring Yun, Tam proceeded into the room. Chul looked up from the table, already set with a teapot and matching cups.

"Mr. Voll! I hope you don't mind, but I ordered us some citrus ginger tea."

Tam noted that the Zinferan nobleman was wearing a bright-plum silk shirt with glittering gold designs. This color suited the young man better than the garish red outfits he had worn before, although it still seemed far too ostentatious for his nature.

"Not at all. My apologies for being late." Tam smartly closed the sliding door with its white paper, catching one last look at the disgruntled expression Yun wore as he loitered outside.

"I overheard you say you were tending to my sister. Is she alright?"

"Oh yes. If you recall, I said yesterday that she has a tendency to overwork herself. I was making sure she didn't start straining herself today. She's stubborn, you see."

"Both our parents are stubborn," Chul informed Tam with a kind smile. "She comes by it honestly. Though her work ethic must come from our grandfather, the previous Lord Nam." Chul lowered his eyes, and Tam didn't need to ask to know that the man must have recently passed.

"Did Yun serve your father before serving you?" Tam asked while pouring his own tea. He didn't want to intrude into Eli's history more than he already had.

"No, his father serves my father. But he's been studying to become my assistant since before I was born."

Tam nodded without revealing his thoughts. "I see."

"Yesterday, you more or less said I should be careful of Yun. I-I know I'm not as dignified as he is, or, or as well spoken, but I am doing the best I can to become a worthy successor of my family!" Chul's hands had curled into fists on his lap, as though he were fighting off the urge to fidget.

"Eli fidgets nonstop," Tam blurted without thinking.

Chul blinked and sat up straighter. "R-really? I was punished all the time for doing it." He smiled, his eyes fixed on the teacup in front of him. "I guess we are a little alike even without us growing up together."

"I'm sorry that your visit with her did not go as planned," Tam said kindly.

Chul swallowed with difficulty. "It's strange. She's absolutely right about how we don't know each, but I've always felt like I've missed her. I suppose I'm odd like that, but... I'd do anything for her. I just hope she is happy."

Tam gave him a sympathetic smile. "I'll do my best to make it so."

Chul nodded then sniffed. He was obviously about to start crying again, as he had the day before. He reached for his teacup, but Tam noticed the tremor in his hands.

"Is there any other reason you would want Eli to return with you to your parents' home?"

Chul blushed tellingly.

Despite having asked on a whim, Tam straightened in alarm. Perhaps the young man was craftier than he let on.

"There is... a small reason, but of course, whatever she wants, I have no problems abiding by. I—I won't have children of my own. So I just wanted her to know her eldest son—Luca?—can inherit the title if he'd like."

Whatever Tam had been expecting, it wasn't that.

And then it all came together.

Yun wanted Eli and the title that would come with her. No wonder he had been after her so aggressively.

But now, Tam and their supposed offspring stood in the way.

A sense of foreboding crept into Tam, and so perhaps he didn't exercise quite as much tact as he should have when he asked, "Why can't you have children?"

Chul ducked his head. "My... My preferences don't align with the gender that would be conducive to—"

He was gay.

Tam blinked.

"O-of course I have two other sisters, so it really is not in any way meant to pressure Elisara, but she deserves to have the first say. I haven't told my parents about this, and I didn't want to say anything yet, but I've always wanted to talk to Elisara, and just felt as though she might understand."

Letting out a breath, Tam realized that he couldn't keep Eli from having this information. He resolved to tell her everything that night.

Though there was still one thing he needed to do.

"Chul, I will communicate with my wife about what you have told me, and I wish you nothing but the best. I bear absolutely no ill will to you... but that said, there is one thing I will recommend you do."

"What's that?" Chul looked at Tam hopefully, his eyes still shining.

If only he knew the weight of Tam's next words.

"You need to fire your assistant."

Chul's jaw dropped, and Tam reached for his own cup. "I think he might be an even bigger antagonist than you realize."

"His family has served ours for three generations! I can't just turn my back on that kind of loyalty."

"If he were truly interested in maintaining loyalty, he wouldn't push you around. He's using you. And I think he wanted to use Eli, too, if he knows your secret about passing along the title to her son."

"No, that can't... It can't be!"

"Are you really going to say you haven't noticed how obsessed he is with her?"

"I... I... He just wants what's best—"

"Chul, I'm not trying to make things difficult, and by all means, think about this for yourself, but... I will say this, because I have a hunch: Ask Yun's father directly if he knew anything about Eli getting sent to the royal family. Hell, Yun might know the details already."

The young man's lips trembled, but he didn't look angry... at first.

"If they did? Then I won't only fire Yun," Chul started quietly. "I will drive their family into the ground, then salt the earth."

Tam spilled some of his tea. The whispery threat from Chul startled him soundly. But when the words fully registered, Tam couldn't help but smile in respect.

Perhaps Eli's brother had secret sides to himself he didn't like showing people... just as she did.

"If my guess turns out to be true, Chul? You let me know, and you best believe I will be helping you however I can."

CHAPTER 42

A CATASTROPHIC CORNERING

Tam clapped a hand on Chul's shoulder as they exited their private tearoom. "Thank you for agreeing to meet with me," he said warmly.

The young man smiled up at him. "Thank you for your wisdom, Mr. Voll."

Yun was just starting to push off from the wall. The fact that he was taking his time to do so gave the action a palpable attitude which spoke volumes of the hierarchy between Chul and Yun.

Tam's steady gaze met with Chul's. If the young man had no idea when he was being slighted, he had no hope.

But Tam watched as he bristled...

He did know.

So all that was left was for him to gain the confidence to stop Yun's disrespectful, overbearing behavior.

I wish I could do more for him, but I have my hands full as it is with—

"Mr. Voll! My goodness! I haven't seen you in days. How have you been?"

Tam's stomach somersaulted as he turned around to see none other than Lord Kim striding along with three attendants.

"Lord Kim." Tam bowed. "Apologies for keeping away. I had some business I had to attend to."

As if on cue, Tam felt his magic flush through his being… And it was strong.

Almost as strong as it had been when he'd last disappeared.

Tam swallowed with difficulty. He hoped none of the black, smoky tendrils were visible yet. He needed to get out. He needed to go home… He wanted to be home.

His magic tugged harder.

"Of course, I know you're a busy man, Mr. Voll, what with your family matters and research." Lord Kim smiled good-naturedly then glanced at Chul. He raised an eyebrow at the brightness of his clothes. "And you are…?"

"Right. Sorry." Tam blinked rapidly, trying to fight off the power. "This is Lord Chul Nam from Bani."

Chul inclined himself politely, but Lord Kim paused, and a coolness Tam had never seen before entered his gaze. "Ah yes. I've heard of the Nam family."

Tam's mind raced.

Even though Chul had claimed that not many people knew he was gay, was it possible Lord Kim knew? The followers of the religion of Acker did not take kindly to those who preferred the same gender.

"How is it you two know each other?" Lord Kim's next question sounded more like an accusation, and Tam knew he'd have to answer carefully.

"Lord Chul and I met the other night at an event, and I'm afraid I was a bit rude, so I invited him out to your fine teahouse to apologize."

Tam could see Yun narrow his gaze.

Lord Kim didn't say anything to Chul, but he did clear his throat and lean forward to Tam. "Would you be able to spare a moment for a private discussion?"

"Of course! I hope you don't mind, Lord Chul." Tam felt relief wash over him, which in turn helped his magic ebb back.

"Not at all," Chul smiled uncertainly at Lord Kim, then Tam. "Will it be alright if I call on you and my sister again?"

Tam felt his heart drop.

Evidently, Chul had forgotten the bit about Eli not wanting to be associated with the Nam family, and *also* was blissfully unaware that he had just risked Tam, Eli, and the Ryu brothers' entire objective in Junya.

"Have a good day, Lord Chul," was all Tam could say as his magic once again pounded in his ears, making him dizzy with the effort it took to resist it.

The young lord cast one last bewildered look at Tam, then made his way down with Yun following—though the assistant paused and leaned in to whisper to Tam, "Don't think I have forgotten about your *magic* trick yesterday. We aren't finished, you and I."

Tam's right hand trembled as he struggled against his power. "Trust me, Yun. You don't want me to finish you."

The assistant hesitated for only a moment before giving a scoff and heading down the stairs after his master.

Once they were gone, Tam turned back to Lord Kim. He had to salvage his relationship with the man, but there was nothing he could do until he learned what it was about the Nam family that had so clearly upset him.

Lord Kim gestured back down the balcony. "Shall we?"

Tam inclined himself and followed Lord Kim at a respectful distance.

Lord Kim had chosen to wear a tasteful pale-green satin coat tied across his wide stomach, and linen pants that looked airy and comfortable… And yet, as one might expect of a lord, his presence filled the space.

Tam tried to focus his thoughts on the conversation he was about to have, but the power welling up in his chest was making it hard to breathe.

I want to be here. I want to be here. I want to be here.

He repeated the mantra over and over, trying to convince himself. But he couldn't help wondering why it felt like his abilities had grown stronger. Had his time in the void increased their potency? But why?

Lord Kim showed him into a discreet corner room that turned out to be not another tearoom, but an office. The two walls across from the door were lined with windows overlooking the streets of Junya and its tiled rooftops. The window ledges were mostly free from clutter save for a jade tree in one corner and a stack of books in the other. The room was warm and welcoming, with two comfortable armchairs in front of a large oak desk. A matching chair with emerald cushions sat behind it.

It struck Tam as odd that the furniture was all Daxarian. Another reminder that Lord Kim was a follower of the Acker religion; the woman who started it had been, in fact, Daxarian.

"Mr. Voll, please take a seat."

The door closed behind Tam, and he noted that the attendants stayed outside.

Stiffly, he made his way over to one of the chairs, and the moment his backside grazed the cushion Lord Kim started to talk.

"I was under the impression that your wife was from Haeson."

Venturing a careful guess, Tam reasoned that a portion of the truth would serve him well.

"She is, but her brother resides in Bani."

"Which is where Lord Geun Nam lives with his wife, son, and two other daughters. So there is something not adding up to these stories." Lord Kim's eyes were cutting, and if Tam truly were a powerless scholar, he'd probably start to feel more than a little concerned.

As it was, he hung his head with a sigh. "My wife had… a bad history with the Nams. She has not been considered part of their family since she was eight." Tam watched as the lord frowned. It had been a gamble that Eli's past wasn't widely known. "Might I ask why you seemed… concerned about Lord Chul's presence?"

Tam hoped to the Gods it wasn't about Chul's romantic preferences.

"The family is rotten," Lord Kim responded bluntly. "They currently support the concubine Soo Hebin and all of her duplicitous dealings, which include human trafficking." The Zinferan nobleman shook his head, missing Tam's shocked reaction. It wasn't often that nobility spoke openly about such things. "All the Nam family cares about is being seen as the most lavish and highly elevated."

Overcoming his surprise, Tam bobbed his head. "My wife did mention a few things like that… She doesn't want much to do with her former family. However, her brother, Lord Chul, was worried about her, and sought her out."

"Don't trust him," Lord Kim warned. "Your wife is wise to want to avoid them."

Tam was relieved to see that the Zinferan looked like he believed him. "I understand. I only wished to alleviate Lord Chul's concerns without having his presence upset my wife."

Lord Kim shot Tam a kind half smile. "You're a good man, Mr. Voll." He leaned forward and pressed the tips of his fingers together, elbows resting on his desk. "I take it the family you were referring to that lived in Haeson is the one that adopted your wife... Ellie? Was it?"

"Yes." Tam nodded without clarifying her family background.

"Well, I am sorry to hear she had such a troublesome past. I must confess, I had heard whispers about the Nam family having an elder daughter who was adopted by our emperor, but that must have been a rumor they made up to seem more prestigious," Lord Kim replied. "There is nothing but greed and toxic pride in their hearts."

Tam lowered his head without offering any more elaboration.

"Was it because she was a witch?"

Tam's gaze snapped back up. "I've never seen her use any kind of magic," he insisted quite honestly.

The lord tilted his head back and forth thoughtfully. "That was the rumor back then. That the eldest Nam daughter was a witch, and her powers were dangerous, so the emperor took her in to use as a weapon. I happen to have friends in court who saw her there, though not often. I'm given to understand that the emperor's mother took a liking to her."

Tam's heart was slowly increasing its pace.

"If your wife *is* who she says she is, and the rumors are true, then it must be quite a story of how she moved from the Nam family, to the palace, to allegedly another family in Haeson. Then somehow found you in Daxaria. Though at least she is alive and well. Only four or five princes and princesses remain in the palace last I heard. The others have either disappeared or married into other families under Soo Hebin's influence."

Tam remained silent, but inwardly he cursed Chul's slip of the tongue.

Then again, it had been his own fault for having tea with him at Lang Tea in the first place.

"So tell me. Has Princess Elisara returned to Zinfera to claim her place as a successor to the throne?"

Tam's magic stuttered in his head as he himself wavered on how best to handle this spiraling situation. If he revealed his true identity, then they were stuck with everyone's eyes on them. If he tried to lie more, there was a chance Lord Kim could order an investigation.

"You aren't simply a scholar, are you?" The nobleman's voice was soft.

"*If* my wife is who you *think* she is, then I would be inclined to inform you that she truly did only return here due to circumstances outside of her control, and she wishes to leave as soon as possible," Tam ventured carefully, hoping to glean some insight from Lord Kim's reaction.

Gods… My mother was always the one who was great at handling these confrontations. My strengths were always to hide in the shadows and observe… What would she do now? Hell. What would my father do to get out of this? "I am here to study, and I will protect my family."

"That is an interesting response. Now I have another question… I recently heard whisperings that the devil has landed here on our Zinferan shores. Stories have spread from not only pirates but also a reputable crew belonging to Daxaria. It's interesting, given how the description of such a man aligns so well with none other than yourself. I didn't think much on it, but if you are connected with the Nam family… well. It only makes sense."

Tam's magic felt like it was swelling under his skin until it ached as he watched Lord Kim stand.

"I'd say sorry, Mr. Voll, but I don't think the *devil* gives two whits about an apology, and nor does he deserve one." The fire in the Zinferan's eyes left Tam with little imagination as to how wrong everything was about to go, given the assumption Lord Kim had just leapt to.

Tam stood. Lord Kim halted, eyeing him warily as he reached behind himself. Tam wasn't certain if it was for a weapon or something else, but he could tell blackness was consuming his vision, he knew he was barely hanging on to his power, and it didn't help when Lord Kim drew out a dagger.

"There is the true you. I see the princess has recruited some dark forces to seek her revenge and claim the throne for herself." Lord Kim's voice was filled with horror, and while inwardly Tam recoiled from it, he knew he had no choice.

He lunged for the lord across the desk right as Lord Kim thrust the blade forward to defend himself. But Tam had been trained, and he was faster. He caught the hand that wielded the dagger, and with his other hand clasping Lord Kim's shoulder, he felt darkness consume them both in a wispy black, silvery rush that stole them both from the world.

CHAPTER 43

THE TRICK TO TRAVEL

Tam landed in the void with so much force that his ankles jarred painfully, but he was still clasping Lord Kim's wrists, and the Zinferan still held the knife.

"Wh—What did you do? Where am I?" The fear and panic in Lord Kim's voice rang out into the blackness.

Underneath his touch, Tam could feel the man start to tremble. Sighing, he released Lord Kim and watched as the Zinferan collapsed onto his knees, the dagger falling to the ground. As soon as he collected himself, Lord Kim started murmuring prayers to the Goddess.

"Prayers don't work. Trust me. I've tried."

Tam turned around and took a few steps away from the nobleman. Then he thought better of turning his back on the Zinferan. In the void, he might not hear an attack from behind.

Unsurprisingly, Lord Kim's fervent prayers continued.

"I'm a witch, not the devil," Tam tried again, not bothering to disguise his growing exasperation. "And if you knock that off, I can try to figure out how I can get you and me out of here."

Lord Kim only cracked an eye to quickly glance at Tam, then continued praying.

Great. Now I need to decide I don't want to be here. But wait… If I appear back in the office with him, he's going to have me arrested. Shit. My only shot at resolving this, is if I tell him more of the truth… Tam groaned inwardly. Revealing more of the truth was going to be problematic.

At the very least this problematic turn of events was distracting him from his anxiety about being back in the void.

"Lord Kim, I'm really not the devil. But it *is* true I lied about my identity."

The nobleman finally stopped muttering and opened his eyes, already looking like he was preparing himself to attack Tam with his bare hands.

Tam sidled a little bit closer, mostly to make sure the Zinferan didn't lunge for the knife that glinted on the ground between them.

"Well? Who are you going to claim to be this time, Satan?" Lord Kim snarled.

Tam sent a silent prayer of his own up to the Goddess, that he wasn't making a massive mistake.

"My name is Lord Tamlin Ashowan. Son of Duke Finlay Ashowan. The house witch. From Daxaria. My mother, Duchess Annika Ashowan, was part Troivackian, hence my black hair and dark eyes."

The words stunned Lord Kim into silence.

Tam held his gaze and straightened his shoulders. "I'm here to investigate the state of the Zinferan court from a distance. Eli, who is posing as my wife, came with me because she knows this kingdom. She's currently working for my family while she tries to obtain Daxarian citizenship."

Lord Kim sank back onto his haunches as his expression grew even more gobsmacked.

"Then we received information regarding Lord Guk and Lord Yangban's work with human trafficking and how the concubine Soo Hebin is working to build her own power to place her son on the throne. We decided to tip the scales a little out of their favor."

"You…" Lord Kim managed, his thoughts racing behind his eyes. "You made me approach you. You knew I was opposed to Her Highness Soo Hebin."

"Yes."

"You wanted to work with me, even though your family openly disapproves of those of the Acker religion," the Zinferan continued.

"It's a ridiculous religion, born to feed hatred that comes from some sort of personal pain. The Goddess does not hate any creation she makes, and if you think she isn't aware of who they love…? Then you are insulting their divinity." Tam could see the way his words once again incited rage in Lord Kim. "However, aside from your terrible beliefs pertaining to those who don't have straightforward sexual preferences… You are not an evil person. There is bad in all of us, but it's rare that that is all we are."

Lord Kim glared at Tam. "I suppose you feel you can lecture me when you have the upper hand. Where are we?" he asked scathingly.

Tam released an agitated breath. "My ability makes me able to move to a place of everything, and nothing. It's very difficult to find my way out, and I've never been able to bring anyone else in with me before."

"You are death."

"I'm not—" Tam paused.

Was that why the carriage driver had come? *Was* he like him…? Wasn't the carriage driver Death?

"I don't know. I've avoided wielding my magic because I don't know how to use it, or the nuances of it."

Tam wearily sat down cross-legged while continuing his explanation. "Eli—or Elisara, as you know her—didn't want to come back to Zinfera. She only did it because the Daxarian king promised her citizenship in exchange for her help. She does not want anything to do with the Zinferan throne. All we are doing is investigating and trying to stop Soo Hebin from gaining supporters to name Junya the capital where more nobility are neutral in their loyalty, but would benefit in the increased value to their businesses, land worth, and investments when the palace would move. Those nobles would be in her pocket if she succeeds doing this and those nobles would offer their resources. We're trying to make it so her only means of power is through human trafficking, which as everyone knows is an incredibly high-risk venture, and in no way secures the throne for her son. You just happened to try to stab me, and so my magic brought us here."

Lord Kim arched an eyebrow, his expression softening fractionally. "What about the boy?"

Tam winced. He'd hoped this question wouldn't come up. "He *is* my son."

"Now I know you lie," Lord Kim scoffed coldly. "If he is your son, then you are not Lord Tamlin Ashowan."

"Aaah." Tam reached up and rubbed his face. "No, no. He is. I found out I had an illegitimate son on my voyage here, after he stowed away on the boat in order to meet me. Prior to this journey, I had no idea he existed, and I'm doing my best to navigate this new complication."

Lord Kim was once again so appalled that he was shocked into momentary quiet. "I doubt the great Ashowan household would ever have something as scandalous—"

"Wow. First time in my life I've been considered the scandalous one in my family." Tam let out a dry laugh.

"If everything you've said is true… What now?"

Tam leaned back and rested his palms against a solid surface that felt like cool glass, but really just appeared as more darkness. "Well, I can start trying to get us back out of this place—which I'd like to. Last time this happened, I was stuck in here for three days."

"That's why you were gone for so long from the library!"

"Yes. And I'd like to get back sooner than that, but I need to know what you will do once we return." Tam's dark eyes rested somberly on the nobleman.

Lord Kim tilted his head, and Tam watched as his chubby index finger occasionally tapped his thigh as he navigated his thoughts. "What did you mean when you said this is a place of everything and nothing?" he finally asked, succeeding in catching Tam off guard.

The future duke opened his mouth, then closed it.

He had the sense it was a bad idea to mention his encounter with Death's carriage driver.

"How I'm understanding it is—if I focus? I can feel, hear, and smell my surroundings. But there are spots in here where there is nothing."

"Like the Grove of Sorrows?"

Tam could tell by his leading tone that the Zinferan nobleman was once again trying to argue that he was Death.

"Apparently the Grove of Sorrows is worse."

Lord Kim frowned. "How do you know such a thing? Have you also met with the Gods? I thought it was only your father who briefly spoke to the Goddess—"

Tam looked toward where the sky theoretically should have been. "If you think everything about my family is flawlessly transparent and reported to everyone, you concern me."

Lord Kim had to concede the point. "With your magic, can you possess people?"

"I don't believe so."

"Can you banish people to this place?"

"Not sure. You're the first to come here, remember?"

"Peculiar... As someone who, lord or not, has a scholar's mind, I'd expect you to have more of an investigative spirit for such a gift."

Tam felt an old wound in his heart resurface. "You were scared when you first got here, right? Well, imagine being a child and being stuck in a void where you had no body. And there was no sense of time. You simply ceased to exist."

Something remarkably similar to compassion welled up in Lord Kim's eyes. "That sounds frightening."

"It was. I didn't want to learn more about it until recently, and to be quite honest, there hasn't been a great deal of time to think about it."

"Does time move slower here...?" Lord Kim peered around curiously.

"It feels that way. Or as if it's a space that occasionally halts time."

Lord Kim carefully lifted the right corner of his mouth. "Well... Lord Tamlin Ashowan. If that is the case, then the answer to your earlier question on what I will do once you free me from this place is this: Let us explore your magic in here as much as possible, and once we return to the land of the living, I will try to help you stop Lord Yangban from gaining any more power, and I will keep your secret. *But*... I want you to promise me you will not grant any favors to the Nam family. Not ever."

"Elisara better be excluded from that detail," Tam warned, his expression turning cold.

Lord Kim balked only for a moment at the shift in the future duke's disposition, but then smiled genuinely. "Ah. So it wasn't entirely a lie that you care deeply for Elisara."

Tam said nothing for a moment. "I do not believe Chul Nam is like his father," he finally replied, "but I will concede that I think his assistant is corrupt."

"Like attracts like, Lord Tamlin. But if the scenario is as you evidently believe, where that boy is pushed around by a bully? You cannot be the one to reach out a hand to save him. Lord Chul must learn to save himself or you will get dragged under. Lord Chul already has a wealth of support, why should he need yours?"

"If he does start trying to free himself, will I be able to help without you considering it a nullification of this agreement?" Tam questioned instead of commenting on Lord Kim's observation.

Lord Kim considered this proposal carefully before responding. "Possibly. He is well connected enough, Lord Tam. Do not give him any tie to you, and if you think you are doing it for Princess Elisara, you are mistaken. It was a blessing she was freed from that family. You keep her as far from them as possible."

Tam wanted to object more, but Lord Kim held out a hand, letting him know this was the deal. And he had no choice but to take it.

The future duke recognized that he might be gaining an ally, but he was also gaining a very risky liability. Still, once they left Zinfera, it wouldn't really matter.

He shook the man's hand.

"Wonderful, now—" Lord Kim began.

"Before we get started, I do just want to confirm that you are aware that if Soo Hebin finds out about any interference on your end, you could find yourself charged with treason."

"For what? Helping exterminate the vermin infestation of human traffickers we have?" Lord Kim wondered mildly. "If we cripple Lord Yangban, she will claim to know nothing about it."

Tam chuckled. There wasn't anything else he could say on the matter, he supposed.

"Alright, Lord Tamlin, can you transform into objects, or is this the middle ground to that end?"

"I doubt that."

"What do you feel or smell right now?"

At first Tam was going to dismiss this question, but he had to admit it wasn't a bad idea to learn more about his abilities.

So he closed his eyes and reached out with his senses.

At first there was nothing, but as he waited, a faint clamor started wafting closer, as though he were still in Lord Kim's office with the bustling streets of Junya just outside... What did he smell?

Varnish? Fresh paper?

He repeated his findings to the Zinferan nobleman, who nodded excitedly. "We must be in a pocket of magic within my office still!"

Tam pondered this discovery. The last time he had been in the void, he had wandered around a lot; was that why he wound up somewhere else? Or... Could he *choose* where he reappeared?

A buzzing sensation sprang to life in Tam's chest, and it started to spread.

"You know, if you ever do happen to find the devil, this would be a marvelous way of holding him hostage, unless of course he is more powerful than yo—"

"Why would you say that?" Tam demanded abruptly, his thoughts snapping to the present in alarm.

Lord Kim didn't react to Tam's disturbance. "The devil's power is to extort fear from people. If he is trapped in a place *without* people, then really, it is the perfect prison. One that no one other than the Gods or yourself could've made."

Tam felt a droplet of cold sweat run down his back as Luca's smiling face flashed through his mind. Then he thought of the mysterious, magical red thread that had dragged him out of the void last time. At one point he had had a similar thought about his void being a prison, and it had struck a chord in him. Now it made him feel sick. Unless perhaps it was used on the first witch...

"I have another idea," he said gruffly, not wanting to dwell on the dangerous possibilities of such a stressful future. "Stand."

The Zinferan nobleman obeyed.

Tam reached out and grasped Lord Kim's arm. He closed his eyes, but this time, instead of searching for what was around him and what he could feel, hear, or smell, he thought of his and Eli's room back at the house.

He thought of the bed with the fluffed duvet, the warm color of the wooden floors, the papered sliding door, the dresser with Eli's new bangles. He remembered the polish Haewon used when dusting the ledges and bed frame, which gave the room its lemon scent...

Then Tam allowed all his desire to return to that room flood his being. How, more than absolutely anything, he wanted to be back in the house with Eli and Luca…

It was just after lunchtime, and it was usually when Luca's tutor had him meditating out in the plum tree, so the inside of the house was quiet. Maybe Eli was taking a nap.

Unlike when Tam's magic leaked out in black shadows and silvery wisps, a different sensation bore down on him. It was the feeling of being weightless as he whipped through nothing and yet not nothing. He heard sounds blare, he could feel all kinds of things bump into him, he even thought he felt sunshine on his face at one point, but that driving flow of magic that he allowed to rush from himself pulled him forward as he clung to the image of the room until…

"Tam? W-what just… Who's that?"

Tam's eyes snapped open, and he found himself standing exactly where he had imagined he would, still holding Lord Kim's arm.

He turned, dumbfounded, to see Eli sit up in bed with her eyes bulging out of her head.

Tam noted that there were fading, silvery wisps around him that eventually disappeared into the air…

He swallowed.

He'd done it.

His magic allowed him to travel to in-between places. To a nothing place. To an everything place… and to places in the land of the living.

Opening his mouth, his head spinning, Tam looked at Eli and said, "Your hair's sticking up at the back of your head."

CHAPTER 44

AN ENCOURAGING EVOLUTION

Tam was seated on the bed beside Eli, who had been woken from her nap by Tam's magical reappearance.

With Lord Kim.

Who was still in their room.

Pacing.

And talking to himself.

"Remarkable. One with all things, and yet nothing... in between life and time itself. Death but not... A new god? No, no, probably not..."

"Er... Lord Kim. I greatly appreciate that you have agreed not to alert anyone to our true identities, but—"

"The implications of such a power. What distance? How often?"

Tam stopped trying to draw the man back to the present. He felt a deep exhaustion settle in him following his brief explanation to Eli of what had happened between himself and Lord Kim and their deal.

He lowered his forehead to his hand and sluggishly wondered if traveling such a distance used up more of his magic. He'd heard Kat could strain her own power to the point of exhaustion after days of rigorous activity and no sleep. Admittedly Lord Kim's questions were exceptionally insightful, but he simply did not have the energy to answer or investigate them, and furthermore…

Did he have to ask them in the bedroom right then?

"Lord Kim." Eli's voice was sharp and imperious.

It took even Tam aback, who with heavy eyes forced himself to look at her. "You are in our room, and my husb—my lord would like to sleep."

That certainly succeeded in making Lord Kim halt.

Then he seemed to suddenly remember Eli's history. He blinked several times and then swept into a bow.

"Your Highness! Welcome back—"

"I am not a princess anymore. I am an assistant to the Ashowan duchy. Please call me Eli."

"You *are* a princess! No matter what others say, you— Did you say this room was for the both of you?" Lord Kim's reverent tone fell flat once he'd interrupted himself.

Tam inwardly groaned. He could tell where this was going, and he had the unpleasant prediction that he was going to have to act aggressively to get the man off the premises.

"It is. We are playing husband and wife for safety and must have even the servants believe it."

"That is not proper! Surely, Lord Tam, you sleep on the balcony, or behind a screen or—"

"I *asked him* to sleep in the bed with me." The sharp edge in Eli's voice carried a note of warning.

Yet another side of her Tam hadn't ever seen before.

Even so, Lord Kim managed to recover. "Regardless, Your Highness, this is not dignified for any young woman, let alone someone who, in my opinion, should be one of the strongest candidates to take the throne!"

"I'm not taking anything. And I am not a princess. I will not tell you again." The force behind her words succeeded in forcing back Lord Kim.

Tam slowly sat up straight again.

"Lord Tam, might I speak with you outside—"

"His lordship is exhausted," Eli broke in. "No doubt from magic use. He will rest and then seek you out for a meeting. I will now escort you out," she commanded smoothly while gesturing toward the door.

It didn't matter that she was in a robe and the back of her hair still fluttered in the wind. She was a formidable force to be reckoned with.

Tam had to rub his mouth to hide his smile.

Lord Kim openly struggled not to say anything, but after Eli continued to stare him down with no signs of budging, he let out a grunting breath through his nose.

"Until next time, Lord Tam." Lord Kim bowed and exited, Eli following closely behind.

Once the door slid closed, leaving Tam alone once more, he chuckled. "Gods, she's impressive." He then slowly slid back onto the bed until his head grazed the pillow.

He knew Eli would be back soon, and she'd most likely have questions, but Tam couldn't help it. Sleep smothered him in its embrace, and by the time Eli returned, he was far from the world of the conscious.

As Eli stared at Tam's still face, she let out the tensely held breath that had built in her lungs.

She wanted to know what the hell had happened. Wanted to ask her employer just exactly how the hell Lord Kim had gotten pulled into the void. But truthfully, she had been in a sound sleep herself when she had simply... jolted awake.

Yawning, Eli eyed the spot in the bed she tended to occupy at night beside Tam, and decided she might as well nap with him.

She had explained Lord Kim's presence to Haewon by saying the lord had kindly brought Tam home when he was ill, and they had simply managed to come in without being noticed.

Scratching the back of her neck, Eli let her hand drift up to the back of her hair. Did it really look that weird? It was the first thing Tam had commented on...

Shaking her head at herself for even bothering with such a pointless thought, Eli climbed back into bed and settled down... Until she realized she had started smiling at some point.

When?

Had it been when she'd reentered the room?

Or when she'd stood for longer than she wanted to admit watching Tam rest? His mouth slightly open, his left hand at his side, palm up, his right hand resting across his abdomen—an abdomen that Eli knew happened to be quite muscular...

She felt heat streak across her cheeks and so she turned onto her side quickly, pressing her face into the cool pillow, grateful that he couldn't see her right then.

Oh Goddess... Do I want to be with him? He's made it abundantly clear I can if I want to. And if he decides he tires of me...? What then? He could ruin me... Then again, his last ex-lover he simply left alone and vanished from her life.

Eli's thoughts started to spiral until she heard the sliding door opening a crack. Sitting up, she found herself looking at Luca, who stared nervously back at her.

She tilted her head in question, but when the child didn't answer and instead his eyes darted to the bed, Eli knew exactly what he wanted. She remembered wanting the same thing as a child, though she had only been four years old when her mother couldn't put up with it anymore.

Swallowing past the lump in her throat, Eli gave a short nod and a single pat to the bed in the space between herself and Tam.

Luca's face split into a grin, and he shuffled in hurriedly, forgetting to close the door behind himself.

Eli didn't bother pointing it out as he scrambled up into the bed and nestled himself between them. She simply turned on her back and closed her eyes.

Why did I let him do this? Tam might not want—

And then she felt it.

Luca's hand reaching into her own and grasping it.

And something in her, very abruptly, broke.

She pressed her eyes tight, hoping that Luca wouldn't notice the tears slipping out.

When she didn't hear him comment, she squeezed his hand back, and for whatever reason, that made the tears come all the more.

She dared to crack open an eye and was grateful to see that Luca was already fast asleep. With his small face and the shape of the still-growing cheekbones, he looked just like his father, sleeping beside him.

But Luca's left hand wasn't lying on his stomach; he had grabbed Tam's hand as well.

And the enormity of the situation ravaged Eli's well-guarded heart, which she'd thought unable to feel anything fractionally as intense as what she felt right then.

This could be *her* family.

This could be her everything, and the fact that the mere daring thought of it made her feel more whole in a way she hadn't in years...

Scared her soundly.

"There has been news, my liege."

With an arched brow, Aradia turned away from the mirror in front of her.

Ansar and Mr. Julian knelt before her. "We received word from an innkeeper that he believes the man thought of as the devil was headed for Junya."

A ruthless grin ventured halfway up. "Excellent. What contacts do we have in Junya?"

"The concubine has her cousin Lord Yangban staying in the city presently. And she has recently heard that an heir to the throne may be there as well, so she will most likely be quite willing to lend us funds and manpower," Ansar explained evenly.

Aradia nodded thoughtfully. "That concubine has a burdensome amount of pride."

"Yes, my liege."

"Ansar. We've talked about this. Call me Aradia."

"Yes, Aradia."

Briefly, the first witch smiled warmly at her devoted servant. Then her expression melted back to seriousness.

"How big a threat does this princess or prince pose to the concubine, truly?"

"That is difficult to say. It is a princess. Princess Elisara. And she may wish to seek revenge, yet have no design on the throne. According to some servants that remember her, she was quite resolute not to assume any power while she was being raised here in the palace, but that could have been something she was taught to say in order to survive."

Aradia considered that suggestion momentarily. "Alright. I don't know what state my brother is in. Or how powerful he is right now. This world is breaking free of the natural laws my parents set, and the wilder it grows, the more complicated things become. We will send five of the men the concubine loaned us, and one or two members of the coven. But don't send the best. Send one experienced man, and the rest with varied levels of competence. We will start to assess my brother from afar and make judgments accordingly. If he tries to flee Junya, only then will we make contact." Aradia gave a lone cursory glance at the mirror, then stood.

"Thomas Julian, what news from Troivack and Daxaria about my dagger and Chronos?"

"Chronos remains with the Coven of Wittica, and the dagger has been moved to another location."

Aradia's eyes moved to the ceiling. "Another location... Have someone investigate the home of Troivack's captain. Leader Gregory Faucher's keep was rebuilt around the time I was imprisoned. It'd make sense that, knowing what they know, they would build an extra room for protecting the dagger. Particularly as Gregory Faucher is one of the few men that the Troivackian king trusts."

"Yes, ma'am."

Aradia placed her hands on her hips, which were wrapped snugly in black lace. "If all else fails, I can summon the dragon. But I will not fail this time. One way or another, my brother is being sent to the Forest of the Afterlife. No matter what stands in my way."

The two men kneeling before her remained silent.

"Anything else to report?" she asked, more as an afterthought.

"Is there anyone in particular you'd like to sit on the throne?" Ansar returned, in much the way a butler would ask his master if she'd like tea or coffee.

The first witch smiled again, this time more calculatingly. "Definitely not that brat who shares blood with Soo Hebin. Check the other princes and princesses and their reputations. I'll make a decision afterward."

"Ma'am?" Thomas Julian's nervous voice pulled Aradia's eyes to his bowed head. "What if members of the Ashowan family are here—and more of them come when they learn about the chaos brewing?"

Aradia ran the tip of her tongue over the jagged edges of her teeth. "I'll plan for them accordingly this time. Don't you worry. Ansar? Make sure we hear about any and all passengers coming into Zinfera that could match any of the Ashowans' descriptions."

"As you wish."

Aradia turned back to the quarters she had been granted in Soo Hebin's palace.

They weren't small, but they were far from dignified or extravagant. Though Aradia knew she wasn't in a position to do anything about it yet, she would soon show the concubine that it was a grave error to treat her, the daughter of the Gods, lightly, or with any measure of disrespect.

Because that was what she saw in the concubine's eyes. This was Soo Hebin's childish, passive-aggressive way of showing dominance.

Aradia emitted a breathy cool laugh to herself. "Oh, one more thing. Contact the Coven of Giong. It's time they started serving their ancestor, particularly in light of the very generous benefactor I've given them."

CHAPTER 45

A SWEET SURRENDER

Yun kicked over the basket that held his crumpled correspondence. His hands tightened into fists as he glared at the mess in the flickering light of the candles in his quarters.

Everything had been *perfect!* His father had had every detail plotted out ages ago...

Yun was supposed to swoop in with the useless Nam son and rescue Elisara after she'd spent years getting that stubbornness beaten out of her.

They'd paid that wretched Duke Icarus a hefty sum to seize her after they helped Soo Hebin abduct the princess from the palace, but the useless Troivackian noble had been caught by his king and she'd been out of Yun's grasp again.

Until lo and behold, he heard whisperings from one of his connections at Ori harbor about a half-Zinferan woman called Eli traveling with some suspicious men.

Why the hell hadn't Icarus mentioned that Elisara had had a child?

Then again... It was probably right around the time that the Troivackian duke had been captured that she'd fallen pregnant.

That ruddy scholar, Joe Voll, probably slipped in and got his hands on her while traveling in Troivack or something to that effect.

Yun gritted his teeth. His eyes cut to his desk, which he typically kept flawlessly neat, but he had bashed it out of his way in a fit of rage, and so its contents lay across it askew.

I thought if I could marry her and simply associate myself with the royal family at a distance like that concubine suggested, it'd be enough, but now I could rule over the entire Nam family. She is far too valuable to leave her to rot in a marriage to that man—who is most likely a witch...

Pausing his furious pacing, Yun's emotions settled abruptly, as they often did.

"There are rumors about the devil... I doubt Soo Hebin is unaware that Elisara is here," Yun muttered to himself. "All I'd need to do is say that I met with the princess, who is plotting to return and take over the throne. I'm sure Soo Hebin would then be willing to lend me some help. If I could have a powerful witch or two help me kill off her husband and son, I can tell Her Highness that Elisara will no longer be a threat. I'll make it known that I only want to become the head of the Nam household and we'd be loyal to her son once he takes the throne... Yes. That should be enough to convince her."

With this new plan, Yun sat down at his desk, a new spark of hope igniting.

I'll fix this, and after I do? Everything will be even better than I had ever planned. Father will be proud.

Tam woke with a start, though his mind tried to hold him under the blanket of slumber. He rarely fell into a deep sleep. Once or twice growing up he had momentarily appeared in the void due to some horrible nightmare, and so he had managed to train himself to wake should a dream start to become stressful or should his environment change even slightly.

So he was more than a little shocked to see not only Eli in bed beside him, but also Luca.

He stared down at the two of them, utterly awestruck; his panic abated only a little as he processed the situation.

Eli's eyes were red and swollen, and her cheeks were flushed. She'd been crying.

Tam wanted to wake her up right there and ask why she had been upset, but then he realized that Luca was holding his hand.

He stared dumbly at the small hand clutching his own, then noticed that Luca was also holding Eli's hand. Tam felt emotions well up. He laughed, though he did his best to do so quietly.

I guess I understand why she might have been emotional—I could start weeping here myself. Though I might just be an obtuse arse in assuming that's what it was...

Tam sighed, wondering how someone could ever cross a chasm of trauma as large as Eli's, when he noticed the rosy evening sky just outside the window.

The future duke knew he needed to start getting ready to break into Lord Guk's house.

Tam looked back at Luca's hand, then at his son's sleeping face, and motivating himself to the task suddenly seemed next to impossible.

Gods, is this what a normal life would be like? A life where I'm not trying to live up to a hero father and a spymaster mother? Not living in fear of my magic?

The idea was utterly intoxicating, and while he didn't want to acknowledge it fully yet, a small seed that was planted at the idea of a quiet family life of his own had already sprouted roots.

Tam gave Luca's hand a gentle squeeze before carefully sliding his fingers free and easing himself off the bed.

He idly sniffed under his arm. He could stand to bathe, but that would have to wait. It was a better idea to prioritize eating before leaving. Besides, he'd see about splashing some water there and that should be enough to—

A quick, whispering movement drew Tam's eyes upward. Eli had leapt up from the bed, her left foot braced on the bed frame, her right hand lifted back as though she were about to cast a powerful magic.

Tam watched this speechlessly, but once he overcame his surprise, he waited for the sleepy confusion to drift from Eli's eyes as her mind rejoined consciousness and understood there was no imminent danger.

When Tam felt certain he wasn't about to be attacked, his mind started to whir into motion.

Eli's power... He hadn't really given it much thought, but if it was strong enough that she'd learned to brace for it? He was inclined to suspect she had wind magic.

Still, she wouldn't be scared of simple wind magic, and furthermore, the Giong Coven would've helped train her. Especially if she was close in line to the throne.

Tam was pulled from his thoughts when Eli set both feet on the ground and glanced just past Tam at the sky outside.

Her eyes widened. She nodded to Tam—*time to get ready*—then padded her way over to the dresser and started quietly withdrawing a black shirt and pants.

Tam pulled his own shirt off and moved toward the wardrobe in the back left corner. Eli turned and started to take off her own shirt. When her sight landed on Tam, they both froze.

Momentarily stunned, self-consciousness flooded Tam, and he felt his face heat as Eli's eyes roved over his bare torso. But his embarrassment ebbed when he saw a glint in her expression that told him...

She was having a reaction to seeing him without a shirt.

He squared himself to her and raised his eyebrows in question, he felt a cheeky smile draw itself on his face.

It was Eli's turn to flush, but she returned the favor by mirroring Tam's position and resumed sliding her shirt over her head.

Shock bolted through Tam and he found himself rooted in place.

Eli had been living openly as a woman, so she didn't have her bindings on. She was standing half naked in front of him.

Tam felt his knees weaken.

What the hell is she doing?

Taking a shuddering breath that did little to help his control, he tried to force himself to turn around, but then he made the mistake of meeting Eli's gaze.

The look in her eyes...

His heart thudded violently in his chest.

She looked shy and vulnerable, but when he again gave her a questioning look of alarm that let her know he hadn't a clue why she was standing there, baring herself to him without a care in the world when she *knew* how he felt...

Gods help him.

She gave a nod.

Delirious panic, hope, excitement, and thought-stopping *want* drowned Tam's senses.

He rubbed his face with one hand then let it rest over his mouth, his eyes never leaving Eli's, save for a brief glance at Luca, who'd flopped onto his stomach as he slept.

Tam dropped his hand.

It took three steps for him to stand nearly toe-to-toe with Eli. She had to tilt her head back to keep looking at him.

His heart skipped a beat when he noticed her trembling and the quick, quiet breaths that accompanied the expression on her face. She had a look of tentative opening, of nervous trust… Tam's head swam.

Lifting his right hand to gently grasp her neck, his thumb pressing lightly against her cheek, Tam twitched his chin down once in silent question as he lowered his face closer to hers. He stopped, mere inches from her mouth, and waited.

Was she certain?

Eli's breath caught in her throat, and it nearly undid Tam right then and there as he held still.

She was shaking under his touch, but Tam knew by the way she leaned into his hand that it wasn't because she didn't want him there.

Wind chimes from outside gently tinkled in the quiet.

Eli looked at his mouth, and then back at Tam's eyes, and again, she nodded.

Tam was done waiting.

He dropped his mouth to hers and kissed her, pure happiness pouring from even the darkest reaches of his being.

Especially when he felt her warm hands rest on his hips, and she kissed him back.

Tam pulled her into himself, needing her to feel the intensity simmering in him, needing her to understand what she was doing to him…

He broke away only when he had to breathe, his eyes opening in the haze of heady emotions to see that her own had darkened, and her dazed longing was edging toward urgent desire…

A muffled sleepy moan sounded from Luca.

Tam and Eli sprang apart. Eli threw her shirt over her head in the blink of an eye. Tam flew across the room and yanked a fresh black shirt over himself.

The pair then turned in unison to see that Luca was still sound asleep, and had only grabbed more of the comforter to hug. His back was to them.

Tam's attention darted back to Eli, who had managed to fully change while Tam had been busy dressing himself.

Though the way her cheeks were still blushing... she looked beautiful.

Tam swallowed. Then straightened, knowingness steadying him.

He returned to stand before Eli, though this time he moved slower, and he watched as she fidgeted, uncertain what he was about to do.

Tam let out a breath, then got down on his knees.

Panic flooded Eli's face. Tam managed to give her a half-reassuring smile as he gave his head a small shake to let her know he wasn't proposing marriage—not quite yet.

Instead, he took her right hand, kissed her knuckles, and rested her palm against his chest so she could feel the thrumming weight of his heartbeat.

Her eyes widened, and Tam smiled up at her before covering her hand with both of his, then bowing his head so that his forehead rested against her middle.

Despite not a word having been spoken, Tam felt as though she understood exactly what he was trying to say...

Remember what I said. You can do and have everything.

Tam basked in the moment, hoping she wasn't already regretting what they were in the middle of, but his worries were quieted as her left hand softly brushed through his hair, making him tilt his face back up to look at her.

Eli crouched down, her expression shifting toward wary concern, and Tam took it to mean...

Slowly. Please. Go slowly.

He smiled and bowed his head briefly in assent.

Whatever she wanted.

Eli smiled back. While she still looked unnerved, there was a spark in her eyes that hadn't been there before. Tam found himself thinking how the woman had absolutely no idea the lengths to which he'd go for her.

But perhaps, for the time being, that was for the best, because the truth was that there were no limits, and she would need to discover this on her own.

Eventually.

When she was ready to accept that he was planning on giving her absolutely anything she wanted that was within his power to give.

CHAPTER 46

A DISASTROUS DISCOVERY

Jumping down from the carriage, Tam gave a cursory glance up and down the street to confirm there really was no one around. All that greeted him were shadows from the walled yards, their trees fluttering in the nighttime wind.

"I'll be here unless someone comes and asks questions. Then I'll go two streets down to the left and wait there," Eli whispered from the driver's seat.

Tam gave her a short nod while avoiding looking directly at her. He needed to focus, and any glimpse of her in that moment would have him bumbling around in a haze of drunken happiness.

Moving swiftly along the wall on his left, Tam made his way to the corner, paused and listened, then risked a quick glance around the bend to see the guards standing a short way down in front of Lord Guk's doors.

Tam eyed the branches of the cherry tree that extended over the stone wall, then took five measured steps back... followed by another three... then one step forward before turning to the stone wall, jumping, grasping its top, and hoisting himself up and over.

He landed where he had hoped to: right behind the golden swan in the garden.

Staying in a crouch behind the statue, he waited to make sure there were no sounds of alarm.

Then he waited even longer, just in case someone had glimpsed him and was still watching.

Staying low, Tam crept forward toward the servants' walkway, the sounds of the night all he could hear. Eventually he reached the very same corner where he and Eli had stood barely a week ago.

It was a fantastic vantage point, and so Tam slowly straightened while continuing to observe around himself.

All he needed to do was get into Lord Guk's room. Once he knew which was his, the next time he came, all he'd have to do would be to break into that balcony.

No one was in the garden, which made perfect sense. Lord Guk was supposed to be out with Lord Yangban, Jeong, and Bong at a local tavern or brothel. They wouldn't return for a long time, so most likely the staff would be resting before preparing late-night food and libations.

Taking a left into the nearest darkened hallway, Tam stopped after five steps as soon as the scent of cooked fish and spices overcame his senses.

This must lead back to the kitchen. Which means there should be a hall to the dining room. Too risky. If only I'd had more time at the party to learn the layout. Bong and Jeong couldn't even see much, as they were reluctant to leave Eli...

The thought of her name brought a smile to Tam's face as he rounded back toward the exit. He gave his head a firm shake. No. He could be happy later.

He paused at the doorway to the courtyard, again checking the garden surroundings, and proceeded along the wall, though he lowered his head in a subservient manner in case anyone glimpsed him from afar. He worked to keep track of his surroundings out of his peripheral vision.

Let's see, a house this size... the best view would undoubtedly be on the south side toward the sea.

Tam lamented that from this theory, he'd have to cover more distance while trying not to be noticed.

He had guessed that Lord Guk would've placed his quarters on the north side as someone who tended toward nightly excursions. It stood to reason that someone who went to bed late would want to avoid being woken early by the sun.

But, Tam reflected, while Lord Guk was indulgent, he was still a competent man. If he knew to appreciate the view, then he could put his discomfort aside.

Tam managed to find a doorway that led to an unlit hall, and he was relatively certain he spotted a set of stairs on the far end.

Slipping into the shadows, he padded farther into the house, his ears honed for any small noise that could signal someone coming.

At the end of the hall, he found that he had successfully located the stairs. Tam started his careful climb up, tentatively testing each stair for squeaks and creaks that could pierce the silence and reveal his presence.

It took him far longer than he would've liked, but it turned out the stairwell he used was for servants and in a state of disrepair. The second step had a nasty squawk, and the fourth and fifth sounded like they were about to collapse… Following that, the seventh had a small whine, and the eleventh, while it didn't make a sound, had a loose nail popping up.

Lord Guk should spend a fraction of his decorating costs and get this death trap sorted, Tam grumbled in his mind upon reaching the top of the stairs.

However, his criticisms were cut short as voices sounded just a few doors down.

Quickly, he reached for the first door across from the stairway, but found it was locked.

The second door was also locked.

Turning around, Tam risked moving closer to the voices to reach the next door, and he was rewarded and relieved to find it was not only open, but the room was dark and empty as well.

Which was perfect, because no sooner had he closed the door from within the room and dropped down behind the wooden paneling, the glow of a lantern moved past the papered door. Two maids murmured to each other about how they hoped they wouldn't have too much to clean up in the morning after Lord Guk brought back some new party with him…

Tam kept himself pressed against the solid wood of the wall until he heard the Gods-awful stairs herald the maids' descent.

Letting out a steadying breath, he took stock of the room he found himself in.

It looked to be a guest room.

But not just any guest room…

He eyed the lavish furniture and wall hangings. The gold goblet by the bed covered by a purple silk coverlet...

Then he spotted the desk in the middle of the room. Glancing once more over his shoulder at the door to make sure there were no other lights with servants attached drifting by, he made his way there and in the faint glow from outside scanned the letter that rested on its surface ...

Your Highness,

Junya remains as we hoped. Busy, and mostly unconcerned by the increase of activity in the desert...

Tam's heart thrummed.

He was in Lord Yangban's room.

His hands flew to the stack of letters and immediately began reading through them, grateful for the white moonlight that came in through the window.

At first, he intended to glance over the missives looking for any specific mention of incriminating actions.

But according to the regular dates of the many letters, there were some missing.

Tam scoffed. Of course they were hidden...

He started knocking under the desk, excitement and intrigue heightening the tension with his every breath.

No secret compartment.

He eyed an ornately carved box with a golden latch and hinges sitting atop a dresser propped against the wall to his left, and while casting another cautious glance at the door, he stood, darted to the side, and plucked it up.

It turned out to be an easy puzzle box that Tam opened by pressing the eyes of the two panthers on either side of its length, which released the bottom latch in the shallow, narrow compartment. Sure enough, this contained the rest of the letters.

Dropping back down to the patch of moonlight, Tam resumed reading, only to find so much more than he was ready for...

A soft laugh of disbelief escaped his lips as he read one particular missive that had clearly been read and reread multiple times... But as Tam reached the bottom of the page, his face paled, and his gut churned.

There was a very big problem…

And he needed to alert his family in Daxaria as soon as possible.

Tam hadn't explained anything to Eli when he had climbed into the carriage. Nor had he said anything at all other than, "We need to get back, and we need to have a meeting with Jeong and Bong as soon as possible."

He could tell that she had wanted to press the matter, but Tam knew his air of panic and grave worry stopped her from doing so.

Even once they had returned and Eli had changed into a dress just in case Haewon had woken up, she didn't ask any questions as she waited at Tam's side while seated at the dining table.

It was late by the time Bong and Jeong stumbled in. Tam momentarily worried they were too drunk for a proper conversation, but decided the news was too important to hold off.

"Mr. Vooooolll," Jeong whispered in a near whine. "Can we have snacks for this?"

Tam didn't say anything as he waited for Bong to quiet down, as he was emitting a prolonged, labored grunt as he exerted the effort to sit down at the table.

"Did everything go *hic* as planned?" Bong asked, his eyes fluttering.

"It did, but I learned something that makes this entire venture significantly more dangerous. We might have to return to Daxaria on the next boat out."

Eli sat upright, her eyes blinking wide.

"The first witch has not only escaped Troivack with the help of concubine Soo Hebin, but she is now here in Zinfera."

The stunned silence dragged on, and no one could bring themselves to say a word.

"I don't know that I can trust the coven here, either—there was mention that the first witch may have helped Soo Hebin earn their loyalty."

Tam felt Eli recoil at his side, the fear in the air around her palpable.

Bong cleared his throat and struggled to enunciate his words. "How… did you learn this?"

"I found Lord Yangban's letters to and from the concubine, but that isn't the only thing I discovered."

Jeong leaned forward, his red face filled with wild panic. "What more could there be? That's awful enough!"

Tam swallowed. "While we wondered if it was just a rumor… It sounds as though there really is a dragon here in Zinfera. And Soo Hebin knows where it is, because the first witch told her."

No one could speak under the crushing weight of what seemed like a sound win for the evil woman who was aiming to take over Zinfera.

Bong leaned forward, resting his arms on the table, his glassy eyes somber.

"Alright… Here *hic* is the plan. Tomorrow. You… and you, dear, *dear* Eli, get on a boat, and go to Daxaria. Tell them what is happening. We will… write about everything and sign our names in an official document for you to take to Daxaria so there is proof for your king. Jeong and I… will finish crippling Lord Guk best we can, and then return to our father. He *hic* Godsdamn hiccups—" Bong muttered to himself before continuing. "Will contact… the coven. If they lie *hic* about things—or if the coven is divided in their alliance—he will… figure it out."

Tam nodded. That plan made the most sense. Especially if the first witch had, like Lord Kim, happened to hear rumors about Tam's incident with the pirates, which had led to the rumors about him being the devil.

If he was in danger, Eli and Luca were also in danger, and he would not take any risks with their safety.

"I'll wake Haewon and let her know," Eli said, bowing her head. "Then, my lord, I'll join you in our room to start packing."

Tam gave her a nod of affirmation, and the two of them stood.

Jeong and Bong struggled to do the same, and at one point Bong fell onto his back and couldn't get up, much like a turtle. Tam and Jeong stayed behind to help him to his feet but deemed it a thankless task when they heard the first snores rumble from the man.

"The world could be ending and he still sleeps through it," Tam groused while setting Bong's arm down by his side.

"Aah." Jeong, hearing Tam's words, waved his hand dismissively. "Better to be rested than stressed as you die."

Tam blinked at Jeong, who blinked back in response, and with a sigh that did bring with it a begrudging smile, Jeong clapped a hand on Tam's shoulder.

"You know… I will miss you all," Jeong lamented. "Once this is all over, you should officially move to Zinfera."

"Ah, I would, but my nephews would kill me."

"They sound wonderful," Jeong said sincerely. "I'm sure they'll love Luca."

Tam smiled genuinely. That was true.

And while he was gravely concerned about everything he had learned, he was looking forward to seeing Antony, Charlie, and Asher again.

With another wave, Jeong took his leave, and Tam managed to quietly make his way back down the hall toward his own room to start packing.

But in the cool silence of the night, anxiety was settling into Tam's mind. And there was something else in the air that made him think that things might not go quite as smoothly as Bong planned.

However, without any idea of what else could be done, Tam carried on preparing to leave Zinfera. There was no one here they could fully trust when the stakes were as high as the heavens themselves.

CHAPTER 47

AN EARLY ESCAPADE

Gently shaking Luca awake, Tam sat on the edge of the bed in the quiet room with Eli standing at his back.

The birds outside were only just starting to chirp, and the sky had barely lightened.

"Mm?" Luca murmured groggily.

"Luca," Tam whispered, "we need to leave now, alright? We're getting on a boat."

"Mmwhat? Boat...? Again...? Sleep... I just... Food?"

Despite the precarious situation they were in, Tam couldn't help but smile as Luca struggled to rejoin the land of the waking. With a glance over his shoulder at Eli, who wore a similar expression, he scooped Luca up in his arms and pushed himself up to standing.

"Do you have his coat? Or a blanket?" Tam asked softly.

Eli nodded, lifting the black coat in her arms that had been fitted for Luca.

Tam gave a half smile in appreciation, then, with his free arm, he reached out and grasped Eli's hand and guided her from the room to where Haewon waited outside. The housekeeper's long hair was for once not styled into a bun at the back of her head, but in a long braid draped over her shoulder, and she wore only her robe and nightshift underneath that.

"I am sorry to hear that family matters have called you away, Mr. and Mrs. Voll." The housekeeper bowed dutifully.

Tam bobbed his head in acknowledgment. "Thank you for all of your attention and diligence to us during our stay."

Haewon lowered her chin in a dignified manner. "I will alert Luca's tutor that he will no longer be requiring his lessons."

From his sleepy spot on Tam's shoulder, Luca suddenly mumbled. "I carried… the two… no, it's not three… Not the cabbage. Please not… cabbage…"

Even Haewon had to work to suppress a smile.

"Thank you again," Eli said politely.

Tam nodded his head once more in thanks, and then proceeded to the front courtyard doors, where Jeong was waiting with a carriage to take them to the docks.

Bong was still collapsed and fast asleep by the table where Tam had left him.

Tam wished he could've said a proper goodbye, but he knew there was no chance of waking the man—he had tried and failed on too many previous nights.

As they climbed into the carriage, Eli was the one to pound the ceiling, alerting Jeong they were ready.

"I instructed Haewon to ship the rest of your books later today," she explained as Tam adjusted Luca so that he was slumped at his side, with his father's arm around him.

"Thank you." Tam directed a full smile at Eli in the faint light that ebbed in through the gauzy curtains. The smell of morning dew hung thick in the air. "How're you feeling?"

"Glad."

Tam's eyebrows drifted upward in surprise.

"I worried you would be like your sister, Her Majesty, and want to stay behind and find a way to fight everything on your own," Eli expounded bluntly.

Tam laughed quietly and shook his head. "I can't take down a dragon, widespread corruption, and the daughter of the Gods on my own. I'm not Kraken or Pina."

Eli tilted her head in serious acknowledgment of the two familiars. The one belonging to the Daxarian queen, Piña Colada, or simply Pina as she was called without the accent for a nickname, was known to have a way with the hearts of people to the point that it bordered on obsession. Finlay Ashowan's own familiar, Kraken, somehow managed to rule the beasts he came across and had long ago dubbed himself emperor. But the extent of Kraken's command when it came to the human realm was murky at best.

"Knowing your family legacy, you'll wind up with the dragon as your familiar," Eli speculated, appearing only partially serious, and leaning forward to glance at Luca, who remained deep asleep.

Tam released a sigh mixed with a laugh and shook his head. "And how are you feeling about... other matters?" he ventured carefully, while noticing with no small amount of giddiness that Eli had not pulled her hand free from his.

Her grip on his hand tensed, and Tam could tell she wanted to fidget.

"I'm... nervous."

Tam tilted his head. "You didn't say that you're horrified, so I'm tentatively optimistic."

Eli slid a flat expression his way. "Can you please promise me something?"

"Anything."

"That's ridiculous. Don't say that kind of romantic garbage that has no meaning."

"You know, most people who say that sort of thing do so to convey the gravity of their feelings. I'll have you know that is not why I said it."

Eli scoffed. "Oh?"

"I said I'd promise you anything because I will promise you anything."

"What if I asked you to kill someone?"

"Depends who it is."

"See?"

"And who do you want me to kill?" Tam asked interestedly while flashing what he hoped was a mischievous smile.

Eli's eyes narrowed.

Tam laughed before persisting. "What is it you wanted me to promise?"

"Promise me you won't tell Luca about us until I say it's alright."

The good humor faded from Tam's face. "Of course. Whenever you're ready, we can tell him. I have a question of my own, though."

"What?" Eli managed without masking her suspicion.

"Well, *now* I'd like to ask why you seem so suspicious of me, but we'll circle back to that."

Eli rolled her eyes.

"How do you want us to be in Daxaria? And at night? And do you want to still be my assistant? Knowing you, I'm assuming so, but I'd like to know your thoughts, and your boundaries."

Eli's eyes widened and she turned to stare ahead of herself. "Good Gods, how anyone hasn't been romantically attached to you by now, I'll never understand."

"I want to take that as a compliment, but I know with you I should double-check."

"It *is* a compliment. Just… Anyway." Eli shook herself free of her amazement. "I want to continue being your assistant, and for the time being, I'd like our relationship to remain private between the two of us."

"And the sleeping arrangement…?" Tam wondered with a mild tone that he paired excellently with a practiced innocent expression.

"We should most likely only share a bed until Daxaria. To keep up the façade of us being a married couple."

Tam nodded reasonably, though his self awareness of his more base instincts prompted him to say, "You're going to have to be *very* clear about what you are and are not alright with when I'm in your bed. And if you can't be? I'll sleep on the floor."

At first Eli blushed scarlet, but then she let out a breathy laugh of disbelief. "Honestly… as I was saying before, with your respectful charm, it is *baffling* that you are unmarried."

"I think my dear son's presence does continue to serve as proof I'm not quite as pure as fresh snow as you think," Tam reminded dryly.

Eli opened her mouth to say something but was forced to stop when the carriage halted. Both Tam and Eli glanced out the window and discovered that they had successfully made it to the harbor.

It served to remind them of their mission: to sneak out of Zinfera and report back to the Daxarian monarchy that there were serious threats present in Zinfera.

The flirting therefore came to a tragic end.

Fortunately, by this point Luca was lifting his head and blinking dazedly around. "Wh—Where are we?" He sat up straighter, his head turning every which way.

The carriage door opened, and Jeong appeared. "Ah! Good morning, Luca!"

Tam gently touched Luca's back, drawing his son's gaze. "Luca… We need to go back to Daxaria. I have an important message to deliver to my family."

Luca's face tensed. "Wh-why?"

Wincing a little, Tam rested his hand on Luca's shoulder. "Because it is a *really* important message."

The young boy slumped forward. "Are Bong and Jeong coming too?"

Behind Luca, Jeong's hand clutched his chest, obviously moved by the boy's sentiment.

"I'm sorry, but they can't. We'll see them again, though. I promise."

Luca's eyes welled up, but he blinked furiously while trying to keep the tears at bay.

He then swung around to Jeong and crumpled into a sob before throwing his slim arms around Jeong's neck.

Caught off guard momentarily by the suddenness, Jeong's beefy arms managed to find their way around the young boy. "I'll miss you, too, Luca, but we'll see each other again, just as your father says."

"You were my first real friend," Luca croaked.

Jeong blinked, his bloodshot eyes looking suspiciously wet.

Tam and Eli decided to not hurry them. They exited from the other side of the carriage, noting the scant number of people milling around. The docks were coated in moisture, and a thick fog whirled around the ship hulls, a foot or so off the ground.

Sadly, Tam was forced to interrupt Jeong and Luca once they'd rounded the back of the carriage. "Which ship is ours?"

Jeong gave Luca a final mussing of hair before stepping back and nodding down the line of ships toward one with a sea serpent figurehead carved in her bow. It was visible thanks to the lit braziers along the dock edge.

"That one there. The captain was out drinking with Bong and me last night; his first mate will be the one casting off this morning. They should be here soon."

Both Tam and Jeong's eyes drifted up toward the quiet deck of the vessel, hoping to see someone who might lower the gangplank for them.

"My lord," Eli whispered, tugging on Tam's sleeve.

"Mm?" he asked with a frown. It was oddly quiet… But perhaps the drizzly weather was delaying most of the ships from leaving.

"Something is wrong."

The future duke turned to Eli, who was peering into the shadows with still alertness. "What is it?"

"I keep seeing men drifting closer, and—"

"They're over there as well," Jeong interrupted as he glanced over his shoulder.

Tam turned and spotted four men who were indeed casually meandering closer to them.

"Four on this side, too," Eli whispered while inching backward toward the carriage.

"There might be more on the other side of the carriage," Tam pointed out softly, his senses prickling. "Luca, get out here right now."

The sharpness in his father's tone had the boy springing from his seat to Tam's side.

"Luca, I want you to climb under the carriage and lie there in the middle. If someone that isn't myself, Jeong, or Eli tries to grab you, scream."

Luca's eyes rounded, and he turned his head to try and see what threat was making his father give such a frightening order, but Tam knelt down in front of Luca, filling his vision and resting his hands on the boy's shoulders. "Don't look, Luca. Alright? Do you promise?"

Behind Luca, Jeong undid the tie of his green coat and tossed it into the carriage while rolling his shoulders.

Tam could feel Luca starting to tremble. He pulled his son into a hug, waited for him to nod, and then watched as Luca sank down onto his belly and crawled under the carriage.

Tam stood, then stripped off his own coat and tossed it into the carriage in anticipation of a fight. "Eli, do you need to be under the carriage with him?"

"Who would have ordered this?" she responded instead, her dread making the question come out a hushed rasp.

"We'll keep one alive and ask them," Jeong replied with surprising ferocity.

"My money is on your brother's assistant, Eli," Tam speculated grimly while pulling his daggers from their sheaths at his back. "I wouldn't put it past him to have us followed."

"But why—"

"Chul wants to name any son you have as the next heir to the Nam household."

Eli rounded on Tam instantly. "What? Who told you that?" The warning note in her voice was not lost on Tam, but he was a mite fixated on the men closing in around them. By now he could see that they were all Zinferan…

But then Tam noticed that one had a peculiar physical characteristic: black nails. "Dammit," he breathed, flipping the blade in his hand. "Witches."

Eli's tentative anger toward Tam morphed to shock. "What?"

"The safest thing might be to reveal my identity," he explained quickly. "Even if they are in the pocket of the first witch, to attack me is to start a war with the Coven of Wittica."

"Then the first witch will know you're here," Eli argued, her voice mounting in volume.

"I know. But we need to survive this."

Eli fully faced Tam, desperation bright in her eyes. "We'll be fine! You're capable and—"

A flame erupted in the palm of the fire witch, who smiled excitedly while revealing flashing gold teeth.

But it was a man wearing a fine dark-blue coat that Tam could see on the right in the light of the fire witch's flames who spoke first. "By the authority of the Coven of Giong, I hereby arrest you, Mr. Joe Voll, under suspicion of your identity being Satan, son of the Gods."

Tam's stomach plummeted.

While he had already known things weren't good, he hadn't known they were going to take *quite* as dramatic a nose dive.

Well… Shit.

CHAPTER 48

A DALLIANCE WITH DARKNESS

Tam noted that the rest of the men surrounding them wore plain black. Perhaps they weren't all witches…

"There seems to be a mistake," he called back to the Zinferan who had addressed them. "I am not Satan, but I confess, I am not Mr. Joe Voll, either."

At the creak of a bow being drawn, Tam jerked his head back to look over his shoulder. His blood filled with ice when he saw the arrow directed at Jeong, who balled his thick hands into fists at his sides and glared at the archer.

Turning quickly back to the man who addressed them, Tam felt his magic seep forward. He wasn't sure where an unfamiliar instinct came from. It would require trusting his magic like never before. But it was welling up inside of him rapidly.

It'd be a blind leap into the darkness, and he'd be risking everyone's lives.

He fought back against the urge, opting for the less risky option. "My name is Lord Tamlin Ashowan. I am traveling in Zinfera with my assistant here, Eli, and a family friend."

Barely anyone dared to breathe.

Tam watched the Zinferan who had spoken to him lower his brows. Beside the man, the fire witch's eyes had grown round. No one was smiling anymore.

"If that *is* the case"—the man who appeared to be in charge strode forward confidently—"Then you are traveling without issuing proper notice to either the Coven of Giong *or* the Zinferan emperor."

"That is because I am not traveling on official business," Tam explained hastily, every muscle in his body taut. He noticed the way Eli shrank back against the carriage. Her attention was fixed on the fire witch, who had a close-cropped beard and an oval face. He stared imperiously at Tam.

Pretty bold if he genuinely thinks I'm the devil, Tam thought suspiciously.

"And you are able to prove your identity?"

"Of course. I have papers with me, as well as other tokens belonging to my family that should be recognizable."

The man raised an eyebrow.

"Might I ask who *I'm* speaking to?" Tam ventured warily, still well aware of the arrow primed for release behind him.

"You can ask." The man said nothing more.

Tam continued staring for a breath of silence. "Is there a reason there is still an arrow aimed at us?"

"Is there a reason your knives are still drawn?"

Tam felt aggravated anger start to burn in his being. They were being mocked and toyed with. "Put down the arrow," he ordered, his voice soft. He felt his magic build from the soles of his feet, up his chest, down his arms, and into his head. He knew that at any moment his eyes would blacken.

"I will, once we are finished asking questions. It is highly suspicious that you travel with your identity hidden, and with a missing princess who belongs here in Zinfera, no less."

Jeong stiffened and Eli froze. Tam sensed the two reactions while his own heart skipped a beat.

This was bad.

Very bad.

"What do you want?" he asked, forcing the fingers holding the hilt of his blade not to flutter.

The man smiled, and the cold look in his eyes made Tam's stomach churn.

"Lord Tamlin, we are happy to let you board your ship after you meet with one of our superiors and the princess agrees to return to the palace. Her Highness Soo Hebin has been worried for her."

"And you are aware that forcing someone working under the protection of my family to do something against her wishes will invoke consequences from Daxaria?"

That at least dimmed the man's slyness, if only slightly.

"She does not have the emperor's permission to leave the royal family."

"She is not property. She is a person. Unless the laws have changed since I last checked. Princess Elisara Taejo left Zinfera nearly a decade ago and is now under the protection of Viscount House Jenoure, Duchy of Ashowan, the Daxarian king, and my father, the Coven of Wittica's diplomat. And—" Tam's power pushed against the confines of his control.

"Tam—" Eli tried to physically insert herself between Tam and the representative, who was holding his ground, though he was looking increasingly uncertain despite Tam not moving a muscle. But Tam wouldn't let her; his forearm coming out just enough to block her.

"—And she is under *my* protection." Tam's words came out a rasping growl thanks to the effort it was taking to fight off his magic.

The fire witch shifted closer, but a single flitting of Tam's eyes in his direction stopped him in place. "You will be coming with us, Lord Tamlin, or you will be charged with espionage and aggressive acts against the emperor and our coven."

Tam leaned forward slowly. "Are you going to put down that fucking arrow, or am I going to do it for you?"

The man's eyebrows twitched, and his right heel slid backward half an inch. "This aggressiveness does not warrant peaceable treatment of—"

Tam let the power consume him, and unlike any time before in his life... he chose to trust his magic.

In a rush of black-and-silvery smoky aura, Tam disappeared.

"Wh-what is— Where'd he go?" the coven's representative demanded, turning to Eli.

The archer darted his startled eyes to her out of sheer panic. The rest of the men were exclaiming in surprise and nervousness.

Before Eli could even think of a response, Tam reappeared...

Behind the archer.

He wrapped the man's head and shoulder in a hold that redirected the arrow to the ground, and with a quick jolt, he pulled the shoulder out of its socket. The archer shouted in pain.

The other assailants instinctively began to retreat as Tam jerked the man's head, then released the body onto the ground, but that was all they had time to do, because Tam disappeared again.

And just as the fire witch started to square himself to Eli, Tam reappeared behind him and slid a dagger into his back.

Before the fire witch's body had even hit the ground, Tam disappeared, and reappeared behind another man... and another... and another, until in a rush of smoke and fog, every assailant but one lay lifeless on the ground.

The man who had cockily taunted Tam stumbled back, his voice caught in his throat before his eyes flew desperately toward Eli.

As though sensing the line of his thoughts, Jeong grabbed the man by the throat and slammed him against the carriage to stop him from acting on any unsavory ideas about grabbing Eli and using her as a shield to escape.

Tam reappeared beside Jeong, who jolted.

The future duke bore down on the final adversary, his eyes filled with black, pooling magic. "Who sent you?" he asked, his voice seeming to echo from everywhere.

"T-t-t-the first witch! S-she is who you will answer to! She is—"

"So Soo Hebin wants Eli, and the first witch wants me? Why?"

"S-she wants the devil."

"And who are you?" Tam persisted, his eyes gradually returning to normal.

"Garam. I serve Her Highness who is an ally of the first witch."

"So concubine Soo Hebin is aiding the *fugitive*, the first witch, and the coven knows about it. Does everyone in the coven know?" Tam demanded. His breath came out as vapor in the chilly morning air.

"M-most. Not all." Garam swallowed. "You can't leave. The coven will come after you. They'll sink your ship. You have no choice but to come to the palace and—"

"No. I have a choice. And that is to leave no witnesses and then find a different way home. Though I appreciate the input. And information."

Tam lifted his blade.

"You cannot possibly be an A-Ashowan! The family represents goodness and—"

"Goodness has a cost, and I happen to be the outlier who pays it." With a short jab, Tam ended Garam's life. Jeong let him fall to the ground in a heap.

Tam turned to look at Eli.

She flinched.

He recoiled at her fearful response, his grip on his dagger tightening before he busied himself wiping his blade clean and sheathing it.

Jeong stared for a long while at Tam, then Eli, his thoughts indiscernible. Tam could tell he was trying to process everything he had just learned about them: Tam could disappear and reappear… and while they had merely talked about the possibility of him killing someone in the past, he had actually gone ahead and done so quickly and efficiently with no hesitation.

Not to mention, Eli was a princess.

"Luca? Close your eyes and crawl out, okay?" Tam called while crouching down.

"What are we going to do now, my lord?" Eli inquired, her neutral tone sounding forced. "Garam was right. They can sink our ship if we try to leave from this port. The coven resides on an island nearby. If we take a ship, we most likely would only have half a day before they come looking for us."

Tam lifted Luca into his arms before gently setting his son back in the carriage and closing the door. "I killed these men so that they can't reveal my identity. That will keep my family, Jeong's family, and Daxaria safe from any accusations of espionage or treason. It was the only way to stop a war breaking out, but we do need to get back… For now, they will just assume it's the devil who did this," Tam reasoned as Jeong folded his arms.

"That doesn't answer the question—what now? They know where to look for Mr. Voll. We can't go back to the house or use that name."

Tam nodded wearily and reached up to rub the back of his neck.

"We could go to my brother," Eli said suddenly.

Tam's eyes snapped up. "No."

Eli blinked then stood taller. "Why not? And how did you know about him planning to leave the title to any son I bear?"

"He told me when we had tea yesterday."

"What?"

Tam watched anger spark in Eli's face.

"Your brother's assistant was obviously using him, and I wanted to warn him about it. I was going to tell you about it after I went to Lord Guk's, but things got—"

"Tam, Eli, we need to leave. It'll be daylight soon," Jeong interrupted softly.

For a moment the couple stared at each other, the heavy weight of their unresolved discussion sinking its claws into them, until Tam sighed then held open the carriage door for Eli.

She gave him one last steely look, then climbed in and sat beside Luca.

Tam closed the door and joined Jeong on the driver's bench.

Once the two men were ready, Jeong slapped the reins gently onto the horses' backs and set them into motion. Heavy raindrops started to drop from the sky as they navigated their way away from the harbor in silence.

It wasn't until they had found a suitably quiet side road that conversation started.

"Eli's a princess?" Jeong ventured quietly.

"Yes."

Jeong's eyes lowered thoughtfully, then lifted once more.

"Where are we going?"

Tam leaned his head back against the carriage as he replayed in his mind the way Eli had flinched under his stare.

"I think I know someone whom we can stay with while we reorganize. We'll go there, and then you'll go get Bong. We're going to have to leave from some other port, or find some safe way to send the message."

Jeong nodded in assent, though he did shoot a look of surprise and uncertainty at Tam when he mentioned their destination.

Tam sighed and closed his eyes to sort through his thoughts.

The way he had used his magic when fighting—it had been…

Exhilarating.

Freeing even.

It had felt so effortless weaving in and out of the void like a needle and thread, reappearing wherever he wanted to be.

He also realized how different this had felt from the times before, when his goal was simply to disappear into the void. His magic had been beckoning him to trust in it—to trust in himself.

"Eli has probably seen worse things than what happened back there," Jeong started carefully. "And I'm sure she'll forgive you eventually for having tea with her brother."

Tam gave a quiet, humorless chuckle. "She has definitely seen worse, but betraying her trust…? She doesn't take that lightly. And I think while she's seen more gore, seeing my magic was—"

"That was incredible." Jeong shook his head, awe in his voice. "Terrifying, absolutely. But as soon as you disappeared, I knew we'd be fine. I had this sense that you became… bigger than the situation, and that you controlled it."

Tam allowed himself a half smile. "It's funny. I've been afraid of my magic for years, but I never thought it'd frighten other people the same way."

Jeong didn't reply.

Instead, they continued through the quiet streets of Junya. The clouds above prevented the light of dawn from reaching them.

Which was probably a blessing as they fled a crime scene.

"What happens if the covens discover what you did?"

"I'll be on trial," Tam answered easily, even though his mind was starting to feel like it was turning to stone, and exhaustion weighed down his limbs. "I'll argue it was in self-defense, but honestly, until things get sorted with the concubine, I don't think it'll go over well."

Jeong winced.

"I'm sorry. I've gotten you involved in a lot more than just touring me around Zinfera and drinking with nobles," Tam said sincerely while addressing the Zinferan he had come to think of so highly.

Jeong smiled. "My father did warn Bong and me that things get messy when the Ashowans are involved. But he also said your bloodline has a way of making everything work out."

Guiltily, Tam winced and looked ahead of himself. "I'm sorry to say it, Jeong, but I don't know that I inherited that ability. If I had, I probably wouldn't be the one in the family who creeps around in the shadows and occasionally kills people."

Leaning to the side, Jeong bumped his shoulder into Tam. "Time will tell."

Tam would've argued, but he didn't have the heart to in that moment, and so he simply allowed Jeong's comforting sentiment to rest between them. The fact that Jeong still seemed to trust that Tam was a decent person and only ended a life in self-defense meant more than he could possibly say.

"I hope Luca didn't see any of it," Tam lamented next.

At this Jeong grimaced. "I hope that, too."

The two men fell into pensive silence as they continued to ride through the streets, though they were becoming increasingly soaked from the rain.

Tam didn't mind. If anything, it helped him stay grounded and not spiral into a state of pure anxiety as his energy was focused on not shivering… that is until they pulled up to their destination.

Jumping down from the driver's seat, Jeong and Tam approached the two guards who stood at the doors.

"I'm here to see Lord Kim," Tam called out. "Please tell him that his scholarly foreign friend is here."

One of the men bowed and called for a steward. Jeong and Tam stood out in the rain in front of the grand wooden doors.

The world started to spin in Tam's vision, and his right knee trembled.

"Are you alright?" Jeong asked, noticing that his companion was looking quite pale.

"Fine… Just tired." Tam gritted his teeth as he battled against the lightness in his head.

Perhaps between spending three days in the void, dragging Lord Kim there, and then fighting using the abilities he had barely touched before was too much.

Despite his efforts, a particularly violent spin in his vision sent Tam down to his left knee on the hard cobblestones. He caught himself with his left hand before he bashed his nose against the ground.

He could distantly hear people's voices around him as colored spots filled his vision, but he couldn't tell who they belonged to. The draining of his energy was so thorough that as it happened, Tam couldn't think of anything other than how he hoped he was right, and that Lord Kim would be willing to host and protect them for a few days, at least until he could formulate a new plan that would keep everyone he cared about as safe as possible.

The colored spots turned to darkness, and then, Tam lost himself to the weighty realm of sleep.

CHAPTER 49

A PLEA FOR PEACE

Petals slowly drifted down from the plum tree toward the square of grass surrounding it. Its boughs swayed back and forth in the air.

A fountain burbled on the opposite side of the courtyard, with a bamboo lever occasionally thunking against the stones artfully placed around it.

Eli sat staring at the tree, her heart thrumming against her chest while she did her best to remain as calm as possible.

It was the morning of the second day since they'd arrived on the doorstep of Lord Kim.

Tam was still unconscious, and Luca was beside himself with worry—though it was a blessing that Jeong and Bong were with them and able to take turns distracting the boy.

Especially because...

Lord Kim was on a devout mission to convince Eli to become the next empress of Zinfera.

She had firmly refused him over and over, and yet he persisted.

And she couldn't flee.

Not until Tam woke.

Her hands curled into fists against the pretty ivory skirt she wore. It was more than a decade out of style, and was far more conservative than the slimmer skirts that had become the trend recently. Of course this reflected Lord Kim's nature. Followers of Acker tended toward more conservative looks.

Still, one particular detail of the religion served Tam and Eli well: Acker followers believed witches to be closer to the Goddess and Green Man, so they gave witches the utmost reverence and respect. Some even believed it acceptable for witches to take same-sex partners, since they presumably were capable of respecting the duality of the masculine and feminine in nature more adeptly than humans, regardless of their partner.

A soft tapping of porcelain being placed on the boards of the raised walkway around Lord Kim's house made Eli turn her head. "I heard you are quite fond of tea," Lord Kim was saying as he seated himself beside Eli. His servants were setting up a short table behind them, with two maids waiting behind him to finish placing it. One was holding a white teapot with a wicker handle, and the other, a three-tiered tower stacked with cakes.

However, Lord Kim had set an already filled cup beside her. The tea had a lovely, soft orange hue, and steam curled up invitingly. Eli raised an eyebrow at it, then allowed her eyes to drift upward to meet Lord Kim's gaze.

"A white tea with peach?" The sweetness of the fruit melted into the softness of the white tea scent in her nose.

It instantly made her mouth water.

Lord Kim didn't mask his surprise before letting out a chuckle. "Lord Tam was not jesting that you are a discerning tea drinker I see."

Her gut twisted, but Eli masked her emotional reaction by plucking up the cup and lifting it to her lips to sip. The tea was smooth; its sweetness wasn't overpowering, but rather light and pleasant. It was perfectly balanced as it glided warmly over her tongue.

"I know he cares for you very much," Lord Kim continued.

Eli's posture straightened and her eyes slid to the nobleman in silent warning about trespassing onto matters that were not his business.

Lord Kim held up a hand as though conceding. "I know I have argued my case for you to inherit the throne a good deal the past two days, but I realize

I have failed as a scholar by not asking a very obvious question… Why do you not wish to take the throne?"

The tea suddenly tasted bitter. Eli set the cup down a little harder than she meant to. "The expectation that I would aim to take the throne was foisted on me as a child, and my fate since then has always been at the mercy of others. Out of curiosity, if I were still the eldest daughter of the Nam family, would you have such expectations of me?"

Lord Kim's face stiffened. "Our emperor's mother thought you were deserving of far more than what your former family could provide you."

Eli bit back a horrible laugh. But Lord Kim seemed to understand from the twitch of her lips just how she felt about that thought.

"Then, Your Highness, what is it you *do* want?"

"I have already said it. If I say it again, will you listen?"

Lord Kim frowned. "You are unmarried. You will not share a bed with Lord Tam, and I am asking about your greater ambitions."

Eli gave a huff of a breath, then leveled a hard stare at the Zinferan nobleman. "As a self-appointed scholar, you should review your philosophy. Look beneath my answer."

Yet again, Lord Kim was stunned. He continued studying Eli, but his thoughts gradually climbed to her challenge. "You… wish to be the next duchess of the Ashowan duchy."

Forcing herself to acknowledge that Lord Kim was at least trying to understand her point of view, Eli indulged him. "In your time coming to know Lord Tam, what is he like?"

"He was pretending to be someone else most of the time he was in my company," Lord Kim pointed out flatly.

Eli shook her head, while a genuine smile started to sprout at the thought of Tam. "He was more himself as Mr. Voll than he ever was as a nobleman. So who was he?"

Lord Kim gave the question another moment of thought with a fond smile of his own lifting a corner of his mouth as he looked out at the flowering plum tree. "A man who loved the study of the stars, adored his wife and son, and was excited to talk about ideas… He found adventure by exploring the mind and its possibilities."

"And with us? In private? When he didn't have to do work for his studies, he stayed up with Luca and me telling us stories of the stars. In the morning, we had long breakfasts with Jeong and Bong, talking, jesting… During the day, I reviewed expenses, studied, and managed paperwork with my choice of tea. I went on walks, became overly invested in Luca's education…" Tears started to tingle in Eli's eyes as she thought about their time in Junya. "I finally felt… happy."

The confession made her throat close and her heart ache.

"You want a peaceful life with Lord Tam. You wish… for simplicity," Lord Kim concluded gently.

Eli lowered her chin and nodded, tears falling from her eyes. She flicked one thumbnail against the other one and clenched her teeth together to stop her jaw trembling. "All my life I have been directed and forced into roles others wanted for me. I've let it happen. Even Chin warned me that those without ambitions of their own will be swallowed by others who are ravenous with the desire for more." Pausing at the vivid memory of the day Chin had said this to her, Eli forced herself to continue.

"Perhaps in another life, I would have been passionate or whole enough to want to change the world. But I'm tired, and the world has taken enough from me already. Can't I just… be happy? Can't I make Tam and Luca's life better and make my own decisions? Can't I have peace? If this is what I want, is it enough to stop being eaten by others?"

She dragged her eyes back to Lord Kim and saw the compassion on his face. "Or do I not deserve to have what I want?"

Lord Kim looked back at the plum tree in the courtyard and allowed silence to drift effortlessly between them.

Eli was rather glad for it. The quiet gave her a chance to blink back tears and get a hold of herself.

Tam… I need you to wake up.

It was midday, and Eli stood with her hands braced on the table in front of her, where a map of Zinfera had been unfurled and weighted down at the corners.

Bong and Jeong gazed at her seriously. "Imperial soldiers and witches are patrolling the streets, and all exits leaving Junya are blocked. Even the ships are stuck at the docks. We should have left the first day," Bong lamented with a shake of his head.

"The first witch could even come herself, given that everyone thinks the dead men on the docks were killed by the devil," Jeong worried openly.

Eli nodded as she listened, but her eyes remained fixed on the map, her mind whirring through possibilities.

"You two could leave easily enough," she pointed out. "Only Tam, Luca, and I are the problem. How are things with Lord Guk going?"

"Lord Kim says his reputation is sinking faster than a gem cargo ship filled with holes. Apparently, he keeps blurting out random truths, then complaining about how his skin itches. Whatever did our dear Tam do to him, I wonder." Bong chuckled thoughtfully to himself.

"He used a form of itching powder in Lord Guk's clothes and sheets. He then replaced some of the soaps in the lord's quarters so it'd have the same component, only more potent. As for the blurting of true thoughts, he infused a drug derived from silo mushrooms into the lord's hair oil. As a result, Lord Guk is hallucinating regularly."

"Wouldn't the maids also be affected as they apply it to his hair?" Jeong wondered worriedly.

Eli shook her head. "They apply it with a comb."

Both the Ryu brothers gave a breathy, impressed laugh.

"You could disguise yourselves and try to leave that way," Bong suggested.

Eli lifted her face, her expression grim. "No. It's too risky. We just have to wait until Tam wakes up. We can escape with Lord Kim's help, but we need Tam to be able to disappear and reappear for it to work."

"I still don't trust Lord Kim," Jeong mumbled.

"Beggars can't be picky," Eli reminded him somberly.

The two men sighed and nodded, then Bong spoke. "I agree that your plan to get the three of you out of Junya could work, but where would you go from there?"

Eli's finger tapped the table. "We travel south of Gondol, go around it, and then try to find a fishing boat or low-ranking merchant ship that'll take us to Daxaria once we come up to the far west side of the kingdom."

Both Jeong and Bong tensed. "You want to go near Gondol?"

"I do *not* want to. But it will be a very confusing path to track. Anyone chasing us will think I'm either avoiding Gondol, or heading straight for it. But going around the long way? It makes so little sense, they won't bother with it. And it will take so long that you two will be able to go contact your father and get a message to Lord Finlay Ashowan. Then even if we can't get a boat, at least we'll know help is on the way."

"It's a tricky plan. The longer you're traveling, the more likely it is that you'll be captured," Bong pointed out seriously.

Pushing off from the table, Eli folded her arms and glanced out the window at fresh green leaves, which brightened the otherwise unremarkable second-story room filled with maps and shelves of books that lined the beige walls. "We'll stick to the forests as much as possible, and only go into small towns where there will be fewer patrols."

Jeong and Bong glanced at each other uncertainly. "That'll be difficult. Tam is a tall man, and being of Troivackian descent, he definitely sticks out."

Eli pursed her lips briefly. "True. In that case, I can go into the towns on my own for supplies."

The two Zinferans frowned. "That's too dangerous. I'll come with you," Jeong proposed firmly.

Eli gave a half smile. "While appreciated, wouldn't that leave Bong exposed?"

Bong shook his head. "If anything, it'll be better. No one would think of me, a lord, traveling alone."

Thinking about this briefly, Eli eventually bobbed her head in assent. "Very well."

While she didn't want to show it, Eli was secretly glad to have Jeong join them. If Tam were to disappear, she'd worry about guarding Luca on her own.

"Alright. So all we need to do is have Lord Guk experience his big bout of madness at the blossom festival, where we can utilize the imperial soldiers' presence. The more witnesses, the more word will spread. With Lord Guk out of the way, the figurehead for naming Junya a capital removed, ideally Soo Hebin will be stopped from expanding her power amongst the nobility anytime soon."

"Lord Yangban's presence is a problem," Bong reminded. "He could pick up where Lord Guk leaves off. Which is probably why he is here in the first place—to make sure the remaining lords agree to the change in capital no matter what."

Hearing the nobleman's name had the familiar effect of making Eli's gut roil.

"It's too bad we can't kill him," she commented darkly.

Jeong and Bong looked up, startled, but after a moment they shrugged and nodded in agreement. The man was a key figure in pushing human trafficking in Zinfera. Because of that, he'd amassed power that he used to support his equally rotten family member Soo Hebin.

"If Tam were here, we could have a chance to make that happen. The way he dealt with those men the other night? It was..." Jeong's eyes lost focus as the memories of the recent attack played in his mind.

"It was like he was death itself. Snuffing them out," Eli said aloud, her expression cool.

The Ryu brothers looked at her, at each other, then back to her.

"Are you alright with what happened the other night?"

Eli's hand tightened around her sleeve, then released. "I don't enjoy violence, but I was..." She trailed off, trying to find the words to describe how she had felt at the time that would make sense.

What even had she felt when Tam kept disappearing and reappearing, dropping lifeless bodies on the ground as he moved? She had been frightened at first. She wouldn't pretend otherwise, but then she had felt...

Electrified.

As though rushing excitement and giddiness had filled her.

Why was that?

Was it just the awe of seeing such power?

Was it shock?

Or was it simply gladness that Tam had at last seemed to master the void...

Eli gave her upper left arm an idle rub as though chilled.

"I think what we all are feeling is... hopeful."

Her eyes snapped up to Jeong who had a subtle smile quirking his bow-shaped mouth. "I think we all have heard countless stories about the abilities of the Ashowan family, and how they are capable of turning the tides however they choose. And yet Tam seemed to fall through the cracks. The rumors always said he was strange and troubled, but it feels like we are seeing the start of great power in him. It's hard not to feel like we may have a chance to fix Zinfera."

Jeong's words left Bong and Eli in stunned silence.

But once she had overcome the heavy insight into what they were all feeling, she added, "Fix Zinfera. Then Luca, Tam, and I are getting out of here, and then—forgive me, but the only problem I want to deal with from then on is how to stop Luca being influenced by the three hellion Daxarian princes."

Jeong and Bong grinned at this. "What? You don't want farm animals finding a way into Tam's home?"

"Or for Luca to experiment with setting people on fire?"

"Or try putting sea slugs in someone's bed?"

"No. No, I would not like any of that," Eli snapped. "You haven't told him those stories, have you?"

The two brothers were suddenly unable to look her in the eye.

"I think I'd like some lunch now, hm?" Bong nodded to his brother, then moved quickly over to the door with Jeong scampering behind him. Eli's glare bored into their backs.

With a final grumble, she cast one last glance at the map.

I can do this. I can get out of Zinfera after getting rid of Soo Hebin, and then… And then I'm going to get what I want. No matter what.

CHAPTER 50

THE ELEGANCE OF ETHER

As Tam struggled back to wakefulness, he relived his last memories. Spots had drowned his sight as he weakly tried to battle them back... Then darkness—not his void, but the darkness of sleep—had claimed him.

The instant he regained the ability to think again, his eyes flew open, and he sat up.

With his heart already pounding, Tam's attention whipped around his surroundings.

He was sleeping in a single-sized bed, in a room that was very sparse, with everything around him either wood-toned or white.

Tam reached up and idly dabbed at his forehead, noting that his clothes had been changed at some point. Now he wore a light, cream-colored sleep shirt and loose brown pants.

Raking a hand through his hair, he tried to stand but became horribly dizzy, and was forced to take slow breaths and wait for the sensation to pass.

While he focused on his breathing, he observed the desk beside his bed, and a dresser with an oval mirror perched on top. Overall, it looked like a senior servant's room.

Tam swallowed and eyed the door. It had a paper covering and was a sliding model, so he doubted he was barred from leaving…

Unless there were guards outside.

Craning his neck, Tam looked over the edge of the bed to see if there was anything he could use for a weapon, or shoes.

But there was nothing.

At least the dresser held a water-filled porcelain bowl and pitcher containing more water. He could use one of those items to bash someone over the head in the worst case scenario. For the present, however, he appreciated being able to rub some water on his face and even drink a little as he realized how parched his mouth felt.

Then Tam stared at himself in the mirror and discovered two things that startled him.

The first was how badly he needed another haircut. That is, if he wanted to keep his hair short. The second…

Was the change he saw in his eyes.

He didn't look timid or frightened.

Back in Daxaria, he had struggled even to look his own reflection in the eyes…

But now?

In a way, Tam's newfound calm and direct stare was similar to his father's.

But there was another strange thing lurking behind Tam's vision that reminded him of the ethereal light behind Finlay Ashowan's eyes, although Tam thought the flicker that moved behind his own was darker. His brown eyes were not quite as deep in color as the shadow that waved through his vision like black candlelight…

Dropping his gaze, Tam seized the towel beside the basin and dried himself off. There were more important things to worry about.

He ran his hands through his hair again, making it slick itself back. Then he moved his attention to the door to the room.

If someone was outside, he would've heard them move or react to the noises he was making. And so Tam cautiously slid the door back two inches, then another three. A glance outside into the hall revealed that no one stood there. After looking both ways down the hall, he opted to go left.

Padding carefully down the narrow space, Tam did his best to bring his mind back into focus. The last thing he clearly remembered was reaching Lord Kim's house. He had fought off the men sent on behalf of concubine Soo Hebin back at the harbor, and discovered that the Giong Coven was loyal to the first witch…

Voices wafted gently down the hall, stopping Tam in his tracks.

He listened but couldn't make out any particular words, and so he eased himself closer to the wall and continued. He reached some stairs that were most likely used by the servants.

He descended. When he could see sand-toned stones, he paused and leaned forward far enough to recognize a kitchen…

And there, standing with a pout on his face, but wearing fine black pants, a silk shirt, and a black vest, was Luca.

"—Why not?" Luca shouted up at a maid who was standing with her arms crossed.

"Because he must rest."

"I napped with him before!" Luca argued.

Tam felt his tense face instantly ease into a smile.

From his position on the stairs, he could see a cooking table and the edge of a stone oven. Just behind Luca was a door that led outside…

A thrilling magical instinct filled Tam.

And he didn't cringe away from it or lower his eyes to make it stop.

He loosed a breath of a laugh, and… fell back into his void.

But only for a moment.

He brushed across the stones of the kitchen, touched the table, smelled the remains of an omelet in the air…

And reappeared behind Luca, making the maid scream. Just before Luca could do the same, Tam plucked him up and tossed him in the air, catching him so that his son could see him.

The boy's dark eyes were wide, but Tam grinned, and the next thing he knew, his son's arms were thrown around his neck.

"I kept my eyes closed the whole time! Just like you told me to!"

Tam blinked, confused, and then remembered the orders he had given Luca right before dispatching their assailants at the docks. Relief flooded through him, knowing that his son hadn't witnessed him killing people.

"That was absolutely the right thing to do, Luca. Thank you for listening."

Tam hugged his son back, relishing the way his heart warmed. Then a throat-clearing pulled his gaze toward the opposite end of the cooking table he stood near.

He had already sensed Lord Kim's presence, but Tam at last locked eyes with the man seated at the table. The nobleman fingered a fan of parchment on its surface while an older woman with a large mole above her lip and gray streaked hair continued to gape in shock at Tam, a cooking knife in her hand hovering uncertainly over a pile of fresh herbs on a nearby stone ledge.

Lord Kim didn't rise, and there was a peculiar glint in his eyes as he perused the future duke.

Tam slowly lowered Luca to the ground, then righted himself and asked, "Where's Eli?"

Lord Kim's eyebrows rose. "Most likely in her room. Your other friends are busy getting ready."

Tam frowned.

"They're going to the festival tonight before they leave town," Lord Kim clarified.

Faltering, Tam struggled to process that he had been unconscious for days. It hadn't felt like it'd been that long...

"Leave us," Lord Kim ordered over his shoulder quietly.

The older woman and the maid Tam had frightened inched out of the room through another doorway, across from where Tam stood. It led to the outdoors and revealed a lush expanse of colorful flowers. Luca slipped his hand into Tam's and pressed himself into his father's side.

Lord Kim smiled gently at the child. "I'll only be a moment, perhaps you should go tell Her Highness that your father is awake, hm?"

Tam could feel Luca stiffen. "I already told you! She's not Her Highness, she's Eli! Or Mom! Tell him, Dad!"

Lord Kim's soft gaze turned to Tam and hardened instantly.

"Luca, go let Eli know I'm awake, alright?"

At first Luca looked like he was going to argue, but eventually he nodded and left Tam alone with Lord Kim.

The Zinferan gestured toward a stool across from himself, and Tam plunked himself down while also eyeing the kitchen's details—he knew his father would ask about it one day.

Folding his arms, Tam leaned back. He had a hunch about what was going to be said, but decided to not be an ungrateful boor and instead started the conversation with "Thank you for taking us in. I'm guessing Jeong filled you in on everything?"

Lord Kim arched an eyebrow and bowed his head in assent.

"If there is any way I can repay you, I'd be more than happy to arrange something once I return to Daxaria, and—"

"Her Highness and I have already come to an agreement."

Tam's shoulders straightened. "What agreement?"

Lord Kim shook his head. "You will have to ask her and see if she wants to share that with you. I have two other things to say to you, however, Lord Tam. The first being, do not confuse your child and have him address Her Highness in such a manner. Not unless you are married should he be given such thoughts as to call Her Highness 'Mom.' I say this not to be prudent, but because I worry for both his and Her Highness's hearts. It is a complicated, beautiful love between a child and their mother, and to start in a hurry or on uncertain footing can be harmful."

While Tam would've been more dismissive if this advice was given with any note of condescension, the sincerity in Lord Kim's eyes stopped him. The man genuinely was suggesting, with pure intentions, what he thought would be best.

"The second thing I have to say is… I know what your magic is."

Tam reared back. "What?"

"Ether." Lord Kim rapped the papers on the table in front of him excitedly. "I've been reading and thinking about your void, and how you described being around everything, and yet nothing… And now, when I just witnessed you appearing, I feel as though I've confirmed my theory."

Tam tried to think of how best to express his confusion, but couldn't, and so he waited for the Zinferan to continue.

"When you disappear, you essentially are a part of everything around you. It is why you could sense things in the surroundings that were there when you disappeared. You travel through these things, disperse through them, and then reassemble yourself. Only, when you go into that 'nothing space'—your void, as you say—you are in a state between life and time itself."

A hum was starting to build in Tam's body, and some deeper part of himself recognized that Lord Kim was absolutely correct. He didn't quite know how, and it was more than a little bit of a frightening notion… but it sounded right.

An ether witch.

That's what he was… And back when the Coven of Wittica had first examined him as a child, hadn't they identified the strongest element in him as air? Wouldn't that make sense, because air travels?

"How did you figure this all out?" Tam asked, not bothering to disguise the awe in his voice.

"Well, you said something interesting when you took me with you—something about it being a nothing place—and as you should know, the Goddess believes in balance. I started to ponder the balance of having such a power, and it taking you to such a place." A small smile started to creep up Lord Kim's face. "I struggled with it until it dawned on me quite simply. All or nothing. You are all, and you are nothing."

Tam wasn't too proud to admit he could barely wrap his head around the reasoning. Yet he couldn't argue that it resonated as truth to him.

"A great amount of chaos has been happening in Junya since you fell unconscious." Lord Kim's tone shifted at mention of this, and he leaned in closer. "There are rumors of the devil here, and concubine Soo Hebin has of course jumped in to send imperial soldiers to scour the streets to find the being who killed not only her own men, but a member of the Coven of Giong."

Closing his eyes, Tam let out a quiet groan.

If he hadn't been asleep for so long, they could've escaped the city before it had gotten swarmed…

"Her Highness has a plan to get you all out and return to Daxaria." Lord Kim eased back in his seat with a smile.

Tam gave a weary look in response. "It won't be easy, will it?"

"No. But Her Highness is intelligent, and the Ryu brothers are capable despite their reputations."

"Thank you. Again." Tam lowered his head respectfully while noting that Jeong and Bong had revealed their true identities to Lord Kim as well.

Lord Kim gave a short, wry laugh. "I'm not doing this for nothing, Lord Tamlin Ashowan. I wouldn't risk my life and the lives of my household just out of the goodness of my heart. I'm doing this to better my own situation and Zinfera. Now, I imagine Her Highness is just about here now." The Zinferan nobleman rose to his feet, prompting Tam to do the same, his gaze drifting to the sunlit doorway behind Tam where the faint sound of feet galloping down the boards could be heard drawing closer.

As Tam turned eagerly, intending to meet Eli halfway, Lord Kim added, "You better marry her soon, Lord Tamlin. Otherwise, I'll find it difficult to support you."

Tam cast an apologetic glance over his shoulder. "I'll do what I can, but I did promise my da I wasn't getting married without my family being there. My sister kind of ruined it for me."

The nobleman opened his mouth as though to argue the point more, but Tam was already moving toward the door. And no sooner had he rounded the corner than he was hit by the rebellious princess he was in love with. Realizing who she'd crashed into, Eli threw her arms around him, startling Tam soundly for a lone breath before he returned the embrace.

Everything would be alright.

They'd find their way home, and whatever Eli had promised in exchange for Lord Kim's help? Tam would make sure she could get out of it, or else he'd share the burden as best he could.

At the sound of light panting, he looked back up to see Luca darting toward them. Eli turned as well, and then, seeing Luca's flushed tearful face, they both opened their arms to the child, and he bolted into them to join the hug.

Regardless of how bad things were, Tam had Eli… and his son.

He had everything.

And so everything was going to turn out just fine one way or another.

CHAPTER 51

AN IMPROVISED IMPARTING

Tam stood with his back pressed against the stones as festivalgoers drifted by on the other side of the wall he hid behind. It was hard keeping to the shadows when the street was so brightly lit with paper lanterns strung between the houses. Still, the crowds would help him disappear, and any sounds he might make would be swallowed up by the music that played over the frothing chatter.

As Tam listened to said music, he found himself feeling his heart start to hammer a bit harder.

There was a twang to the instrument that was being plucked and reverberating as a solo, but it was the occasional thud of a drum that made the mood intensify.

Giving his head a shake, Tam tuned this out to the best of his ability and resumed creeping along the wall.

Earlier that day, after a quick debrief from Jeong and Bong on the plan to force Lord Guk into a public episode of acting outlandishly, Tam had changed the method they were going to use to minimize the risk for Jeong and Bong.

Instead of letting the brothers get anywhere near the poison and risking discovery by imperial soldiers, they would simply give Lord Guk a particular drink. It had only just started to become popular in Daxaria, but its effects were not well known in Zinfera.

Espresso.

A potent beverage made from coffee grounds that could jolt the human body into wakefulness.

Tam had been a part of its development, and thanks to Lord Kim owning a teahouse, he had access to the tools and coffee grounds he required to create it.

For this particular night, Tam recommended doubling the serving. With the drugs he had already integrated into Lord Guk's daily life, the man would already be jittery and nervous. Tam would only need to fire one more little pellet dosed with drugs to launch the man into a spectacular scene.

Lord Yangban was a whole other issue, but Tam had an idea on how best to deal with him without resorting to murder.

Despite Eli having casually suggested it to him, Tam confessed he wasn't much on the idea of assassination. Killing in self-defense was one thing, but making a point of going out to kill someone was another entirely.

Tam's mind briefly grazed on these varying thoughts as he moved painstakingly slowly along the wall. Technically he was passing through people's front yards, but the majority of the population was attending the festival; in addition, most front yards had tall clay barrels of fermenting pastes and beans that Tam could duck behind as he made his way to the seaside, where the wealthier lords were preparing to climb aboard their boats for the fireworks show. It would begin when the crescent moon hit the peak of the starry night sky.

The window of time to act was small, but the real concern was rushing back to Lord Kim's house while remaining unseen, so they could make their escape from Junya—a detail Eli had emphasized as she worked with Lord Kim to get everything ready.

At long last, Tam reached the final house in the stretch of road. There, wedged in the corner behind a walnut tree, beside a tall clay pot and a broken statue of a frog, Tam crouched waiting for Jeong and Bong's signal.

And the cough followed by a low whistle came much sooner than he expected. He had barely arrived in time.

"Lord Guk! You *must* try this! It is a new beverage from Daxaria and— Oh."

The hesitation in Jeong's speech made Tam's ears perk up. Should he risk a glance over the wall before he shot at the nobleman?

Then Lord Guk's frenzied voice sailed over the wall. "Have you heard about the dragon? You know, the dragon in Gondol? Is it the monster attacking ships? Could it be my ships? Do you think—" The harried, paranoid stream of questions was stopped by another speaker.

"Lord Guk, do you perhaps think you should cease imbibing for tonight and go to bed?" The voice was smooth and authoritative.

Without even hearing a name, Tam guessed this person was Lord Yangban.

The hairs on the back of Tam's neck prickled, and his body became restless. Particularly when he reminded himself this was the man who'd been instrumental in selling Eli off.

"Ah! Lord Yangban! This beverage my brother is offering for you to try is not alcoholic. In fact, some people find it speeds up the processing of alcohol."

There was Bong, helping things along, and even taking on a more formal tone with the Zinferan nobleman.

Tam couldn't resist: He lifted himself slightly and glimpsed the back of a head. The man Tam was guessing to be Lord Yangban had a patchy, receding hairline that had already retreated past the middle of his head; what hair did remain was black and sheared short. He wore a long teal coat, with loose black pants that Tam could only make out thanks to the lanterns.

Lord Yangban stood under a raised canopy beside Lord Guk while facing Jeong and Bong.

And during that quick glimpse, Tam understood what had startled Jeong. Lord Guk's hair looked greasy, and the long sides stuck straight out as though he had been pulling on it. His customary light-green coat was untied, revealing a rumpled shirt underneath. The man's eyes were wide and shifty, while a patch of red, scratched skin on his neck had been clawed at until it bled.

Tam saw this thanks to Lord Guk's profile being turned to stare wildly at Lord Yangban. This drastic change in appearance made Tam wonder if the lord had begun partaking in drugs that had nothing to do with his own intervention, but most definitely had not helped.

"Would you mind if I had a sip of this drink you are offering?" Lord Yangban's careful question made Tam duck down again.

"Of course not, my lord!" Jeong retorted cheerily.

Tam waited with bated breath to see what would be said. "Mm. It is quite bitter and sharp on the tongue, but I agree, it does seem as though it might help Lord Guk feel... more like himself again."

Tam inwardly celebrated and waited. Rustling sounds and the clinks of porcelain changing hands could be heard.

"I don't like it! It tastes like acid mud! It... It... Oh, I've finished it. At least it is over quickly. Do you think the dragon will be summoned by the fireworks?"

Tam heard Lord Yangban sigh.

"You know, I recently heard that the devil is here in Junya!" Bong interrupted quickly. "Which is why Her Highness, Soo Hebin, has increased the imperial soldiers' presence. What do you make of this?"

Lord Yangban took his time answering, but Tam was happy to find after another quick cursory peek that the lord's attention was fully affixed to Jeong and Bong.

"There is some speculation about that, but of course the concern lies mostly in catching whoever is responsible for killing Her Highness's men and a member of the Coven of Giong. I'm sure they will be apprehended soon, so pay it no mind. We have more important matters regarding rumors that the disgraced princess Elisara Taejo has been seen once more."

Rage overcame Tam so instantaneously, he struggled not to vault over the wall and beat Lord Yangban to a pulp.

"Disgraced? I thought she was simply missing?" Bong speculated loudly, his tone light.

Tam was willing to bet money that Jeong was feeling relatively violent himself.

"Why, yes. She ran off with a servant boy to get married, but it seems she wants to stake a claim on the throne now that she has had her fun."

"What a strange rumor. I've heard nothing like it... In fact, I thought I'd heard that she was somewhere in Troivack." Jeong's voice was tense, and as much as Tam appreciated him for trying to find a way to defend Eli, he also knew saying such a thing was making them seem suspicious.

"Oh? Where did you learn of such a thing?" Lord Yangban's inquiry may have sounded mild, but there was a frostiness in his voice that Tam could identify even without seeing his face.

"Not sure, to be honest. Where is it you happened to hear that Princess Elisara ran off with a servant boy? It would certainly seem less likely given the kidnappings that have taken place around—"

"Forgive my brother, Lord Yangban, he gets too nosy for his own good," Bong cut in swiftly.

Meanwhile Tam had a new plan in mind as he pulled free the slingshot and counted the number of pellets in the slender glass vial he had withdrawn from his pocket.

Standing up slowly, Tam took aim…

And fired at Lord Yangban.

"Such questions are fine when shared between us. But I do recommend that your brother mind himself elsewhere. As Her Highness's cousin, I happen to know a little bit more accurately what goes on behind palace walls. Unlike whatever sailor or drunkard your brother may cross paths with."

Tam knew he'd hit Lord Yangban, but the man gave no sign of it.

Tam felt a tight grin lift his mouth. That was for the better. He stood one more time and with a quick creak of wood by his ear hit Lord Guk, though he momentarily noticed Bong's eyes flit to his and his eyebrows twitch in question. The look was so brief, though, that Tam didn't even bother trying to linger.

"BUGS! BUGS AGAIN! WILL THEY NOT STOP?" Lord Guk burst out, slapping a hand to the back of his neck just in time for Tam to hide himself once more and, without wasting a breath, start shuffling carefully down the wall.

He knew Bong and Jeong would meet him seven houses down. He could tell them then the change to the plan he had just made.

Though he didn't celebrate yet.

He knew better. His mother had taught him that things can go especially wrong right when you grow confident that everything is over.

And so he waited in the yard of the seventh house until he heard a particular pattern of coughs. He then eased up slowly in the shadows of two plum trees, though he didn't allow himself to stand to his full height.

Jeong and Bong stood face-to-face, feigning a discussion that would make their responses to Tam appear natural.

"Why did you shoot Lord Yangban?" Bong asked immediately upon Tam's head clearing the wall.

"Remember how I suggested we start more rumors about him to discredit his influence?"

"Yes?"

"We could simply tie him to Lord Guk. The madness he is experiencing? It's contagious."

Bong and Jeong fell silent. "That is brilliant, though what will we do? We are all leaving, and one instance of madness is not enough to—"

"We leave it to Lord Kim, who happens to run the most influential teahouse in Junya. We give his staff some of the drugs and, well, soon Lord Yangban's position could become… uncertain."

"I must caution you again about putting so much stock in Lord Kim." Bong didn't mask his concern in his tone.

"He made a deal with Eli. And remember how you said he was adamantly against Soo Hebin's rise to power? Don't trust that he will help out of the goodness of his heart. Trust that he is doing it out of self-interest."

"That is a very risky thing to bet on," Bong persisted.

"Also remember that as a devout follower of the religion of Acker, he will be more inclined to think highly of me as a witch. But all that aside, he already has the power to destroy all of us. He knows almost everything. He knows who I am. He knows who Eli is. We're already beholden to him. May as well see it through."

"Handing him drugs to distribute is another matter entirely," Bong pointed out bluntly.

"Do you have a better idea?" Tam countered.

Bong fell silent.

"I will give him the opportunity, and if he wants to say no, he can, but if there is any chance he will agree and help weaken the group that's trafficking humans and trying to destroy Eli's reputation through gossip? I want to take it."

At this reminder of Lord Yangban's horrific offenses as well as his new plan to discredit Eli and stop her from gaining any kind of power, Bong acquiesced. "Alright," he said. "We will start the rumors in the crowd tonight. You go back. I do believe that this is now our goodbye. I thought we would get to say our final farewells with Luca and Eli, but with us needing to spread the new rumor that changes things." Bong sighed.

Tam lowered his chin in respectful regard. "I hope we cross paths again. Thank you for everything, Bong. I know we have not seen eye to eye at all times, but you are a wise friend."

"Tam, I'll catch up with you and Eli later," Jeong said with a serious nod to Tam, who gave a half smile of appreciation.

"May I make a request for the next time we see each other?" Bong asked, his mood seeming to lighten.

"Yes?"

"Can we have a lot more fun next time? I sincerely think you, Eli, and Luca could all spend some time being less serious."

Tam grinned more openly. "I think I could be persuaded—though you're on your own when it comes to sledding down desert dunes."

Bong's shoulders slumped forward. "That's a pity. Well… Until next time. And Tam?"

The future duke raised his eyebrows expectantly.

Bong grinned. "Good luck with your new family. I think you two will be quite happy together."

Tam's smile broadened. "I certainly hope so, though I'll miss your guidance when I inevitably mess things up."

"Don't worry! I'll be there!" Jeong reminded happily.

Tam chuckled. "Well… I'd best be off. Take care, Bong."

The Zinferan bowed his head with a subtle smile, then turned to melt back into the festival crowds with Jeong at his side.

Tam watched them disappear, and despite the seriousness of what was still happening, he made sure to take a moment to appreciate the wonderful Ryu brothers, and how lucky he had been to have them at his back during the most bizarre time in his life.

CHAPTER 52

A FAMILIAR FRIEND

Hidden inside a compartment beneath the carriage seat, Tam clutched Luca to his chest, hoping the boy wouldn't feel how hard his heart pounded as the carriage rocked to and fro on the road.

He tried to mentally tally where they were by how long they had been riding, but with the stop and start of the vehicle—most likely thanks to the festival crowds clogging the streets—it was a hopeless task.

"Dad?" Luca whispered.

"Ssh," Tam murmured.

His son shifted against him as they traveled.

In a way, Tam hoped he wouldn't be able to tell when they were stopped at the gates of the city, because that would mean he wouldn't have to disappear into his void and his poor child wouldn't be forced to come along with him.

Sadly, it was easy for Tam to sense.

The carriage stopped, and he could feel the door latch lift as it reverberated down the wood into his shoulder.

He could hear the murmur of voices.

One rumbled, one spoke tersely, and one softly.

The soft voice was most definitely Lord Kim.

The carriage bounced.

Someone had gotten off.

It bounced one more time.

Judging by the silence, Tam gathered that everyone save for one person remained in the carriage.

Now it was a game of waiting to see whether the person searching the carriage would check inside the seat where Luca and Tam were scrunched up together.

The instant someone touched the bench, Tam would disappear with Luca into his void.

He waited… And waited.

And nothing happened.

Until Luca's heel accidentally tapped the back of the wall.

Tam heard a slight shift in the wood of the carriage, and the hair on the back of his neck stood up, his instincts screamed terribly, and so… He whisked both Luca and himself into the void without bothering to find out what had been about to happen.

"Is there a particular reason you are leaving the city during the spring blossom festival, Lord Kim?" the imperial soldier asked, his demeanor calm but his dark eyes appraising.

Behind the lord with his footman and maid, three guards scoured the carriage for any stowaways.

Lord Kim inclined himself respectfully. The guard wore a long, loose red shirt, a chest plate, and a matching helmet, with a sword at his hip and a spear in his hand.

"The noise is unacceptable and the number of drunkards vomiting on our beautiful streets leaves me no choice but to flee for my home in Gondol. Perhaps by the time I arrive there, things will have regained some sense of order and propriety!" Lord Kim huffed.

The man's moralistic reputation bolstered his claims well, and Eli had no doubt that he was actually quite sincere about his thoughts on the festival.

The soldier appeared not to have heard of Lord Kim's reputation, however, as he raised a doubtful eyebrow before sliding his gaze over to his comrades and lifting the torch in his hand higher, further illuminating the east gate of Junya.

One of the other soldiers circled to the back of the carriage and started pulling trunks from the back of the vehicle.

"I beg your pardon? What do you think you are doing?" Lord Kim seethed openly while rounding toward the guard.

"Inspecting what you are taking from the city," the guard answered without a hint of emotion.

Fury sparked bright in Lord Kim's eyes as he whirled back around to face the first soldier he'd been speaking to. "On whose authority do you search a noble's things? Her Highness Soo Hebin? If so, then you have *grossly* overstepped your bounds, as this is not an order from our emperor himself!"

At the very least, this point did make the soldier pause, and even raise a hand to stop the men from opening the trunks.

"Her Highness's men were murdered, along with an esteemed member of the Coven of Giong. Her Highness is to be commended for being so proactive in retaining good relations with the coven. Do you not agree?"

"I do not agree with orders issued behind our emperor's back. It almost sounds like *treason*." Lord Kim loomed over the guard, who, while wiry, was at least half a foot shorter than the nobleman. He was particularly small for a soldier, but given that he seemed to be in charge, he must have been that much more intelligent.

A soldier within the carriage suddenly held up a hand, drawing every soldier's attention.

His gaze was fixed on the seat cushion where Lord Kim had been sitting.

The nobleman rounded, as did his footman and maid… who happened to be Eli in disguise…

The soldier then lifted his sword, took aim, and plunged it into the seat.

"Honestly!" Lord Kim threw his hands in the air in exasperation. "I am fining you! You will pay for the upholstery of my carriage!"

Everyone ignored him.

The guard lifted the cushion attached to the lid of the compartment, his blade at the ready, only for everyone to see him relax as he realized he was staring at an empty space.

Kneeling on the carriage floor, he knocked on the walls of the compartment while frowning.

Meanwhile, the commander who had been dealing with Lord Kim strode purposefully over to the vehicle. When it was concluded there was nothing suspicious in it despite the stab through the seat, the soldier investigating the carriage shook his head at his commander.

Lord Kim waited with his arms crossed, glaring with unmasked disapproval.

The guards all shared glum expressions.

"Well?" Lord Kim insisted irritably.

"We still have to go through your luggage."

Lord Kim took in a deep breath, looked to the stars, and carried on with his tirade.

Eli stood behind him.

She was certain much of his rage was inspired by Soo Hebin, but at the same time, it was doing a marvelous job of aggravating and distracting the guards from taking a closer look at herself.

And so she bided her time, hoping that Tam would be able to find his way out of the void with Luca, and that he had indeed mastered his magic enough to appear back in the carriage. Even more important… that his magic wouldn't run out.

Tam had explained to her that the reason he had fallen unconscious before was he had overexerted his power as of late, and so he didn't have a great deal to muster…

Eli's pulse raced to the point of making her dizzy, but there was nothing she could do other than keep her hands clasped in front of her plain gray skirts, watching the imperial soldiers tear through Lord Kim's belongings.

"Keep your eyes closed, Luca," Tam ordered the moment they appeared in the void—though he did release his son from his firm hold against his chest. He didn't want Luca feeling the tremors running through his body that felt akin to the end of a gruesome workout that left his muscles weak. Still, he knew it was a risk letting go of Luca in that moment, as his control started slipping and his exhaustion grew.

"What's happening?" Luca asked, fear making his voice come out a croak.

While Luca was able to come up to his knees, his eyes firmly closed, Tam remained lying down to regain some measure of strength.

He had hoped that returning to the void might help him restore some power, but unfortunately, that wasn't the case.

It would seem his magic needed to recover the good old-fashioned way.

By resting.

"We are just somewhere safe for a little while, but we will be back in the carriage soon, alright?"

"If it's safe, why can't I open my eyes?" Luca's hands started to fidget, and Tam wished he could force himself to sound calm and comforting, but his vision was starting to spin.

He didn't know how much longer he could keep himself awake.

But if he fell unconscious in the void, would he just reappear somewhere, with Luca stuck here?

Would they both reappear in the world where trouble awaited them?

His teeth started to chatter.

"You have to keep them closed because it's a hard place to see. Just... Just... wait," Tam managed.

"Dad, are you okay?"

"Very tired... It'll be alright, Luca. I promise."

"I really want to open my eyes, Dad."

"No, Luca. I'm serious. Do not open your eyes."

Luca fidgeted even more, and even in his weakened state Tam could see his son's eyes moving under his eyelids.

Summoning some of his remaining strength, Tam managed to roll onto his side and start pushing himself up.

Why was he so drained? He had been perfectly fine before! Was it like an overextended muscle he had accidentally pulled again before it had time to properly heal...?

"Luca, I'm going to hug you again, and really soon, we are going to return to the carriage," Tam repeated. He took the time to enunciate his words so that he could keep the warble from his voice.

Luca's fidgeting turned to outright pants-gripping. "Dad, I'm scared."

"I'm sorry, I understand that it is scary, but everything is going to be okay. Do you trust me?"

A peculiar look overtook Luca's face then.

It was not unlike the time aboard the ship coming to Zinfera after the attack of the pirates, or the time in the street when he'd been talking about his odd dreams... Though at least Luca still didn't open his eyes.

"Luca, are you alright?"

For a moment Luca struggled to come back to himself, and Tam gingerly reached forward to rest a hand on his shoulder. Only this had the very bad effect of making Luca's eyes snap open.

Seeing this, Tam grabbed him, pulling Luca into his chest, blocking his sight in a panic, but the movement made him completely lose his grip on his power. Tam felt both himself and Luca be snapped out of the void. Belatedly, Tam attempted to grasp where they were going to reappear by paying attention to the feelings and smells that flooded by him in a rush.

Fresh air? The cool touch of stones?

But it was all over too soon... And then he was on his back.

Luca was still in his arms as he lay in the grass, his boots stretched over the edge of the road.

Tam opened his eyes and saw the wide expanse of starry skies but also noted the glow of torchlight a short way to the left.

He could hear voices, and he fought against unconsciousness to sit up and turn his head toward the sounds.

There was the gate of Junya.

There were the imperial soldiers.

Tam's heart slammed against his chest, which unfortunately did nothing to help his waning energy.

At least they were far enough away that there was a chance that the guards couldn't see them in the darkness!

But... where was the carriage?

Tam's stomach roiled, and he did his best, regardless of the cold sweat sprouting along his brow, to ease his feet off the road while lying low in the grass.

"Why aren't we in the carriage?" Luca at least had the good sense to speak softly.

"I didn't do something right. Just a moment... I'm going to try and find the carriage, but we need to be very, *very* quiet."

Luca, being the smart lad that he was, nodded for his response, then managed to move onto his belly. At his father's side in the grass, he slowly moved the same direction of Tam.

Meanwhile, Tam's mind raced.

Had Eli and Lord Kim left already? Or had they been apprehended?

Taking long, steadying breaths, Tam glanced up enough to spot the edge of a forest just over a nearby slope. Redirecting his trajectory toward the trees, Tam gestured for Luca to follow him. Tam hoped he could rest for a little while once they'd slid over the ledge before continuing to move deeper into the darkness away from Junya...

And so he did.

Thankfully, it seemed the soldiers stationed at the gate were too busy keeping an eye on things in the city to give any special thought to what was happening just outside the city wall. The lights from Junya faded into the distance behind them as they carefully climbed down the hill through the trees to the bottom, and Tam felt comfortable enough to rest.

"Wake me if I'm not already up by dawn, alright?" Tam ordered softly while still holding on to his son to keep the poor child warm in the chill of the night.

"Okay... What are we going to do if Mom and Lord Kim are gone ahead of us, though? How did we get out of the carriage? Where did we go? Was it magic?" Luca's questions grew brighter in tone with excitement, but Tam had to gently stroke his head in response.

"Sorry, but... I will have to answer... your questions... in the morning... Alright?"

Luca obediently fell silent, and Tam started to relax enough that he felt his body submit itself to the pending unconsciousness, even though he wished he could've continued walking well into the night until they caught up with the carriage...

"Dad?"

"Hm?"

"I know things are kind of scary right now... But I know you're going to make everything okay."

Tam smiled sleepily and resumed gently rubbing Luca's head.

"Can you try to wake me before dawn?"

Tam felt Luca nod under his palm. He broadened his tight-lipped smile despite already being half asleep.

Everything had been going according to plan, aside from Tam's inability to wield his magic properly during their escape. Being a perfectionist with his work, that should have troubled him a lot more, but at least Luca was safe.

I'll find Eli and Lord Kim tomorrow, and we'll continue traveling until the next town to meet up with Jeong… Today is just a slight hiccup. It isn't that bad. I can still fix this. Eli… wherever you are… please… if you can… come find us.

And so Tam at last succumbed to sleep, his body twitching and his forehead perspiring, but he hoped that a simple night's rest would be all he needed to rally again the next day. They weren't out of danger yet… but with any luck, Eli and Lord Kim had escaped without a problem.

Tam woke with a jolt the next day and found that for all his fervent wishes, he may as well have hoped for the rumored dragon of Zinfera to walk up and introduce itself.

Upon feeling Luca's hands tug at his arm, Tam discovered himself surrounded by guards with lowered spears and another bunch with four torches raised above their heads.

Tam bit back a curse word as Luca shrank into a ball at his side.

Sitting up and clearing his throat, Tam plastered an easygoing smile on his face.

"Good morning!" he greeted brightly while also wrapping an arm around Luca. "How are you fine… armed… gentlemen doing today?"

"Sir, you will be coming with us to Junya for questioning," one of the soldiers informed Tam calmly.

"Oh?" Tam didn't bother reaching for his knives. A single wrong move, and things would escalate.

"There have been several murders in Junya, and we are going to investigate anyone suspicious who—"

"But I've never been to Junya. I was with a traveling troupe until—"

"On your feet," the soldier ordered.

Tam held his hands up in the air to show he was unarmed. "I will be glad to, but my boy here is a bit afraid. Mind lowering your weapons?" He tried relaxing his formal pronunciation to make himself seem less threatening and peculiar.

The group didn't budge.

Tam's mind raced.

He couldn't risk using his magic. He might pass out and instantly condemn himself. And without anyone to care for Luca, it was out of the question.

Tam slowly rose to his feet with his hands in the air. Luca slipped behind him and burrowed his head into Tam's lower back.

"Now, sirs, there really isn't a need for—"

There came a flash of black fur and a loud, snarling growl as a massive animal tackled two of the soldiers to the ground.

Tam flinched back, his right arm reaching back protectively for Luca, and yet he felt oddly calm after the initial startle.

The beast continued swiping at the men with massive paws. They scattered, forced to defend themselves as individuals rather than a cohesive group.

Which was perfectly fine for the beast, what with each of its claws being the length of a man's finger and its fangs almost the same size. If not longer.

It systematically darted and leapt among the men, powerful muscles rippling with each attack.

Transfixed, Tam watched the long, ropy black tail swish right before it pounced on the last two men, who had started to run away.

The soldiers littering the ground were either unconscious or dead, and yet Tam waited with a thudding heart as the beast turned and stalked back over to him, a low rumble in its great chest.

It looked like a giant cat—a panther of some sort? Or something even bigger. Then again, Tam had never seen a panther himself in real life.

He knew he should've been frightened. Especially without his magic. Luca was letting out shivering sobs behind him, and yet when the animal lifted its face, and its large, glittering yellow eyes met his, a rush of knowingness surged through Tam.

Electricity hummed throughout his being.

My familiar, he thought dumbly to himself. The creature gazed back at him as though in equal awe.

Tam had no idea how long they stared at each other, but he relished the potent happiness of at last finding his familiar, already sensing what a powerful connection it was...

But then the back of the beast twitched, and its legs shook...

Tam frowned. What was wrong with—

It transformed.

And in front of him, kneeling on the grass staring up at him in open shock, remarkably fully clothed once more...

Was Eli.

Other works by Delemhach

The House Witch Trilogy
Volume 1, Volume 2, Volume 3

Kraken's Guide to The House Witch
This work is exclusively available on Campfire

The Princess of Potential
Standalone

The Burning Witch Trilogy
Volume 1, Volume 2, Volume 3